PAYBACK

EDIE BAYLIS

Boldwood

First published in Great Britain in 2023 by Boldwood Books Ltd.

A CIP catalogue record for this book is available from the British Library.

Paperback ISBN 978-1-80280-186-6

Large Print ISBN 978-1-80280-187-3

Hardback ISBN 978-1-80280-184-2

Ebook ISBN 978-1-80280-188-0

Kindle ISBN 978-1-80280-189-7

Audio CD ISBN 978-1-80280-180-4

MP3 CD ISBN 978-1-80280-181-1

Digital audio download ISBN 978-1-80280-182-8

Boldwood Books Ltd
23 Bowerdean Street
London SW6 3TN
www.boldwoodbooks.com

For Tanya x

PROLOGUE

Seb Stoker stared with impatience at the sweating, shivering man cowering beneath him. 'I won't ask you again, so I suggest you think very clearly before you answer.'

He casually inspected his fingernails, frowning at the hint of dirt underneath a nail on his right hand. Something else to put on the list of things to get straight. 'I'd also suggest you do so quickly. I'm a busy man, so time spent on you is limited.'

Seb's green eyes flicked over the back of the large Erdington lockup to the wall where the rack of metal cabinets that housed his firm's collection of safes had once stood.

His fists clenched. As instructed, the area was now cleared. He didn't need a constant reminder of what the firm – or rather, *he*, had lost. Or, more accurately, had been *stolen*.

And if the theory was correct, the theft was aided by this lowlife.

Seb returned his glare to the trembling man. The mere sight of this loser – a paid member of their firm, who, it seemed, had made the unforgivable error of opening his fat gob to cause this disaster, boiled his piss further.

He was acutely aware that his brother, Neil, had been lax for leaving the safes' codes on his mobile phone long enough for this yellow-bellied turd to learn of them, but gross stupidity had not warranted or forced this piece of shit to take it upon himself to wander around flapping his gums.

And flapping his gums to a certain *somebody* who'd turned him over.

This runner, Simon Parker, may not have physically lifted the contents of the safes whilst the Stokers' casino had burnt down around them, but his big mouth had certainly enabled the act.

And for that he would pay.

Seb glanced at his twin brothers, standing either side of the runner, waiting impatiently for the nod to start work on information, Andrew more so than Neil. But Seb had already decided that this time, he would do the job himself – if only to release some steadily festering pent-up bitterness and frustration that had mounted up during the rapid chain of events over the last month.

At this precise second, the firm had lost its spare stash of millions, his casino was razed to the ground, half his staff were being temporarily employed at the Violet Orchid, courtesy of his fiancée, Samantha, and, if he didn't sort this shit out, his and Sam's home would be the next thing to cop it.

And that he drew the line at.

Someone would suffer, and this wanker made a decent starting point.

Seb's eyes narrowed back to the man in front of him, his swift turn towards one of the many workbenches causing a gibbering sound to escape from the trussed-up man's mouth.

Yeah, this bloke knew what was coming. *Everybody* knew what happened if you fucked with the Stokers. Or at least they had... But being as someone believed they'd escape retribution after pulling a robbery and arson, the city needed a fast and sharp reminder.

And Simon Parker would be the poster boy.

Yanking a pair of pliers from a holdall, Seb dropped to his haunches in front of the bound man, making sure to balance his weight more on the leg that hadn't taken a bullet the night everything hit the fan. It might not have been long since Andrew had fished the metal from his thigh, but thankfully, short of it still being a bit stiff, there were no ongoing problems. He'd been lucky.

This man, however, would *not* be so lucky...

'Still nothing to say?' Seb's teeth glinted in the illumination from the bank of fluorescent strip lights overhead as his eyes rested on Simon Parker. 'Try thinking about what you did after nosing through my brother's phone whilst you sat all comfy-like in the van. Remember? The night you were instructed to bring him here to drop off money?'

Simon's eyes darted to Neil and Andrew as they moved to flank Seb. 'I didn't... I...'

As Simon tried to move away from the jaws of the pliers, Seb grinned. The prick couldn't move anywhere, the gaffer tape securing his arms to the chair put paid to that.

It also held them in the perfect position for *this*...

Clasping the tips of the pliers over Simon's right thumbnail, Seb ripped the large nail clean off its bed with minimum effort.

The howl of pain was pleasurable, but if the man found *that* painful, he was in for a rude awakening.

'Now, let's think about this carefully,' Seb smiled coldly. 'After going through my brother's phone and getting the codes, who did you deem it wise to pass them to?'

Simon howled again as the next two fingernails were removed. His shaking increased. He wasn't stupid enough to believe Seb Stoker had even warmed up yet. 'I – I didn't nose through the phone. Neil dropped it... I mean, Mr Stoker dropped it. I just picked it up from the footwell and...'

'Let's not be finicky,' Seb said, his rage a simmering timebomb as he glared at Neil for good measure. *Dropped the phone in the fucking footwell? Christ!* 'How you got the code is irrelevant, but who you gave it to isn't!'

'I – I didn't give it to anyone. I...'

The crack to Simon's jaw from Seb's fist echoed around the storage unit. The chair rocked unsteadily whilst Seb stared at the blood trickling from the man's mouth. 'We paid you good money to work for us. We employed you for fucking years and this is how you repaid us?' he screamed, his controlled demeanour deserting him.

Grabbing a fistful of hair, Seb wrenched Simon's head back. 'Andrew? Sort the teeth!'

Andrew stepped forward with a wide grin. It had been a while since he'd removed anyone's teeth and he was looking forward to it.

Simon's eyes widened at the long-nosed pliers in Andrew Stoker's hand. 'No! Please! I...'

Jamming the pliers into the man's mouth, Andrew yanked out a front tooth, the scream going straight through his head. 'Urgh, these are fucking rotten. They're like cottage cheese!'

Seb snatched the thin pliers from Andrew's hand. 'Give me those! I might as well lift the whole fucking lot, being as this prick has nothing to say.' He tugged harder on Simon's hair, scowling as the man fruitlessly tried to close his mouth, rivulets of blood cascading down his chin.

'Ygggh! Nhhgh!' Simon squawked.

'What? What did you fucking say?' Seb roared. 'I can't understand you. Oh, fuck this! Grab the bolt cutters, Neil. Do this wanker's fingers whilst I do his fucking gob.'

'No, noguggh!' Simon wailed, the chair jumping around despite Andrew's firm grasp of his shoulders.

Seb released Simon's hair and slowly walked around the front of the man. 'Two seconds is what you've got to talk.' His eyes narrowed malevolently. 'Which firm did you sell us out to? Who paid you?'

'I – I didn't sell them!' Simon gabbled, his mouth a sea of pain. 'I didn't, I swear, Mr Stoker. The only thing I think I did was I said something. I was pissed up and I...'

'You were pissed up and you *think* you said "something" to "someone"?' Seb raged incredulously. 'Are you taking the mick?'

'He's talking shite!' Andrew barked. 'Let's just get on with it.'

'No! I did! I'm sure I did. No, I *know* I did!' Simon blathered, sweat running down his brow to mix with the blood dripping onto his T-shirt.

Seb pushed himself into the runner's face. 'Well?'

Simon racked his brains. It was true that he hadn't sold the codes, but he *had* said something once. He might as well say, because he had nothing to lose. The Stokers appreciated honesty. Everyone knew they were fair. 'It... it was this bloke...'

'Which. Bloke. Did. You. Tell!' Seb spat each word through clenched teeth. Whoever was told was the crux of the shit he was now dealing with – the shit put on Sam and the shit he was about to unleash on *all* of them to dig them out of this mess. And it was all down to this waste of fucking oxygen.

'I was in the Whistling Pig having a drink with a bird called Marlene when some geezers called me over.'

'What geezers?' Neil pressed, the weight of his part of this disaster weighing heavily on his shoulders.

'I – I don't know. No one important – just blokes. But there was a guy with them asking about the poker tournaments. I – I said I could get him a VIP pass...' The words spilt from Simon's broken mouth. *He could still save himself, he knew he could.*

His eyes darted between the three Stoker men pleadingly.

'Please, you've got to believe me. I never meant to say anything out of turn. I was drunk and showing off.'

'The name of this man?' Seb flexed the pair of bolt cutters now in his hand.

Simon couldn't move his gaze from the jaws of the vicious-looking implement. He'd lose his fingers and probably his toes if he didn't talk. He'd heard they'd done this before. 'I... I think his name was Dan. No, it was, I'm sure of it.'

Andrew rolled his eyes. 'Dan? Dan fucking who?'

'I – I don't know. I'd never seen him before. I said I was a trusted member of the firm and could prove it because I knew the codes for the safes...' Simon's face burnt with humiliation. 'I don't remember giving him the actual numbers, but I must have. I'm so sorry. I'm sorry. I...'

'You pathetic bastard!' Seb's hands shook with rage. If this prick was to be believed, then his firm had lost its capital and the casino, and his family and the woman he loved would soon be put in jeopardy, all because of a boast?

'This is bollocks,' Neil muttered.

'It's not, I swear! I know it sounds pathetic. I – I've always wanted to be someone – like you lot. I've got a wife and three kids... Please! I'll do anything to make it up to you. I...'

'And you don't know anything else about this Dan bloke?' Seb's rage morphed into a dangerously quiet calm. Dan wasn't a name of anyone in any of the firms he knew, and he knew pretty much all of them – major and minor.

'No. No, I'd tell you if I did,' Simon gibbered. 'I'm not stupid. I'm telling you everything. I'd never seen him before, but I'd recognise him again because he only had one hand. Look, please. I...'

Seb jerked his head at Andrew. 'Let him up.' He watched his brothers staring at him in stunned silence. 'Untie him.'

'You're letting him go?' Andrew gasped. 'After what he's responsible for?'

Seb shrugged. 'Ripping him to pieces won't change anything. We need to locate this one-armed tosser. He's the one.'

'That's if it's true,' Neil muttered, reluctantly slicing the taping around Simon's wrists and ankles.

'Thank you, Mr Stoker. You don't know what this means. I'll do anything to put this right,' Simon cried.

'There's very little you can do to fix what you've caused.' Stony-faced, Seb watched Simon stagger from the chair, stumbling as the feeling returned to his stiff legs. Ignoring the disdain over his decision plastered across his brothers' faces, a small smirk tugged at the corner of his mouth.

'Thanks again, Mr Stoker,' Simon stuttered, barely able to believe his good fortune. 'People always say you're fair and...'

'Not as much as you perhaps think,' Seb said. He'd been fair over many things in his life, but not this fair. *Oh, brothers, ye of little faith...*

Simon Parker didn't even get the chance to flinch when a bullet shot a hole clean through the centre of his forehead and he crumpled silently to the floor.

1

ONE WEEK LATER

Not for the first time, Marina Devlin scowled at the large-breasted woman with bleached hair sitting at the kitchen table in her over-tight skirt and barely-there top. The tart was twenty, if she was a day, and Mickey was old enough to be the woman's father.

Unfortunately, Mickey was *Marina's* father and each time she saw him, she was reminded exactly how disappointing that fact was. But desperate times meant desperate measures and her good for nothing, pointless, selfish bastard of a father had been the only one to turn to in her hour of need.

For once, he'd delivered – in as much as he'd dragged his sorry arse up from London, but not without bringing this brainless limpet with him, for reasons Marina was yet to deduce.

A week now, the three of them had been holed up in this shit-hole of a flat in Bearwood, and yet nothing had been done to locate her waster boyfriend, Dan Marlow, who had done one with the Stokers' money that should have been hers.

Nothing at all.

Not that *she'd* seen Dan as a 'boyfriend' for some time. And regardless of whether the bozo still believed somewhere in that dense head of his that there could possibly be anything left between them after any of *this*, then he had even less brain cells remaining than Marina had thought.

But none of that changed that she'd been forced to put up with watching this bimbo Mickey had dragged along with him draping herself over him and listening to the dulcet tones of them shagging every single bloody night. It was getting right on her wick.

More so, considering she was stuck here, unable to risk setting foot outside due to having two major Birmingham firms after her blood. And the final insult, short of Samantha Reynold – up until relatively recently, her previously unknown and thoroughly undeserving sister – still lording it up around the city, was that Dan wasn't already six feet under.

Furthermore, as a final twist of the knife, the day he'd buggered off, Dan had also pinched her one remaining credit card with a few quid left on it.

Marina's brows narrowed. If Dan had any sense, he'd have disappeared off to a sun-drenched Brazilian beach – somewhere he couldn't be located. But despite him somehow pulling this off behind her and her brother Grant's back, she had the distinct impression he was still in this city.

And she had to find him.

There was no way she was letting that loser wander off with the money that should have been hers. Not in a million years. But without Grant around to help, she really was on her own.

Her mind digressed once again to spare a thought over what had happened to Grant. Of course, after she'd shot him, his body would have been quickly disposed of by those Stoker bastards. By now, her brother had most likely been dumped, along with a sack of rocks, amongst the general rubble at the bottom of the Gas Basin.

She raised her chin. Grant shouldn't have got in the bloody way, should he? Had he just remained where he'd stood and let her crack on with shooting Samantha Reynold through the head, he'd still be here.

Her mouth formed a narrow line.

Grant didn't deserve her sympathy, or even a thought. He'd been the one to waver in his loyalties. If her stupid, deluded brother hadn't been so desperate to protect that woman, then none of this would have happened. Samantha would be dead as a door nail and they would have had it away on their toes with Stoker's money, like they'd planned.

Instead, now Dan was in receipt of millions, and she was stuck here. With *them*...

'How long is she going to be here?' Marina snapped, watching her father shovel the remains of last night's Chinese takeaway into his mouth. The thought of eating that shit at any time of the day, let alone for breakfast, was one step beyond. 'You're supposed to be sorting this out, not here for a holiday or a fucking shag fest with your latest tart!'

Mickey Devlin's fork paused halfway to his mouth, a noodle dropping down the front of his stained vest. 'Be patient, dear daughter,' he smirked. 'Things take time to plan. Don't stress, it's all in hand.'

'The only thing in your hands are her tits!' Marina glared at the blonde, who was oblivious to what was being said, her concentration solely on the latest copy of *Hello* magazine. 'Why is she actually here?'

Mickey ran his tongue slowly along his teeth. 'Sophie is here for distraction.' He held his hands up. 'And before you come out with another bitchy comment, not just as a distraction to me, a distraction in the big scheme of things.'

Marina's eyes narrowed. 'Then I'd appreciate knowing exactly what part of your alleged plan relies on using a thick bitch with plastic tits?'

Standing up, Mickey brushed the clods of noodles from his vest, rubbing the mess into the carpet with his boot. 'Like I said... patience... All you've got to do is trust me. You'll see.'

The harsh truth was that he didn't have a plan. Not yet. But he would. This miserable bitch of a daughter of his was too highly strung to understand that the best-laid plans appeared from the ether. That was what he relied on, anyway. Dan Marlow would be tracked down somehow.

But in the interim...

Grabbing Sophie's arm, Mickey winked suggestively. 'Come on, sugar-tits. Get your arse into gear. I haven't finished with you yet.'

Marina scowled at the back of Sophie's head, focusing on the dark roots of her yellow hair as the pair left the room. Great... Another round of listening to disgusting noises through the cardboard walls.

She snatched her cigarettes from the Formica tabletop. Her father had better come up with something and do it soon because otherwise everything would be down to her and her alone. *As usual...*

* * *

Samantha Reynold walked through the games room of the Violet Orchid Casino, nodding to her staff.

It had been a decent day so far. Having earlier spoken to the rehab clinic, she was pleased with the account of her mother's progress. According to what was said, Linda wasn't yet at the point where she could have visitors, but progress had been made and all being well, this would change next week.

It was good news. Although the clinic cost a fortune, it was worth every penny to remove the addiction issues her mother had always struggled with. That, and right some of the wrongs that bastard, Tom Bedworth, had caused for Linda.

Sam chewed her bottom lip as she continued out of the games room and along the staff corridor to her office.

Over the last two weeks, she'd put feelers out for the character from her mother's past who had shown up again like a bad smell; the bastard who, not content with keeping Linda prisoner and drugged up to the eyeballs in the attic of his filthy doss hole of a brothel, had spent the rest of his time orchestrating, running and profiting from a place specialising in grooming young girls to sell themselves to equally foul men.

After Linda's experience, the crux of why Sam had not even been aware of her real mother's existence until relatively recently, meant the subject was both a pet hate *and* a mission.

Now she knew where Tom Bedworth operated from, she'd felt able to get revenge. Seb had gone to the dump on the Hagley Road as promised, but Bedworth's club, the Aurora, had been abandoned. The building was as deserted as the Mary Celeste, so the man she was desperate to make pay was still at large. *Somewhere.*

And she wouldn't rest until he suffered.

Until both he *and* Marina suffered.

Because that was another person she owed...

Marina Devlin, another of Linda's daughters – a sister Sam had been unaware of, storming into the Orchid and trying to kill her had made things even worse.

Remorse and sadness filtered her thoughts, remembering Trevor Jensen getting shot at the hands of this psychotic woman. But he hadn't been Trevor, had he? He had been Grant – *Grant Devlin*. Marina's brother.

Her brother...

Sam had liked the man, but both he and Marina had wanted

her killed. And that hurt.

Seb also getting shot that night as collateral damage in Marina's twisted plan also meant there could be no forgiveness for the woman. She had to pay for what she'd done. But Marina had escaped. She was still out there somewhere and the nagging worry of her returning to complete what she'd started was never far from Sam's mind.

This burning need for revenge didn't change that the priority was split with getting the Stokers back up and running. Sam knew that Seb's firm and casino were down the pan because of her. The only reason he'd been shot was because of her too.

Sam's heels clicked loudly on the corridor as she hastened towards her office. The meet was due the minute Seb returned with, what she hoped would be, the full details for the heist – the one he'd kept close to his chest until he knew exactly which way it would happen.

And no – there was no way she would ever have taken him up on his instruction to walk away whilst she still could.

Seb Stoker was her life – the reason her heart beat. She loved him like no other. To walk away to save her own neck was unthinkable. Whatever happened, they were in this together and neither hell nor high water would detract from that.

Sam's face set determinedly as she reached her office door. Seb had moved mountains to keep her safe and protected, so if he went down, she was going with him.

Plus, if he didn't rectify what had been lost, it would be his undoing.

Seb wasn't the sort to cope with being second best or taking a back seat. It would eat away at his soul until there was nothing left, and she would never allow that to happen.

Sam would do whatever she had to do to help, regardless of what that was.

2

As they rushed from the foyer out underneath the front canopy of the hotel, leaving the Hyatt receptionist staring after them in confusion, Dan Marlow grabbed Tom Bedworth's sleeve. 'What are we doing?' he hissed. 'You said we couldn't leave until you were sure the coast was clear?'

Tom shrugged the fingers of Dan's intact hand off his jacket. 'We haven't got a lot of fucking choice!'

From the window of their junior suite on the twenty-third floor, he'd seen the police car roll up outside the hotel for the second day in a row, the officers making their way into the reception. He'd hardly dared move for what seemed like an indeterminate amount of time, paranoid even the sound of his breathing would expose his presence, as well as the location of the holdalls in the wardrobe that were stuffed with the contents of the Stokers' safes.

As well as successfully burning the Stokers' casino to the ground, thanks to Dan's 'helpful' inside information, he'd lifted the entire stash of those wankers' money from under their noses.

And he couldn't think of more deserving victims than Seb

Stoker and his thug family, who thought themselves clever by involving themselves with Tom's unwanted daughter, Samantha.

But the last thing Tom wanted was anyone finding out that he'd been behind any of it. The police included...

If the Old Bill were here *again* digging around, even if they weren't digging for him, it still might inadvertently highlight the trail leading to the owner of the car which had disappeared from the hotel's underground car park a week and a half ago – the motor used to dispatch a two-faced little whore. The one he'd taken the opportunity to mow down before she caused further problems.

As well as becoming surplus to requirements at his *own* club, before that went to shit, Deb Banner had been involved in *something* – something that also included the Stokers, so she'd had to go via any available means.

He only hoped she'd been removed in time.

No, he didn't want *any* of those things coming to light.

A layer of sweat beaded on Tom's forehead as he furtively glanced around.

Christ, he'd been all but sorted. Everything was in place. Aside from still being lumbered with this moronic fool, he'd been a gnat's cock away from utopia.

Tom glared at Dan with building resentment. That was why they'd been holed up in this bloody hotel waiting for the passports to arrive to spirit them away to a new life elsewhere.

His jaw clenched. That was until the passports were delayed...

There had been no update since the man tasked with supplying the fake passports before the shit hit the fan got himself shot in a boozer. The fucker could have carked it by now, for all Tom knew, so he had to draw the line. He could no longer sit waiting like a target.

They had to shift, and the minute the police car left, Tom knew it was time to move.

The Hyatt doorman manoeuvred closer, his gloved hand gesturing to a line of waiting black cabs queuing hopefully in front of the hotel's entrance. 'Taxi, sir?'

Tom swung around; his nerves frayed. 'No! No, we're fine, thank you.'

'Perhaps I can help you to your car with your bags?' The doorman reached towards Tom's holdalls.

'I said, I'm fine!' Tom swiped the bags as far away as possible and without looking back, stomped down the entrance steps with Dan close on his heels.

'What are you doing?' Dan hissed. 'We need a taxi. Not that I've got a clue where we're going, but we can't be seen around here.' He glanced opposite at the blackened remains of the Royal Peacock Casino. 'The Stokers could be watching us right now.'

'If they were watching us or knew who we were, we'd already have a hole in the back of our heads!' Tom upped his pace across the hotel's turning circle to Broad Street. 'The doorman could pass our destination to the Stokers or even the fucking cops, so it's safer to get a cab from the road.'

Dan's sallow face coloured with a tinge of green. 'Cops? Why do you thi...'

'Stop asking bloody questions!' Tom waved down an oncoming black cab. 'Always fucking asking things.'

The cab hadn't fully stopped before Tom yanked open the door and clambered in, throwing the heavy holdalls into the footwell. 'Frankley, please, mate. Put your foot down.'

Dan lurched into one of the backward-facing seats as the taxi accelerated. *Frankley? Why were they going to Frankley?* 'Have you found us somewhere else to stay?'

'Nah, we're going for a fucking picnic!' Turning away, Tom stared out of the window. Dan really was a thick prick. And no, he didn't know for certain whether they'd got anywhere to stay, but the place they were heading to was the only location he could think of where there was little chance of them being turned away.

* * *

Andrew Stoker steepled his fingers under his chin and mulled over what had been said. He glanced at Neil, the expression on his twin's face one of equal concern.

He couldn't say he blamed his brother – this was risky to say the least.

In fact, risky barely touched the sides of what might unfurl if things went wrong. Seb's planning of this heist to swap out a container-load of cocaine under the noses of the real owners was immense. It was true that only something of this magnitude could pull in the amount of money needed to get the firm and casino back on track and fix what had happened, but this was one hell of a biggie.

Andrew then looked at Sam, her stunning face showing no hint of alarm, reminding him how wrong he'd been to try and impede Seb from having anything to do with the woman. His initial belief that she was detrimental to his brother, the firm and the family had been a gross oversight.

Admittedly, the chain of events sparking the collapse of their family had stemmed from Sam, but it could have easily spawned from *any* of them. This kind of life always held those risks and possibilities.

But Sam's steadfast devotion to Seb was a godsend. She'd proved her love and loyalty fourfold and he suspected she would have no issue with what was being put into motion. He focused back on his eldest brother. 'Do we know when it will take place?'

Seb gave a slight shake of his head. 'Not yet. It's a question of keeping my ear close to the ground and awaiting the nod from my contact. Once I get that, it's all systems go.'

'Fuck me, this is heavy shit!' Neil muttered. 'You're sure we're not being set up?'

'As sure as I can be. Unfortunately, nothing is guaranteed, but it's a risk we need to take.' Seb stared at Neil long and hard. He required all hands on deck for this one like never before and couldn't have any dampeners put on anything. Well, not all hands on deck – that would be far too dangerous. Only their inner circle would be party to it.

Involving anyone else only heightened the chance of betrayal. They knew only too well that people's heads could be turned for the right price.

Even the firm's trusted accountant would have no knowledge of this. Until afterwards...

Kevin scanned the sheet of paper containing the figures Seb handed out and shrugged his huge shoulders. 'All I'll say is that this will definitely provide the required money with plenty to spare!'

Seb nodded. *That it would.* And he just had to pray that luck, as well as a lot of other things, was on their side.

'The container is coming from Paraguay?' Sam asked, still astounded at the colossal amount they stood to gain if this worked. And it *had* to work. Seb was right. There was no other way to raise the needed capital so quickly.

Seb poured himself a large whisky from the decanter and sipped at it thoughtfully. 'I don't know exactly where it's originating from yet. Paraguay, Ecuador or Colombia. Either way, it's routing via Portugal before docking in England.'

Neil frowned. 'Who exactly are we ripping off? The Colombians? We don't want to start a war with them! It will jeopardise the dealings we already hold with them.'

Seb bristled. Yes, they did have deals with the Colombians and always had done. The Stoker and Reynold firms held a monopoly over the coke trade in Birmingham, but drugs had always been a smaller part of the facets of the Stoker firm – the Irish gun deals taking the majority of side turnover. But their long and profitable relationship with the Irish had turned sour of late.

In their infinite wisdom, the men from the Emerald Isle had decided to retract their prior offer of laundering a big chunk of surplus money after the arson and robbery to the Stoker firm, most probably feeling it unlikely the favour would ever be returned.

Seb scowled. Despite their past dealings, *anyone* who believed him finished or held such little faith in his ability to recover from such a disaster was not someone he would go out of his way to deal with. Unfortunate, but that's how it had to be, so the decision to pull back from concentrating on arms and up their stake in the cocaine trade was made.

Besides, not only was there more markup, but with what Seb had got planned, a wider and better network of supply routes was needed.

And as for ripping people off...

Seb didn't much like ripping *anyone* off and appreciated Neil rubbing his face in that even less. 'We're not short-changing or pulling one over on the Colombians or any of our South American counterparts,' he snapped. 'The deal has already been done. The only people to lose out here will be people we already owe payback to.'

A smile crept over his face. 'It's time to call in an old debt from our father's day.' He moved his gaze to Andrew. 'Jog any memories?'

'You're not by any chance referring to what I think you're refer-ring to, are you? The story we heard every time Dad got pissed?'

'You've got it in one,' Seb grinned.

Sam sat forward, confused. 'What am I missing?'

Seb gave Sam's hand a squeeze. 'Wolverhampton. Those fuckers have never been happy not having the monopoly over the coke trade in Brum as well as the Black Country. They've been trying to take over for years.'

Andrew nodded. 'Our dad got ripped off by them way back when he first started the firm. He agreed a deal with the Ross firm, but they stiffed him. It very nearly finished his firm before it even started. Dad ended up taking out half the Ross firm over it, including the main man, to regain his foothold. After that, an uneasy truce was made. Even with this, it always rankled Dad, but a deal is a deal.'

Sam frowned. 'So, why now?'

Seb's smile dropped. 'The long and short of it is, over the years, the firm have developed a selective memory about their side of the deal and reverted to pushing for territory some time ago. They've always failed, as it's been easy enough to hold them off, but doing this kills two birds with one stone.'

Finishing his whisky, Seb placed the glass back on the desk with a steady hand. Being as he was forced to turn someone over, out of all of the unpalatable options, this one was the most well-deserved and wasn't something he would lose sleep over.

Sam frowned. 'If it's an old score or could be construed as such, then I don't understand why this is so risky?'

'Because,' Neil muttered, 'the Rosses are a bunch of sneaky fuckers. If they find out we're behind this, it will declare war between us. That's always been on the cusp, but never materialised. The thing is, they've got stronger in recent years and are itching to take us on. As you can appreciate, with our current position, now is *really* not a good time for that to happen, hence the risk.'

Seb's lips pursed in irritation. 'You'd be right, Neil, but I don't intend on letting that happen. We'll be doing the switch at Bristol docks and if it's done to plan, no one will be any the wiser.'

And the amount of brass the coke coming in that container should fetch would make everything just fine.

3

Catching sight of herself in a shop window as she mixed with the throng of people pushing up and down the ramp in the centre of Birmingham made Marina cringe.

With her beige mac, dodgy sunglasses and a pink headscarf, she looked like a washerwoman, but the choice of clothes the charity shop on Bearwood High Street had in her size for less than a tenner was limited.

It wasn't a big deal. Not short term, anyway. It was more important not to be recognised. The chances of bumping into the Stokers or Samantha Reynold on the number 440 bus from Bearwood into the city centre was remote, but then, so were plenty of other things and *they* had still happened. It was best not to take chances.

Once she was kitted out with a decent disguise, she'd be in a better position to wander around unsuspected without looking like Hilda Ogden and stinking of mothballs.

Getting a waft of the tell-tale smell of McDonald's as she neared the top of the ramp, Marina glanced with contempt at the people sitting in the window cramming their faces. It was so busy in there, most customers were standing up and the orders barked by the overworked staff rushing around behind the long counter spilt through the open doors, hurting her ears. She'd never been a fan of McDonald's, but she was that starving, for once she'd consider making an exception.

But she couldn't. Finding an acceptable disguise was more important. Plus, it wasn't like she had much money to play with now. Getting anything at all out of her tight-fisted father was difficult enough as it was.

Shoving her way through the open doors into the Pallasades, Marina headed to the escalators. She knew exactly where she was going. The kiosks on the lower ground floor not only sold cheap stuff, but all manner of things. And there was one kiosk which sold wigs. At least, there had been when she'd come in here a few weeks ago.

Travelling past the other set of escalators leading down to New Street Station, Marina glanced into one of the shops around the outskirts of the open-plan area that stocked thigh boots and platform shoes in various colours, all suitable for her new look.

She had to make money as well as keep her ears to the ground. As much as her idea wasn't top of the list, she had a decent figure, nice tits and could dance, so this was a workable solution.

Getting onside with the sort of women who might reveal an inkling as to the movement of her errant thief of an ex-boyfriend was the only way.

Dan had always believed her unaware, but she knew he frequented strip clubs and got through tarts like multi-pack crisps. She didn't imagine anything had changed since his disappearance and if the man was still in Birmingham, which she was certain he was, then it wouldn't cross his tiny mind to keep out of sight and not frequent the most obvious places anyone with half a brain would think of looking first.

Her chipped nails dug into the palms of her hand. Oh yes, Dan would no doubt be busy boasting of his exploits and flashing his stolen cash around like the fool he was. Hopefully, with insider info, his stupidity would lead her straight to him.

And it had to, because it wasn't like her father had offered an alternative solution. All that joker was doing was using her electric, so she needed a backup plan in the event he brought nothing to the table.

With renewed determination, Marina strolled into the wig shop, her sights already set on the long auburn tresses perched on a polystyrene head at the back of the shop.

Providing it didn't look too plastic close up, that would do nicely. It was the other end of the scale from her long blonde hair and with a bit of fiddling in other areas, coupled with some nasty clothes, she'd have the perfect disguise.

Luke Banner dragged the back of his sleeve across his face, smearing a thick line of snot over his cheek.

He pulled himself to his feet. Why couldn't the papers leave him alone? He'd already given his response of how he felt about his only child being murdered and refused to talk about it any more. His comment to the *Birmingham Mail* was the only one he was willing to give.

What did they expect him to say, anyway? That he was fucking happy that his only daughter – the daughter he'd all but brought up by himself for the last few years since his wife had left him in the lurch – had been run over and killed by a pissed-up bastard or drugged-up twat?

And not just run over by *accident*, but run over, reversed on and then run over again – left like an animal to die in the road.

Well, he wasn't happy. How could he be?

Since Deb had stomped out of this house six months ago with her sights set on better things than he could offer, he'd remained ever hopeful that one day – preferably before too long, he'd be reunited with his little girl.

He no longer cared what she'd done. He'd got over her buggering off with that boyfriend. He'd forgiven that – he'd forgive *anything* if it meant he could bring her back to life.

Luke staggered towards the front door, unable to get a hint of who was on the other side of the yellowing net curtains with his drink-addled vision. But whoever it was wasn't about to give up and leave.

His teeth grated at the incessant banging, waiting for the door to fall in. It was about time the council replaced the bloody thing. Fucking rotten as hell, it was.

Luke pulled the door open, its progress thwarted by a snagged offcut of carpet covering the hallway floor. 'What the bloody hell do you w...' He stopped abruptly, blinking at the two men on his doorstep. 'What the...?'

'Finally!' Tom barked, barging inside. He glanced over his shoulder, making sure Dan followed him and that no one was lurking around outside who might recognise him. 'Planning to leave us standing there all day, were you?'

Shutting the door, Luke stared at the men who had pushed into his hallway. 'What are you doing here?'

Tom pasted on a sickly grin as he slapped his arm around Luke's shoulder. 'This is my mate, Dan. Dan, this is Luke.'

Dan smiled uncomfortably at the drunk man.

'I thought we'd swing by,' Tom continued. 'We need a place to crash for a few days and I didn't think you'd mind.'

Pulling away, Luke swayed, his hand reaching to steady himself against the wall. He hadn't seen Tom Bedworth since the man had turned him over with that crack shop contract. And that was part of the reason Deb had walked out in the first place, believing he could no longer be trusted to provide for her. 'It's not a good time at the moment,' Luke said, moving back towards the door. 'Maybe another time.'

Tom slammed Luke against the wall, the reverberation dislodging a plastic-framed print of Birmingham City FC from its nail. 'Actually, now is the *perfect* time.'

He replaced the snarl on his face with a practised grin and then smoothed down the lapels of Luke's stained sports jacket. 'Let's not fall out over this, my old mate. I don't hold it against you with what happened with our little "venture".'

'Against *me*?' Luke gasped. '*You* were the one who pulled the crack production, then binned me off and y...'

'You're confused,' Tom smiled coldly. Ignoring Dan's concerned expression, he took Luke's arm and steered him towards where he remembered the living room to be in the small semi-detached house. 'You're a bit worse for wear. Have things been getting on top of you?'

Dan followed the two men into the cluttered sitting room where empty cider cans and takeaway cartons littered the grubby carpet. *Who the fuck was this bloke and what was all this about crack?* He didn't want to get involved in any more shit. They had a shed-load of money on them and if this bloke was a drug-addled nut-job, he could also be a thief. What was Tom thinking? 'Look, maybe we should just go.'

'Nonsense!' Smiling viciously, Tom pushed Luke into the nearest chair. 'Luke's a good friend of mine. And it looks like you could do with some company, couldn't you, my old son?'

Luke winced as Tom slapped him on the back, the slap feeling like a thousand needles. He didn't want Bedworth here, but he didn't want any trouble either. He couldn't take it.

Tom jerked his head in the direction of the kitchen. 'Grab some cans from the fridge, Dan. We'll have a drink and chat about old times.' He waited until Dan reluctantly left the room before turning back to Luke. 'Now don't fuck me about,' he hissed. 'We're staying here for as long as we need. I'm trusting you don't have a problem with that?' His stained teeth bared into a mouldy grimace. 'You don't want further misfortune befalling you or your family, do you?'

Luke shook his head. Tom *could* make things worse by doing what he'd previously threatened and tell the council he'd been using the house to cook crack. He'd be sure to get kicked out then and, if that happened, all traces of what was left of his daughter and where she'd grown up would be taken from him. That was one prospect too much to bear, so he'd have to do what Tom said, however much he didn't want to.

His eyes moved to the framed picture on the wall of Deb standing with him and his ex-wife, taken when they'd been a family – before everything went wrong.

'I thought you were still running that place up the Hagley Road?' Luke muttered, wishing he had the balls to sling Bedworth, his lies and fake promises out of his house, but he'd never had the backbone to stand up to the man – even when they'd been at school and certainly not now.

Something else Deb had thrown at him just before she'd walked out. *She'd said he was a coward and she'd been right.*

'The Aurora's hit a bit of a stumbling block, that's all, but things will be okay soon,' Tom said, enjoying Luke's discomfort. It was pleasurable sitting in this man's home knowing *he'd* been the one to offload the man's trog of a daughter.

Obviously, he'd pretend he had no idea about Deb's demise. Despite what he'd threatened the little scrubber with in the past, if Tom understood correctly, Luke was unaware his darling daughter had worked at the Aurora and it was best to keep it that way. The thick fuck didn't have the first clue. It was laughable.

'Is that your daughter?' Dan returned to the room, seeing where Luke's eyes rested. 'She's a little stunner!' He handed Luke and Tom a can of Strongbow, failing to notice the warning glare on Tom's face, nor the tears brimming in Luke's eyes. He studied the photograph and frowned. 'She don't half look like a girl I saw at your place a few weeks back, Tom.'

'Nah, most definitely not,' Tom said hastily. *If Dan didn't shut the fuck up, he'd throttle him.*

'My daughter's dead...' Luke said hollowly.

'Oh, shit, mate! I'm sorry to hear that,' Tom exclaimed, the lies tripping easily from his mouth.

'Oh my God!' Dan gasped. 'What happened?'

Tom scowled harder. *Shut. The. Fuck. Up. Dan. You. Prick.*

'A hit and run.' Luke's voice was barely audible. His shaking fingers struggled to open the fresh can in his hand. 'Some bastard mowed her down. The funeral's tomorrow and I don't know how I'll get through it.'

'Dreadful, just dreadful,' Tom wittered. Taking Luke's can, he opened it and then deposited it back in the man's hand. 'But there you go, see? You shouldn't be on your own at a time like this. That must be why I was drawn to come here.'

Dan listened to Tom's bullshit. Shrugging, he turned back to stare at the photograph, sure he'd seen that girl at the Aurora.

4

Waiting until Seb had ended the call and placed his mobile on the bedside table, Sam pushed herself up onto her elbows and pressed her lips to his. 'Problems?'

Seb traced his fingers down Sam's cheek, wishing he could remain exactly where he was. 'No, but I do have to go.'

Sam frowned. 'I didn't think we were going anywhere until late morning?'

Moving to the edge of the bed, Seb reluctantly got up and stared back at his phone. 'Neither did I, but that was Neil. Baker wants to talk to me.'

Sam tensed. Although she was aware Seb paid Detective Inspector Baker a large chunk of money every month to be kept informed of any goings on concerning the firm and made larger ad hoc payments to ensure certain things were 'overlooked' when the need arose, what could he possibly want to see Seb for all of a sudden?

The relationship with Baker had done them all favours in the past, but it also had its flaws. The detective's clout wasn't foolproof and keeping the Stokers off radar had gone wrong on a couple of occasions. Those episodes could have been disastrous had they not been averted, so the prospect of the man making an impromptu visit unnerved her. Even more so when plans for a massive heist were underway. 'What's happened, Seb?' she asked. 'Baker's coming to the Orchid?'

'Yes, but it won't be about anything important. Since the Peacock burnt down, I haven't had a chance to touch base with him, so he'll want to remind me that our arrangement still stands, I expect.'

Sam bit her bottom lip. 'You don't think it's anything to do with that runner, do you?'

Seb grinned the easy smile he reserved only for her. 'No, I don't. That was sorted. Baker hasn't any cause to be aware of that, so don't worry, okay?'

Nodding, Sam leant back against the headboard whilst the en suite shower sprang to life, hoping Seb was right with his presumption.

She knew he'd dealt with the runner who had given up the safes' codes, and although she didn't know the details, she could guess. She just prayed Seb's need for retaliation didn't consume him. How he dealt with things was not what she'd been used to, but he was fair, and she didn't want that to change. But she'd trust his judgement. Her past mistrust had almost ruined them, and she would never make that mistake again.

Getting out of bed, Sam pulled on her satin robe and glanced in the cheval mirror before padding across the landing. She then moved down the stairs and grabbed the paper sticking through the letterbox.

Making her way into the kitchen, she flicked on the kettle and gazed through the window into the established garden, dappled with the morning winter sun. Plants always brought a sense of

calm and Sam needed that today because she couldn't shift the
sense of foreboding creeping along her veins.

Hearing the kettle come to the boil, Sam made a cup of tea and
sat down at the large kitchen table to flick through the paper.
Randomly scanning the pages, she stopped at the photograph of
the girl killed on the night of the fire.

Belatedly wishing she hadn't looked, nausea rose. Her instincts
were spot on. She'd thought the previously printed vague description of the victim had matched that of the girl she'd screamed all
manner of insults at that night, believing her to have been the one
Seb had betrayed her with.

Even though she now knew what was true, the image of
walking into that bedroom in her very own house, to see what
appeared to be the man she loved beyond anything in bed with a
girl only just old enough to have left school, had floored her
beyond everything.

Thankfully, as that fateful night unfolded, Sam had realised
her error. Seb had not betrayed her with this girl or anyone. The
girl had been a victim herself – a victim of an elaborate plan. And
this photo proved she was indeed that same girl. The girl used by
Sam's sister – a previously unknown sister – who had been trying
to kill her, kill Seb – kill *all* of them.

Sam traced her finger over Deb Banner's photograph.

Marina Devlin hadn't killed Deb. She might have killed her
own brother, but being as the woman had inveigled her way into
Sam's office and was busy hellbent on putting a bullet in her brain,
then she couldn't have killed the girl.

Even Marina Devlin couldn't be in two places at once. But Sam
couldn't help feel convinced it was all somehow connected.

She shuddered, the memory of that night continuing to haunt
her in a never-ending series of flashbacks. Witnessing Seb get shot

had been the worst. The thought of losing him forever, unthinkable.

Sam sipped her tea, grateful the searing liquid distracted her from the tumult of disturbing thoughts.

Of course, Seb was right. Marina would have retreated back to London by now. The woman wouldn't risk remaining in Birmingham. Not after *that*.

But that she was out there *somewhere*, possibly planning to finish what she'd failed to do last time, continued to play on Sam's mind.

Shaking her head, Sam returned to the paper. There wasn't anything she could do about what had happened, nor about Marina Devlin still being around, but what she *could* do was get further information on the disgusting creature who ran Deb Banner's place of work – the man intrinsically linked to a lot of things. The one from her mother's past... Tom Bedworth.

Sam read the article accompanying the photograph:

The victim killed on the night of 6 February in Granville Street, city centre, can now be named as Deborah Banner, 16, originally from Frankley.

Ms Banner, the recipient of a vicious and purposeful attack, was run over repeatedly before the driver fled the scene.

Deborah's father, Luke, is set to bury his only child tomorrow at St Leonard's Church, Frankley.

Mr Banner said: 'I cannot begin to explain how devastated I am. The person responsible must be brought to justice.'

The incident is still under investigation and anyone with information, or who witnessed anything that night, is urged to contact West Midlands Police as soon as possible...

Sam tapped her finger on the newsprint. *Luke Banner?* Did this man know what his daughter did for a living? Did he know this Tom Bedworth person that Deb had worked for?

She chewed the inside of her cheek. It would make an awkward conversation, but if she could locate Luke and get him to talk, she might get leads to where the scum, Bedworth, was hiding.

Perhaps Luke Banner believed Bedworth had something to do with his daughter's murder too? He might have even seen Deb with Marina?

All these people seemed to be linked and if Sam could just speak to the man, she might learn something useful.

Seb had his hands full with the heist and, like she'd promised, she'd be there in whatever way was required, but she still had her own mission. Ridding Birmingham of the lowlifes grooming young girls like Deb Banner to work in the sex trade was important to her, and if any of these things were connected, it gave even more reason to pursue it.

Either way, it wouldn't hurt to test the water by locating Luke Banner.

Sam frowned. She could turn up at Deb's funeral, but grilling a man busy burying his daughter wasn't the best. It would also expose to onlookers that she was digging around.

Instead, she needed to find out where Luke Banner lived. Frankley wasn't a big place, so it couldn't be that difficult.

* * *

Seb folded his arms and waited impatiently for Baker to get to the point. If he'd been pulled from his morning off purely to chat about the bleeding weather or the unfairness of insurance claims, then Baker could sling his bloody hook.

If he couldn't spend time with Sam, like he'd prefer, then he'd rather be fine-tuning his plan to intercept the container landing at

Bristol docks and getting the lowdown on those no-necks from Wolverhampton.

'Yeah, insurance firms are notorious for not paying out, short of incidents with time-stamped footage!' Baker continued, laughing at his own analogy. His beady eyes scrutinised Samantha Reynold's office. 'It's good of your wife-to-be to allow you to use her premises whilst you're in this position. When's your wedding again?'

Seb's jaw tightened. Did Baker think it amusing to rub his face in the fact that he had sod all to his name at the moment? Putting this whole business straight couldn't come quick enough. And as for the wedding, it would be soon, but if Baker was angling for an invite, he would be sorely disappointed.

He eyed the balding detective scornfully. 'Are you here for anything of importance, Baker, or are you just here to nose around and state the fucking obvious?'

Baker flinched, disguising his reaction by scratching his chin. He shifted his overweight frame in the chair. 'Well, I...'

'Our agreement still stands, if that's what's bothering you.' Seb sighed. 'Just because some fucker torched my casino and the insurance think it's arson doesn't mean I won't uphold my liabilities.'

But it was getting that way. After shelling out the preliminary payment for the rebuild two weeks ago and covering the staff wages for the month, things were tight. But he'd rather hack his own tongue out than admit that. *Especially to Baker.*

DI Baker submissively raised his hands. 'That thought never crossed my mind,' he lied, smiling weakly. 'We go back a long way, Mr Stoker. Despite our ups and downs, I'd like to think we have a good relationship.'

Seb returned the smile, but failed to conceal the sneer it contained. There was no such thing as having a 'good relationship' with the police. Not from his side of the fence. A necessary one, perhaps, but good or through choice – *never*. 'Okay, so now get to the point!'

Baker exhaled loudly, the air passing through his teeth making a strange whistling noise. 'This isn't my doing, Mr Stoker, so I'll just come out with it.'

Seb clenched his teeth and cracked his knuckles, wishing to God that Baker would hurry up and do so.

'It's been brought to my attention that you're due to be questioned about an incident at the Aurora.'

Seb retained a neutral expression at the mention of the Aurora, yet his mind whirred frantically. *The Aurora?*

'I take it you're aware of the place?' Baker raised an eyebrow.

Seb swallowed his annoyance. Baker clearly expected him to deny knowledge of the place when it was obvious he knew otherwise. *But what incident was he referring to?* 'I'm aware of the Aurora, yes, but I can't say I've had any dealings with whoever runs it.' *Because if he had, the bastard would already be six feet under.* 'It's hardly on par with anything of interest to me.'

Baker chuckled, the noise grating Seb's jangling nerves. 'I have to agree, Mr Stoker. The Aurora is nowhere near the standard of clubs like yours.'

Seb removed a cigarette from his monogrammed gold case and raised it to his mouth, keeping his steely gaze on Baker. 'You mentioned an incident? What incident is this and why would I be questioned in relation to it?'

Baker's uncomfortableness returned. 'Erm... Well, we received a rather disturbing phone call concerning the Aurora. When my officers arrived to check out the report, they found the place deserted. They also discovered the body of a woman concealed in a wardrobe in the attic...'

Seb stiffened. 'A body?'

Baker nodded. 'A woman. At a guess, in her late forties or early fifties. By the state of her, I'd say she'd been there a while. Unsure of the cause of death at the moment, apart from that it was foul play.' He looked at Seb questioningly. 'There were also signs that in addition to this body, someone else had been kept in the attic against their will, but there was no sign of another corpse. Not that we've found yet, anyway.'

Seb hoped the twitch on his face wasn't visible. That 'prisoner' had been Sam's mother, Linda, but he didn't know anything about a dead body. 'What has any of this got to do with me?'

Baker had the good grace to avert his eyes when he next spoke. He knew he wouldn't like the expression his words engendered on Seb's face. 'The last person reported to be seen at the premises was you, Mr Stoker.'

'Me?' Seb gasped. He *had* gone there, like he'd promised Sam, to see if he could catch the man who had tortured Linda, but there hadn't been a soul about. Wherever Bedworth had gone, he was no longer at the Aurora. And it was there the trail had ended.

'It was also reported your brothers were seen at the property on earlier occasions,' Baker added. 'What's your interest in the place?'

Seb's eyes narrowed. Andrew and Neil had indeed gone there months ago, but they hadn't set foot in it since. That was a fact.

It was *him* who had stupidly pulled the Aurora from the equation as not worth bothering with, yet now the bloody place was at the helm of *everything*. 'You're talking about reports, but exactly *who* reported my brothers being there a million years ago and that I just happened to be the last one seen before a corpse was discovered?' Seb laughed mirthlessly. 'Let me guess. One of my competitors from the casino strip, by any chance? Bill Shipley? Or perhaps one of those tossers from that place down by the Arcadian? Well, you can tell them that th...'

'Actually, since the building was purchased last year, we've had reports filed almost on a daily basis about the toings and froings there,' Baker interjected. 'One of the neighbours is well known for calling us to complain about the "unsavoury goings on" and the "house of ill repute". She's made it her life's work to document everything.' He rolled his eyes. 'We usually put her reports to one side, but now a body has been discovered, we have no choice but to treat this woman as a witness.'

'You're saying I'm a murder suspect?' Seb snorted derisively. 'Oh, come on, Baker! Out of *everything* that's gone on in the past, you're lumping something like this on me?'

Baker shrugged his shoulders. '*I'm* not lumping anything on you. I'm *warning* you that this one's out of my hands. That's why I'm here. I'm just keeping my end of our arrangement by letting you know.'

Seb nodded abruptly, showing no sign of being rattled. He chewed the inside of his cheek, the gnawing growing in the base of his stomach. *Fuck.*

Whatever had gone on at the Aurora was sod all to do with him, but it didn't look good. The last thing he needed was cops following him around when he was poised to pull a massive job. 'Look, Baker, this is nothing to do with me!'

'For the record, I believe you,' Baker said. 'The problem is, the force will want to know, if that's the case, why you were there at all?'

Seb dug his nails into his palms, knowing he couldn't say why he'd been at the Aurora without opening a can of fucking worms.

Shit, this was bad.

5

'What do you look like?' Mickey guffawed, eyeing his daughter with ill-concealed mirth. 'You so don't look like you!'

'That's the general idea!' Marina snapped, resenting Mickey finding her new look so amusing. Did he really think she'd choose to look like this if she wasn't so desperate to find Dan and her bloody money?

'I think she looks amazing!' Sophie gushed, openly admiring Marina's look. 'The hair is great and I *love* the clothes!'

Marina scowled. *Wow, what a compliment...* Just what she wanted – the green light from a vacant, plastic bitch...

It was hardly surprising this thick slapper was impressed. This clobber was the sort of get-up the tart would wear herself, and that alone only angered her further.

Sophie's fake pink nails scraped against Marina's sparkly halter-neck top. 'The material is beautiful too. Oh, I'd so love a top like this!' She batted her fake eyelashes in Mickey's direction. 'Don't you think I'd look good in this, babe?'

Mickey grinned. *That she would.* And he might have to treat her to one just like it once he'd got a bit more ready cash. In fact, if Marina wasn't his daughter, he'd quite fancy a go with her. The deep red of the wig completely changed her face and she no longer resembled her vindictive bitch of a mother. But when all was said and done, Marina *was* his daughter. *Sophie, however, was not...*

Openly squeezing Sophie's buttock, he slipped his hand inside her crop top to tweak her nipple. 'Maybe I'll treat you to some new clothes, if you're a good girl.'

Marina rolled her eyes at her father and his fawning Barbie doll. The material of this top wasn't nice either. It was scratchy, cheap and thoroughly bloody horrible. *Much like Sophie...* 'If you're going to treat this flat like a knocking shop, then you might as well fuck off,' she spat. 'I'm trying to sort out this shit, so what are you doing to help?'

Sophie grinned inanely, oblivious to Marina's scathing words or thoughts. 'Your tits look amazing too! Where did you get yours done? I got a great deal with a surgeon in...'

'They're real, thank you!' Marina cried, unable to quite believe the ridiculous question. *Christ, how much worse could this get?*

Flouncing across the room in her sky-high heels, she snatched her new sequined bag from the table.

'Where are you going?' Mickey asked, only half-interested now Sophie's hand was massaging his groin.

'To do what *you* should be doing!' Marina shouted, strutting down the hallway. 'Finding my bloody money!'

And although she wasn't looking forward to doing this herself, it was the only way of getting anywhere.

* * *

It seemed like a hundred years since Sam had been to Northfield or any of the surrounding areas. So much had happened since receiving that letter from someone claiming to be her mother and meeting the woman in question, Linda, at the Hen and Chicks.

But some things remained the same...

Sam clambered back into the taxi, glad she'd told the driver to wait. 'Can you take me to the Horseshoe in Frankley, please?'

As the taxi turned around and pulled out of the pot-holed car park, Sam glanced back at the looming façade of the Hen and Chicks.

Going in there just now, she'd been greeted with the same immediate silence she'd received the first time. Everyone knew who she was and who she was involved with, which caused a heavy aura of distrust or over-nicety. It never failed to make her feel uncomfortable.

At least no one had asked after Linda. Sam had no wish to recount what had happened to her mother or that she was, at present, in a private rehab clinic. But one thing was for definite – no one knew of Luke Banner's whereabouts. He certainly didn't drink in the Hen and Chicks.

It had only been when Sam was leaving that someone had suggested she try where she was heading right now.

Smoothing down her jacket, Sam watched as the taxi crossed the Bristol Road and headed into Frankley, the streets a never-ending maze of houses.

'The pub's just down here, lady,' the driver said, his eyes meeting Sam's in the rear-view mirror. 'Do you want me to wait, or are you staying?'

'Wait, please,' Sam confirmed as the car pulled up outside a 1960s-built pub slap bang in the middle of a housing estate. 'I won't be long.'

Getting out of the taxi, she walked to the entrance of the Horseshoe, nodding at two men leaning against the door with pints in their hands. She glanced at her watch. Deb Banner's funeral would have finished, so Luke could be here drowning his sorrows by now.

She moved into the bar, the smoke in the taproom thick. Ignoring the inquisitive stares and whispers, she inched past a group of men around the pool table, ignoring the remarks, 'That's the woman from the Orchid,' and 'That's Stoker's missus.'

The landlord, a heavy-set man with straggly thinning hair, ran his eyes over Sam appreciatively as she reached the bar. 'Yes, love, what can I get you?'

'I'm looking for Luke Banner,' Sam said, immediately noticing the conversation level dwindling.

The landlord's appreciative gaze morphed into suspicion. 'Luke Banner?'

Sam refused to turn to face the many sets of eyes burning into her back. These people suspected she was here to bring trouble, courtesy of herself or the Stokers, so she'd try a different approach.

Smiling at the landlord, she continued. 'I heard about what happened to Mr Banner's daughter and I'd like to pay my respects.' Hearing murmuring from behind, she pressed on, unfazed. 'I know it was Deb's funeral today and being a local girl, I felt it right to offer my condolences.' Linda *had* lived in Northfield, so what she'd just said was kind of true...

Sam kept a relaxed look about her, even though she felt anything but. She finally glanced around, the many eyes immediately looking away. 'It's a bit of a poor show if I can't show my respects, is it not? Is there a wake?'

'Luke ain't having no wake,' a burly man piped up. 'He's in too much of a state. Besides, he ain't got the money.'

'Perhaps I can help out on that score?' Sam smiled sweetly. *Sometimes feminine guiles were necessary.* 'Will he be in here later? I can wait.'

The man studied Sam for what seemed like an age. 'I doubt it, but...' He glanced at his mate. 'I suppose I could tell you where he lives.'

Sam concealed her excitement and smiled. 'That would be great!' *Finally! She was getting somewhere.*

6

'You're a suspect in a murder case?' Andrew cried, throwing his hands in the air. 'What the fuck, Seb?'

Seb closed his eyes in frustration. 'That's about the crux of it, yes.'

Neil looked between Seb and Andrew. 'Why hasn't Baker sorted this out? Isn't that what we fucking pay him for?'

'There's only so much he can conceal,' Seb muttered. Not that any of that helped.

'And there was me thinking the worst-case scenario was that someone was deranged enough to notice Simon Parker had gone missing.' Hearing a notification, Andrew glanced at his phone. 'Ah! It looks like I might have just received info about the Wolverhampton crew's movements.'

Seb raised his eyebrows. 'You've put word out?'

'Only keeping my ear to the ground. Subtly, of course.' Andrew leant on the desk with his elbows. 'But more to the point, where do we go with your little problem?'

'It's relatively straightforward...' Neil said. 'Sam.'

'Sam?' Seb cried. 'I haven't told her anything yet, but what's she got to do with it?'

'She hasn't, but *Linda* has.' Neil grinned. 'Get Sam to ask Linda what she knows. *She* was the one locked in the Aurora's fucking attic, so if a woman was killed and shoved in a cupboard, then she must have seen something.'

Andrew nodded. 'That's a good point! You can bet your life this woman's death is something to do with that fucker, Bedworth. All Linda's got to do is tell the cops what happened to her at his hands, and that will sort it!'

'It will also explain why you were there. Admit you went looking for Bedworth. It stands to reason you'd want to find the man responsible for keeping your mother-in-law locked in an attic,' Neil suggested, proud of his acumen. 'But make sure to add that the place was abandoned when you got there and you never saw him.'

'Neither did you have anything to do with women in wardrobes,' Andrew added.

Seb chewed his bottom lip. 'Bedworth or not, I ain't no grass. I don't give names to the police.'

'But *you* won't be!' Neil cried. 'Linda will, therefore your conscience is clear.'

Seb raked his fingers through his hair. 'But if the cops get their hands on Bedworth, then I can't. I want to be able to do that for Sam.'

'You'll be doing fuck all for Sam if you're on a trumped-up murder charge,' Andrew reasoned. 'See sense, bruv!'

Seb stared at Andrew, his mind ticking over. 'Hmm, perhaps... Providing we get our mitts on the twat before the cops do and it doesn't uncover additional snippets of info we would rather not become knowledge.' *And there were several of those...*

'You'll just have to make sure that doesn't happen.'

Seb nodded. That was a definite. He had to get rid of any suspicion fast. Every passing second delayed moving forward with the heist, which was detrimental to the reopening of the Peacock, as well as the recommencement of his life, without feeling like an abject failure. 'I'll speak to Sam when she gets back.'

* * *

Luke wearily dragged himself to the front door. He wouldn't have bothered answering at all had Tom not placed an order to the offy for another crate of lager to be delivered. By hell, he needed another drink!

Today was the worst. The police's presence at the funeral being the final insult. Aside from the cops, the only other mourner present was him.

His teeth gritted. No one liked him and it appeared no one had liked Deb either. Even Deb's wanker of a boyfriend hadn't shown his sorry arse. It was the least the bastard could have done, considering he'd stolen Deb away in the first place.

Pulling open the door, Luke squinted through the bright sunlight at the unknown woman on his doorstep, disappointment at it not being the off-licence delivery burgeoning. 'Yeah?'

Sam smiled at the dishevelled man wavering in the doorway. 'Mr Banner?'

Luke struggled to focus. 'If you've come for another story, then I'm not interested. Just fuck off and leave me alone!'

Sam stopped the door from slamming in her face by positioning her foot to stop it closing without lopping off her toes. 'I'm not from the newspapers. I'm very sorry to disturb you on a day such as today, but I really need to talk to you.'

Luke blinked and used the door frame to steady himself.

'My name is Samantha Reynold. I knew your daughter and I want to help find out what happened to her.'

Luke faltered. *Samantha Reynold?* As in Samantha Reynold and Seb Stoker? Jesus Christ. Did she know something about how Deb had died?

Deciding he'd got little to lose, he stepped back into the hallway. 'You'd better come in.' Luke staggered into the sitting room and gestured towards a chair, wondering where Tom and Dan had disappeared to. 'Take a seat.'

Nudging an empty Pot Noodle out of the way, Sam perched on the edge of the green velour armchair, trying not to make it obvious she was taking in the general state of the place, or counting the pile of empty beer cans on the coffee table. 'I won't take up much of your time, Mr Banner. I appreciate this must be difficult.'

'What have you found out about my Deb?' Luke asked. 'The police won't tell me jack shit and I have the right to know.'

'I was hoping you'd be able to tell me that,' Sam frowned. 'I need to know more about where Deb worked and particularly the man she worked for.'

7

Bursting into the large shed at the bottom of the garden, Luke stumbled through the dust-covered remains of the crack shop he'd made a nice living out of before Tom had pulled the plug on it. 'You fucking cocksucker!' he roared, launching himself at Tom.

The cigarette dangling from Tom's mouth dropped to the floor as he was ripped from his perch on the workbench. Momentarily dazed as he was pinned to the floor, he looked up into Luke's face. 'What the f...?'

'You never told me Deb was working for you at the Aurora!' Luke screamed. 'You bastard! How could you allow that? You *knew* she was my daughter and you let her sell herself?'

Seeing Luke raise his fist, his face twisted with rage, Tom regained control. He grabbed Luke's wrist, deftly twisting his arm. 'Don't be a cunt all your life, Banner,' he snarled, twisting harder to reverse the control. 'Forget about that tart daughter of yours for a moment and tell me what the fuck Samantha Reynold wanted!' His eyes narrowed. The second he'd heard her voice, he'd grabbed Dan's arm and yanked him unceremoniously from the lounge. 'You let that stupid bitch into the house? Are you fucking thick? What did you say?'

Dan stared open mouthed at the unfolding scene. Half an hour he'd been in this weird shed place whilst Tom paced up and down, chain smoking and muttering. As he'd been dragged from the house to find himself crashing through the back door into the litter-strewn garden, not once, despite being asked several times, had Tom given an inkling why they were hiding in here like fugitives. Now Luke had gone apeshit? 'What the hell is going on?'

'Ask *him*!' Luke screamed, hatred for the person who had pimped his daughter overriding his longstanding fear of the man. Even the pain in his arm wouldn't stop him this time. 'You fucking lied! You pretended you didn't know Deb had gone AWOL, yet she was at yours all along?'

Tom laughed. 'So the fuck what? She turned up, so I was hardly going to turn her away.' He increased the twist on Luke's arm. 'Very popular with the punters she was, too!'

Luke struggled underneath Tom, his face a paroxysm of rage. 'You bast...'

'I had more than a few goes with her myself, mate. Right little goer she was – like her slag of a mother, no doubt!' Tom ramped up his hold as Luke's fury gave him power he wouldn't have believed the man possessed. He leant closer. 'Tell me what you told Sam Reynold. Did you say I was here?'

'I should have!' Luke spat, his body thrashing around in an attempt to release himself. 'I always got the gist you had an issue with the Stokers and now it seems you've got the Reynolds on your case too. I should have fucking told that woman everything because she's after you. After you *big* time!'

Dan's eyes flicked between Tom's rabid expression and the raw hatred on Luke's face. *This was fucked up.* Why would Samantha Reynold be after Tom? He knew Tom hated the Stokers, but...

Unless...

'Fuck, Tom, do you think they've found out it was me who torched the Peacock? They might have seen me getting into your car. Shit! We need to get out of here and...'

'Shut the fuck up!' Tom yelled. Dan had just admitted he'd torched the Peacock? Holy mother of God. The man was a retard.

'It all makes sense now,' Luke roared. 'I might have known you were behind that. Sam Reynold thinks you're linked to everything. She even suggested you knew something about Deb's murder!'

The flash of fear on Tom's face gave Luke the added impetus to find the additional strength required to dislodge the man. 'Seems a lot of people are after you, you utter cunt!'

Suddenly leaping up, Luke wrenched his arm free, catching Tom unaware with a swift right hook. 'Did you kill my daughter, Bedworth?'

Tom scrabbled around on the floor like an upturned beetle, his fear multiplying as Luke grabbed a crowbar from the workbench.

'I'm telling Sam Reynold and the Stokers where you are. But only after I've killed you!' Luke growled.

Not taking his eyes from Luke, Tom's fingers closed around the handle of a wrench on the floor underneath the workbench near where he lay. *Luke was planning on telling Samantha?* That couldn't happen. The thick fuck hadn't given him up whilst she'd been sitting in his living room, so the man had lost his chance. He wouldn't get another one.

Despite wanting to run out of the shed and in the opposite direction away from this pair of lunatics, Dan stepped forward. If Luke Banner told Sam Reynold, then the Stokers would be coming – not only for Tom, but for *him*. *Fuck. Fuck. Fuck!* 'Look, guys, let's calm down. I think that we...'

Dan's voice deflected Luke for long enough for Tom to react.

As Tom lurched to his feet, Dan could only watch in horror as the heavy metal head of a wrench was brought down on Luke's skull. The noise of cracking bone was a sound he hadn't heard before in his life and one he had no urge to ever hear again.

With bile racing up his throat, Dan staggered back against the workbench as Tom continued smashing the heavy tool onto Luke's head, blood splattering over him like a garden sprinkler.

* * *

Sam stormed into her office, her face thunderous. 'I knew it, I just *knew* it!' She looked from Seb to Andrew and Neil. 'I've just been to see Luke Banner – the father of that girl mowed down around the back of here. You know, the girl that... that you...'

'I know who she is,' Seb muttered, not needing reminding of what had almost ruined his chance of marriage before even getting down the aisle. 'You went to see her father? Why would you do that?'

Sam slapped her handbag down on the desk and shrugged off her jacket, her face full of determination. 'Whilst you're tied up planning the heist, I thought I'd do some digging. I haven't forgotten about getting to the bottom of who was behind what happened to my mother.'

'*I* haven't forgotten about that either,' Seb said. 'But getting things put into place with the heist must come first.' He ignored the look on Andrew's face questioning why he hadn't stopped Sam in her tracks and broached speaking to her about Linda.

He would, but all in good time.

'I knew Bedworth must be connected with everything and it looks like I was right,' Sam continued. 'Get this! It turns out Luke Banner had no idea his daughter worked at the Aurora. No idea at all!' She flapped her hand. 'And, yeah, I get that perhaps that isn't too surprising, but you should have seen his face when I asked about Bedworth!'

She paced the room, her excitement palpable. 'Luke knows him! He may have tried to conceal it, but he couldn't hide the blind rage behind his drunken eyes when I hinted Bedworth might have something to do with Deb's death!'

'We don't know that for certain,' Neil reasoned. 'It's a theory, yes, but...'

'Tom Bedworth *is* connected, I'm sure of it. I wanted to see Luke's reaction and I got it. I bloody got it loud and clear!' Sam grabbed Seb's hand. 'Don't you see? Luke knows where Bedworth is! We've got to get onto that. Seb, go and check him out yourself. We can't let this go. I know you're planning the jump, but I want Bedworth to pay for what he did to Linda and...'

Seeing the Stoker brothers exchange glances, she paused. 'Don't you want to put a stop to it? I do! I need payback for Linda, and he probably killed that Deb girl as well. In fact, it wouldn't surprise me if he was behind robbing your money! Talking of which, what did the police want?' She glanced around. 'They're not still here, are they? I didn't see anyone when I came through reception.'

Neil stood up. If Seb didn't broach this issue with Sam now, then he never would. Whatever happened, until police suspicion was removed, Seb couldn't sniff around *anyone* with connections to the Aurora. None of them could. It would raise too many red flags. Sam had to back off until it was sorted.

He jerked his head at Andrew. 'Let's leave them to it.'

Andrew and Neil's hasty retreat from the office showed Sam something was amiss. Nerves fluttered in her stomach. 'Seb? What's going on?'

Seb sighed. Sam would like what he was about to tell her and what he would ask less than a hole in the head, but it had to be done. 'You'd best sit down.'

8

'Sirendale Clinic.'

Pressing back down on the intercom button, Sam cleared her throat. 'Samantha Reynold, here to see Linda Matthews. I spoke to the manager earlier about a visit.'

After a slight pause, a buzzing sound released the door. Pulling it open, Sam walked into the airy reception, the leather sofas and palm trees in brightly coloured ceramic pots making the place resemble a spa, rather than a rehabilitation clinic for drug dependency and its associated problems.

Sam moved towards the brunette perched behind the reception desk, who extended a gold pen from her manicured hand.

'Good morning, Ms Reynold. If you could just sign in for me, please? I've informed Mrs Brunswick of your arrival. She'll be down in just a moment to escort you to see Linda.'

'Thank you,' Sam said, hastily scrawling her name in the leather visitors' book.

She very nearly hadn't got anywhere when requesting an urgent visit this morning. There was another full week before Linda was officially allowed visitors and therefore a fair bit of pulling rank with her standing in the city was necessary in order to override the clinic's strict rule. But she'd done it and that was the important thing.

Still reeling from the bombshell Seb had dropped on her yesterday, Sam had so far controlled her panic, but it was becoming difficult. Especially as Linda was the only person who could put a halt to it.

A woman with auburn hair curled into a chignon and a suit on par with her own glided into the reception. 'Ms Reynold, I presume? Please follow me.'

Sam waited for Mrs Brunswick to enter a code into the door leading off from the reception, then followed her down the brightly lit carpeted corridor with doors on both sides like a hotel.

'This is most unusual, Ms Reynold.' Mrs Brunswick glanced at Sam. 'I trust your visit won't jeopardise Linda's recovery?'

'No, it won't,' Sam replied tersely, not liking the woman's tone. She didn't know how her mother would react to her request, but as much as she didn't wish to impede Linda's progress, she had no choice but to ask this of her.

If Seb was pulled in for suspected murder, it would trash everything. It was not something she could stand by and let happen. Not when she held the key to doing something about it. Or rather *Linda* did...

Mrs Brunswick stopped outside room thirty-one, the numbers attached to the door on a brass plaque. 'Linda's in here. Press the buzzer if you need anything.' She smiled tightly. 'You have half an hour.'

Biting her lip to stop from responding with a rude retort, Sam took a deep breath and waited for Mrs Brunswick to move away before knocking on the door.

* * *

Dan threw the can of lager on the floor in frustration. He'd been trying to open it for ages with his one good hand, but his fingers shook so much, he couldn't do it. Meanwhile, Tom had sat there the whole time, watching him struggle.

Dan's eyes tracked through the kitchen window to the dilapidated shed and nausea brewed amongst the contents of the many cans of lager he'd already downed. The shed might as well have a neon sign on top of it for the police helicopter to spot: *Dead body in here...*

This was not what he constituted as starting afresh! He hadn't signed up for this shit. He'd come to Birmingham to escape the growing list of people he'd ripped off at poker, but now things were worse than ever.

'Look at the state of you,' Tom sneered. 'You're a bag of fucking nerves. Call yourself a hard case? Pretending to be in with the big shots from London, when realistically, you're shitting your kecks because you've got a corpse on your hands.' He stared pointedly at Dan's missing fingers. 'Sorry, I should say, "hand".'

Dan scowled. 'It wasn't me who killed the bloke! It was *you*. And by what Luke said before you bashed him to death, pretty soon we'll have the Stokers and Reynolds on our backs. What if that woman comes back? What if she brings the Stokers? What if th...'

'Oh, shut up!' Tom barked. 'You saw Banner pick up that crowbar, so what else could I do?'

He'd have killed the stupid bastard regardless. The second Samantha entered the house meant it was only a matter of time before Banner had to be removed. He'd become a downright liability and would have given them up sooner rather than later. Tom had only brought forward the inevitable. It was a mercy killing.

But this had caused a further problem. His brow furrowed.

'We'll have to find somewhere else to stay.'

'That's another thing!' Dan jumped to his feet to retrieve the can which had rolled into the corner of the room. 'You knew that girl was your mate's daughter and you gave her a job? That's out of order!'

Tom laughed heartily. 'Wow! Listen to Mr Morality! Next you'll be saying *I* killed that silly little tart as well, like Samantha Reynold reckons!'

Against his better judgement, Dan remained silent. Until yesterday, he hadn't made the connection that the girl killed in the hit and run was from the Aurora. Not until he'd seen that photo in Luke's lounge.

It was also playing on his mind that the same night it had happened – the night he'd torched the Peacock – he remembered gunk on Tom's car windscreen, as well as a crack... Neither of which had been there before...

And it had only been when Tom's car had gone AWOL from the Hyatt's underground car park that the man had become so insistent they leave.

Why was that, then?

Dan finally opened his can of lager and tipped the warm liquid into his mouth.

Surely Tom wouldn't have purposefully killed the girl and then lodged at her father's house?

No. Not even Tom was that sick in the head.

Tom batted the can out of Dan's hand, his eyes narrow slits. 'Fucking answer me! Do you reckon I killed Deb? Because if that's what you think, then you can fuck off!'

'No, of course I don't,' Dan lied, wiping the spilt beer from his chin.

'That's all right, then!' Tom watched Dan's face fluttering with panic. What a bloody arsehole. Whatever the man thought and despite his pretence of being the big 'I am', Dan Marlow was full of bullshit. He didn't have the balls to do shag all on his own. He was too much of a spineless bastard to think or say anything and it was about time he capitalised on that.

Slumping into a chair, he flexed his knuckles. 'I'm going to pay one of my mates over the Black Country a visit whilst you dig around for someone else who makes passports.'

'B-but I thought we couldn't risk going anywhere?'

'*I* can't,' Tom said, casually cracking open a fresh can of beer for himself. 'Not in Brum, anyway, but being as you've been saying how sick you are of being cooped up, now's your chance to get out for a while.'

Dan stared at Tom. 'But what if someone recognises me?'

Tom laughed coldly. 'You give yourself too much credit. No one knows you, so why would they recognise you?' He looked Dan up and down. 'Let's face it, your only distinguishing feature and point of interest is your missing hand! But I've already thought of that.'

Fishing a rubber glove from his pocket, Tom threw it at Dan, who stared at the yellow Marigold glove with horror. It was filled with something and looked like a body part found after several weeks at the bottom of a canal. 'What the fuck is this?'

'It's a glove, you twat! What do you think it is? I've shoved plasticine where your fingers should be. Good, ain't it? I made it myself, so don't say I don't do nothing for you. Wear it under those poncy white gloves you like sporting.'

Dan eyed the yellow rubbery monstrosity with repulsion. 'For God's sake! Are you serious? How am I supposed to have a piss with that thing on my hand?'

'The same way you do usually, I expect.' Tom's eyes narrowed. 'Just wear it and don't even *think* about taking it off in public. You might be a nobody, but I don't want even the most miniscule chance of someone placing you. Got it?'

Reasserting his authority over this muppet was long overdue. Dan had been stepping over the line for too long and had to be held in check. The bloke needed reminding he was a nobody – a *nothing*. 'I'll give you a couple of places and people to try. Meanwhile, I'll get on with the important stuff.'

Nodding miserably, Dan bypassed the fact that he was being sent out in a city where players in major firms could already have a warrant out for him and instead concentrated on the surge of unexpected freedom he'd been granted.

Tom was putting *him* in the firing line and despite, for now at least, having no choice but to do this man's bidding, he was getting heartily sick of the man's attitude and presumptions – he wasn't wearing *that*.

He glared at the horrible pretend hand once more. He might have over-embellished his standing in London, but he wasn't comfortable with people being knocked off left, right and centre. All he wanted was the easy life – cards, beer, money and women in whichever order and he didn't have to wear that thing to get those. If he was such a nobody, then he didn't need the crap disguise.

He'd let Tom think he would follow this latest absurd 'errand', but the man could screw himself. Since coming to this dump of a city, he'd fallen party to all manner of complicated things that he wanted no association with. Now Tom was lumping more stuff on him?

He knew where all the stolen cash was hidden and Tom could do little about it if he helped himself to one of those holdalls. There would be no cash at all if it wasn't for him.

But before anything else, he was having a well-earned night out for himself. He'd had enough stress.

Marina was gone, and like Tom said, he was irrelevant, so providing he kept clear of the Orchid, there was no reason he couldn't enjoy himself without the aid of a fucking creepy glove.

9

Linda's fingers trembled as she reached for her glass of iced water. She had been overjoyed to learn Sam was visiting earlier than expected, but she hadn't bargained for *this*...

She didn't want to let Sam down, but if she agreed to what was being asked, there would be repercussions. *Big* ones.

She had to think. *Quickly.*

Guilt flooded Sam, sensing her mother's stress. Linda looked so much better, or she *had*. 'I'm sorry to put you in this position. If there was another way...'

'But going to the police...' Linda's voice was quiet. 'Telling them everything that happened in that attic...'

'I realise raking that up is the last thing you need, especially as you're finally on the mend,' Sam said. 'I know you don't want anyone to know what that bastard did to you, but Seb can't be accused of a murder he didn't commit, he just can't!'

Her heart thumped. Seb might have committed several others, but not this one – and it was *this* they wanted him for. This happening in the middle of his plan to regenerate the Peacock would destroy him. Even being formally charged, even if nothing came of it, would tarnish his ability to return from what had happened. Time was of the essence.

'If the police knew what Bedworth did, they'd have to accept *he* must have murdered that woman, not Seb!' Sam cried. 'Think, Mum, *please*! Can you remember anything that happened to the woman they found in the wardrobe? Anything at all? It must have happened in front of you, so you must recall something?'

Linda forced the water into her mouth to buy extra time whilst she processed her options.

Yes, she had seen it – she'd seen everything. Tom *had* killed Amelia, and Linda had been able to do little about it. In reality, she probably wouldn't have, even if she could have, but she hadn't told Sam any of this. There had been too many other things to deal with.

It wasn't that she wouldn't tell Sam, but the police...?

Her daughter was way off with the reasons behind her reticence.

Speaking to the police, having to say what Tom had done and it being recorded down in black and white for all and sundry to see, although not great, wasn't the cause of her reluctance. That was a mere inconvenience compared to what else she'd endured.

It was what it *could* and most probably *would* uncover.

Telling the police she'd witnessed Tom kill Amelia wouldn't satisfy them. She'd then be expected to explain why she hadn't reported it in the first place... That was easy enough – at the time, she hadn't been in a fit state to think past the end of her nose, but the police would then start digging around in general...

They'd want to unearth why Tom had been torturing her in the first place. They'd want to know her connection with him – her history... One way or another, everything would come out and Linda couldn't, just *couldn't*, let that happen. Because if it did, Sam would discover Tom Bedworth was her real father and Linda had promised to shield her daughter from that truth, whatever the cost.

The craving for crack stirred, the prodding finger of the promise of oblivion becoming ever more insistent.

No. No. No! She would not give into that again. Not ever.

'Mum?' Sam said, wanting to break the unbearable silence. 'I really need your help.'

Linda felt like she may pass out. There was no solution to this. Whichever way she dealt with this, it would end in tears. She couldn't risk the truth about Tom being exposed. 'My word won't count for anything, Sam. A lawyer would override evidence from a drugged-up prisoner as an inadmissible or unreliable source. I'm sorry.'

'But you could try!' Sam exclaimed. 'Surely you could?'

Linda's panic spiralled. If she didn't speak up and tell the police what she'd witnessed, then Seb could be done for the murder of Amelia. But if she *did*, her daughter's life would be ruined regardless.

Wait... There was something... Perhaps she could solve this without sacrificing her daughter.

'There may be another way,' Linda blurted. 'Find Tina.'

'Tina? Who's Tina?'

Linda grasped Sam's hand. 'One of Amelia's daughters. She was there the night I escaped. She knew what Tom was like and that I was being held prisoner. Tina also knew Amelia was trying to help me. She knew Tom killed her mother.'

Sam's eyes widened. 'Tom killed this woman because she was helping *you*?'

'I don't know,' Linda muttered. 'Probably part of it, but...'

Sam's spirits soared. 'This could work! She'd be an independent witness. Where is this Tina?'

Linda shrugged. 'I don't know that either. I begged her to

escape before Tom returned, but she refused. I don't know whether she did or whether she...'

'Well, she's not there now. The place is deserted.'

'What? Where have all the girls gone? And Tom?'

Sam shook her head despondently. 'That I don't know, that's why Seb went there in the first place. I wanted to help the other girls and find Bedworth.' Seeing her mother's renewed panic, she squeezed Linda's hand. 'Don't worry, he won't be coming for you.'

Linda chewed her lip with what remained of her teeth. Now she really *did* have to put this right. Seb was in the frame because Sam wanted retaliation for what happened to *her*? 'If Tom hasn't finished Tina off, she'll have disappeared out of town completely. Either that, or she's still around doing the same thing as she was at the Aurora.'

And Linda hoped for Sam's sake as well as her own that Tina *was* still around. 'Check out all the low-end strip clubs and red-light areas. If Tina's still in Brum, she'll have ended up in one of those.'

* * *

Tom didn't want to acknowledge it, but the truth remained the same. He was worried. *Really* worried.

He now knew for certain that Samantha was gunning for him, which meant so were the Stokers. But why were the Stokers still on the scene, considering he'd left them with nothing?

Since systematically removing everything from underneath them, they should have skulked from the city with their tails between their legs. Their casino was gone, he'd swiped their dosh, so what did they have left?

Fuck all, so why were they still around?

Even weirder, why was Samantha giving that Stoker prick the

time of day? If she was that stupid to remain involved with a man holding no collateral or ability to prosper, then she had inherited few genes from him, that was for sure.

Tom stared from the taxi window as they left the Aston Expressway to join the M6 at Spaghetti Junction.

How he'd love to bury every single one of those Stoker fuckers in the uprights holding up this concrete monstrosity. Sadly, he'd missed the boat by nigh on thirty years, but there probably wouldn't have been room anyway, not with the amount of people who'd got 'lost' that way, forever entombed in the base of one of the weirdest flyovers in the world.

Still, nothing he could do about that now.

He pulled the baseball cap lower over his eyes and glared at the back of the taxi driver's head.

So, who had given his name up to Samantha and the Stokers?

Tom drummed his fingers on the plastic of the inner door. He'd already removed all those stupid enough to talk – even those constituting the slightest risk. Anyone left knew nothing or was too thick to do much about it, so how had this happened?

His brow furrowed, emphasising the deep concertina grooves on his forehead. Why had the police been digging around at the Aurora in the first place to find that fat cow's body in the wardrobe?

Tom's nerves jangled. There had been no mention of Linda in the report either. The raddled old cow had but hours left to remain on the planet when he'd made the decision to let nature take its course, rather than expending energy offloading her, but maybe he should have?

He picked at the dry skin around his fingernails.

No, Linda hadn't been going anywhere. She'd been as good as dead. The only possible explanation for her not being mentioned in the paper must be because they hadn't identified the old bitch. She'd been little more than a bag of bones and after smashing her mouldy fucking teeth from her stupid head, he'd successfully ruled out identification by that means too.

He was overthinking this, but *someone* must have said something.

Suddenly, the truth dawned. That was it! *Get a grip, Tom*, he chided. It must have been Deb Banner. He'd suspected the tart was up to no good the minute she'd done a runner, that was why he'd made it his business to look for her. That was also why he'd spotted her near the casinos. She'd been there flapping her bloody gums.

His jaw tightened. The fucking slag. It was a good job he'd already killed her, otherwise he'd *definitely* be doing it now. It was just unfortunate he hadn't mangled her into the tarmac before she'd opened her gob and made him prime suspect to his own fucking daughter!

Samantha wouldn't be so quick to be cross with him if she knew he was her kin, would she?

A glimmer of an idea formed before Tom quickly dismissed it. Enlightening Sam to their shared blood wouldn't do him any favours. Besides, he'd already got most of what he'd wanted from her and her loony boyfriend and that was safely stashed in holdalls at Banner's house. Telling Sam would achieve nothing. It wasn't like Linda could open her mouth now, was it?

Tom suddenly burst out laughing.

'You all right, mate?'

Tom's head shot up to meet the scrutinising eyes of the taxi driver in the rear-view mirror. 'Why wouldn't I be?'

'You've looked like someone shit on your cornflakes since you got in the cab and now you're laughing? Are you an escaped axe murderer or something?' the driver laughed.

Quickly composing himself, Tom returned the laugh. *The bloke wasn't spot on, but he wasn't far off either.*

'Right, we're coming into Wolverhampton,' the driver continued. 'Where to?'

'Primo Autoshop, please,' Tom said, glancing out of the
window.

'Picking your motor up?'

'Something like that.' Tom's smile dropped. No doubt the
miserable, greedy bastard he was hoping to see would be lording it
up in his Portakabin. If not, then he'd try the pub.

He just had to hope Potter Ross was in a good mood and that it
wouldn't be necessary to part with any wedge as a bargaining chip.

10

Marina found it difficult to stop her face from curling into a mask of utter contempt as she touched up her trowelled-on makeup. This foundation was so thick that if she scraped her nail down it, she fully expected to dig a deep groove before reaching her real skin.

If she ended up with acne or a pile of blackheads after this, then she really would rip Dan's cock off for putting her in this position. But that would happen anyway once she caught up with the weasely bastard.

Peering closer in the mirror, made difficult by half of the surrounding bulbs being missing or blown, Marina ignored the dark marks on the glass and checked her face.

'Are you the new girl?'

Marina didn't want to turn in the direction of the gormless tart next to her, but she had to make the effort. That was why she was here, after all.

'I love your hair!' the voice continued, the scratchy timbre jangling Marina's already tried patience.

Swivelling around on the broken chair, the castors squeaked

loudly, further pushing Marina towards driving her fist into the woman's face. Instead, she plastered on a smile, wide enough to fool even the most astute of audiences. And these people were as far removed from astute as anything. 'Thanks,' she purred, patting her carefully secured wig. 'Yes, this is my first night. I'm Ava and I'm a bit nervous.'

Marina hated her latest assumed name, but it was all she could think of off the top of her head when asking for a job. It wasn't like she could use her real one.

'Don't be nervous! You're stunning! No wonder you got the job,' the girl gushed. 'Shane's right fussy about maintaining standards. You should see some of the women who come here asking for work!'

Marina almost choked. *Standards? From what she'd seen, there were none. And Shane O'Shea was a lecherous pervert...*

Putting up with that greasy bastard's hands all over her whilst he gave her a thorough inspection to ensure she was suitable to dance in his shitty club had pissed her right off. Still, she'd do whatever was required to get where she needed to be.

She only hoped this was it...

'Yeah, some of the women who try their luck are right mingers,' the woman continued, rolling her eyes dramatically. 'Shane hit the jackpot with you, though. The punters won't believe their luck!'

The punters would be having no luck – not with me, anyway, Marina thought. Spying a metal nail file on the dressing table, she wondered how messy it would be if she plunged it deep into this bimbo's neck.

Getting up, wobbling on her skyscraper heels, the woman moved closer and extended her hand. 'I'm Tina, by the way. You're partnered with me tonight. Shane wants me to show you the ropes.' She smiled mischievously. 'We'll have a great giggle together.'

Marina stared at Tina's chipped nails. *Remember the plan.* 'I think you might be right,' she lied. 'Being new to town, I could do with a good mate.'

Tina checked none of the other dancers were paying attention, then pulled open a small drawer in her own dressing table. Quickly unscrewing the lid of supermarket own-brand vodka, she took a swig before passing it to Marina. 'It's always good to have a tot before the show.'

'Cheers!' Marina reluctantly put her lips on the bottle, hoping this nasty tart didn't have foot and mouth disease or the plague. It was possible she had both. Still, she wouldn't dwell on that.

Swallowing the spirit, which tasted suspiciously of meths, Marina quickly handed it back. 'How long have you been working here, Tina? Is it good?' *Yeah, right...*

Tina perched on the edge of Marina's dressing unit and crossed one of her long legs over the opposite knee. 'Yes, it's good. Apart from the footwear. Christ, these kill my fucking feet,' she moaned, inspecting the transparent platforms of her teetering heels. 'I've only been here a few weeks myself.'

'You're new to Birmingham?' Marina asked, glancing around to weigh up who else she might have to get pally with. This silly cow was no good if she'd only just arrived on the scene.

'Me? New to town?' Tina laughed. 'Nah, I've been in Brum all me life. I worked somewhere else before this, but...' Her face dropped. 'It erm... didn't work out.'

'Oh? Why?'

Dropping her voice, Tina leant forward. 'Well, Bedworth – the guy running it – was a total wanker and that ain't the half of it! I probably shouldn't say anything in case you know him.'

'Say anything you like,' Marina grinned, despising Tina more every second. 'Mates, aren't we? Besides, I don't know anyone around here.'

'Well, I heard that he's done a runner so I don't suppose it matters. Anyway, it ended up a total nightmare because...'

A shrill bell cut Tina off in her tracks and she jumped from her perch to grab Marina's hand. 'Come on, that's our call. The show's about to start.'

A heavy ball of nerves rolled in Marina's stomach. She was actually doing this? Dancing and taking her clothes off in front of dirty old men?

'Hurry!' Tina pulled Marina to her feet. 'The first show's always the worst, but it will be over in half an hour, then the rest of the sets tonight will be water off a duck's back.'

Marina grimaced as she was pulled towards the stage door. *This really was not good.*

* * *

Potter Ross used his front teeth to press the end of the ballpoint pen in and out, the repetitive clicking in the heavy silence making Tom even more uncomfortable.

To divert from the oppressing situation, Tom looked around the makeshift office, pretending to admire the setup, when it looked exactly what it was – an end-of-life Portakabin with a naff table and a few filing cabinets, probably filched out of a skip from one of his additional businesses.

Considering the Rosses were the main firm in Wolverhampton and now possibly the whole of the Black Country, their frugal surroundings were polar opposites of the grotesque amount of money they raked in from their underhand dealings. And Tom *hated* the lot of them.

Namely because they'd overcharged him for the coke they'd supplied a while ago when his usual route had become temporarily stuck. He'd held a bone of contention towards the greedy twat in front of him ever since. But now wasn't the time to quibble over past dealings. As much as he resented taking whatever this toerag chucked in his general direction up the shitter, he had little choice.

He wasn't exactly overloaded with alternatives, but the bloke could at least answer him. He'd asked a question ages ago and the fat turd was enjoying making him sweat.

Tom's eyes tracked back to Potter in his oversized leather chair – again, a huge contrast to the other meagre furnishings. His huge belly spilled over the straining waistband of his trousers and a stain reminiscent of fried egg clung to the front of his creased shirt. The man's beady eyes watched every move – he was probably even reading his goddamn mind. 'So, Potter, what do you think of my proposition?'

Potter drummed his fingers, the pudgy digits resembling overstuffed sausages. 'What I think, Bedworth, is that you're not being honest.'

Tom feigned shock. 'What do you mean?' *Of course he wasn't being honest!* Why the fuck would he tell this greedy bastard he had millions stashed in a wardrobe in Frankley? He might be in need of cover, but he hadn't had a lobotomy.

Potter's nails tapping on the desk grew louder. 'What I mean is, you've come in here pretending I will benefit from giving you and some bloke I've never heard of a place to stay for reasons you won't divulge. You don't think that a bit odd?'

Tom frowned. 'Odd? Why? It's no secret I've had problems at the Aurora. I just need a few days to get my shit straight. Come on, mate, we've known each other donkeys' years, so why the hell not?'

Potter laughed, the sound like rubbish being crushed in the back of a dustcart. 'Yeah, we've known each other for years. I've always thought you were a cunt and I still do. Especially after you went round trapping off that I'd ripped you off when you came crawling to me a few months back to tide you over with coke for your crack shop.'

Tom cringed, heat rushing to his cheeks. *How the hell had Potter heard about that?* He laughed, pretending they shared a joke. 'That wasn't serious. Christ, mate, I think we've known each other long enough to be able to have a bloody laugh!'

'Do you?' A sneer appeared at the side of Potter's mouth. 'Hmm...' He resumed tapping the desk – this time with the pen.

Tom wanted to scream. This was not working out well at all. If only he wasn't in such dire need, he'd shove the fat fuck's hand in the laminator and tell him to go do one. Instead, he would have to offer up some of his hard-earned coin. 'What about a business deal?'

Potter raised an eyebrow. 'Wait! You're so lucrative that you have nowhere to live, but you can offer me a business deal? This should be good!'

'I never said I had no readies, Potter. I said I needed somewhere to stay!' Tom snapped. There was only so much jibing he would take. He'd rather buy a fucking wig, call himself Priscilla and rent a room somewhere to sell his arse than put up with this condescending bastard.

Potter folded his arms and rested them on his mountainous belly. 'Go on, I'm listening.'

'Give me somewhere to crash and I'll stump up half the cash for your next incoming shipment. How's that for generous?'

Potter frowned. 'What makes you think I have something like that on the horizon?'

Tom laughed, this time genuinely. 'Where else would you get gear from in the quantities you do? You might think me a thick twat, Potter, but I ain't.'

Potter studied Tom silently before speaking. 'Let's say hypothetically that I agree to this, what percentage of the profit would you expect for your "investment"?'

'Fifty per cent, of course. Half the outlay equals half the reward. Easy! An equal split.'

'Right... So you put in half the money into a deal you haven't brokered, you get a place to live thrown in, plus half the returns?' Potter chuckled. 'And your funds are from where exactly?'

Tom flinched. 'Where they're from is irrelevant.'

'Thirty per cent.'

'Forty-five,' Tom countered. 'Thirty per cent is taking the piss. I ain't standing for that.'

Potter's eyes narrowed. 'My offer has now reduced to 20 per cent because you're a greedy, rude bastard.' With considerable effort, he hefted his huge frame out of the chair. 'Take it or leave it, Bedworth, but you've got precisely ten seconds to decide because you're getting on my tits.'

Tom's teeth grated. *Bollocks, shit and fuck.* This wanker had him by the short and curlies and he knew it. The worst thing was, he had no choice but to accept.

11

Taking a tumbler from the display cabinet, Sam poured Seb a glass of whisky then topped up her wine. Placing the glass on the table, she wrapped her arms around his waist. 'Had a good day?'

Seb pressed his lips against Sam's, the feel of her mouth on his just the tonic. Finally pulling away, he smiled. 'Not bad, under the circumstances.'

And it hadn't been. Having received further information needed for the heist, he was almost in a position to set the schedule. All that was left was a call to confirm the requested meet with his contact at Bristol docks, then he was good to go. It hadn't come through yet, but once it had, he'd feel a lot better.

He shrugged off his suit jacket and slung it across the back of an armchair. Undoing his silver cufflinks, he placed them on the side, then rolled his shirt sleeves up. Loosening his tie, he undid his top button and flopped into the chair, grateful to be back in his own home.

Things were now heading in the right direction. Apart from *one* unexpected thing. And that bothered him more than anything else because it was an unknown variable – one he had no control over.

And he'd be the first to admit that he struggled when control was out of his hands.

Taking a long swig of whisky, Seb lit a cigarette and pulled the ashtray across the table towards him. 'Tell me your news. You've been out all day. I half expected you to call with an update.' He looked at Sam quizzically. 'How did you get on with Linda?'

He resented asking this of Sam, but his hands were tied. He just hoped she had a palatable answer to give him. If Linda refused to play ball, he didn't know what other options were available, if any.

Sipping her wine, Sam gave a slight shrug. 'Linda won't do it. She doesn't think her account will be accepted and will be over-ruled as untrustworthy.' She smiled sadly. 'The thing is, she has a point and...'

'Shit!' Seb hissed.

'Wait!' Sam continued. 'Linda can't do it, but she has suggested someone who *could*.'

Seb sat forward. 'Who?'

'A girl called Tina. She's the daughter of that woman in the wardrobe. This girl knew Linda was being kept prisoner by Bedworth too.'

'She witnessed Bedworth murdering that woman? Her mother?'

Sam held her hand up. 'No – at least not from what I gathered, but Linda said that Tina knew it was Bedworth. I tried to find out more, but Linda couldn't remember much.'

Seb studied Sam's face. 'You don't believe her?'

'I – I'm not sure.' Sam had seen Linda's internal argument and couldn't deduce what it was over. Being unexpectedly asked to go to the police could have knocked her sideways; she might have been flaky due to the strain of rehab, or she was hiding something.

And Sam, whether she wanted to or not, felt Linda *was* hiding something.

She could be wrong, but there was a fine line – one she was loath to cross by applying further pressure at such a crucial point in her mother's recovery. This meant she was stuck between a rock and a hard place. She couldn't achieve anything without either damaging Linda, who had already been through more than enough, or helping to ruin the man she loved and owed everything to, who had already lost so much because of her.

'Hey.' Seb moved next to Sam on the sofa and pulled her against his chest. 'You did your best.'

Sam closed her eyes. *But had she?* Either way, she wasn't stopping here. She sat back up. 'All I've got is a name and a vague description of the woman Linda mentioned, but I'll find her.'

'Oh, Princess, she'll be long gone by now.' Seb swigged his whisky to hide his disappointment. Sam was clearly devastated by Linda's reluctance to speak to the police, but he had to accept he'd have to deal with it and just hope he could get things rectified before he got formally charged.

How ironic. Charged for a murder he'd had no hand in. But whatever happened, he would not let Sam take the guilt. She felt responsible for too many things already. He'd sort it out one way or another.

'I've been looking for this woman all afternoon, but I haven't given up. I've got a few more places to try,' Sam continued.

'What places?' Seb tensed. 'Where have you been?'

'A couple of strip clubs and red-light areas, but there's been nothing so far.'

'Fuck, Sam!' Seb barked. 'I don't want you wandering around places like that. You're enough of a target as it is!'

'I'm continuing to look,' Sam said determinedly. 'You concentrate on your plans and I'll concentrate on mine.'

* * *

Lounging back on the PVC-upholstered bench seat, Dan grinned. *This* place was more like it.

His eyes moved greedily over the gyrating bodies of the scantily clad women. Underneath the table, he pressed his palm down on his aching groin. From what he'd gathered about the general gist of this place, as well as this very pleasurable show, extras were also on the menu and he was long overdue for some action.

Yep, this place would do nicely. It was ten times better than the first gaff he'd tried down the Chinese Quarter. Twenty quid to get into that dump, yet most of the birds in there looked like they were from a bad version of *Antiques Roadshow.*

No fucking thanks!

Here, on the other hand, was more up his street and made up for the enforced poker drought. At least for now…

Dan ran his tongue over his bottom lip as a shapely blonde bent over and wiggled her backside suggestively. How he'd like to ease that red G-string down her thighs and give her a good time. Perhaps he'd do just that if the chance arose?

Beckoning over a waitress wearing only a black thong and a tiny white apron, he found himself unable to pull his gaze from the breasts bouncing enticingly close to his face. 'Another pint, please, love.'

The waitress beamed vacantly before scurrying off to do his bidding and Dan chuckled. Being holed up with Tom for so long had made him paranoid when there was absolutely no need. Not one person had batted an eyelid as he'd walked along the streets. *Not one.* Plus, he'd been nowhere near Broad Street and had no intention of going there either, so there was nothing to worry about.

He must have been stupid to think otherwise, which only further underlined the control Bedworth had quietly ramped up on him.

Dan scanned the club's interior once again. The black walls festooned with spangly strips of silver formed a backdrop to the 'Sunset Boulevard' signage attached behind the stage at the back of the room. The fluttering glitz may be plastic and the place wasn't the Moulin Rouge, but the girls were half-decent and that's what counted.

His focus fell on the next pair of women moving onto the stage. The blonde wrapped herself around the central pole, whilst the other, a redhead, pressed herself against the other girl's fishnet stocking-covered legs.

Nice, very nice, Dan thought, his interest as well as his arousal growing. He'd definitely find out if those two were up for extras.

'Here's your beer, sir.' The waitress leant over the table, giving Dan another eyeful of her bare breasts. 'Is there anything else I can get you?'

'Not right now.' Dan winked. 'Maybe later.' She was hot, but not as hot as *them*.

His concentration returned to the pair on the stage.

Wait a minute...

Dan squinted through the fug of cigarette smoke.

That looked a bit like...

Dan could barely wait until the set ended and a further two women appeared on the stage. Getting up, he made his way through the mass of men just as the two women were about to disappear through the backstage door.

It was! It was her! He could barely believe his luck.

Dan grabbed the blonde's arm. 'Tina?'

Tina swung around, glaring at whoever had hold of her. Punters weren't allowed to touch until a price had been agreed. 'Sir, you...' Stopping, her eyes widened. 'Dan? Is that you?'

Squealing, she flung her arms around his neck. 'Oh my God! I can't believe you're here! I thought you'd disappeared! Ava, you'll never believe... oh!'

Tina caught a glimpse of her new friend disappearing through the backstage door and frowned, before returning her attention to Dan. She hadn't seen him since the Aurora.

She froze. *The Aurora!*

Did that mean Tom was here? If he was, then she'd have to make herself scarce. And *fast.*

'Come and sit at my table.' Seeing Tina's face pale, Dan frowned. 'What's the matter? Aren't you allowed to talk to customers? I was under the impression you could offer extras if you saw fit?'

Tina's eyes darted around in the direction Dan gestured. 'Erm... I... Who are you with?'

Dan frowned. 'No one. Why?'

Standing on tiptoe, Tina pressed herself against Dan to whisper directly in his ear. 'Is Tom with you?'

Tina's breath against his earlobe caused further movement in Dan's groin. *Tina was worried about Tom?* Well, Tom wasn't ruining his chances of a shag. As far as he was concerned, Tom had pissed him off too much lately, so it was fair game to delete him from any dealings – at least as far as *this* one was concerned. 'I haven't seen Tom for ages! From what I gather, he did a runner,' he lied.

The immediate relief on Tina's faced backed up Dan's theory. 'Come and have a drink with me and tell me how you are.' *With any luck, he'd get payment in kind for his concern.*

Following Dan to his table, Tina inwardly glowed, thanking God to hear the confirmation Tom was no longer in Birmingham. She'd been on edge ever since leaving the Aurora, panicking that he could still be around and would find her and do the same to her as what he'd done to her mother. But now he'd legged it? That was brilliant!

Dan was different. Furthermore, he was bloody loaded.

What a fabulous twist of fate that he should appear in the Sunset Boulevard!

Tina's smile grew wide. Could her fortunes and luck be on the up?

12

Dan pulled more money from his pocket. Tom wouldn't notice that he'd helped himself to a wedge from one of the holdalls. He would once one of the bags went entirely missing, along with *him*, but he wasn't going to be involved with the man for much longer.

He didn't know what he'd been thinking. It was *Tom* everyone was after – that was obvious from what Luke said. He'd been utterly stupid entertaining the prospect the Stokers knew he'd torched the casino. They thought it was Tom.

'You need to wear this glove I've made you...' Dan mimicked Tom's scratchy voice under his breath.

Sod that. And sod Tom!

As the topless waitress approached again, Dan waited for her to place the bottle of champagne on the table, along with two glasses, before tucking a fifty-pound note in the waistband of her little apron.

He winked at Tina, knowing as always she'd be impressed with his display of wealth and silently congratulated himself for coming to the Sunset Boulevard. He'd missed this girl's attentions since the Aurora closed and now he could pick back up where he'd left off –

a guaranteed shag from the chick who'd been so eager to please him in the past.

Champagne was expensive – even the cheap shit they charged extortionate prices for here – but it was worth it. It was refreshing not to be cooped up and stuck in that house with the body in the shed.

Dan poured two glasses, twisting the neck of the bottle with a flourish, then handed a glass to Tina. 'For you, madam!'

His smile dropped, seeing Tina glance around like she'd rather be elsewhere. She didn't seem herself. Since her excited reaction on seeing him, she'd become jittery and subdued – what he'd even class as *worried*.

Was she now involved with someone else? Maybe she was being run by another bloke since Tom had stepped off the scene?

It could even be one of the men here.

Fuck. He didn't want anything spoiling his first night of freedom. 'Is there a problem?'

Tina's eyes darted to Dan like she'd only just noticed his presence. 'No. No, I'm fine.' She grabbed the flute of champagne and swigged at it, desperate to play down her nerves. 'I *love* champagne!'

Dan frowned at Tina's forced smile. 'You might as well tell me what the matter is. If you've got a better offer, then just say.' Even as he said it, the thought pissed him off. He'd seen the other blokes in here. If Tina thought any of the scabby munters were nicer looking than him, that was really depressing.

His eyes narrowed. Tina would change her mind if she knew what he'd got in the holdalls at Luke's house. 'You're not the same as you were at the Aurora. You...' Seeing another flash of fear on Tina's face with the mention of Tom's club, Dan paused and reached for her hand. 'Why don't you tell me what's bothering you, because something is.' And he strongly suspected it was to do with Bedworth. And if it was, then he needed to know exactly why.

He might have lied when he'd said Tom was no longer on the scene, but from what he'd seen happen to Luke and the other nagging doubts over everything, it was in his interests to know the score, being as he was still far too connected with the man.

Tina's eyes suddenly filled with tears. Her outward show of bravado and telling herself her happiness to see Dan again was because of what might be in his wallet, she suddenly realised wasn't entirely true.

Dan was the only man who had ever shown concern for her and seemed genuinely worried, like he *cared*.

Her bottom lip trembled. A man had never been nice to her, not *genuinely*. In fact, she'd never had *anyone* be nice to her without wanting something in return. It was a strange feeling, both saddening her as well as offering a glimmer of hope. But she couldn't forget that she, under Tom's instructions, had gleaned knowledge from Dan about his plans to rob the Stokers. Using her feminine guiles, she'd infiltrated the information and then passed it back to Tom, like he'd insisted.

Tina swallowed uncomfortably. For weeks, she'd pushed that unpalatable truth to the back of her mind, but seeing Dan again, it hit her between the eyes. There was no getting away from it.

Why had she been so blinkered all that time to believe it was important to get Tom's seal of approval? She'd wanted to impress him – actually wanted to *impress* the man and go up in his estimation.

The fact that she'd even *thought* like that was both humiliating and exasperating. If she hadn't been so ridiculous, she might have stopped what had happened to her mother. Had Amelia hung around just that little bit too long at the Aurora to try to get her daughters to see sense and leave, rather than taking the opportunity to escape when she had the chance?

Tina's bottom lip trembled. Her delusions might have meant she'd helped her mother to die...

Without a doubt, she'd betrayed Dan and she wished more than anything that she hadn't. She wished she hadn't done *any* of it and that she'd never set foot in that bloody place.

Would Dan ever forgive her?

Tina frowned. She didn't even know whether the plan to rob the Stokers had been successful.

Like a thunderbolt out of the blue, despite what she'd spent years telling herself was all that mattered, she realised right here and now that it *didn't* matter.

The Peacock had burnt down, she knew that, but that was nothing to do with the lockups where Dan had said the safes were kept.

But it didn't matter whether he'd got the money or not. *Not now.*

Whether Dan was loaded or not made no difference any more. That he cared enough to ask what was troubling her was the only thing that mattered.

All Tina knew was that she had to be honest about what Tom had insisted upon and what she'd done. She wanted to tell Dan about what had happened to her mother and the woman in the attic. She wanted to tell him *everything.*

She hadn't breathed a word about it to anyone and it was slowly eating her up from the inside. But first, she had to tell Dan how she'd betrayed him. Only then would her conscience be clear and he'd understand why she was so terrified of Tom finding her.

She raised her eyes, bolstered by the renewed concern in Dan's eyes, and taking a deep breath, began to speak.

* * *

Leaning against the wall the other side of the stage door, Marina's heart crashed in her chest, the muffled music behind the thick wood still far too loud for her speeding mind.

She'd spotted Dan long before Tina had. The only thing stopping her from launching herself to kill him on the spot was that if he was dead, she'd never know where the money was.

When that was safely back in her possession, she'd deal with him.

Marina closed her eyes to quell her escalating fury. She'd just *known* Dan had remained in Birmingham. Only someone as stupid as him wouldn't have hopped onto the first plane and instead remained to ponce around backstreet strip joints.

Despite her rage, her lips curled into a sneer. For the first time since stepping into this grubby hole of perverts, she was glad to be here. Her instinct of knowing where to focus had been bang on because within one day of working at this dump, she'd spotted her target.

Dan was in the city, which meant so was her money...

Even wrapping herself around Tina with her tits out in front of the dregs of society was worth it to hit the bullseye.

But it had been close.

For a second, on leaving the stage, Marina had been sure Dan was heading straight for her. She'd panicked, until she remembered it was past his ability to see through her auburn wig and stripper shoes. Leaving nothing to chance, she'd got out of sight regardless.

But how did Dan know Tina?

Marina edged back towards the door and opened it. She had to get back out there...

Taking a deep breath, she stepped through the door and, glancing around, picked her way through the tables, batting away the hands grasping for her thighs, arms or backside.

Remembering her alter ego, Marina propped herself against the bar with one of her shiny stockinged legs and lounged seductively against the sticky surface. She could see Tina deep in conversation with that scheming toad. She wanted to hear what they were saying, but she couldn't go any closer and risk interrupting.

Tina was saying *something*. Something, from the look of anguish on her overly made-up face, that was both important and distressing.

What could she possibly be telling Dan? It had to be something major. Or rather something *Tina* classed as major.

Marina swallowed a chuckle. Tina was probably running low on foundation and tapping Dan up for a few quid to restock.

No. It wasn't anything like that. Tina was telling Dan something of interest because...

She focused through the fug, the cigarette smoke stinging her eyes.

Dan looked concerned! He'd grabbed Tina's hand and looked bothered – like he *cared*.

He'd never looked at *her* like that; never acted like he gave a flying fig about how she felt about anything. *Ever!* What the fuck was this about?

Marina's nails dug into her palms through her clenching fists. It shouldn't bother her, but it did.

She went to snatch a drink off the bar, not caring who it belonged to, when someone pressed up against her; a hand snaking around her thigh, another on her left breast. The tell-tale hardness of arousal dug distinctly against the back of her spangly thong.

Swinging around, Marina found a man, not a day less than sixty, with saliva dribbling from the corner of his mouth.

'On your own?' he slurred, his sickly breath making Marina wince. 'We can't have that now, can we?'

Marina snatched the hand from her breast. 'Get your fucking hands off me, you dirty fucking per...'

'Hey, that's not friendly. I don't think the management would appreciate your tone,' the man snarled, his pleasant demeanour dissolving.

As the hand on Marina's thigh tightened, overlong dirty nails tearing a ladder in her expensive stockings, she wasted no time slipping her hand under the man's overhanging belly to grab hold of the penis tenting his stained trousers.

Clamping her nails down, she twisted hard and moved closer, despite the stench of the man's breath. 'I said, get your fucking hands off me before I rip your pathetic cock clean off!' Enjoying the shock and pain twisting the man's repugnant features, Marina added a further twist for good measure.

Finally letting go, the man staggered back and hastily retreated into the crowd. No doubt he'd put in a complaint, but she didn't care.

Now, back to *this*...

Turning back to find the table Dan and Tina had been sitting at now empty, her eyes darted around the busy room.

Where had they gone? Shit!

She had to find Tina, pretend she didn't know Dan and find out what they'd been discussing.

Storming past another approaching man, Marina rushed towards the stage door. With any luck, Tina was already here because they were due back out for the second set in fifteen minutes.

13

Dan wasn't sure how he was acting so normally, but behaving any other way would alert Tom to the realisation that Dan now knew *everything*.

But did he believe what Tina told him last night?

Dan's teeth clenched. *Yes, he did.* There was no way she would have that knowledge if it wasn't true.

He'd been set up, though. It was irrelevant how much Tina had apologised for her actions because the damage was done. Had it not been for her, he'd have had the money from those safes to himself; he wouldn't have been roped into torching a casino, plus he'd have been out of here with no connection to a man that every criminally insane person in the city was after.

And to learn that Tom had kept a woman chained to a bed in the attic pumped full of drugs? Tina had also said he'd killed her mother too – that fat old bird who had run the Aurora.

Christ...

The night Tom had killed Tina's mother and shoved her in the wardrobe to fucking rot, *he'd* been downstairs...

The sudden need to bring forward the robbery to that very night made sense now.

On top of that, from what Tina also said about Deb Banner going missing, it seemed his growing fear that whilst he'd been busy setting fire to the Peacock, Tom had also been the one mowing young girls down, was true.

The gunk and the crack on the windscreen...

Dan shuddered.

Fuck.

And what about Luke Banner?

Forget about Tina relaying his drunken boasts to Tom. Her underhand ways paled into insignificance with the rest of this shit.

Tom was a fucking psycho.

Dan's eyes centred on Tom chuckling over the daily cartoon in the morning paper and his stomach churned. He had to get the fuck away from this loon whilst he still could.

Tom suddenly looked up, catching Dan staring. 'Are you planning on informing me whether you got anywhere last night or am I expected to read your fucking mind?'

Dan flinched. He'd got further last night than he'd thought, just not on the subject Tom wanted. If this psycho discovered he'd spent the night in a strip club on Edgbaston Street with a woman holding enough knowledge to put him away until hell froze over or that he hadn't followed orders, things wouldn't end well.

Dan floundered. *Think, think, think!*

Sparking up another cigarette off the back of the one he was stubbing out, he shrugged, hoping his shoulders didn't show they bore the weight of a medium-sized landfill. 'Not much to report,' he said casually. 'I checked out a couple of places for the people you mentioned, but there was no one about.'

He took a rapid four drags from his fag, the end becoming a

glowing orange carrot. 'I didn't want to draw suspicion by openly inquiring, but I'll try again tonight.'

Placated, Tom turned back to his paper, leaving Dan to quietly exhale. *Okay. It was okay...* 'Erm, how did you get on?'

Tom's head darted back up. 'What? What with?'

Dan shrugged once more. 'You said you were going over the Black Country last night, so I wondered how it went, that's all?'

Tom scowled. 'Yeah, it went all right.' *If being forced into handing over thousands of fucking quid to a fat bastard and settling for a shit percentage at the end of it counted as acceptable?* 'We've got somewhere else to go now.'

Dan paled. He wasn't going anywhere with Tom again. He hadn't wanted to in the first place, but especially not now. It was preferable remaining in a house with a decaying corpse in the shed. 'When?'

Tom eyed Dan suspiciously. 'Later on today or tomorrow.'

Feeling like his veins were filled with weedkiller, Dan pretended to turn his attention elsewhere. He had to think how he could remain here whilst Tom left.

His eyes moved in the direction of the garden shed.

Okay, so preferably not *here*, but somewhere. *Anywhere* that didn't include Tom.

He stared at the remains of his right hand, wanting to drum his fingers on the table, but that was, of course, impossible – even if he wore that crap glove.

After last night, things were even more complicated. Along with the unsavoury events slotting together about the man he found himself linked to, another surprising issue had come to light.

And as much as he'd ignored it so far, it was true.

He was worried about Tina. Actually *worried* about her.

And that was an alien concept.

Seeing the fear and sadness in her eyes last night, then how she'd entrusted him with what had been done to her mother and that other woman, had shifted something deep in the recesses of his brain.

Tina had been so pleased to see him and then, when her countenance had suddenly changed, he'd been upset.

Yes, *upset*.

Passing off his immediate reaction as being annoyed over another bloke's wallet catching Tina's attention over him was easier, but it wasn't that. Much to Dan's astonishment, it had dawned on him that he wanted Tina to want him – to *be* with him.

Even her betrayal didn't matter.

Not any more.

Dan wanted Tina to like him for him – not whether he was flush or not.

And she *did*.

Aside from the gravity of the circumstances and everything else on his back, he felt a warm glow radiate from inside. For the first time, he genuinely wanted to be with someone; to look after them and to be there for them.

It felt good.

All he needed to do was distance himself from Tom. Going to Wolverhampton and further away from Tina was not an option.

Dan stared at Tom's bowed head, still engrossed in the paper.

Whatever happened, he was having one of those holdalls. It was the least he was owed.

He'd be all right then, as would Tina.

All he had to do now was convince Tom it was imperative he remained in Birmingham for a while longer.

* * *

'Tell me again when this is happening?' Andrew asked, seeing Seb glance at his watch for the third time in the last few minutes.

Considering they were on the brink of pulling this heist off, Seb seemed on edge and distracted. Had something changed that the rest of them weren't aware of? Andrew hoped not – they needed this job to play out more than ever.

Seb looked up. 'I still haven't got the exact date. That's what I'm waiting for. That, and confirmation from our man on the inside at the docks.' He chewed his lip. 'I was hoping to have had both by now.'

Neil glanced from Andrew to Seb and then to Kevin, Craig and Daz. Although he'd have preferred keeping everyone apart from family out of this, he also appreciated more hands on deck were needed for something of this magnitude. But no one – absolutely *no one*, apart from the people here – could be in the know. Any more was far too risky. 'How much is coming?'

Seb shrugged. 'Enough. It's a standard shipment for the Ross firm. Bob, our contact in Bristol, clocks the Wolverhampton containers each time they come in. The gear will be supplied within dog food.'

'Dog food?' Neil cried. 'A container of fucking *dog food*?'

Seb grinned, despite the mounting stress. 'Dog food comes in all the time from abroad. Knowing the South Americans, it's probably minced dog!' He chuckled before becoming serious once again. 'Joking aside, the container holds pallets of big drums – some of which will contain coke.'

'I presume the drums will be marked?' Andrew frowned, the prospect of sifting through dog food not an enjoyable one. 'How many are there?'

'I've no idea, but the usual lift is approximately one tonne of cocaine.' Seb's smile grew. 'It will bring a good resale value and an even better street value.'

Neil's eyes lit up. 'Perhaps even better, depending how we cut it?'

'We won't be shifting on anything less than our usual standard.' Seb glared at his brother. 'We have a reputation to protect – one which will evade us if we don't get back on track soon. We're not diluting our rep any more than it already has been by selling substandard coke to our buyers. What they do with it after is their call, but there will be no overcutting to bulk it out from our side. We'll get enough of a wedge not to need to.'

Andrew blew through his teeth appreciatively. Admittedly, he hadn't been over enamoured about this job. The risk was *huge*, but for this sort of payout, it was worth it.

He did a quick calculation. 'The going rate for coke at the moment is at $40K a kilo, so say there's roughly a tonne, that will be... erm... What's the exchange rate?'

'About £1.53 to the dollar.'

Andrew snatched the calculator off the desk. 'So, one tonne at around $40K a kilo would be...' He tapped frantically. 'Shit! About £20 million!'

'Seriously?' Neil squawked, scarcely able to believe the sort of money up for grabs.

'Even half a tonne would be more than enough,' Seb said.

Andrew nodded. And it would, but that amount of coke would take a long time to shift. In the meantime, they'd have to hold it, which was an even *bigger* risk...

'Once we've cut it and even if we offload it at less than our normal rate, the street value will still coin us £25 to £30 million,' Seb grinned. 'Not bad for zilch outlay!'

'It's fucking immense!' Andrew gasped. 'But the Wolver-hampton bastards will go ape when they clock their gear's been lifted.'

'Shame...' Seb laughed. 'We'll make sure they can't connect us. Or even *think* about connecting us.'

'They'll connect us regardless.' Kev didn't wish to be pessimistic, but it was true. He'd never wanted to be involved in something *this* big. He shrugged his massive shoulders. 'What about Sam? Is she aware of the implications?'

Seb frowned. 'Sam is Sam. She knows the score.' He'd tried to make her walk away. Not that he wanted her to – she was his life, but she wouldn't hear of it. But now he had additional worries where she was concerned. 'Sam's leaving us to it, but in the meantime, she's digging around in things I'd prefer she didn't.'

Kevin sat forward. 'What do you mean?'

Seb quickly explained what had happened with Linda.

'You're letting her wander around shitholes?' Kevin exclaimed. 'On her *own*?'

Seb's eyes narrowed. 'I'm not "letting" her do anything, Kevin. Unless you haven't noticed, Sam does what she chooses, but I can't say I'm comfortable with it either.'

Kevin nodded his bull head in agreement. 'Craig will accompany her. Just let me know when.'

'She'll be here soon, so you can ask her yourself.' Diverted by a text notification, Seb grabbed his mobile and read the message, a smile spreading over his face. *Finally!* 'It's Bob confirming the meet. We're on!'

14

It had taken Marina almost an hour last night to scrape her thick makeup off, but despite spending a further age in the shower this morning, a tinge of orange still remained along her hairline.

Disgusting. The whole thing was bloody disgusting!

Including *this*...

She glared at her father, slouching at the kitchen table with Sophie draped over him, her boobs spilling from her crop top. 'I see you're busy, as usual!'

Mickey glanced up. 'Good morning, dear daughter. How did your evening dancing for the lovely men of Birmingham go?'

Marina's scowl deepened as she inwardly seethed. She wouldn't bother answering that. How did he *think* it had gone? Mickey was as much use as he'd always been and she'd been stupid to think now would be any different.

However, she did have an answer to one outstanding question. Not that she would tell her father she'd located Dan. She'd made that decision coming home in the taxi last night. When, and it would be *when*, she retrieved the money from Dan, Mickey would get nothing. Despite his promises, he hadn't done a thing to help, so he could go swing.

She'd be doing this the way she did everything.

On her Jack Jones.

But none of this changed her other problem: Tina hadn't gone backstage after all last night. She'd gone AWOL.

With Dan...

Marina's eyebrows knitted together. To make it worse, Tina's absence had ballsed up her second set and she'd been forced on stage with another girl with the physique of an Amazonian warrior who had nearly broken her ribs.

She quickly shook the image away.

Marina had to pray Tina was back tonight, because she needed to prise from her what she'd been saying to Dan.

This was a nightmare. The woman who might hold the key to where Dan's ill-gotten stash was kept was not only nowhere to be seen, but was also as thick as shit. Furthermore, presuming she got the info required, how would she lure Dan to where she needed him? And then what would she do?

Dan might not have recognised her last night, but if she got too close or started acting suspiciously, he, or worse, *Tina*, would work out she wasn't who she said she was. Dan had already proved he wasn't quite as brain dead as she'd once thought.

Marina's mind whirred as she stomped over to the fridge, yanking it open to find the last of the milk gone. 'Where's the bloody milk?' she screeched.

Mickey rolled his eyes. 'Hark at her!' He grinned at Sophie. 'Late nights and strenuous dancing clearly don't suit my daughter!'

Sophie batted her large eyes, the heavy fake lashes fluttering. 'Oh, I'd *love* to be one of those glamorous dancers, Mickey.' She traced a fake nail along Mickey's stained T-shirt. 'Imagine how sexy

I'd look in killer heels and sparkly stuff! Hey, I'd even keep the kit on for you when I got home...'

Groaning appreciatively with the thought, Mickey pulled Sophie onto his lap.

Oh, please, Marina thought, turning away before she vomited in her own mouth. She couldn't stand this. The pair of them had to go. She opened her mouth to tell her father and his slut to pack their bags and get the hell out of her flat, when she stopped herself just in time.

Sophie wanted to dance, did she? Could the woman lure Dan into a trap? Once it was discovered where he was hiding, which she'd get out of Tina eventually, then Sophie could be the go-between.

Marina eyed Sophie's voluptuous figure and plastic breasts. The scrounging bitch clearly had a sugar daddy in her pocket at some point to be in receipt of *those*. It wasn't like she'd have been able to foot the bill herself. But if Sophie believed she'd be the beneficiary of anything along those lines from Mickey, then the dim troll was in for a disappointment. The man was tighter than a badger's arsehole.

However, *Dan* was a different story. Sophie was just Dan's type, plus the bimbo had several points on Tina in the looks department too. Whatever Dan's prior association was with Tina, Marina knew him well enough to guarantee he'd be easily diverted by the promise of a real-life Barbie doll to play with.

Plastering on a smile that hurt her face, she sidled over to the table and forced herself to place her hand on Sophie's shoulder. 'If you're serious, maybe I could get you a job at the Boulevard?'

Sophie's head darted up in surprise. 'Me? You'd get me a job there? To work with you?'

Marina pushed her face into a wider smile. 'Why not? I know we didn't get off on the right foot to start with. That was my fault, so it would be fun to do this together, don't you think?'

Sophie leapt from the table and flung her arms around Marina's neck. 'Oh, thanks, babe!' she squealed. 'I'd love that!'

Marina spluttered on a chunk of nylon hair extensions that flipped from Sophie's head into her mouth and prayed the silly tart unpeeled herself before she was left with no choice but to stab her. 'No problem,' she choked. 'I'll ask about it tonight.'

Sophie skipped back over to Mickey. 'How about that then, babe? I'm going to be a glamorous dancer!'

Marina turned away so her sneer of disgust wasn't spotted. *Yeah, because didn't all little girls dream of growing up to take their kit off for seedy men in a doss hole?*

* * *

Seb slammed the phone down. 'Change of plan.' Standing up, he shrugged on his jacket. 'That was Baker giving me the heads up to expect a visit from the Old Bill this afternoon.'

'Shit!' Andrew hissed. 'What's the plan, then?'

'I need more time before I speak to them. I cannot afford to be charged, even if it's dropped at a later date.' Seb scraped his car keys from the desk into his suit jacket pocket. 'I'll head to Bristol now. Neil, contact Bob and tell him I need tomorrow's meet brought forward to this afternoon.'

He saw the confusion on his brother's face. 'Once the cops have been here, regardless of what is said, I'm not giving them the opportunity to tail me, otherwise we're fucked.'

Because whether or not he liked Sam looking for the tart Linda mentioned, it was now vital the girl was located. It was Seb's only hope of disassociating himself from the Aurora killing.

Nothing could impede the operation and planning of this heist.

'What if Bob can't do this arvo?' Neil asked.

'He will.' Seb turned to Andrew. 'Deal with the cops when they show up. Fob them off. Tell them I'm doing wedding stuff or that I've been abducted by aliens! I couldn't give a shit what you say, just get rid of them. Baker will be with them, so that should help. This time, he'd better earn his bastard money!'

He moved to the door. 'Oh, and let Kev know what's happened and to bring Sam up to speed when she returns. I'll be back as soon as I can.'

Leaving the office, Seb strode up the corridor, his grimace deepening. *This was shit.* He could only hope Sam found that girl. Christ, why couldn't Linda have just done her bit? It wouldn't have hurt her.

He barged past the staff in the Orchid's lobby, not having time for pleasantries. He had to get to Bristol and hope he didn't get snarled up on the motorway. He needed the lowdown from Bob bloody fast. If Sam hadn't located the girl, then it wouldn't be long before the cops sniffed around just about everything he did for the foreseeable. And that only spelt disaster.

If he got copped lifting a ton of cocaine from the docks, then his chances of seeing the light of day again were miniscule. And that he could not afford to happen for himself, Sam *or* his firm.

Seb's eyes narrowed. The Royal Peacock must be rebuilt and he had to get his firm back where it should be. Furthermore, he wanted the life with Sam he'd promised her and no fucker was stopping that.

15

Shane O'Shea moved closer to corner Marina between the wall and the only viable exit from his office at the rear of the Sunset Boulevard.

He blocked her path with his arm and strategically leant in. His well-worn face creasing into a leer as his bulbous eyes devoured Marina's Lycra-clad body. 'You've only been here a couple of days, Ava, yet you're asking for a job for your mate?'

'Just thought you might be interested, that's all.' Marina raised an eyebrow suggestively. She knew how to play the game, even though all she wanted to do was poke her long thumbnail in this greasy loser's eyeball.

She may have to be nice and allow this turd into her personal space, but despite pretending otherwise, this *was* important. She'd never dreamt she'd need Sophie to do anything, short of fucking off out of her life and taking Mickey with her, but now the daft bitch was the best option in getting her hands on Dan, she had to get Miss Plastic Fantastic into this dump one way or the other. And if that meant allowing this muppet another grope, then so be it.

Something else to add to the list of what was Dan's fucking fault.

A hand shoving between Marina's legs ricocheted her concentration back to the room.

'I'm interested, all right?' Shane said, his tongue running over his fat bottom lip.

'Now, now,' Marina grinned, expertly twisting herself away from Shane's probing fingers. 'Patience gets you everywhere.' *And what he'd just done would put him in a fucking coffin, but first things first.* 'I'm on stage soon, so you'll have to wait your turn!'

Before Shane could block her escape again, Marina skittered to the door, her thick makeup deflecting from the snarl itching to present itself whilst she drove her stiletto heel into his groin. 'So, how about my friend? Can she work here?' she purred, her voice oozing charm, whilst inwardly plotting this fucking dirty fat bastard's very painful demise.

Shane salivated as Marina showcased one of her long legs against the door. 'Yeah, why not! If the bird's anywhere near as hot as you, then she'll go down a treat!' He thumped his chest with mirth. 'Ah-ha, see? Go down? Yeah, that would be good an' all!'

Marina chose to ignore Shane's latest comment for now and smiled seductively through her revulsion. 'I'll bring her tomorrow night. Right, must dash!'

Slamming the door behind her, Marina blocked the memory of Shane's fingers stabbing against her lace knickers from burning into her mind and instead allowed her inner anger to fester. 'It's all for the greater good, remember?' she muttered under her breath as she tottered up the corridor to the dressing room.

That perv would get his at a date yet to be confirmed. Something to look forward to.

Pulling open the dressing room door, Marina replaced her

scowl with a happy face. 'Tina!' she cooed. 'Where have you been, babe? I've been really worried about you!'

No, I haven't. I'm thoroughly fucked off that you left me in the lurch on stage last night with a fucking mud wrestler whilst you disappeared with my ex-boyfriend who nicked millions from me...

Keeping her thoughts to herself, she perched on the edge of Tina's dressing table. 'So, come on then! Are you okay?' *Hopefully not. With any luck, Dan has given you herpes...*

'You'll never believe who came in here last night!' Tina cried.

Marina smiled sweetly. She wouldn't have any problem listening to Tina tonight, as long as she heard what she needed to know.

* * *

Sam hadn't wanted Craig to accompany her. She'd been irritated by Seb's insistence that he did, but in retrospect, she was glad.

In the matter of seconds it took to get out of the car before Craig hefted his huge frame from the driver's seat, she'd been accosted by two separate men in passing cars enquiring after her services.

She stared after the disappearing tail-lights. 'Jesus,' she hissed.

'Take no notice,' Craig muttered in his usual matter-of-fact tone. 'They presume everyone's up for grabs here.'

Sam's anger bristled. Not for herself, but for what her mother must have put up with during the time she walked the streets. This area might be well known for the 'services' it offered, but the people who preyed on or ran these women never ceased to rankle her.

She peered further up the dark street, the many broken streetlamps not helping the overall situation. Through the gloom, she could just about make out several women. 'Come on,' she said, upping her pace. 'I need to speak to as many women as I can.'

Craig lumbered after Sam, his bulk dwarfing her. As she neared the group of women, they took one look at the approaching pair and began to disperse.

'Wait!' Sam shouted. 'I need to speak to you.'

The women continued scattering in various directions. 'I'm looking for my friend,' Sam lied, breaking into a run. 'Someone called Tina. I can't find her and I'm worried. I'm not the police, I promise you. *Please!*'

Seeing two women stop, Sam continued, leaving Craig to catch up. Brute strength he may have, but running ability, he did not.

Reaching the women, she leant against the brick wall of the back of a shop, out of breath. She smoothed down her hair to collect herself, then turned to the two women eyeing her with suspicion.

'I'm looking for a girl called Tina. She might have come here a couple of weeks ago,' Sam said. Tina might have been here for a few weeks or two days, if at all, but it would have been after the Aurora had shut. 'She's about so high.' She held her hand level with her own head. 'And she's got blonde hair.'

Not much of a description, but Linda couldn't recall much detail. 'Have you seen her?'

A tall, overly thin woman with straggly brown hair scowled. 'That could be anyone!'

Sam stared at the woman, guessing her to be in her mid-thirties, but she could have been a lot younger. 'Tina is about seventeen.' *Seventeen – all but a child.*

'What's it to you, anyway?' the tall woman snarled.

Sam frowned, not having time for games. 'I'm looking for her because I need to speak to her. I want to help her and I want her to help me.'

Folding her arms, the woman looked Sam up and down for the second time. '*Help* her?' She nudged her companion. 'Another fucking patronising do-gooder, coming here with all her posh clobber on and bringing...' she gave Craig the once over, 'her pet monkey!' She then winked. 'Although you ain't too bad for a monkey, are you, sweetheart! Interested?'

'Cut the shit!' Sam barked. 'Just tell me if you've seen her.'

The woman stepped forward. 'Listen, sister, I say who works this patch and I'm the first to know about any new brasses wanting to muscle in and th...' She stopped when her mate tugged her arm.

'That's the woman who runs the Orchid. That bird in the papers? The one getting hitched to Seb Stoker!'

Even though it was whispered, Sam heard the words. 'Yes, I *am* that "woman from the Orchid" and both me and Seb are looking for Tina, so if you'd answer the fucking question, I'd appreciate it.'

Realising her mistake, the tall woman paled. 'Why didn't you say so!' she laughed, attempting to play down her rudeness.

Sam looked between the two women once more. 'Well?'

'There was a new face here last week, but...'

Sam's heart leapt. 'Yes?'

'She was at least forty, so it couldn't be the bird you're looking for.'

Sam glanced at Craig in desperation before turning back to the women. 'There's been no one else?'

'Nope.'

The tall woman ground her cigarette out with her pink patent stiletto, the scraping noise against the rough pavement making Sam's teeth on edge. She couldn't help but wonder how these women didn't catch their death standing out here in freezing temperatures with clothes that barely sufficed in a heatwave.

Suddenly, Sam thought of something. It was a long shot, but worth a try. 'Do you know a Tom Bedworth?'

The younger woman shook her head, but the older woman's expression showed otherwise.

'Wherever Bedworth is, he ain't here, thank fuck,' she spat. 'And he'd best not show up either!' Her face twisted into a scowl. 'Nasty piece of work, that one. Ripped me off once and I've never forgotten it. He fucked off years back and good bloody riddance.'

Defeat washed over Sam. No hint or knowledge of Tina and no one had seen Tom Bedworth either. Not lately, anyway. But it seemed his reputation preceded him even back then.

Pulling two business cards from her pocket, she handed them to the women. 'Thanks for your time. If you remember anything, please get in touch.'

As Sam walked away, the tall woman regained her confidence. 'Hey, we've told you what we know and you hand us a poxy card? We could have missed a punter whilst gabbing to you! We've got kids to feed, lady! What with all your money, you could at least...'

'Here!' Sam snapped, shoving a twenty-pound note in each woman's hand. 'Come on, Craig, let's go!' Swiftly turning on her heels, she began walking back to the car.

'Oh, and lady,' the woman called, 'there's one place popular with the younger ones you could try.'

Sam stopped. 'Where's that?'

'The Sunset Boulevard on Edgbaston Street.'

Nodding, Sam continued back to the car, deflated, but at least with a recommendation of somewhere else to look.

16

'Thursday next week.' Potter glared at his brother, offended that this was the third time the same question had been asked. 'I've told you twice now, so why the fuck are you asking me again?'

Mark shrugged. 'Dunno. I just wondered whether anything had changed.'

'Why would anything have changed?' Potter heaved himself out of his chair and stomped over the other side of the Portakabin to help himself to a drink, the damp floor sagging underneath him.

Yanking open one of the many battered filing cabinets, he growled as the rusty hinges stuttered on their runners. Taking out a bottle of rum, he unscrewed the top and swigged down a large mouthful. He wouldn't offer Mark any. His brother could buy his fucking own. This wasn't the bastard Salvation Army.

Potter's beady eyes homed in on his brother, whose gaze remained fixed on the bottle in his hand. 'Well? You got something to say, then fucking say it!'

Mark folded his arms, the leather of his bomber jacket squeaking. 'All right, then. I saw Bedworth here yesterday. Word has it that he's in on the next shipment. Is that true?'

'Yeah, so?' Potter scowled, knowing it wouldn't take long for this lot here to jump to conclusions. Except this time, they'd been right. *Sort of...*

'But he's a cock!' Mark cried. 'You know he went round saying we'd cunted him off with prices over that coke he begged from us. Then he tried to undercut us by setting up his own crack shop! You said you'd slap the taste out of his mouth if he ever came round here asking for owt again, yet you've allowed him an in with our next haul?'

Potter placed the bottle of rum back in the filing cabinet before he wrapped it around Mark's head. 'That's the problem with you, ain't it?' he barked. 'Always jumping to fucking conclusions! Had you bothered waiting until the meeting, I'd have told you!'

Moving back to his desk, he ripped open the bottom drawer, the force making the Portakabin walls rattle. Pulling out a folder, he slammed it down, a plume of dust exploding in Mark's face. 'Yes, Bedworth's in on this next shipment. And yes, he's a cunt. And yes, I *am* having him for previous – he just doesn't know it yet!'

Mark coughed as he waved the cloud of dust motes away from his face. 'How? What do y...'

Potter grinned. 'The thick twat is putting up half the outlay, but receiving only 20 per cent of the profit of resale.'

'That doesn't cancel out bad-mouthing us! I don't know why you're dealing with him at all.'

'Bad-mouthing *me*, you mean?' Potter glared at Mark. '*I'm* the head of this firm, so any slights are against *me*, not you. But, if you'd let me finish, I'd have said that's what *he's* agreed to. What he doesn't know is that he won't be getting jack shit from the profits at all.'

A snide grin spread across Mark's face. 'Ah, so he'll be paying half for nothing?'

'Brilliant analysis... but it's even better than that. Bedworth needs somewhere to stay. It appears he's outstayed his welcome in Brum, so I'm giving him one of the flats to use, but...' Seeing Mark about to protest, Potter held his hand up. 'Bedworth being Bedworth couldn't resist an opportunity to boast and let's just say I'm guessing he's got a massive stash of money in addition to what he's put on the table for this deal. It doesn't take rocket science to work out why a) he needs to exit Brum and b) why he's so flush.'

Mark frowned. 'Doesn't it?'

Potter sighed. His brother really hadn't received a fair percentage of brains when they'd been handed out. 'The fire at the Peacock and all of that?'

Mark's frown deepened. 'Yeah, we've all heard they got torched, but wh...'

'For fuck's sake! It's obvious it was Bedworth who did it!' Potter barked, his patience lapsed. 'Bedworth must have torched the Stokers' place and, using that as a distraction, robbed the safes. That's why he's making a sharp exit and creeping around like Dracula!'

Mark blew through his teeth. 'Fucking hell! Do you really think Bedworth had the balls to do that? Or the ability?'

Potter shrugged his big shoulders. 'Why not? A fire gave the perfect excuse to rob the fucking place. The Stokers must have kept their money in the casino. Where else would they put it? And okay, so I don't know Bedworth robbed them for definite, but how else did he get his hands on all of this money?'

Mark sat thoughtfully. 'It adds up, but I still don't know why you'd...'

'*I'll* be having the remainder of Bedworth's money and that remainder will be large. Then I'll make a call to the Stokers to tell them Bedworth's location.' Potter sat back in the chair, a self-satisfied grin covering his pudgy face. 'That, I think you'll find, will be the end of Tom fucking Bedworth. Plus, the Stokers will then owe us one.'

'Ah, I see,' Mark mumbled. 'But won't they want to know where the money's gone? Won't they put two and two together and realise we must have it?'

'They can do as much maths as they want, but they'll have to fucking prove it!' Potter grinned. 'And they can't... Furthermore, they'll *know* they can't. I hate the fucking Stokers! I'll never forget what they did to this firm and to our father. And I hate Bedworth. This way, I win and no one can do sod all about it.'

He beat his fist against his chest. 'This is my chance to get Birmingham and I'm having it. For years, the Stokers have kept us on the periphery, but at the moment, thanks to the burning of the Peacock, they're weak. If my theory is correct and Bedworth half inched their clobber whilst torching the gaff, they'll have shag all to get back on their feet with.'

His face creased into an ugly frown. 'I also heard from one of my lads that it looked like the Stokers sent someone to dig around our turf the other day, so they must be checking for openings they believe they can cash in on. That will not happen!'

His face split into a wide grin. 'This is my time to shine. By this time next month, bruv, the Rosses will not only be running Wolverhampton, but we'll have the whole of Brum on our payroll too! There may be a couple of other two-bit fringe firms knocking around, but they ain't no threat and never have been.'

He laughed heartily. 'Let's face it, the only firms in Brum with clout are the Stokers and Reynolds. The Stokers are utterly fucked and the Reynolds – well, that's now run by some lame bird, so we don't have anything to worry about there!'

With a flourish, Potter pulled open a narrow drawer at the top of his desk and retrieved a cash box. Rooting through bunches of keys, he fished out a set and chucked it to his brother. 'Bedworth can have this fleapit to live in during the week he's got left on the planet. Give Daphne a call and tell her to get her arse there to give it a once over. It probably still stinks of shit since that old codger carked it and no one found him for two months!'

Nodding, Mark got to his feet. He'd have to be civil to Bedworth, but he could manage that as long as Potter's theory was right. It would only be for a few days, anyway.

'Oh, and I shouldn't have to say this, but I will anyway.' Potter stared at Mark as he stopped at the door. 'This goes no further. No discussing it outside of these four walls and with *no one*. Got it?'

It was bleeding obvious really, but where Mark was concerned, everything had to be spelt out slowly and loudly. There could be no room for error, otherwise they would be as fucked as Bedworth was about to find himself.

For once, the Stokers would not get things their way. They could do what the fuck they liked with Bedworth, but *his* hands would be squeaky clean on every single part of it.

It was perfect because Potter didn't want grubby fingerprints on the immense stash of money about to land in his lap.

* * *

'But it makes sense!' Dan reasoned, desperate to make Tom feel this was his decision, rather than what *he* needed.

'Does it fuck!' Tom pulled one holdall after another out of the wardrobe. 'We're leaving *now*. I've sourced us somewhere to lie low, so grab your clothes and stop buggering around.'

Dan pulled his eyes away from the holdalls Tom placed on the bed. The hard-earned haul was about to leave the building and be lost forever if he didn't accompany the lunatic.

But he couldn't be linked to this man any longer and there was no way he wanted to leave Tina – not now he'd realised how he felt and how *she* felt. He couldn't.

Quickly, think.

His eyes darted back to the holdalls whilst Tom shoved the last remaining pieces of his clothing into a carrier bag.

'Get your fucking arse into gear. The taxi will be here any minute.' Tom turned to Dan, a pair of well-worn underpants in his hand. 'Do I really need to spell out again why we can't hang about with a fucking corpse in the shed or, as you so enjoyed pointing out yesterday, Samantha Reynold and half of Birmingham are looking for me?'

Tom nodded towards the holdalls. 'They'll take our money and not only will they kill me, but they'll kill you as well. I enjoy my life too much for that to happen.'

And of course he had the further trick up his sleeve to make another nice little fortune very soon, thanks to his association with Potter. Once that had come to fruition, Dan could fuck off. But he wasn't having the guy balls things up by insisting they stick around here and wait for everything to be taken. No fucking way.

Dan tried to regulate his breathing, each breath catching in his throat. It wasn't 'our' money, it was *his* – all his, not Tom's. He must act rational.

Smiling, he held his hands out. 'I get what you're saying, mate, but just think about it. Yes, Sam Reynold mistakenly believes that you're behind a lot of shit.' *And she'd be right*, he thought bitterly. 'But we can't get out of the country until I've sorted the passports out. Like you said, no one knows me and I've got that ace glove you made to conceal the only thing anyone could recognise. If we both go to Wolverhampton, how will it work? This mate who's helping you out – is he arranging our passports? Do you trust him, or have you got someone else over there you know well enough to safely approach? Someone who won't allow word to get back to the Stokers of our whereabouts?'

Dan pretended to chew his lip thoughtfully. 'We'll also have to be careful keeping all the money in one place, especially if there's people around we don't know. If anyone finds out about it, we'd be like sitting ducks...'

Tom faltered. He'd been about to punch Dan in the face until his words sank in. The man had a point. Potter Ross hated him almost as much as he, himself, hated the fat bastard. Potter certainly wasn't a friend. He didn't trust him either.

Sensing Tom's hesitancy, Dan took the opportunity to continue. 'How about this for an idea? I was all set to go out again tonight. Like I said, I think I'll be able to touch base with at least one of those people you mentioned to get the passports done, so why don't *you* go to Wolverhampton? I'll get the passports sorted and then join you in a day or two?' *Or, like, never...*

Tom mulled over Dan's idea. Potter Ross aside, he couldn't go out over the Black Country because he didn't know many people. Those he *did* know would sell him up the river to the Stokers for a fucking fiver. *Shit – Dan was right.*

'Oh, and,' Dan continued, his confidence growing at the acceptance creeping onto Tom's face, 'don't forget, if and I mean *if* anyone turns up here looking for you, they'll only find me. Sam Reynold doesn't know me from Adam. She's never even seen me, remember, so if you leave the money here, it will be safe.'

'You must be joking! You could do a runner!' Tom barked.

'Where to and with what? I can't go anywhere either until I've got a passport! We really can't risk having all the cash in one place. Look, leave me half – at least that way we cover our backs. If your lot gets lifted, then we'll still have what's here. Remember, no one's looking for me. It's just *you*.'

Tom scowled. *For fuck's sake. That was true as well.* In fact, he wouldn't put it past Potter to find his stash and rob the fucking lot. 'All right, but I want word the minute you get the passports.' Putting his hand in his pocket, he pulled out a card and handed it to Dan. 'If I don't hear from you by Sunday at the latest, I'll track you down and fucking kill you!'

'Christ, Tom. Do you not think I'd have sold you out long before if that was my game? I brought you the option of robbing this money in the first place, didn't I? I could equally think *you* might run off on me, but I don't.'

He wished Tom would, though. Dan wished more than anything that Tom would scuttle off the side of the planet with immediate effect – after leaving all of the money, of course. But half was better than nothing. Hell, he'd even take a quarter to rid himself of this freak of nature.

Tom went to argue the point a little further, when the staccato beep of a car horn interrupted him. 'That must be the taxi.'

Making his decision, he shoved the remaining underwear in the bag, zipped it up and grabbed two of the holdalls, making sure the one he'd already taken the cash from to pay into Potter's shipment was one of the two left on the bed. Dan wouldn't notice until he'd gone and he'd follow as soon as he could, like the obedient puppy he was. The bozo didn't need to know that the minute he turned up with their passports and the shipment was safely in, he'd be dispatched.

Tom smiled. And once that was sorted, he'd be free to leave the country for good – a rich man.

Watching Tom stagger out of the front door with the heavy bags towards the waiting taxi, Dan waved. 'See you in a couple of days then, mate,' he called, glancing down at the card Tom had handed him:

Primo Autoshop

Now that mental fucktard had gone, leaving him half the dosh, he could put his life back in order and get away from everybody as soon as physically possible.

Apart from Tina.

Dan would ensure *she* accompanied him wherever he went and neither he nor Tina would have to set eyes on Tom Bedworth ever again.

17

Peering through the stage door, Tina scanned the Sunset Boulevard. Dan had promised faithfully he'd be back, so where was he?

Her heart pounded. After all the hurt – all the years of feeling unworthy, all the years she'd been trained to let no man into her heart because they'd always be the cause of pain – she'd allowed the exact opposite to gain momentum by thinking that maybe, just *maybe*, this time was different...

She knew it was a cynical way of thinking for someone with three years to go before hitting her second decade, but so far, her life had proved the warnings her mother had spent her life instilling to be true.

But despite her and Dan's initial way of meeting, he seemed different. Was he the one to break the mould?

Her mother would say no and that all men were the same, but then her mother had had one hell of a life. And look how that had ended...

At the thought, Tina swallowed the lump forming in her throat and continued searching the room for a glimpse of the man she hoped would be her knight in shining armour.

'What are you doing?' Ava hissed. 'We're on in a minute!'

'I know, I know. I'm just looking...'

Seeing hope and longing in Tina's eyes, Marina almost felt slight pity for the silly cow pinning her hopes on a loser such as Dan.

How she'd managed not to choke when Tina confessed what had happened last night, she didn't know. Tina had admitted the man she had been instructed to shag for info so her boss at the Aurora could benefit had turned up last night, glad to see her. Marina hadn't been surprised in the slightest about this, but what she *was* surprised about was that Tina believed Dan wasn't like other men and that he'd forgiven her for turning him over and setting him up...

Marina snarled maliciously. Fat chance!

Dan *was* different from other men. He was *worse*.

But that wasn't *her* problem. She couldn't care less if Tina got murdered or chucked down a sewer. The woman was a thick skanky tart, worth nothing more than the grubby plaything she was so adept at being. But if the silly cow thought she'd benefit from Dan's thieving ways, she had another thing coming.

Marina had convincingly forced herself to look interested whilst Tina had continued gabbling on about Tom Bedworth and his instructions. Apparently, he was the same man who had allegedly killed the girl's mother and the man who had been holding some druggy prisoner in the attic of that brothel.

And then Sophie had interrupted.

Marina could have killed the plastic bitch! She'd stuck her hooter in just as Tina was getting to the bit about where Dan was living. Despite this setback, she was still glad she'd had the foresight to bring Sophie on board.

Marina glared at the back of Tina's bleached head resentfully. Now Tina had a thing for her pointless ex-boyfriend, she was out of the running for the job. But Sophie didn't hold a torch for the moron, so getting *her* to do it was now a necessity. But she couldn't do a fat thing if Tina glued herself to the door, staring hopefully out into the crowd like a dog at a rescue centre.

'Come on.' Marina irritably tugged at Tina's arm and pulled her from the door. 'You can't stand there all night!'

As they hurried along the corridor for final touch-ups to their makeup, Sophie tottered towards them again, her big blue eyes glittering. 'I thought I'd missed you!' she squealed, her sparkly platforms clacking against the concrete floor. 'I'm on with you tonight, aren't I? Oh my God, I'm so nervous, Mari...'

Delivering a hefty nudge to Sophie's bare ribs made her immediately realise her mistake. 'Ava, I meant Ava!'

Frowning, Tina looked from the new girl to Marina. 'I kind of guessed Ava wasn't your real name, but I thought you might have told me,' she said sulkily.

'Okay, it's Mary.' Marina glared at Sophie, even though the daggers in her death stare floated straight through the woman's air-filled brain. 'Mary's hardly a good name for a dancer!' She tried to laugh, but it sounded more like a choke. 'I call myself Ava most of the time in real life, anyway,' she lied.

'Then why...' Tina tailed off and frowned. 'I thought you said you were new to Brum. Do you two know each other?'

'Yes!' Sophie exclaimed. 'I'm the...'

Marina cut in. 'Sophie's my new flatmate. She's just moved in, haven't you, Soph?'

'What?' Sophie blinked, belatedly remembering what she was supposed to say. 'Oh, yeah, I've just moved in. I didn't know M... Ava before that. Not even slightly...'

'We need to hurry up,' Marina barked, pulling Sophie in the direction of the dressing room, leaving Tina to follow behind.

The stupid, thick cow! If the gormless bitch couldn't remember the basics, how would she cope with the story planned to feed Dan?

If the thick trollop let her down on this, she'd go apeshit. She hadn't put up with Shane O'Shea's lecherous bullshit in order to get Sophie a job in this fleapit for fuck all.

* * *

'Fine! If you need to send someone to their home, then be my guest!' Andrew shrugged, appearing nonplussed. He rested his eyes on DI Baker, the awkwardness clear in the man's pudgy face. 'I'm surprised you're allowing this harassment.'

'I'm afraid it's routine when waiting to speak to someone, Mr Stoker. I have no doubt, though, that if you say your brother and Ms Reynold are not at their house or here either at the moment, then it's the truth.' Baker nodded abruptly at the three officers accompanying him. 'Go and make the required checks and then report back to me. I'll remain here in case they return in the interim.'

Andrew kept his face steady, his jaw clenched. Baker was covering his own back as per usual. He hoped to hell Sam was still with Craig scouring for that tart, rather than back at the house, otherwise she'd be lumbered with a grilling. He didn't want anything said that didn't match with what he'd fed the cops. There was no way of reaching Sam or Craig to fill them in. Or Seb, for that matter, but at least he should be in Bristol by now.

Baker waited in silence as his officers left the room before turning to Andrew. 'Sorry about this...'

'It's a bloody liberty, Baker,' Andrew scowled. 'You know Seb had fuck all to do with this.'

Baker sighed. 'That's all very well, but something else has come to light, that's why I'm here. As well as being under pressure with those above me making sure procedures are followed and boxes checked to the nth degree, now I've got the bleeding press on my case.'

'The press?' Andrew exclaimed, concern rising. 'Please tell me that they haven't got wind that Seb is under scrutiny for this bullshit?'

Baker shook his head. 'It will only be a matter of time before they make their own conclusions. Everything and everyone's on my case today. Listen – a motor's turned up. It was found abandoned in a ditch over Yardley and we have reason to believe it's the same car used to mow down that girl around the back of here.'

'You're not insinuating that was Seb as well, are you?' Andrew snorted in derision, stopping abruptly with Baker's expression. 'Wait... You're serious?'

'Well, I...'

'I don't believe this!' Andrew cried. 'All the motors that didn't get trashed in the blaze are accounted for. Check if you like. Go on!' Standing up, he grabbed the back of Baker's jacket, pulling him from the seat.

'Stop!' Baker shrugged himself from Andrew's grasp. 'I'm warning you about it, that's all, but the fact remains the same. The girl photographed at Seb's housewarming – the one it was alleged he slept with – suddenly ends up dead on the road at the back of your casino... The newspaper hacks are all over it like a fucking rash! Hell knows how they got wind of it, but they have! As well as mounting speculation, the thumbscrews are on me for answers.'

Andrew momentarily shut his eyes in despair. *This was all they needed...* 'You'd better tell me everything you know so far, then.'

18

Sam edged into the Sunset Boulevard, making a concerted effort to find somewhere to stand with her back against the wall, both to give her the most thorough view as well as ensuring she avoided as many salacious stares and wandering hands as possible.

She smiled thinly as Craig took up position next to her. Now it was a question of seeing if she could spot anyone matching the description of Tina.

And that was a tall order...

Her eyes wandered to the stage, where two girls writhed around each other, their lithe bodies gleaming with oil, their costumes glittering with sequins from the lights illuminating them in the otherwise dim room.

Those women were both brunettes. Linda had said Tina was blonde. Tina might not even be working tonight. Or worse, might not even work here at all...

The prospect of scouring more red-light street corners jabbed at the back of Sam's mind. Her thoughts returned to Seb once more.

Since Kevin had informed her the Bristol meet had been brought forward, she'd been even more on edge. She expected the police had been to the Orchid by now too and all she could do was hope Seb hadn't been stopped on the road to Bristol.

No, he'd have got to Bristol fine and would be sorting things out right this very minute. She must stop worrying and concentrate on her side of things. That was more important than ever now.

A tinge of resentment for Linda resurfaced. Although she understood Linda's reasons, it tipped the balance in the wrong direction. Why couldn't her mother have just done what was asked? It would have made things so much easier.

Time was ticking. What if she couldn't locate this Tina woman? What if she was too late and Seb was pulled in for something he hadn't done?

Last week, the rebuilding of the Peacock had started in earnest and the next payment on that massive project was expected soon. It was an immense amount of money – not something she could rustle up in the short term. Not without the house funds to pull on.

Sam frantically scoured every visible woman in the run-down club. Then, seeing an opportunity, she grabbed the arm of a passing topless waitress. 'Is Tina in tonight?' *Did Tina even use her real name? Perhaps, perhaps not. It was the only one to try.* 'She's blonde and about so high...'

'Tina?' the waitress frowned, her eyes darting to the wobbling tray laden with customers' drinks. 'I'm not su...'

'She's a dancer,' Sam pushed, aware the waitress was eyeing Craig suspiciously, no doubt wondering who he was. 'She hasn't been working here long. I'm... er, I'm her flatmate and she's forgotten her keys. I've got to go to work, so won't be able to let her in when she gets back.'

'Oh, okay,' the waitress exclaimed, winking conspiringly. 'We're not supposed to give out personal details, not that I'm saying you're a punter, but Tina will kill me if she can't get back into her place.' She nodded towards a table over the far end of the room. 'There she is. She's been on stage, so now she's "entertaining".'

Following the waitress's eyes, Sam exhaled with relief to see the back of a blonde deep in conversation with a man. She pulled her own keys from her handbag as a prop. 'Thanks. I'll go and give these to her now.'

Sam then looked to Craig. 'Stay here. I won't be a moment.'

Picking her way between the tables, she moved towards Tina, working out how to say what was needed.

She had to get the girl on her own, so first she needed that bloke to shove off for a while.

* * *

'There they are,' Marina hissed. 'That bloke Tina's draping herself over is the one I told you about.'

Turning around, Sophie leant forward and squinted in the direction of Dan's table. 'Which one?'

'What's the matter with you?' Marina spat. 'Don't make it fucking obvious you're looking!'

'I can't see much without my specs,' Sophie said, her cheeks reddening. 'Don't tell Mickey. He doesn't know I'm supposed to wear glasses.'

Marina swallowed the urge to laugh, imagining Sophie in a pair of heavy-rimmed glasses. Nothing would help her to look intelligent. Secondly, Mickey wouldn't give a rat's arse if Sophie wore specs or not. He rarely looked at her face! 'Like I said, it's the guy who's got Tina sitting on his lap. The bloke with one hand.'

'He's got one *hand*?'

'Just go over there and do what we agreed,' Marina snapped, losing patience. 'Get rid of Tina and make a play for Dan.'

When she'd told Sophie what she wanted her to do, the daft cow had been enthralled, like she had an innate attraction to men she perceived as 'gangsters'. Dan was about as much of a gangster as Captain Birdseye, as was her father, but if Sophie wanted to perceive those sad pair of wasters as Al Capone wannabes, then Marina didn't care. As long as Sophie enticed that loser of an ex-boyfriend and got him to a place where she could get her hands on him, and more importantly, her bloody money, then that was all what mattered.

Not that she had a place lined up for that yet, but one step at a time.

'Go on.' Marina nudged Sophie none too gently in the ribs. 'What the bloody hell are you waiting for?'

Sophie frowned. 'Who's that?'

Marina glanced over Sophie's shoulder towards Dan's table and froze.

Fuck! What was she doing here?

'Shall I still go over and...' Turning, Sophie stopped mid-sentence as Marina bolted through the stage door.

* * *

Tina stared at Dan like he'd just dropped out of the nearest tree, wondering if it actually *was* him and not a fairy godmother. Or that someone had spiked her drink and she was hallucinating.

The whole time she'd been onstage with Ava and the other new girl, she'd tried her best, but her mind wasn't on the job. She'd missed several moves and knew Shane was watching from some-where – if not in the audience, then via one of the CCTV monitors where he frequently kept an equally close eye on things.

She needed this job. *Really* needed it, but she'd been unable to concentrate on anything, not whilst being on the lookout for Dan. She'd felt so dejected by the end of her set that she wasn't even interested in the propositions from punters afterwards. It wasn't like her to turn anything down – something else Shane would be less than pleased about.

It was only when she'd spotted Dan making his way towards her that her heart had begun to race.

But *this*? She hadn't expected anything like this.

'I'm being deadly serious.' Dan reached over the table and took Tina's hand. 'I want to be with you and get you away from this. I've got the means to do it.'

He scrutinised Tina. She didn't believe him, he could tell. She thought he couldn't possibly mean what he'd said. Tina and the girls here probably got told things like that all the time, but he was different. He meant it and he'd *prove* it.

But he couldn't prove it here and time was short. Tom was expecting him to come to Wolverhampton in the next day or so and when he failed to show up, he'd be dead if he remained in this city.

Dan squeezed Tina's hand a little harder. 'You've got to believe me, babe. I can't tell you everything right now, but if we can talk later, I will. I swear I won't let you down. We can get away from Birmingham and make a fresh start.'

Tina's teeth dug into her lip. How she'd love to believe Dan, she really would, but why would someone that she'd already betrayed and who was in cahoots with Tom Bedworth suddenly appear out of the blue and offer something like this?

Cold washed over her. Maybe that was it? Perhaps this was a way of getting back at her for what she'd done? She knew too much, so it could be a trap to take her somewhere that Tom was waiting to finish her off, like he'd done to her mother.

But... but what if Dan was telling the truth? What if he really *did* mean it?

But leaving Birmingham and a job that paid well? She had a room in a house too, plus, she hadn't yet caught up with Stella. Tina had no idea what had happened to her younger sister since the Aurora closed. How could she leave and abandon Stella without knowing for certain that she was all right? Their mother would turn in her grave if she knew Tina was considering disappearing and leaving her sister on the word of a man.

Plus, if Dan was lying, she'd be left with nothing.

Or dead...

Tina pulled her eyes away from staring at Dan's hand and looked into his face, seeing only genuine concern. Or was it nerves?

Oh God, she didn't know. She was no good at this. How was she supposed to tell the difference? She had to weigh this up. Maybe Ava would know what to do? The woman was older, so she'd have more experience of this kind of stuff.

'Well?' Dan pressed.

Tina smiled weakly. 'I want to... It's just...'

'We haven't got time to hang around,' Dan cried. 'We must go as soon as possible. *Please*! You have t...'

'I can't just drop everything!' Tina exclaimed, alarm bells ringing. *What was the rush if there wasn't a catch?* 'I've got a life here an...'

'But I want to be with you! I want you to come with me,' Dan pleaded, realising he sounded both desperate and possibly even a little bit creepy. 'At least meet me later and we can talk about it?'

His heart thumped uncomfortably. If he could get Tina out of here, then he could explain everything and she'd see why they had to go.

'Okay, okay,' Tina said. 'But I'm not sure about... Oh!'

She wasn't imagining it. *The woman approaching the table was*

Samantha Reynold. She'd seen her in the papers enough to recognise her a mile off.

'I'm sorry to interrupt,' Sam said, reaching the table. 'Tina, isn't it? Can I have a word? Somewhere private?'

'With *me*?' Tina cried. She turned to Dan, only to find he was nowhere to be seen.

19

Potter scratched the crotch of his trousers for far longer than he should whilst his other hand trailed down the back of the paper where the form for the dogs running was listed.

He had a percentage share in a couple of greyhounds racing tonight and at least one of them had better deliver, otherwise those jokers from Hall Green wouldn't get another penny for the upkeep of the mangy animals.

Never trust a Brummie, he always said. Folk from the Black Country were on the level and knew what they were about.

Talking of Brummies...

Potter glanced up as Tom entered the Portakabin and plonked himself on a chair. 'How's your new drum? Good enough for you, is it?'

'Yeah, the flat's great, mate. Thanks,' Tom muttered, secretly wishing he could kill Potter Ross and be done with it. The flat he'd been assigned wasn't great at all. It made Linda's fleapit look like the Ritz.

And the smell... Christ knows who'd lived there before, but whoever it was must have shat on the carpet for the last thirty years. Possibly longer. Also, the muppet who'd thought it wise to explode a can of air freshener to mask the stench of the place ten seconds before he'd arrived had wasted their time. Still, it was only for a few days, thank God. The less time he remained in that stinking hovel or pretending to be pleasant to Potter, the better.

Potter eyed Tom suspiciously. 'I thought you were bringing your mate?'

'Yeah, I am,' Tom said hastily. 'He's just tying up a few loose ends and then he'll be here.' And he'd better be because if Dan dragged this out longer than necessary, there would be hell to pay.

'Hmm, I'd have thought if things were so "difficult" in Brum, your mate wouldn't stick around either...' Potter's eyes glinted maliciously, loving seeing Bedworth squirm. He could see the twat was lying and had expected nothing less.

Flipping the newspaper over, Potter rooted through the news from the rival city. He insisted the *Birmingham Mail* was delivered without fail every day. It paid dividends to keep abreast of what was going on in that stinking hole.

Tom watched Potter in silence. Wasn't he going to mention when this haul was due? 'When's this delivery coming in?'

Potter looked up, one furry eyebrow raising mockingly. 'Soon, Bedworth. Soon...'

'What do you mean, "soon"? I've handed over a huge chunk of cash, yet you're not saying when I'll see any return for my outlay?'

Heaving himself out of his chair, Potter grabbed Tom in a headlock and ruffled his hair, making out it was a playful gesture, when really it held a clear undercurrent of warning. 'He who doesn't trust the hand who feeds him ends up hungry, Thomas.'

Applying extra pressure before releasing his hold, Potter then slapped Tom on the back. 'In all seriousness, don't sweat. It will happen next week. I'll have the confirmation later on today, all right?'

Huffing, Tom rearranged his crumpled jacket and pretended Potter's meaty arm hadn't almost crushed his windpipe. And no, it wasn't all right! *Next week? Seven more days in that shitty flat? Christ!*

Dan had better be in touch tomorrow or the day after at the very latest. The bloody idiot best have sorted the passports too because the second that container docked and he'd got his money, he was out of here.

Tom chewed his lip, wondering if there were any travel agents nearby to check what flights were available next week. He hoped the only options weren't Iraq or anywhere bloody cold. That would be typical.

When Potter started chuckling, Tom scowled. *Was the twat laughing at him?*

'Oh, this is quality, this!' Potter said, beating his hefty fist against his chest in mirth. 'Listen to this. What a fucking wally!'

Tom rolled his eyes at Potter who was stabbing his finger at an article in the paper. *Yeah, whatever it was must be hysterical... Not...*

Potter was laughing so much he could barely get his words out. 'Fancy pinching a shitty Astra, only to find out it was used in a hit and run! Imagine it? Gutted!'

Tom had all but switched off from Potter's droning voice, until certain words seeped into his brain. *Pinched motor? Astra? Hit and run?*

Shit!

'Let's have a look.' Tom snatched the paper from Potter's hand and feverishly scanned the page.

PRESSURE ON POLICE FOR DETAILS

After a car was found abandoned in a Yardley ditch earlier this week, pressure is mounting on the West Midlands Police to apprehend the driver of the vehicle.

Our source informed the Birmingham Mail that this vehicle is believed to be the car involved in the hit and run on Granville Street earlier this month, resulting in the death of Deborah Banner.

We have pieced together that the E reg Vauxhall Astra was registered to a woman who died six months ago, and who therefore could not possibly be responsible for the purposeful murder of Miss Banner...

'Isn't that fucking hilarious?' Potter guffawed. 'Geez, talk about crap luck! Fancy robbing a murder weapon!'

'Actually, whoever stole the car could have been the killer! Not think of that?' Tom spluttered, unable to face reading the rest of the article. *Shit, shit and more shit!*

This was bad. He'd bought that car cheap from a garage when he'd left the Aurora. He hadn't even bothered sending off the V5. A bloody good job too.

But the garage owner might remember him and give the cops a description...

Fuck. If he got collared for that, he was in deep shit.

Trust that little tart to get one over on him from the grave. He'd been just about to dispose of the fucking thing as well when it got half inched from the Hyatt car park. Damn the fuckturd gluesniffer who'd pinched it. He hoped the bastard choked on his own fucking fumes.

Potter suddenly stopped laughing and eyed Tom. 'You're sweating like a stuck pig, Bedworth. This was nothing to do with you, was it?'

'Me?' Tom choked. 'Do I look like I drive a fucking E reg bastard Astra? And why the fuck would I need to run over some teenage girl? Have a day off, Potter!'

Potter chuckled once again, but kept his eyes on Tom.

Yeah, Bedworth had something to hide all right – a *lot* more than he'd first thought. But he'd play the game for as long as necessary and keep this snippet handy to add to the list of what to use against the pointless piece of shit when the time came. In the interim, once this loser fucked off out of his Portakabin, he'd get Mark to mooch through that shitty flat and see if he could find what he believed was stashed in there.

* * *

Sam ignored Kevin's stares. She was irritating herself fiddling with her handbag's clasp, the clicking noise driving her and everyone else crazy.

She had to do something to keep her hands busy. It was either that or pace the office again. She glanced at the clock. Nearly 11 a.m. and Seb *still* hadn't returned from Bristol.

She hadn't been too concerned when he wasn't home by the time she went to bed last night, sure he must have got word to one of his brothers regarding the delay, or would have slipped in during the night. But waking up to find his half of the bed still empty this morning and now, after hearing that Andrew, Neil and everyone else had heard nothing either, deep-seated worry set in.

Had Seb been arrested? Arrested and *charged*? What if they hadn't granted him the one allowed phone call?

What if he'd had an accident?

He could be lying dead down an embankment off the M5 and no one would know.

Nausea bubbled.

Sam had been quietly overjoyed, having arranged to meet Tina to discuss things further this afternoon. She'd been eager to tell Seb that he'd soon be home and dry, but if he was dead, then it wouldn't matter...

Nothing would matter...

Oh God, please let him be all right, she repeated within her mind, her panic escalating.

'For Christ's sake, Sam! Quit messing with that bag!' Andrew bellowed, Seb's absence also weighing heavily. 'Why don't you tell us about this Tina woman instead, rather than us all sitting here like idiots expecting the worst?'

'Well, I...'

Everyone's heads swung around as the office door suddenly burst open.

'Seb!' Sam jumped from her seat to throw her arms around the man she loved. 'Thank God you're okay!'

'That's a most welcome greeting for a knackered bloke.' Seb smiled. Sensing Sam's palpable relief, he held her at arm's length, concern marring his handsome features at the distress on her face. 'Hey, what's the matter?' He glanced around the other drawn faces in the room, his stomach plummeting. 'What the fuck's happened?'

'Nothing,' Neil snapped. 'Short of us wondering why you didn't leave word you weren't coming back last night...'

'Why didn't you call?' Andrew added. 'You've got a bloody mobile! You knew the cops were coming. We thought you'd been pulled in.'

Wearily, Seb pulled his phone from his pocket and chucked it on the desk. 'The battery's fucked and I didn't have any change to use a call box – not that there were any.' He pulled Sam back into his arms. 'I got a flat tyre and was stuck on the hard shoulder of the M5 since four this fucking morning.'

He pressed his lips to Sam's. 'I'm sorry, Princess, I didn't mean to worry you. There was nothing I could do.' He nodded at his brothers, not impressed with them treating him like a naughty child. 'Lone men aren't priority for breakdown services and garages tend to be closed at 4 a.m., even when you've made the effort to trek miles up the hard shoulder to find an emergency telephone!'

Reaching for the decanter, he helped himself to a much-needed whisky. 'I've had no kip. I've got blisters on my blisters, *but* the good news is that everything's set. It's happening on Thursday.'

Andrew grimaced. 'That's if the cops haven't pulled you in by then.'

Groaning, Seb ran his fingers through his unbrushed hair and flopped into a seat. 'You got rid of them?'

Andrew nodded. 'We said that you'd taken Sam for a wedding dress fitting, but I don't think they believed us because they ended up going round your house.'

'You didn't mention that!' Sam exclaimed.

'You were out! I could hardly call in case the lines were tapped.' Andrew turned to Seb. 'But when those other cops left to check the house, it gave Baker the chance to tell us they're looking at pinning that hit and run on you as well.'

'*What*?' Seb gasped. 'Are you serious?'

'Yep. Look.' Neil pushed the paper across the desk, open at the page of the relevant article. 'Somehow the press got wind of the police info and so it's only a matter of time before they bandy your name around in relation to it. You know, because of all the other business with that girl and...'

'We don't need to revisit that!' Sam interrupted, her cheeks colouring. She needed no reminder that, thanks to the press, the whole city had believed Seb to have cheated on her with a teenager. And much to her shame, so had *she* for a short while.

'For fuck's sake, this will scupper everything!' Seb slammed his glass on the desk. 'It's only a week until the heist, and the Old Bill will be even more over me because of this. It will never work now. Fuck!'

'It might...' Sam grinned, her panic stabilising now Seb's safe return had registered. 'I've found her – the girl Linda told me about. She's provisionally agreed to talk to the police about the Aurora and Bedworth.'

'You found Tina? That's fantastic! Where?' Heart racing, Seb jumped up and planted his lips on Sam's. If this girl could be convinced to talk to the cops, then all these snowballing accusations against him would be dropped.

'In a place called the Sunset Boulevard on Edgbaston Street,' Sam explained. 'We got a tip-off to look there and it was spot on. I spoke to Tina briefly, but she was with a man. He disappeared, thank God, so he didn't hear anything, but the girl seemed agitated.' She shrugged. 'I guess it's because it's her place of work and she didn't want to lose punters.'

Seb frowned. 'But why has she only agreed provisionally?'

'Because I haven't told her all of the details yet. I'm meeting her later on today when I'll explain exactly what we need her to do. I think she'll comply.'

'She'll have to be quick,' Seb said. 'I can't have her "thinking it over" for weeks on end.'

Sam nodded. 'No, I'll make sure of that. Now, tell us what's been arranged with your contact at the docks.'

Seb grinned widely. 'It's a sterling set up. When the container lands on Thursday, Bob will be on duty and...'

'I just need to add something...'

Everyone turned to look at Craig in amazement. Interrupting Seb when he was speaking, especially when he was discussing something of such immense importance, was not something that was done. *Ever.*

Unperturbed, Craig continued. 'This Tina woman... There was a man...'

'I've already said that,' Sam snapped irritably. 'Look, I've arranged to meet the girl, Seb will be off the police radar and then ɔur lives will be back on track, so we need to know *exactly* how this heist is going down now. Isn't that the priority?'

'I'm not sure... Something came to me in the middle of the night.'

'For God's sake, man! Stop talking in riddles,' Seb barked. 'If something is so important to interrupt me, at least have the fucking good grace to get on with it!'

A nerve twitched in Craig's neck, but his face remained passive. 'The man sitting with that bird got up from the table as Sam approached. I was watching from over by the bar.' He flexed his shovel-sized hands. 'I thought he looked suspect and so I followed him.'

'I told you to stay where you were!' Sam cried.

Craig shrugged. 'I wasn't gone long. I just wanted a closer look.' He looked between Seb, Andrew, Neil and lastly Kevin, where his gaze remained. 'He was lurking around outside the bogs, looking paranoid as fuck!'

'Most fuckers frequenting strip joints are paranoid in case someone their missus knows spots them!' Neil scoffed.

Craig shook his head. 'Nah, not this one. This was the guy I pulled in on suspicion of card sharking the night of the house-warming party.'

'The one I told you not to bother with and you did it anyway, you mean?' Kevin snapped. This wasn't the first time Craig had gone against instructions and now he'd interrupted Seb Stoker. 'I called Andrew as Sam was, erm, otherwise engaged.'

Sam bristled. *Another reference to the night she would rather forget...*

Andrew sighed. 'I know you were pissed off about having to leave the bloke as we had other stuff going on, Craig, but it's done, so what's the big deal?'

'The deal is that the guy had one hand, or most of one missing,' Craig continued. 'I remembered him because he'd worn weird white gloves to try and hide his missing fingers. He didn't have those on last night, but it was *definitely* the same bloke.' His eyes fell to Seb. 'Didn't your runner say the safe codes were given to a bloke with one hand?'

There were a few seconds of stunned silence before Sam spoke. 'Why didn't you tell me this last night?'

'As I said, I couldn't place him until it came to me in the small hours.'

'Fuck!' Seb glanced at his brothers. If it *was* the same man – this Dan person – then not only was it the man they were after in relation to the theft of their millions, but if he knew a girl who'd worked at the Aurora, then he had to be linked to that bastard Bedworth, and was possibly even behind torching the Peacock.

How many people were there with one hand around here? In reality, probably a few, given the number of industrial accidents, but there couldn't be many one-handed guys linked with the Aurora *and* Tina... 'We need to pull this bloke in.'

'What about Tina's statement?' Sam cried. If Seb went in all guns blazing, it would give the cops more reason to hold him, then the heist wouldn't be able to go ahead at all. 'We must wait until all of this is done. I...'

'You think I'll give that scrote the chance to disappear?' Seb stood up, his eyes flashing. 'Not bloody likely! He saw you coming and legged it, so it's got to be the right bloke. Don't worry, nothing will happen until we know for definite he's the man we want.'

Sam's heart sank. It would happen... And if it did, it would ruin *everything*.

20

'I know what you said, babe,' Sophie said as she patched up the scuffs on her fuchsia nails. 'But I got the impression last night that Dan was only interested in Tina.'

Marina grabbed one of Sophie's large silicone breasts. 'With tits like this, you think he'll need much convincing?' *More like she hadn't tried very hard, the lazy bitch.*

Sophie giggled proudly, then frowned. 'It's only my opinion, but he really did seem too distracted to notice me.'

Marina gritted her teeth. *Opinion?* Sophie lacked the ability to spell the word 'opinion', let alone have one. She fought the urge to smash the woman's simpering face into the kitchen table. And if she called her 'babe' just one more time...

But as much as it choked her, she had to play things nicely because she needed Sophie's help. 'What exactly did you say?'

Sophie beamed, elated to be deemed such an intrinsic part of something so exciting. 'When Tina disappeared with that other woman, I went over. I laid it on thick, like you said. Whilst my hand was under the table stroking his leg, I hinted that perhaps we could get to know each other later, but...'

Her face fell. 'He kept looking over his shoulder, like he wasn't listening.' Her plumped-up lips pouted. 'Didn't I look good enough in all my get-up last night? I thought I looked ace. Who is Dan, anyway? I mean, I know from what you said during the week to Mickey that he owes you money, but...'

'Yeah, you looked fantastic,' Marina lied. 'Dan must be blind. And don't worry about who he is. Like you said, he's just someone who owes me.' Marina had clearly failed to notice Sophie taking in more than she'd thought. *She must be more careful.*

Her brain whirred. But what the fuck had happened to Dan? Distracted? Only interested in Tina? Had he had a personality transplant?

'You'll have to up your efforts tonight and get super friendly with him. Do whatever it takes. Once you've got him gagging for it, lure him to a hotel or somewhere and then I ca...'

'I don't know about this, babe.' Sophie twisted a hair extension around in her fingers, not noticing her wet nail varnish leaving pink smears on the yellow nylon. 'Why can't Mickey know about this? If he finds out... Dancing and taking my kit off is one thing, but I'm not a prostitute!'

Forgetting the plan to remain nice, Marina shot out of her chair and grabbed a handful of Sophie's hair, yanking a couple of extensions out in the process. 'You are for the time being, until I say otherwise!'

'Ow!' Sophie yelped, clutching at her scalp.

Marina pushed herself into Sophie's shocked face. 'Now be a good girl and do what I say. I've got a lot riding on this and you don't want anything said to put Mickey off, do you? He listens to me, remember?'

Tears formed in Sophie's big blue eyes. She didn't want to do this. Mickey wouldn't like it, but Marina was scaring her. She'd seemed so nice lately, too. 'M-maybe if I explained what you want me to do and why, then Mickey might understand. I don't want him to th...'

Marina cut Sophie's whining voice off when she grabbed her around the throat. 'Are you deaf? You won't say a fucking word! This is between me and you. As far as Mickey's concerned, all you're doing is dancing at the club.'

Mickey wasn't finding out about this under *any* circumstances. If he knew she'd located Dan and had a plan, the greedy bastard would jump on that gravy train quicker than she could shake a stick at. He'd done fuck all towards this, therefore he wasn't having a penny.

Marina's eyes bored into Sophie. 'I need results and I need them fast. Am I making myself clear?'

Holding back a sob, Sophie nodded reluctantly. What else could she do, apart from what this woman wanted?

Groaning, Dan turned over, his back stiff as a board. It was nowhere near as uncomfortable as his head, though, which felt as if it had been smashed open with a sledgehammer.

He gingerly opened his eyes, squinting as the daylight burned his eyeballs, and blinked, trying to make sense of the unfamiliar ceiling.

A pink lampshade? What the fuck? This wasn't Luke Banner's house! Where the hell was he?

Sitting up far too quickly, blood surged through Dan's head and he winced, waiting for the increased pain of his already blistering headache to subside. Even moving his eyes hurt.

He glanced around the room, the reason for his back resembling a calcified plank becoming obvious.

He was lying on the floor...

'You're alive, then?' Tina moved into the room and stood over Dan. 'I tried to get you into bed, but you were a dead weight. I couldn't shift you.'

Dan smiled, despite feeling worse than the contents of a hospital incinerator. God, he had it bad for Tina. If Marina had left him on the floor all night, he'd have punched her in the trap. But that was Marina and she was completely different to Tina. Tina was perfect...

Suddenly the alcohol-clouded memories of last night avalanched over him.

Shit! Samantha Reynold...

Sam had been in the Sunset Boulevard and had come over to talk to Tina. After making a hasty exit, he'd watched Tina go off somewhere with the Reynold woman. The only thing he remembered after that was being back at the table, slugging down drink after drink from pure panic. Tina wasn't there, but some other bird was – a blonde with tits to die for.

Even with the nice view, all he'd been able to do was knock back the drinks and scan the room for Tina. He couldn't even remember her returning, but she must have done, otherwise he wouldn't be here.

But had Sam Reynold been with her? And what had she wanted? Was it to do with him?

Sweat broke on his brow.

'Hey, I really did try to get you off the floor,' Tina said, dropping to her haunches. 'Are you mad with me?'

Dan could have cried. Tina was worried that he'd had a bad night's sleep? But what *had* happened? He had to know what Sam wanted. Did she know who he was? If she did, then surely he'd have been carted off by now?

'Dan?'

'Sorry, sorry.' Dan dragged the back of his arm across his sweaty brow. 'I can't remember... I...'

'You were in a right state last night!' Tina chuckled. 'I thought you were going to chuck up and...'

'What did I say last night? Who...?'

'Relax!' Tina laughed. 'You were just banging on about needing to leave. You made no sense! Honestly, I disappeared for half an hour and by the time I got back, you were wrecked! What are you like?'

Dan forced his addled mind to function as the enormity of what he needed to do resurfaced. His plan for last night had been simple. Once they were on their own, he'd planned to tell Tina everything: explain what Tom had done to Luke, to Deb Banner, and that he, himself, had been roped into torching the Peacock and now the Stokers and Reynolds were after them.

He'd been all set to admit that he'd lied about Tom being off the scene and that he was expected in Wolverhampton by the weekend.

Like, *tomorrow*...

He had no intention of going, but that was just it. He had to do something. But he had the money – half of it, at least – so Tina had to come with him. He *wanted* her to come with him. He'd never wanted anything more.

Dan looked into Tina's face. She looked as fresh as a daisy, whereas he imagined he resembled how he felt – a *corpse*. And very soon he would be a fucking corpse, unless he moved on this. 'Tina, listen... I...'

'Let me make you a cup of tea. You look like you're going to pass out.'

'I don't want a cup of tea. I need to talk to you. I...'

'I can't right now.' Tina stood back up. 'It's nearly five o'clock and I've promised to meet Sam Reynold.' She pulled her hair into a ponytail. 'I'm so nervous, but I'm doing the right thing. It will put a stop once and for all to all of this crap with that bastard, Tom Bedworth. He deserves everything he gets!'

Clanging drums smashed in Dan's head. *Tina was seeing Sam Reynold again?* He dragged himself up to prop his back against the wall. 'What? What did you say? Why are you going to see her?'

Tina rolled her eyes. 'I tried to tell you last night. I really wanted to discuss it with someone, but you weren't capable... *Of anything...*'

Dan grabbed Tina's leg, aware he was acting like a nutter, but he couldn't help it. 'Don't go, please. Just tell me what you said and why you're meeting her.'

'I haven't got time.' Tina shook Dan's hand from her leg and moved towards the door. 'We'll talk later, okay?'

Scrabbling off the floor, Dan staggered across the room after Tina, his head splitting, but he was too late. By the time he reached the landing, all he saw was the back of her disappearing through the front door.

Hyperventilating, he stumbled over to the window to see her walking briskly down the road. He banged on the glass and waved his arms in a futile attempt to get her attention, but it was pointless.

For Christ's sake! Why had he got so slaughtered last night?

If he hadn't, then he could have told her everything, like he'd planned, and then she wouldn't even *consider* speaking to Sam Reynold. If Tina knew exactly how much doing that would implicate him, then she wouldn't, he *knew* she wouldn't.

Sighing, Dan slithered down the wall to the floor and put his head in his hands. All he could do now was wait until Tina returned and hope to hell the conversation she'd gone to have didn't include anything to do with him.

21

Spooning cold sardines from the tin into his mouth, Mickey's irritation grew. His daughter was a stroppy mare. She was getting more like her tramp of a mother every day. That was not a good sign. She'd even *look* like Linda soon if she carried on, and that she most definitely did not want if she planned to continue dancing at a strip club.

Mickey scowled further as a sardine bone jammed between his teeth.

Marina's attitude was getting right on his tits. It had been *her* who'd asked for his help, not the other way around. She'd called him all in a flap when her twat of a boyfriend had got the better of her and swiped Stoker's money from under her nose. But *he'd* done exactly what she'd asked – left London and come to Brum to help her, yet she acted like he was something she'd trod in.

Mickey's brow knitted. But Marina did have a point. Whether he liked it or not, he knew he hadn't done a fat lot to find Dan.

Nothing, in fact...

But Sophie was such a distraction...

That was half the point, though. Apart from getting a shag on tap, his ploy of using Sophie as a decoy to get him in the orbit of the casinos to dig the dirt on Dan was no longer needed since Marina got the idea to look for the wanker another way. And she'd successfully blagged her way into just the type of place that muppet would go.

But he should make the effort to do *something*...

Marina wasn't getting her hands on that money without him. He wouldn't put it past her to swipe the lot behind his back, the sneaky bitch.

His daughter had best not forget that it was *him* who'd supplied the info regarding Sam Reynold in the first place, so she'd better not have a selective memory about that when it came to it.

Flicking a chunk of sardine from his lap to the floor, Mickey glanced up as Sophie entered the lounge. 'What's up with you?'

'What? Nothing,' Sophie said, smoothing down her hair extensions, then screeched as Mickey pulled her onto his lap. 'Pack it in! You stink of fish! I don't want it all over me!'

Mickey frowned when Sophie scrambled off him. She wasn't usually flustered and on edge. 'Time of the month, is it?'

Ignoring Mickey, Sophie turned away to hide the tears brimming in her eyes. How could she tell him what Marina had asked of her? How could she say that his daughter was scary, and in all truthfulness, *unhinged*? Or that she truly believed it was only a matter of time before the woman hurt someone or, dare she think it, *killed* someone...

Marina was a loose cannon – unpredictable.

And it freaked her out.

But if Mickey discovered she'd promised to seduce someone else – and from what had been made clear, *sleep* with them, if necessary – then he would go nuts.

Sophie's breath caught in her throat. She relied on Mickey for money, as well as a roof over her head, and she couldn't jeopardise that.

She chewed the inside of her cheek, worry mounting. She'd love to know exactly what this Dan person had done. Or, furthermore, what Marina was planning on doing to *him*.

She suspected that whatever it was probably wouldn't be very nice.

Perspiration beaded between her shoulder blades, the edges of her crop top becoming damp.

Should she ask Mickey if he knew this bloke?

She risked a glimpse at Mickey and, finding him studying her, quickly looked away. If she asked questions, he might get suspicious and think she'd got something to hide.

Which she had... She just didn't know *what*...

'Are you not enjoying working at the Boulevard?'

Mickey's voice made Sophie jump. 'What?'

'You seemed pleased to be working there with Marina at first,' Mickey continued, becoming serious. 'Has something changed? Have perverts been pawing you or giving you grief?'

Sophie forced a smile. 'No, nothing like that. Everything's fine,' she lied. 'I'm just tired and my feet hurt.'

'You'd best go and soak them in the bath being as you're working again tonight. I'll come and scrub your back in a moment,' Mickey winked.

'Okay.' Sophie pushed her face into a smile and walked from the room, the fact that she was working tonight and was expected to deliver a lot more than a dance resting heavily on her shoulders.

Mickey drummed his fingers on the table as the bath water started to run.

Although he never had issues bagging the birds whilst he was flush, he wasn't getting any younger and Sophie seemed to genuinely like him. She had a decent rack on her too and didn't look like a moose, so perhaps he should give her more attention?

What was it they said women liked? Men to pay an interest in their lives, their jobs and that sort of crap?

A smile replaced his frown.

That was it. He'd pay the Boulevard a visit. Sophie would like that. Not only would he get to see her in action, which he quite fancied, but it would also give him the excuse to see what else was on offer too.

Plus, whilst he was at it, he could keep tabs on Marina to make sure she wasn't doing anything to cause him to lose out on his cut.

* * *

Sam was counting on everything falling into place. Now Seb was on the warpath for this one-handed bloke, time was limited.

She hoped she wouldn't have to get heavy-handed with Tina, but she would if she had to – there was too much riding on it. But she'd do things the more palatable way first.

Pulling her coat tighter, she came to the conclusion that a park bench on a February evening wasn't the most sensible place for a 'chat', but it wasn't like there were many alternatives.

She eyed Tina curiously. The young woman looked terrified. Should she broach asking about the man sitting with her at the table last night or not? There wasn't much point. It was unlikely Tina knew much about him. 'So, like I've explained, I really need your help. I want the person who has been abusing women as much as I expect you do for what he did to your mother.'

Tina nodded, unable to look at Sam Reynold. The woman exuded success. She felt unworthy even being in her presence. But to her surprise, Sam didn't have airs and graces and spoke to her

ike a *person*, rather than a commodity. And it was this which made
her want to do what was being asked.

But worry niggled like a stubborn itch.

Why had Dan been so tetchy about this meeting? Why was he
so bothered? She didn't understand it. If Dan hadn't got so
muntered last night, they could have discussed it.

Yes, she knew he'd planned to rob Seb Stoker's safes and
although she felt guilty, considering how nice Sam was being, this
meeting was nothing to do with the robbery. She wouldn't be
sitting here if it was.

This was to do with Tom Bedworth and if Sam was offering the
opportunity to punish Bedworth for what he'd done, she'd be crazy
not to take it.

Even so, it was way out of her comfort zone.

'I – I understand why you don't want Mr Stoker to be accused
of what was done to my mother,' Tina said meekly. 'But I... oh, the
police...? What about my job? Will they even listen to me?'

Sam bristled. 'They have to! Look, I need to know – did you
actually see Bedworth kill your mother?'

Tina shook her head. 'No. The other woman did. She told me
about it before she escaped. Actually, I don't know whether she
escaped, but I hope she did. Maybe you could look for her and...'

'She did escape, but she won't talk,' Sam snapped. 'It was her
who gave me *your* name.'

Tina blinked. 'That woman came to see *you*?'

Sam sighed. There was only so much she could hide. 'Look, I'm
surprised you don't already know because it was all over the papers
not long ago.'

'I – I don't read the papers. I...'

'That woman – Linda, is my mother. I was adopted.' Sam
shrugged. 'The press ran a story when we first reunited and before
Bedworth locked her in that fucking attic.'

Tina flinched, her mouth falling open. 'Your *mother*?' She couldn't pull her gaze away from the hate spilling from Sam's eyes that could kill a man stone dead at ten paces. 'What did Tom Bedworth have to do with your mother?'

'It's a long story – much of which I still don't know, but either way, I want to fuck Bedworth up. Plus, I will not have Seb being collared for murdering your mother!'

'But Mr Stoker didn't murder my mother. He couldn't have... If...' Tina's voice trailed off, her fingers picking at her chewed nails.

'If *what*?'

Tina stared forlornly up to the ceiling, her eyes welling with unshed tears. 'Oh, I don't know... I just don't know what to think any more... I don't even know who I am any longer and I...'

'For God's sake, stop muttering! It's irrelevant *what* your opinion is or what you think! The police want to pin it on Seb, so are you helping me or what? I haven't got time for this!' Sam snapped. Seeing Tina's shocked face, she softened and pressed a card into the girl's hand. 'Sorry, I didn't mean to shout, but I need your help and I need it now.'

With shaking fingers, Tina stared at the card, dread pooling in her stomach. 'Detective Inspector Baker?' *This was getting pretty heavy...*

Deciding there was no more time for niceties, Sam's eyes narrowed. 'He's the one you need to speak to. And you're going to do it now.'

22

Pulling up on the road housing the Sunset Boulevard, Seb jumped from the car, fully focused on the task ahead.

'You don't think we should have waited until Sam returned?' Neil asked, walking alongside Seb.

'No, I don't!' Seb scowled. 'I'm not suggesting we drag the dickhead off in front of everyone, but I want to make sure he's here, then see where he goes. Only *then* will we take him.'

But he wasn't quite sure how he would stop himself if he set eyes on the man who it appeared had lifted his money.

Reaching the scuffed front door of the Boulevard, Seb glanced at the dilapidated frontage with contempt. What a shithole! Not the worst he'd seen, but a shithole all the same. He glanced over his shoulder, making sure Craig and Neil were behind him. 'You'll be able to spot this bloke?'

Craig nodded. 'Without a doubt! I just hope the fucker's here tonight.'

The tell-tale nerve in Seb's jaw twitched.

So did he...

Walking up to the door, Seb glared at two men waiting to enter the club who immediately moved to let the group through, but as he passed the threshold, an arm blocked his way.

'Membership card?'

Stopping, Seb stared at the squat man who appeared from behind the doorway like the resident troll. He fixed the man with a glare. 'Are you talking to me?'

'Yeah, mate, I'm talking to you. If you ain't got no membership card, then it's a tenner entry. Each...'

A grin cracked Seb's face as the heavy-set man folded his arms over his chest to stand firm. *Like this fat tosser could impede entry...*

Seb could easily cause a scene. It wouldn't take much, but he wouldn't. In a weird way, it was novel not to be recognised.

Craig stepped forward. 'Are you tapped, mate? Don't you know who this...'

'It's not a problem, Craig.' Shoving his hand in his trouser pocket, Seb fished out his wallet and retrieved a crisp fifty-pound note. 'I don't have membership for this superb establishment, my good man, but this will pay entry for all three of us.' He pressed the money into the troll's hand. 'Keep the change.'

Chuckling under his breath at the man's expression, Seb sauntered into the club with Neil and Craig following closely behind. The muppet on the door had provided a sliver of much-needed amusement, but now it was back to business.

He waved away the attendant beckoning to the makeshift cloakroom that consisted of a cupboard with the door removed. If he left his jacket there, even the lining would have gone by the time he retrieved it.

His eyes narrowed as he made his way towards the double doors leading off from the entrance reception.

Now to find this one-armed bandit.

* * *

Dan hadn't known what else to do, apart from go to the Boulevard. Tina hadn't returned from her meeting with Sam, but being as she was due to dance tonight, he figured he'd come and wait for her here. All he could do was act as normal as possible, hope Tina was okay and that she'd be here before long.

He slugged down his glass of rum, waving away a top-up from the grinning waitress, although God knew he wanted to drink plenty.

'Hey, you're back,' Sophie purred, sliding into the empty seat at Dan's table. The line of coke Marina had pushed on her ten minutes prior had done wonders to restore her flagging confidence and override her jangling nerves. Tonight, she'd butter this guy up by whatever means necessary. The sooner she was done with whatever she'd been roped into, the better.

Leaning across the table to ensure her cleavage was on full show in her low-cut top, she traced her finger down Dan's cheek. 'How about treating me to a nice bottle of champagne?' she asked, fluttering her eyelashes.

Dan stared at the same woman who'd approached him last night and, despite his anxiety, found his eyes moving from her pumped-up lips to the breasts spilling from her corset top. It wouldn't hurt to just have a drink, would it? It might take his mind off why Tina wasn't here yet and what she might have said to Sam Reynold.

'Why not?' he said, a smile creeping onto his face. It was nice to know he was deemed a catch for the women – especially bloody nice-looking ones...

Raising his hand, he beckoned a waitress. He could still keep watch for Tina and the minute she arrived, he'd concentrate fully on her.

Sophie glanced up to see Marina watching avidly from the

other side of the room, but quickly looked away, not wanting anything to put her off what she'd resolved to do.

She smiled as the waitress deposited the champagne in the centre of the table. 'So,' Sophie said, her hand moving underneath the table, as planned. 'What brings you back to the Boulevard again, Dan?'

Dan wasn't surprised this woman's hand had found its way onto his rapidly hardening crotch and couldn't help but admit that it was a welcome distraction, but there was one thing that *did* surprise him. 'How do you know my name?'

The seductive smile on Sophie's scarlet mouth froze. *Shit.* She knew she'd fluff it up. Coke booster or not, her nerves fluttered.

She'd be all right. She could do this. She just needed to relax and pretend Marina wasn't watching her like a hawk. 'Erm, you told me yesterday.' *There. That was quick thinking.*

'Did I?' Dan shrugged. He was that hammered last night, he could have said anything. *Wait!* 'What else did I say?'

Sophie frowned. What should she say now? What did Marina say to ask and how to play it? Her heart raced. 'Erm… you mentioned about going back to your place. Where is it? Shall we go there now?' *Was that too pushy? Too suspicious? Oh God, she didn't know.*

'My place?' Dan frowned. There was no way he could take this woman back to Luke Banner's house. Why would he have suggested that? He hadn't even risked taking Tina there. *Shit! Tina…*

Remembering himself, he reluctantly shifted from the hand pleasurably kneading his cock.

Flinching as Dan edged away, Sophie pressed on regardless. 'How about a hotel then…?'

Dan chugged down the glass of champagne, the acrid taste of

the cheap imitation plonk stinging his taste buds. 'I can't. I'm meeting someone...'

On one hand, it was devastating to turn down a woman who was his ideal in the looks department, but on the flip side, he was proud of not falling foul to temptation. He'd never felt about someone the way he did about Tina and he couldn't afford to alienate her now. Neither did he want to. But this was a vast learning curve.

Sophie stared at Dan. *Now what?* 'Don't worry about Tina.' She leant forward further and winked. 'I won't tell her if you don't... Besides, she's got plenty of blokes on the go here and has never mentioned you...'

Dan blinked. *Never mentioned him?* He'd have thought that Tina might have at least said he was special to her. Didn't women talk about things like that?

Fear trundled up his spine. Was that why she hadn't bitten his arm off to leave? Because she didn't think him special? Maybe Tina *was* setting him up again?

Feeling rather sick, Dan floundered. Glancing up, he scanned the large room for any sign of her. Tina wasn't coming. She'd turned him over again. She'd...

What the fuck?

Paralysed with dread, Dan watched the distinctive figures of not one, but two Stokers moving into the room, followed by another man... the man who had locked him in that basement during that Orchid poker tournament...

And it wasn't just any old Stoker – it was the man himself – Seb Stoker.

Fuck, fuck, fuck.

Tina had told Sam Reynold about what he'd done. She must have. They were on to him and they'd come for him. *Now.*

'What are you doing?' Sophie cried as Dan scrambled from the table, his face a weird shade of green. 'I already told you I won't say anything to Tina. Let's just get out of here! Let's go to a hotel. I...'

With one eye on the Stoker clan, who had now reached the bar and were busy scanning the room, Dan bolted from the table, not leaving another second where they, or rather the bloke at the back could spot him.

Clocking Marina frantically gesturing in her direction, Sophie snatched her handbag and dashed after Dan. 'Wait!' she yelled over the loud music.

Dan surged through the tables towards the exit, pushing past everyone in his way. He hoped to fuck that security didn't decide now was an opportune moment to stop him and make him fork out to replace the glasses he'd knocked off tables and from punters' hands.

If the Stokers saw him, he was dead.

Stone cold dead...

Dan's breath burnt in his throat as he forced air into his raisin-sized lungs. The exit was there – the pavement only the other side. *He could do this.*

'Dan! Where are you going? Don't rush off!'

Dan's eyes darted around in panic, only to find the girl from the table blocking the route in front of him. How she'd got through the crowds and overtaken him in those skyscraper heels, he didn't know, but she had. 'Move!' he roared.

He lurched towards Sophie to shove her aside from the only exit from this nightmare, when the door opened from outside and Sophie all but fell backwards through it.

'Fucking hell!' a voice yelled. 'I've heard of nice welcomes, but please don't tell me I've missed your set?'

Sophie looked past the arms which had broken her fall, her eyes widening. 'Mickey! What are you doing here?'

'Come to see you, of course! You're not leaving, are y...?' Stepping through the door, Mickey stopped as he saw the man who had been darting out of the door with Sophie. 'Marlow!' he growled, his eyes narrowing. 'You fucking wanker!'

Sophie gasped. *Mickey was here and he knew Dan?* 'What's going on?'

Dan was fairly certain he might die on the spot. Why was Mickey Devlin in Birmingham? And how did he know this girl?

His eyes darted from Mickey to Sophie and then, remembering why he was in such a rush to leave in the first place, he glanced over his shoulder.

Fuck, fuck and more fucks! Mickey must know he'd lifted the money from under Grant and Marina's nose and come to retrieve it.

Like the Stokers...

Dan's tongue dropped down the back of his throat in horror. *Devlin or the Stokers? Neither was good, but he knew who was the worst and it wasn't Devlin!*

As Mickey lurched forward, Dan did likewise, his forehead meeting with a resounding crack on the bridge of Mickey's nose.

Taken off guard, Mickey staggered, blood spurting, and with Sophie screaming her lungs out, along with heavy footsteps of security approaching from behind, Dan smashed out of the double doors to the pavement outside and took up the fastest run of his life.

23

Lying on the floor, her body a shaking mess, Sophie held her breath and listened once again to Mickey's breathing.

Since dragging her from the Boulevard back to the flat last night, he'd been on at her. It had now been around an hour since he'd finally flaked out and if she didn't make her escape now, she never would.

Gently touching the horrible swelling on her cheekbone, she pulled herself to her feet and risked a glance at Mickey. Lying snoring on the bed, the dried blood on his shirt from his smashed nose and from her own face made him resemble something from a horror film.

With her heart in her mouth, Sophie tiptoed across the bedroom in her bare feet. She'd leave without shoes if she must, but she had to go *now*.

Where, she didn't know. Marina was nowhere to be seen and hadn't returned last night, leaving her to deal with Mickey's fury alone – rage spawning from what Marina had forced her to do in the first place.

Sophie's pulse raced, thudding heavy in her temples. She'd almost reached the door when she heard movement. She turned, but was too late as Mickey jumped off the bed and wrapped his fist tightly in her hair, pulling her head down at a strange angle.

'Still taking the piss?' he roared.

'No, no, I'm not. I wouldn't, Mickey, honest!' Sophie begged. 'What I said last night was the truth.' The fake nails that hadn't already snapped from her fingers scrabbled to relieve the pressure off her scalp from the hair twisting mercilessly at the roots. Clumps of extensions fluttered to the floor, as well as a considerable amount of real hair.

'You lying whore!' Mickey raged. 'You and that bitch daughter of mine are laughing at me, aren't you?' Oh, yeah, it was no coincidence Dan Marlow happened to be in the club where Marina and Sophie now worked. He'd been right all along – Marina was turning him over like a cunt and this slut was in on it too. 'Shagging that prick your next move, was it?'

'No!' Sophie lied, the act of dragging air into her lungs becoming more difficult by the second as her panic and pain increased. None of this was her idea. She hadn't wanted to do any of it.

With horror, she cowered lower as Mickey's free hand curled into a fist. 'Mickey! *Please!*'

'What the fuck is this?'

Mickey released his grip of Sophie, leaving her to crumple to the floor, sobbing hysterically. He swung around and faced Marina. 'Decided to show your face, you lying cunt of a...'

'Don't you fucking dare!' Marina screeched, swiping a bread knife precariously close to her father's face. 'Don't talk like that to me.' Her eyes moved across Sophie's swollen face and the clumps of hair strewn across the patchy carpet. 'You deserve fuck all from me, *father*. You never have. You were supposed to help sort this, so don't give me shit about how *I* do it!'

Mickey lunged towards Marina. 'Just like your mother, you are – a money-grabbing, lying sl...'

'I mean it!' Marina screeched. 'I'll fucking cut you up. If I can kill my own brother and not lose sleep over it, you think I'd give a toss about doing the same to you?'

Sophie pressed her face into the carpet, even though it was agony. Her heart shuddered almost to a stop from pure fright. *Marina had killed her own brother?*

Mickey paused, thinking perhaps Marina really was unhinged enough to follow through with her threats. Scowling, he barged past her towards the door. 'I ain't finished with either of you. Sort your fucking selves out! When I get back, make sure you're behaving reasonably and then you can tell me exactly what you know about where that bastard, Dan, is.'

Slamming the door behind him, his footsteps thundered down the stone stairwell of the flats to the pavement outside.

It was only as they faded to nothing that Sophie sagged with relief. With difficulty, she pushed herself into a sitting position. 'Thank you,' she sobbed. 'I thought he would kill me.'

'You think that was for *your* benefit? Don't be fucking stupid!' Marina sneered. 'My father has pissed me off once too often.'

Grasping Sophie's arm, she dragged the terrified woman to her feet and eyed her scornfully. 'Look at the state of your fucking face. If that cheekbone's broken, it will take ages to heal. And ages, we haven't got.'

Sophie steadied herself against the wall. *Ages for what?* 'What do y...'

'Come on!' Marina snatched Sophie's clothes from the floor. 'Get cleaned up. We'll go round there.'

Sophie shook in earnest. 'I can't go back to the Boulevard. Not now Mickey thinks I...'

'Not to the Boulevard, you thick bitch!' Marina threw the clothes in Sophie's face. 'I'm talking about Dan. Where the fuck do you think I've been all bloody night? Having a party?' Her father might be a useless bastard, but if Sophie pulled herself together, she could still be utilised.

Flouncing over to the 1960s dressing table, Marina stared into the grainy mirror and rearranged her wig. 'After that prick legged it from the club, I followed him. I know where he's staying now – and it's with that sneaky little cow, *Tina*, so you're going round there to finish off what you started!'

Dan was hiding in that dozy tart's house. Wherever he was, the money would also be and this miserable, bleating slapper wasn't spoiling that.

For the fourth time this morning, Tom rolled back the carpet in the corner of the living room. It wasn't difficult, as the scraggy piece of shit was barely attached.

Ignoring the waft of urine that must have soaked into the moth-eaten floor at some point in time, his fingers scraped against the board he'd prised up the minute he'd been given the keys to this dump.

He knew the holdalls were still there, thank fuck, unless they had evaporated in the half an hour since he'd last checked, but he couldn't stop himself from looking again.

His teeth grated. He'd expected Potter and his cronies to dig around and he'd been 100 per cent correct in thinking that because they, or *someone*, had been in here for certain. He'd known that

immediately on returning last night. He'd *sensed* it the minute he'd
walked through the stinking door.

He'd been stupid to fall for the idea that it was safe to go to the
pub at the end of the road. Potter owned it and had assured him
there were no Brummies in there, therefore no one to send word
back of his whereabouts. All the punters were on his payroll, so it
was fine, he'd said.

What Potter had failed to mention was that it was more the
case of wanting him out of the way for an hour or two so that one
of those bastards could rifle through the flat.

How fucking convenient...

On the armchair in the living room, Tom's spare jacket had
moved. Only slightly, but moved all the same. He'd left a plate with
a half-eaten sandwich balanced on the sofa too. It was still there,
but not *exactly* where he'd put it... Plus, the creases in his duvet had
changed, signifying someone had been under the bed...

He had an eye for details such as this.

Tom swallowed, his throat dry. He'd been so in need of a beer
away from this hellhole, he'd fallen for it, hook, line and sinker.

But Potter, or whoever had sneaked around, hadn't found
anything. However, it did prove they either knew or had guessed
he'd got more stash on top of what he'd already forked out for the
deal. It also showed that because they'd failed to find it, they would
continue looking until they *did*.

Now, he could barely set foot out of here until Dan arrived.
Someone must remain here at all times to guard the money.

Slamming the floorboard back in place, Tom got off his aching
knees and kicked the carpet back over the wood, holding his
breath as he did so.

Where was Dan, anyway? He'd made it clear the man was to be
in Wolverhampton by today at the latest. There were no messages
left at the Primo Autoshop when he'd checked yesterday after-

noon, so the prat had better be on his bloody way and have the damned passports with him as well.

Tom paced up and down the small room, realising that with or without Dan, he'd have to venture out occasionally – even if it was only for very short bursts. He needed to keep an eye on Potter. There was no way this deal could go ahead without him.

No fucking way.

24

'I'm telling you now, he wasn't there!' Sam insisted, her stress mounting. 'We've been through this half the night, Seb. There's no point in keeping calling him.'

Seb slammed the phone down and put his head in his hands. 'Fucking Baker, the cunt! How dare he go off radar just when he's needed.' His head whipped up. 'I'll kill him, I will. I swear! I...'

'Just calm down!' Sam urged, her head banging. Hardly an hour's sleep they'd had, both from Seb's ranting and from her own worry. It was typical that after finally talking Tina into going to the police station – or rather, frogmarching the woman there, then waiting on tenterhooks for nearly an hour – they'd discovered Baker wasn't there.

Admittedly, she'd initially thought Tina was lying. Sam knew the girl was reluctant to talk to the police, but her own subsequent investigation proved what had been said was true. Baker's daughter was unwell and word had it that he wouldn't be reachable for twenty-four hours. Even that wasn't certain.

Terrible timing, but there was nothing they could do.

'I can't quite believe you let that girl go!' Seb continued.

Sam moved to the edge of the bed where Seb sat and laid her hand on his shoulder. 'Tina's promised to go back tonight.'

'And you believed her? Left her alone to disappear on you? Christ, Sam! Have you learnt nothing?'

'I've learnt plenty, thank you! Enough to know that women do not respond well to being held hostage!' Sam snapped. 'Tina said she'd go, so I have no reason to think otherwise.'

Seb drew in a deep breath, knowing he was out of line. 'I'm sorry, Princess. It's just what with not seeing that one-armed bloke last night, this on top is the last straw.' It hadn't helped they couldn't hang around at the club as long as they'd planned either. After getting wind of a scuffle in the Boulevard reception, he couldn't risk staying anywhere the Old Bill could turn up.

Softening, Sam smiled. 'It will be all right, you'll see. Tina will return and if Baker's still not there, she'll try again tomorrow. Think about it – after what Bedworth did to her mother, she's got as much reason as any of us for wanting him taken in.'

'*I'll* be the one taking him, not the police,' Seb growled. As soon as Tina had proved Bedworth to be the murderer and *his* name was off the suspects list, the police wouldn't get the chance to pull the man in. He'd be doing that, no one else. *And that was a promise.*

'As for this Dan, just because he wasn't there last night doesn't mean he won't be another night,' Sam continued. 'Neither is it set in stone that he's the one you're after. Craig could have been wrong.'

She wouldn't say so, but Sam was secretly glad the man wasn't around last night. Him not muddying the equation meant more time to get Seb removed from the suspect list and pull off the heist without any distractions.

Seb nodded reluctantly. 'Yeah, I know you're right.' He pulled Sam onto his lap. 'Now, help me take my mind off things for a while, would you?'

* * *

'What are you doing?' Tina cried, watching Dan stare vacantly at the wall, muttering to himself. 'Stop messing about! Go and sober up!'

Weren't things difficult enough? She didn't know what had gone on last night; according to Ava, some nutter had kicked off at the Boulevard and headbutted a geezer in reception. Shane had already been on her case for turning up late and then Ava and Sophie's caginess had made it even worse. The whole night had been dreadful and she hadn't been able to wait to get home.

After leaving Dan in such a weird state, she'd hoped he might have been at the Boulevard, but Ava and Sophie had both insisted he hadn't come in. Then she'd finally got home, only to find him paralytic again.

As much as it pained her, Tina was now really worried that she'd got Dan wrong. She hoped not, but she had no idea what was eating him. If she took him up on his offer and left with him, she could be jumping out of the frying pan into the fire.

Either way, leaving was something she couldn't even *consider* until she'd done what Sam Reynold wanted. But she couldn't believe she'd have to go back to the police station. Still, she'd promised and so, therefore, she must.

Sighing loudly, she focused back on Dan. 'Why are you being like this?' she cried. 'You're acting like a basket case!'

'Just tell me what went on last night.' Dan muttered his first coherent words since yesterday. His bloodshot eyes looked into Tina's. 'I have to know what you said to Sam Reynold. What did you say about Tom? About *me*...'

Tina sighed even louder. 'Oh for God's sake. Not this again! I told you! Bedworth deserves everything coming to him.'

'Tina, *please!*' Dan begged, his eyes wide. 'If you've said anything to Sam about Tom, then I'm dead meat.'

Tina laughed, then stopped, realising Dan wasn't joking. 'What do you mean?'

Dan sighed. *No putting it off any longer.* 'I lied. Tom hasn't gone – he's still around and I'm trying to get away from him. The Reynolds and Stokers are after him, which means they'll be after *me* too. If you've told Sam anything, you'll get me killed!'

'W-what?' Tina slumped against the door, her mind spinning. 'But this isn't about the robbery. This is about my mother. Sam wants me to tell the police that it was Tom who killed my mother and also tell them about the woman kept in the attic. That's all it's about, so don't worry. I went to the police station last night, like she wanted, but the detective Sam wanted me to speak to wasn't there, so I'm going back today.'

She stared down at her hands. 'To be fair, I should have done this long before now. I should have gone straight to them the night I found out my mother was dead, but... but I was too scared. Scared of Tom... Of everything... And I wanted to give that woman time to escape.'

'So the prisoner in the attic got out?' Dan blurted, sure Tom was under the impression that woman had died. 'Where is this woman now? Has she spoken to the police?'

Tina shook her head. 'No, that's why Sam needs *me* to do it. That prisoner was Sam's mother!' A smile cracked her face. 'Bedworth is in deep shit!'

Dan almost choked. Tom had drugged up and kept Sam Reynold's *mother* prisoner in the Aurora's attic? Oh God, this was *really* bad. 'You don't understand! The whole lot will come out and there's more. A lot more!' He grasped Tina's hands. 'Tom was the hit and run driver who killed that girl! He did it whilst I set fire to the Royal Peacock.'

'*What*?' Tina gasped. '*You* set fire to the Peacock and ran over Deb Banner?'

Dan shook his head so hard he thought it might fall off. 'No, well, yes. I set fire to the Peacock – Tom made me, but I swear I had nothing to do with running the girl over! I only pieced it together myself the other day.'

Once he'd started, he couldn't stop. The words spewed from his mouth like verbal dysentery. 'Me and Tom stayed at Deb's dad's house for a bit until Sam Reynold turned up to speak to him. I'm sure she knows everything!' Sweat poured freely down his face. 'Then Tom killed Luke Banner in front of me! God, it was horrible. Look, I've got half the money from the robbery here! Tom's got the rest. He's expecting me to go to Wolverhampton to join him, but I can't. I don't want anything to do with him! He's a fucking nut job, but when I don't show up, he'll kill me. And so will the Stokers. They even turned up at the Boulevard last night.'

Dan spoke so fast, he dribbled everywhere. 'I came to wait for you, but when they showed up, I had to leg it.'

Tina couldn't comprehend this. *Ava and Sophie said Dan wasn't there.* 'What happened to your head?'

Dan's fingers gingerly trailed over the bruise on his forehead, courtesy of Mickey's nose. 'That's something else. My ex's father turned up too. I, erm, pinched the idea of robbing the safes from Marina and her brother. They were planning on splitting the spoils with him...'

Tina slumped against the door. 'Jesus Christ!'

'So, don't you see?' Dan continued. 'You *can't* tell Sam a thing! Tom must think you've left town, but when he finds out that you're behind this, which he *will*, he'll kill you before he gets killed. We'll all be fucking dead!'

Tina felt sick. She'd been over the moon Sam had wanted to

talk to her. Fancy that – someone like Sam Reynold needing help from the likes of *her*. Now she wished the polar opposite.

Why had Dan lied about Bedworth? Oh, sure, Tom may assume that she'd left town, but once he found out she hadn't...

Nausea spread through Tina's body, the taste of bile strong. So, she had the choice of giving Dan up or not getting justice for her mother? That, and if she didn't help Sam Reynold and Seb Stoker, then *she'd* be on their hit list too. And if *they* didn't kill her, Tom Bedworth would. Or this Mickey person would kill Dan...

'Please!' Dan begged once more. 'Just think about it. We could go now! Just me and you. We could get away from everyone.' He searched Tina's face as he reached out to touch her cheek. 'I want to be with you.'

Tina remained frozen. She wanted to be with Dan too, but how could she leave like this? She couldn't let her mother's memory down, leave Seb Stoker to rot in jail for something he hadn't done and abandon her sister. Neither could she let Tom Bedworth get away with everything he'd done.

But she didn't want to die or spend the rest of her life looking over her shoulder.

Did she?

25

Seb was in a better mood than he'd been first thing this morning. Despite the cock-up with Baker and making an early exit from that dump of a strip club on Edgbaston Street, spending time buried inside Sam always grounded him. It served to remind him that whatever other shit went on in his life, he had her. And for that, he couldn't be more thankful.

Instead of going straight into the Orchid, Seb continued a couple of hundred yards further down to the Peacock. The cordon surrounding it blocked most of the view, shielding his eyes from yet again witnessing the ravaged shell of his destroyed building.

The clanging of tools and machinery did, however, show that behind the green makeshift cover and fencing, the rebuilding work was well underway.

Folding his arms, he gazed up at the place which had once been his sparkling and successful casino, as well as the nerve centre for his firm, and wondered exactly how long it would be before he was back behind his desk in there. He also wondered how different it would look once everything had been completed.

Although he had specified the rebuild should be as close as

possible to its original look, it wouldn't be *exactly* the same. That pained him, but at least the Peacock would be back and so would he – along with his staff, most of whom he was paying to sit on their arses at home. Still, it had to be done.

His eyes narrowed. As had catching up with the fucker behind this as well as laying his hands on the funds in order to enable the rebuild to progress.

'Things are coming on nicely, Mr Stoker.'

Seb turned to find the foreman and the project manager standing alongside him. 'Do you have a date as to when it will be ready?'

The two men exchanged glances. 'Not as yet, Mr Stoker. We need to enter phase two of the rebuild. Once that's underway, we'll be in a better position to give you a time frame. It's just...'

Seb let the foreman's words trail off, the man's awkwardness clear. Yes, he knew phase two could not commence in earnest until the next payment was made. And that couldn't happen until he'd pulled the heist off. 'Just let me know when you expect to complete, fellas. Okay?' he said flippantly, wanting to see if either of them possessed the nerve to ask outright for the money rather than take it as read that it would be there when needed.

And it *had* to be there. That, he had to make sure of.

'Erm, would you like to come and see the progress so far, Mr Stoker?' the foreman asked nervously.

'Nope. I don't want to see anything until it's finished.' Turning away, Seb strode purposely towards the Orchid, not wishing to spend a further moment outside the sad skeleton of his beloved club.

He loped up the stairs, making quick work of crossing the reception, and disappeared into the staff corridor before anyone could delay him.

Striding into Sam's office, he closed the door behind him and slung his jacket over the back of a chair. 'I want someone sent to scout the Rosses again,' he said, looking at Andrew. 'I need them watched over the next few days. We want to ensure we're one step ahead in getting to the docks the day of the switch. We'll arrange for them to be held up if they show any sign of movement. I suggest we send one of the Orchid boys, rather than one of ours. Potter Ross won't know who to look for from the Reynold firm, so it's better that way.'

'Sounds like a plan,' Andrew nodded. 'I'll speak to Kev.'

When Andrew left the office, Seb retrieved his notebook from the bottom drawer of Sam's desk and looked at the sums to remind himself again exactly how much he needed to get phase two of the rebuild up and running.

Seb stared at the horrendous figure emblazoned on the lined paper.

£4.2 million.

That would be easy enough to pull from what was in that container, but deals would have to be set up for a good amount of this new coke to be shifted straight away. And that needed to be put in place. *Now.*

Where was Neil? He could get that in motion.

As Seb reached for the phone, it rang just as he got to it. He snatched up the receiver, hearing the voice of the Orchid's receptionist. He frowned. 'What? What, *here*? Now? I...'

He didn't get chance to hear anything further as the office door burst open and several police officers burst into the room.

He jumped to his feet. 'What the f...'

'Mr Stoker?' An officer stepped forward. 'We'd like you to accompany us to the station.'

'What the fuck for? I...'

'You can refuse, but I wouldn't advise it, otherwise we will have no option but to arrest you.'

Travelling back to the Orchid from the Sirendale Clinic, Sam was pleased that Linda looked even better than she had the other day. She was definitely improving. But although she'd have rather not spoken about it, all Linda wanted to talk about during the visit was whether Tina had been located.

Sam had been purposefully vague in what she'd recounted. For one, she was avoiding causing additional stress and could tell by the worry on her mother's face that not being the one to speak up still plagued her, but also because everything was still up in the air.

Seb's attitude wasn't helping. She'd asked him if he wanted to accompany her to visit Linda, but the answer had been a resounding 'no'. She knew her mother wasn't at the top of his Christmas card list at present, but perhaps if Tina got him off the hook with the police, then he'd feel less spiky and his general, and perhaps unfair, resentment towards Linda for the lack of help would mellow.

But things weren't looking promising. She'd attempted to find out if DI Baker was back at the station, but the last time she'd got through to someone, there was still no update on his expected return. She had to be careful who she spoke to for that information, not wanting anyone connecting Tina's wish to speak with Baker to *her*.

The other nagging issue was that regardless of what Tina had promised, Sam had to make sure the woman didn't backtrack. Sam hadn't outwardly shown it in front of Seb, but his reticence to put trust in the girl preyed on her mind. Whether she liked it or not, she was starting to worry that maybe she'd been blasé in assuming the girl would adhere to their agreement. So much so that paying an impromptu visit to Tina's house was the only way forward to ensure the girl hadn't developed cold feet.

It hadn't been difficult to get Tina's address from the disgusting creature who owned the Boulevard. The combined forces of the Reynold and Stoker names alone exerted adequate threat. And once she'd checked in with Kevin and seen if Seb was around, she'd go straight there.

Seb was so stressed about all of this. She couldn't say she blamed him, but she'd ensure this side of things was dealt with so he could plough his energy into the coming heist.

'Hi, Elaine,' Sam smiled as she walked through the Orchid's reception.

'Oh, Ms Reynold! I'm so glad you're back! Mr Stoker has been arrested and...'

'*What*?' Sam yelled. 'Arrested? When? What happened? Where's Andrew and Neil and...'

Elaine was visibly shaken. 'I – I think he was arrested, but can't be sure. He left here with several officers. I...'

'Sam!' Kev appeared from the staff corridor into the reception, beckoning her to follow.

'What's going on?' Sam gasped once they were in the privacy of the corridor.

'I haven't got a bloody clue. All I know is that I was with Andrew, sending Stu out to watch the Rosses, and then the next thing I knew, Elaine rushed in, panicking.'

'So has Seb been arrested? Charged?' Sam couldn't believe this. She'd tried so hard to get this sorted in time.

'I don't know. Elaine said he wasn't handcuffed, but that means shag all. Andrew called the brief and then him and Neil followed to the station.'

Looking at the ceiling in despair, Sam willed her racing heart to slow.

She could go to the police station too, but what would that achieve? If Andrew and Neil were there and the brief was on the way, then she'd be better off fetching Tina. If Tina made a statement now, there might be time to stop this. As long as it happened before Seb was formally arrested or charged, then... *That's if he hadn't been already...*

'Where are you going?' Kev asked as Sam turned on her heels. 'I don't think th...'

'I'm off to sort something out that I hope will fix this,' Sam said as she slammed through the doors back into the reception.

26

Seb was steaming. He glared at the two detectives who led him into a room containing a wall of one-way glass. 'This cannot proceed without me speaking to my brief. I know my rights.'

The young detective smirked. 'The way you operate, Mr Stoker, I've no doubt you're well acquainted with your rights, but when the request comes from the top, I think you'll find we can do what we like!'

It was gratifying being sarcastic to Birmingham's top crim without there being repercussions. This guy was shagged on every level and the whole station knew it. He didn't have a leg to stand on and if it was noted that *he'd* helped collar Sebastian Stoker, the following promotions would be endless.

'I demand to speak to my brief and to Baker,' Seb growled, his rage building to boiling point. 'I came here of my own volition. I didn't have to. I haven't been arrested or charged. Neither was it mentioned that I would be subjected to a fucking identity parade, so you can piss off!'

'In the interim, it would be easy to arrest you for impeding police investigations and using abusive language,' the other detective grinned as Seb made to push past to get to the door. 'It's more sensible to "help out" by your own choice, Mr Stoker. Let's not forget that Baker isn't here to fight your corner, like he usually is…'

Seb's jaw tightened. That was *exactly* why this identity shit was happening. Baker would have put a stop to it if he were here. *Oh, they'd timed this nicely, hadn't they?*

His mind raged with inner turmoil. Whichever top brass had called this had their sights set on taking him down whichever way they could. *They could hold him for days… What about the heist?*

Who the fuck was behind that one-way glass? Anyone? Or another copper faking paperwork to confirm a positive ID?

He clenched his fists, wanting to knock these streak of piss coppers out cold. He could do it without even breaking a sweat, but that wouldn't look good. The press would have a field day reporting yet another 'slip' of the Stoker firm's ability to uphold what was left of their image – the reputation he needed to maintain for when he was back up and running.

Plus, if he belted this pair, then he would *definitely* be arrested and the heist would have to be abandoned. If he played this bunch of pricks at their game, there was a chance he would walk. Behind the scenes, his brief must be putting things in motion right this very minute. Even coppers couldn't argue with certain facts of the law. How could he be ID'd as the murderer when he wasn't even there?

Impossible.

Smiling thinly, Seb shoved his hands in his trouser pockets to keep them from wrapping themselves around these jokers' throats. 'Have it your own way, gentlemen,' he said, moving to stand on the marked position in front of the one-way glass partition. 'I hope you don't mind being disappointed.'

* * *

Dan had sat for what seemed like an age, literally doing nothing but staring at the wall. Tina's room had fast morphed into another prison. He'd been searching for a feasible way to justify her decision, but had exhausted everything, meaning there was no other route left to take.

Dan picked at the zip of his jacket. The only time in his life that he'd felt an affinity towards a woman to the extent that he *cared* what happened and she'd shit on him. Whether he liked it or not, now the Stokers were on his case and Tina was on her way to the cop shop, he had to go to Wolverhampton and lie low with Tom Bedworth.

It would only be a matter of time before Mickey Devlin caught up with him too, so the only way out now was to leave the country with Tom.

That he hadn't sourced any passports was by the by. He'd just have to try his luck in Wolverhampton on that one.

Having made this decision, Dan jumped to his feet, refusing to look at Tina's clothes and makeup scattered around the room. Her actions making it blatant he didn't signify, stinging at a level he hadn't realised existed.

Walking over to the small wardrobe in the corner of the room, Dan yanked open the door and chucked the pile of clothes and shoes out of the way that he'd used to bury the holdalls underneath. It hadn't been the best place to hide anything in the event someone came looking, but he wasn't exactly overrun with options.

There were even fewer now.

Shoving a few clothes in the one holdall he'd already noticed to be half-empty, Dan froze at the distinctive ring of the doorbell.

Shit! Was that the cops?

The minute Tina had left to stab him in the back, he should have legged it.

Bollocks. Shit. Fuck.

Were Tina's housemates in? Those two other women she shared this place with could let the police in. They might be already halfway up the stairs by now...

Dashing to the window, Dan flattened himself against the wall, then crept along the window frame, enabling one eye to peer down from the front-facing bedroom onto the road below.

No cop cars. It wasn't the police...

Relief cascaded, only to stiffen as the doorbell sounded again.

There was no movement from downstairs, so it looked like the house was empty. The minute whoever was at the door had gone, he'd slip down and call a taxi.

Pushing his forehead against the windowpane, he willed the one eye that could see down to the garden below to spot something – *anything.*

Thinking it must be safe, being as the doorbell had not rung a further time, Dan was just about to slope away from the window when a figure moved down the front path and looked up at the house.

Ducking sideways and cracking the side of his head on the corner shelf as he did so, Dan winced, but the sharp pain was nowhere near enough to deflect from who he'd seen standing in the front garden.

Samantha Reynold.

Tina had told Sam Reynold where he was?

He was dead. Totally and utterly flattened hedgehog fucking dead!

This couldn't be happening. Even if Sam left, thinking him not here, she'd undoubtedly be back with the Stokers in tow.

Sweat patches formed under Dan's armpits, the shirt clinging to his skin. Despite the cold fear racing through his body, his brain burnt at 100°C.

He had to get out of here and hope to hell no one was watching.

* * *

'I said get back! She mustn't see us,' Marina spat, shoving Sophie back into the mud beneath the hedge opposite the row of small houses. The last person she'd expected to see at Tina's place was Samantha-fucking-Reynold.

Her teeth gnashed. She wasn't having this. She just wasn't having it. That woman wasn't getting the better of her again.

'Why is sh...'

'Shh,' Marina hissed, glancing at the house. It was then that she spotted it. The very slight, almost indistinct movement at the bedroom window.

That fucker was in there.

Tina might not be in, but *Dan* was. And that was all she needed to know. 'Do not move!'

The thumping of Marina's heart almost drowned out her voice. Had Sam seen what *she'd* seen? Had she seen Dan?

She watched with bated breath as Sam stared up at the house, a frown on the face harbouring eyes so similar to her own.

Marina's face cracked into a wide grin as Sam walked down the path. Her shitty sister hadn't got one over on her after all. She was too fucking blind to see that waste of space in the window.

But Marina had. Oh, yes, *she* had.

Why Sam was here, Marina didn't know, but what she *did* know, was that the stupid cow had screwed up. 'You might have escaped my bullet, you bitch, but you won't win this one,' she muttered, the age-old urge to rid the world of Samantha Reynold resurfacing with shocking clarity.

But what did she want more? The money or Samantha Reynold?

Both. She wanted *both*. And there was no reason why she couldn't achieve that.

'What did you say?' Sophie gibbered. 'Did you just say, "bullet"?' Panic crawled further up her limbs. Soon it would be in her brain and then she wouldn't be able to control the need to throw herself out of the safety of this bush and run to the nearest person, demanding they get her away from this nutter. 'W-who is that woman?'

Her eyes remained fixed on the woman now walking along the pavement, closer to where they hid. *She looked just like that woman in the papers...*

'It's my sister! I can't let her see us!' Marina whispered.

Sophie's eyes widened. It *was* the woman from the papers, Sam Reynold. 'Sam Reynold is your sister?' she choked, her mind spinning with weird blotchy colours.

'*Half*-sister. I share nothing with her, short of a crackhead mother,' Marina said sharply and a bit too loudly.

As Sam paused to look around, Marina clenched her jaw so tightly it clicked. See what happened when she got distracted? Careless and stupid. She wouldn't let Samantha distract her any more.

Her previous decision to push Dan's removal further down the list had been a bad mistake and not one to be repeated. This time, Dan would be number one. Everybody else could be sorted afterwards.

Marina's annoyance with herself faded when Sam continued down the road to slip into a waiting car.

Probably a chauffeur, the fucking posh bitch, she thought, shaking her head before the all-encompassing hatred took hold once again.

Make no mistake, Dan, it's your turn now.

As the car pulled away, Marina turned to Sophie, wanting to slap the panic from her stupid mug. 'Right! Now *we're* going in. But we won't bother knocking.'

27

Tina loitered outside the police station, her mind in chaos. Several times she'd made it up the steps, only to retrace them to lean against the wall of the building out of sight of the entrance doors.

The same selection of things revolved around her brain in a never-ending circle. But no matter how many times each burning question came to the forefront and she convinced herself it was the correct way to go, it was neutralised by the next question in the turning carousel.

There was no right or wrong way to do this. Righting one wrong destroyed another or unearthed another problem.

But who was she making these decisions for? Herself? To protect her own back and stop the repercussions if she didn't do Sam's bidding? Was she using what happened to her mother to justify speaking to the police, or was her sense of loyalty true?

She didn't know.

And what about the rest of it?

Tina fumbled in her bag for a cigarette. She didn't smoke often, saving it for when she felt it might impress a punter, but right now she really needed one. Or was she looking for something for her hands to do, rather than press the buzzer on the police reception desk?

What about Dan? The man was terrified beyond all wits of what might befall him if she spoke to the police about Bedworth and that it would implicate not just him, but both him *and* her.

Tina fully believed Tom would make sure of both of their deaths long before the police picked him up. But one thing that she had no wavering on was she wanted Bedworth to suffer. She wanted him to die slowly and painfully for everything he'd done.

And if she could help achieve that...

But the police?

Dan would hate her...

But he'd lied to her. He hadn't been truthful about Tom still being on the scene, so what did that say about anything they could possibly have together? Could they even make a go of things after this?

But then, *she* hadn't been honest either...

Setting Dan up in the first place pushed back into her mind. She was hardly blameless. The base realisation remained the same. Had she not done what she'd done, Dan wouldn't be involved with Tom.

Yet, if she did what Dan wanted and they took the money and disappeared, they could start a new life together away from all this.

Tina leant against the wall, grateful for the cool bricks against her back. Looking up at the sky, she inhaled slowly to calm her speeding mind.

She'd seen the money. Dan had insisted on showing her the contents of those holdalls, containing more than enough to last them wherever they went.

Choosing that option seemed like a no-brainer, but it was just...

It was just not the right thing to do.

For once, Tina felt overwhelmed to do the right thing. If her and Dan were meant to be and everything was genuinely put right, then there could be no come-back on either of them. It was the law of karma.

Finally making her mind up, Tina ground her cigarette out and walked purposefully up the steps and through the door of the police station. She didn't even let the steely-faced desk sergeant looking her up and down put her off. Nothing would deter her now. She owed it to her mother.

To *herself*.

She cleared her throat, the words still unwilling to move from her voice box into the world, but she pushed through the barrier regardless. 'I'd like to report a crime against my mother and another woman that happened at the Aurora.'

The desk sergeant blinked, his eyes scanning the list of internal memos that all staff were issued with about open cases. He frowned. 'Did you say, *the Aurora*?'

Tina nodded. 'Yes. The Aurora on the Hagley Road. The man you want in connection with your investigation is Thomas Bedworth.'

'Bear with me one moment, Miss,' the desk sergeant said, turning to pick up the phone.

Tina almost jumped out of her skin at the sudden hand on her shoulder. Spinning around, she came face to face with Sam Reynold.

'I'm so glad you're here,' Sam said, hiding the relief coursing through her veins. Hearing that Seb been taken for an ID parade without any form of representation, and finding Tina's house empty, the girl had arrived here just when Sam had started to believe it was too late for anything.

She turned to the desk sergeant as he replaced the handset. 'Please inform Mr Stoker's solicitor, who I know is inside this building, that he is also going to act for and bear witness to this woman's statement.'

Now the police would listen. She would make sure of it.

* * *

Seb smirked as he passed the detectives, their sullen expressions radiating defeat. 'Glad to be of assistance, gentlemen,' he said, his green eyes twinkling. 'I trust this is the end of the matter?'

Nodding morosely, the detectives slammed the door, eager to rid themselves of the gloating image of Sebastian Stoker.

'Seb!' Sam cried, jumping from the chair the moment she heard his voice.

Following his brother, Andrew nodded to the brief. 'Thanks, mate. Send your bill to us, care of the Orchid for the time being, please.'

Sam smiled at the solicitor and waited until he left before following the Stokers out of the police station. 'Well? Have all the allegations over this business at the Aurora been dropped? Everything?'

Seb pulled Sam against him and pressed his lips against her throat, the relief of not having lies hanging over his head acting like an injection of adrenaline. 'The only person on the wanted list now is our friend, Bedworth.'

'Thank God for that!' Sam breathed.

'Right, let's go. We've got things to plan.' Seb winked at his brothers. They needed to fine tune the details for Thursday, as well as find out whether Stu had gathered intel on movement from the Rosses' side.

'Go on ahead.' Sam squeezed Seb's hand. 'I'll wait for Tina. She's been put in a difficult position by doing this, so I want to make sure she's okay.'

Seb nodded. 'Pass on my thanks too. I would hang around myself, but we really do need to get back and see if Stu's seen any movement from Wolverhampton. If he has, we need to add other options into the mix.'

Sam watched Seb and his brothers walk down the road back to the car whilst she remained. Hopefully Tina wouldn't be too much longer. They'd been stuck in the cop shop most of the day. It was already dark and she was exhausted, but she owed the girl the decency of a show of solidarity.

Suddenly spotting Tina through the police station door, Sam waited until Tina reached the pavement before approaching. 'I wanted to thank you for doing wh...' Stopping, she studied Tina's tear-stained face. 'Are you all right?'

Tina dragged her hand under her nose, smearing a trail of snot across her face. 'Yes,' she lied. In reality, she felt anything but. Despite wanting to behave calm and collected, she burst into tears.

Clutching Tina's arm, Sam steered her along the pavement. 'You haven't been charged with anything, have you? Implicated for withholding information?'

Tina shook her head. 'No. I thought they were going to, but then they said what with my mother and all that, they thought I'd been through enough... It's just... it all feels so wrong.'

That was an understatement. She felt dreadful on every level. Seb Stoker might have been absolved from the implications surrounding her mother's murder – and that was only fair, but Tina couldn't dislodge the deep-seated fear that despite not saying anything to implicate Dan, the police would dig further into the Aurora – including its customers...

It had also been uncomfortable admitting she'd worked at the place. Now they all knew what she'd done for her money...

Sam placed her arm around Tina's shoulders and flagged down a taxi. She could guess what the girl was thinking. 'They'll only be looking at Bedworth now, not anything *you* might have done. They'll have him on everything. By the way, did you remember to mention about the girl who got run over?'

'Only that Tom had a problem with Deb and that he'd gone looking for her the night she was killed.' Tina hoped that wouldn't implicate Dan with anything linked to that incident either.

As the taxi pulled up against the kerb, Tina shuffled into the back, grateful to take the weight off her shaking legs. She hoped Sam Reynold didn't grill her about the robbery next because that she *did* know about. Something else she felt dreadful about. 'You don't need to come back with me,' she said, her voice small.

Sam clambered into the car. 'Nonsense. I want to make sure you get home okay.'

It didn't take long to reach the house, but Tina's mind was so scrambled, time had no meaning. Almost before she realised it, they'd pulled up outside, where Sam urged her from the car.

Sam pressed money into the driver's hand. 'Please wait here. I'll just see my friend in and then I'll be back.'

Tina smiled at Sam as they neared her front door. 'Thanks. I'll be fine now. My boyfriend should still be here.' *At least she hoped so, anyway.*

Sam handed Tina a business card. 'Anything you need, call.'

She waited until Tina had opened the front door before walking back to the taxi, feeling that today was as successful as it possibly could have been. Now, full concentration could be given to the heist, getting the Peacock back up and running and bringing Bedworth to justice before the police did.

All of these things were now fully achievable.

Sam was about to open the car door when a blood-curdling scream emanating from Tina's house stopped her in her tracks.

* * *

'Yes, as soon as possible. Just the two of them – you know who. It's a delicate clean-up.' Sam replaced the receiver and moved into the lounge where Tina sat on the sofa, her face deathly pale. She looked around for a bottle of spirits, but could see none. 'When will your housemates be back?'

Receiving no response, Sam frowned. 'Tina? Your housemates? Where are they?'

'Oh, they won't be back until morning.' Tina's voice was hollow – almost robotic. 'One's a nurse at the QE and the other is a carer on nights at the moment.'

Sam perched next to Tina. *That was one thing, then.* The body of Tina's boyfriend would prove difficult to hide if other people came into the house before she'd had a chance to get rid of it.

She'd known something bad had happened the minute she'd heard the scream. Using who she was, as well as an extra fifty quid, had reminded the taxi driver that he had heard nothing. But now she had to get rid of this mess.

Daz and Craig would be here shortly. With any luck, within fifteen minutes. Her wording on the phone to Kevin was obvious to all in the business that it was urgent and that a very *specific* clean-up was required.

'Have you any idea who did this?' Sam asked gently, her own suspicions rising.

She hoped more than anything this was nothing to do with what she had pushed Tina into, but the question pressed against her conscience regardless. *Was this Bedworth?* Had he discovered Tina had spoken to the police? For her? For Seb?

Or had Seb done this...?

Her head pounded. No, he couldn't have. Seb didn't have Tina's address, neither would he have had time since leaving the police station.

Which meant it *had* to be Bedworth.

Tina remained motionless, the image of Dan's body the first thing she'd seen when she'd switched on the hallway light. It would be forever ingrained in her mind. The dead body of her mother was bad enough, but she hadn't been butchered...

Dan had...

Vomit raced up Tina's throat and her hand flew to her mouth.

There was so much blood...

Sam might have managed to drag her away within seconds of entering the house, quickly covering Dan's body with a throw from the sofa, but Tina could still see the lump underneath the furry blanket out of the corner of her eye.

And she knew what was underneath the blanket...

There had been so many stab wounds – so many they all merged into one. Or was it just blood? She didn't know, but Dan's glassy eyes locked towards the ceiling, his mouth gaping – the fear preserved on his face – would haunt her eternally.

This was her fault. *Hers.* If she hadn't gone to the police... If she...

Unable to control herself, Tina started shaking – an all-over trembling that ricocheted through her body.

'Tina. *Tina!*' Sam urged. 'Listen to me. Just calm down. You didn't answer. Do you know who could have done this?'

A sob burst from Tina's throat. 'That man! Him!' she gibbered, her eyes wide. 'But it can't be. He's not here... Dan should have been in Wolverhampton... Those were the instructions.' She grasped Sam's hand tightly. 'He didn't want to go. He was planning not to. He wanted to get away – that was the plan... to leave... He wanted me to go with him. Now it's too late... Oh God...'

It would be *her* next, just like Dan had warned. Now he was dead and she'd never know whether they would have had a future together.

'Hey, it's okay,' Sam soothed, pulling Tina against her to stroke her hair. The girl was talking utter nonsense. She was clearly over-wrought and distressed. 'Some of my men are on their way. They will clear everything up and put it right, you'll see.'

She didn't need Tina's confirmation of who she believed to be behind this. It was more important to make sure the girl didn't breathe a word about this to anyone, whilst Sam put everything right.

28

Seb's brow remained knitted in the deepest frown, the same way it had been since Sam returned last night. Now the one-armed Dan person had been extinguished by someone other than *him*, getting the lowdown as to where his fucking money was and who the man had been working with or for, was gone.

Seb's skin bristled. He'd been counting on getting his hands on the twat and now some fucker had pipped him to the post by removing the cunt from the planet.

He hadn't thought things could get any worse, but it looked like he'd got that wrong as well.

All night, he'd desperately tried to justify Sam's unexpected decision, but he still didn't understand it. *Couldn't* understand it. It bordered on treachery, and he resented feeling even the hint of that negative emotion about the woman he loved.

'I know none of you like it, but what else could I do?' Sam cried, looking around the faces in her office. 'Tina supplied information to get you off the hook, Seb. None of us expected her to find *that* on her return home, did we?'

'But giving the girlfriend of the bastard who robbed us a room here, as well as a job?' Andrew barked, his tone less than friendly. He glanced up at the ceiling, where two floors above, several small flats were used for people to stay. 'It's insane and it's also not on.'

'We don't know for certain whether Tina knew anything!' Sam countered. 'From all reports, she only hooked up with that man the other day.'

'Yeah, but she knew him from the Aurora, we know that much, so it stands to reason she *had* to be aware of the robbery,' Seb grumbled. 'I'm not happy, Sam.'

Sam folded her arms. 'After seeing the guy she was with lying dead in her hallway, convinced she'd be next, I wasn't leaving the girl alone, the state she was in. Tina did us a huge favour and I can't help but think her boyfriend's death was in retribution for that.' Acknowledging that Tina speaking to the police might have caused this, was uncomfortable.

But it was true.

Andrew raised an eyebrow. 'You think it was Bedworth?'

'I don't know.' Sam bit down on her lip. 'I don't see how he could have got wind of what she'd done so quickly, but neither can I think of another alternative.' And no, she didn't like that the body of the man she'd asked Craig and Daz to remove last night had been immediately recognised to be the very same one-handed bloke pulled up in her own club for card sharking not long ago either.

Seb was right that it must be the man who Simon Parker released the codes of the safe to, but what she *really* didn't want to admit to Seb or anyone was worse...

Sam *knew* Tina was aware of the robbery because the girl had blurted it out as she'd been shepherded upstairs during the clean-up operation. She'd sobbed – beside herself with guilt for not saying anything beforehand and apologising for being dishonest to someone who had been so kind.

Sam had only wondered, if *she* had been in Tina's shoes, whether she would have behaved any differently? Would she drop Seb in the shit because a stranger was good to her, regardless of whether it was the right thing to do?

The answer was a resounding no. She'd live with the guilt. But Tina *had* told her and Sam wished she hadn't, because it was now *her* hiding it from everyone else.

Even though Sam felt a huge amount of affinity and responsibility towards the fragile girl who'd spent her life pretending to the outside world she'd got everything sorted, concealing this wasn't just to protect Tina. It was because Tina was convinced Bedworth was the one behind it and would come for her next. The girl had been all set to flee Birmingham.

And that couldn't happen.

The one thing no one else in this room had considered was that although Seb was off the hook, Tina could be called to testify and back up her statement. If she did a flit or, worse, got taken out by Bedworth, things could point back to Seb and then they'd be back to square one. She could not risk tearing a chink in the armour that was stopping Seb from being put behind bars.

But Seb was acting like she'd betrayed him by bringing Tina under her wing and she couldn't explain why. With the Stokers' usual way of thinking, her reasoning would be brushed aside as irrelevant.

Sam suddenly realised everyone was staring at her. 'Look, even if you lot don't appreciate it, Tina did what was needed to get you removed from suspicion.' *For now...* 'It seems that turned out to be to her own detriment too.' She jutted out her chin determinedly. 'This is *my* club and if I say she can stay and work here for a while, then that's what will happen.'

Seb fixed Sam with a long cool stare before getting up and

grabbing his jacket. 'Then you've made your position on this matter crystal clear. It's good to know where I, and the rest of us, stand in your list of priorities.'

He jerked his head in his brothers' direction. 'Let's get moving. As Craig found no sign of the money at that house last night, we can only assume Bedworth has lifted it. In the meantime, arrange with Kev for Stu do more scouting over Wolverhampton.'

He cut Sam another look. 'I'll see you later, that is if you're not too tied up with your "friend"...'

Sam swallowed Seb's harsh words, keeping her eyes fixed on him without any shadow of a waver. Only as the door slammed shut behind him and his brothers did she sigh. She understood why he disliked Tina's presence, but it was for his own protection, even if he couldn't see that yet.

Mickey had waited long enough and wasn't waiting any longer. 'Fuck this,' he muttered, upending the table in the kitchen. 'If that's the way they want to play it, they'll soon wish they hadn't.'

Returning to the flat last night, he'd fully expected grovelling apologies. Not so much from his daughter – she'd have been as acid-tongued and remorseless as ever, but he had expected *Sophie* to fall over herself to get back in his good books. He'd been sure she'd have been waiting ready with her legs akimbo and her fine breasts out for him to grab hold of as a means of making up for her sneaky behaviour. But that hadn't happened.

There had been no sign of either of them.

There still wasn't...

And Mickey wasn't impressed at all.

Snatching the one remaining bottle of beer from the fridge, he ripped the cap off with his teeth and glared around the room. He had a good mind to wreck this shit-tip even more so that Marina got stiffed by her money-grabbing landlords who would have no hesitation in taking her to court to replace their junk shop furniture.

But doing that would waste valuable energy – energy that was better used ploughing into what he could do to remedy this.

His eyes narrowed. So that two-faced worm, Dan, was still on the scene like a dose of herpes? Marina had clearly succeeded in her plan of catching up with him and judging by his liar of a daughter and Sophie's absence, it was feasible they'd got the money back from the thieving toerag. That or fucked off somewhere with him.

Well, it stopped here.

Finishing his beer, Mickey tossed the bottle across the kitchen to smash and scatter brown glass over the ripped lino.

They couldn't have got far. Knowing Marina, she would presume him too thick to put two and two together and think he'd put their absence down to punishing him for taking his anger out on Sophie.

As if Marina gave a toss! She'd made it obvious she hated Sophie, which was why it was so surprising when she'd got the girl a job at the Boulevard.

However, it wasn't surprising now... It was all part of their bloody plan!

Sophie must have fallen for Marina's manipulative ways. She might have a decent face and tits to die for, but she wasn't blessed in the brains department.

Mickey slammed his fist on the only work top the kitchen possessed. Why was he making excuses for Sophie's involvement?

She was as guilty as his daughter. And there was him feeling he might have been a tad hard on her last night. His face screwed into a scowl. He should have broken her bleeding neck.

Snatching his jacket off the peg, Mickey stormed from the flat. To where, he wasn't sure, but he wasn't staying here any longer.

29

Potter glanced at Tom from the corner of his eye. He didn't want a conversation in front of the turd, but it was either that or lose sight of him and he had to make sure Bedworth was in view each and every second. He wasn't giving the bloke a single opportunity to move that money which was concealed *somewhere*.

It couldn't be on him. It wasn't difficult to deduce that even the biggest pocket wasn't sufficient to hold the amount of cash Bedworth must be sitting on. The man wasn't brain dead enough to trust a mate or anyone else to hang onto the cash either – not if he ever expected to see it again. Neither would he stash it some- where else. Which meant the brass *must* still be in the flat.

But where, Potter didn't know.

Mark reckoned he'd looked everywhere, but there had to be *somewhere* his brother had failed to look.

Potter kept his eye on Tom as he continued his telephone conversation, hoping Mark got the drift. 'I know what you said yesterday, but I'm telling you to double check.'

Under the table, Potter clenched his fists, hoping Mark didn't question what he meant. If he needed to ask that, there really wasn't one shred of hope for the idiot brother his parents had lumbered him with.

Watching Potter closely, Tom hid his sneer. The man could attempt to blank him out as much as he liked, but he wasn't falling for it. He was on to him and the fat gimp would get no further chances to lay his greedy hands on the cash.

And that's where he was going right now – back to the flat. If Potter thought he hadn't noticed the veiled attempt at telling whoever was on the other end of the line to search the flat again, then he really was thicker than shit.

Potter continued listening to Mark down the other end of the line, his face suddenly dropping, the colour fading rapidly from his normally puce-coloured cheeks. 'You fucking what? How? How do you know?'

His eyes drifted to Tom, who as predicted was openly listening to his conversation, but he didn't care. What Mark had just said overrode keeping even Bedworth out of the goings on. At least in this instance...

Listening intently to the rest of his brother's explanation, Potter's ire increased by the second. *Those cheeky bastards!* Determined to cause a ruck, were they? Well, he'd give them something to think about. The Rosses weren't here on a dress rehearsal, and it was about time Birmingham and its lowlife inhabitants realised that. 'You're 100 per cent sure that's where they're from?'

A vein throbbed dangerously in Potter's temple. Mark stuttered like a fucking moron when he was playing with the truth. He'd been exactly the same as a kid and had never grown out of the unfortunate feature. Admittedly, it wasn't much use during a rival interrogation, but it was useful from *his* side to ensure he got the truth from his pond-skater brother. And Mark wasn't stuttering now...

'You know what you need to do, so do it. I'll send a note as an accompaniment.' Potter's mouth curled into a sneer. 'Send this one as a special delivery...'

Slamming the phone down, his head throbbed as he scribbled on a piece of paper. Snatching the phone up again, he stabbed at the buttons. 'Get in here now. I have an errand.'

Potter had barely replaced the receiver before a skinny young lad burst into the Portakabin. 'Yes, Mr Ross?'

'Take this to Mark. He's at the Pack Horse. Do it immediately!' Potter barked.

Taking the note, the young lad glanced at Tom, then raced out of the Portakabin.

Tom studied Potter. Impressive turnaround with orders, but the man was still a fat prick. But something had rattled him and he wanted to know what it was. 'Problems?' he asked, like it wasn't obvious.

'You could say that, yes.' Potter forced himself to temporarily bypass how much he hated Bedworth because, on this particular occasion, he might know something of use. 'What do you know about the Reynold firm?'

'The Reynolds?' Tom repeated, surprised. 'A bit. Why?' *In reality, he knew far too much about that bloody lot.* Mainly that his bitch of a daughter ran it, but that pearl of wisdom he'd keep close to his chest.

'One of their lot has been clocked for the third time hanging around. Someone was snooping around last week and then again yesterday. Today, this same prick was over the scrap yard,' Potter snarled, the knowledge grating like an ill-fitting shoe.

Tom felt sick. If the Reynolds were hanging around, it could be because they'd got wind *he* was here.

Was that why Dan hadn't shown up? Only out of the goodness of his heart had he allowed a few more hours' grace for the rest of the money and the promised passports to arrive before contemplating that the fuckturd had the audacity to do a runner. He hadn't believed the one-handed goon possessed the balls to pull a stunt like that, but if the Reynolds were on the prowl, then maybe he had?

What if Dan had been pulled in and bleated about his whereabouts?

The blood in Tom's veins felt stodgy – the very liquid of life congealing as things started grinding to a halt. Had Dan spilled his guts like roadkill and sent everyone hot on his trail?

He shoved his hands in his pockets in a bid to stop himself from clawing at his eyeballs in sheer panic. *Breathe. Breathe!* 'You're sure it was one of the Reynolds?' He forced the words from his mouth, surprised they sounded normal and not a strangled squeak.

'It wasn't any of the Stoker wankers. Mark knows their enforcers and most of their runners by sight,' Potter raged.

A decent ruck with those Stoker fuckers was long overdue, but that couldn't happen until he'd eked out as much dues as possible from them in return for the loser sitting in front of him. But the Reynolds? Why were they casing him all of a sudden?

Potter frowned. 'I can only presume that with some daft bint at the helm, the Reynolds are on the lookout for what they believe to be easy territory. They'll wish they fucking hadn't, though, I can tell you that much!'

Tom would have preferred not to divulge information. It would have been vastly more enjoyable watching Potter get fucked over. That was providing he wasn't also sitting here like a bonus target shot, which he was. So, for now at least, and as much as it pained him, he'd have to make sure Potter remained breathing in order to shield himself from repercussions.

'You're a bit behind, Potter. That bint you mentioned is engaged to the head Stoker. They run their firms almost as one now,' Tom said casually.

Potter's fleshy mouth dropped open in surprise. The Reynolds and Stokers weren't sworn enemies any longer? *Why was he not aware of this?*

He scraped his hand across his face. A Reynold scout could be scouting for the Stokers' benefit and he'd just given Mark the order to top the man...

Shit!

He snatched the phone back up. If the scout was linked to the Stokers, then killing the fucker would start a war. He couldn't have that until he'd got what he wanted from the Stokers, which he would have the minute he handed them Bedworth in three days' time.

Declaring war now would ruin that.

Whatever happened, he'd need to send some of his boys to watch the Orchid to pre-empt what they were playing at.

Potter listened as Mark's phone rang out. *Bollocks.*

'What are you doing?' Tom frowned, watching Potter heave his massive body out of the chair.

'Trying to stop something happening before it's too late,' Potter muttered, stomping to the Portakabin door.

30

Marina lay on the hotel bed surrounded by the contents of Dan's holdalls – the notes amounting to a sum she'd spent years dreaming of, scattered across the soft duvet. Clutching a handful, she threw them up in the air, leaving them to flutter down over her like confetti.

Her smile of contentment grew as she pressed a fifty-pound note against her nose. The dirty smell of money was almost orgasmic. The feeling more fulfilling than any man had ever raised.

This was what it was all about.

She had the money, or rather *some* of it. Where the rest was, she wasn't sure, but this was still good. *More than good.*

She had this and Dan had none.

Ha ha ha!

The surprise on Dan's face last night had been picture perfect. If she could have bottled the expression on his lying, treacherous mug and the heady smell of his unadulterated fear, she'd wear it as perfume. Bathe in it, even. It was the most wonderful smell *ever*.

How satisfying it had been plunging that knife into his heart, his chest... Even her wrist jarring as the blade caught Dan's ribs over and over had been exhilarating. It was a pain she'd never get bored of, and one she'd happily have continued for longer, had it been possible.

And she *would* have done exactly that if she hadn't run out of room for more satisfying pops as the knife sliced through Dan's flesh into his organs. It only took minutes of this frenzied stabbing fest until the exhilarating feeling waned. Each subsequent puncture was like trying to pop a deflated balloon.

Losing this thrill was depressing, so she'd moved to concentrate on his neck – the aim to continue until she decapitated him.

A shrill laugh burst from Marina's mouth as she relived the joyous scene once more.

Dan hadn't expected that! She'd got him with bells on. Got him good and proper!

She'd probably still be at it too had Sophie's piercing screaming not seeped into her fractured consciousness and she'd watched, as if through a strobe light, Sophie stagger, all jerky and puppet-like, into the night.

Madder than a frog, that one, but not anyone requiring a second thought. The tart wasn't the sort to cause come-back.

Marina threw another handful of notes into the air, the excitement within the core of her being building.

But it had to end somewhere. Everything always did. Although she'd had one of the, no, *the* best time ever, she'd known it was time to leave.

She'd never thought she'd *ever* be grateful for truck-stops, but there was always room for exceptions. Had she not been able to access the grotty shower cubicles and somewhere to change in peace around the back of a petrol station, then it would have made it awkward and most likely impossible to check into a nice hotel.

Or rather, to check into *anywhere* without ending up in a police cell.

Yes, those filthy showers had been worth every single penny of the two quid it cost her to wash the remnants of Dan's demise from her skin and hair, as well as enabling her to change her clothes.

Resentment suddenly fluttered. Having to stop and walk away when something amazing ended prematurely was as disappointing as when the generator at the fair broke down and all the rides packed up. She'd been all set to start on Dan's cock next too. Cutting that pointless thing into little slivers like salami would have been hilarious.

Still, she'd been lucky to have as much uninterrupted fun as she'd had. It was just surprising Sophie's hellcat screeching hadn't alerted the neighbours. Whether it had or hadn't, Marina hadn't been about to hang around to find out. She couldn't let *anything* ruin such a special and rewarding day.

Another giggle escaped her lips.

Tina would have had the surprise of her life when she'd got home. How Marina would have loved to watch. Maybe the thick bitch would now think twice before getting involved with losers destined to die because of their own stupidity.

Tina and Dan must have been drawn to each other, like moths to a flame. They shared the same mentality.

Marina smiled. But *she* was okay. *She* was now in a lovely boutique hotel – the first step in enjoying her long-awaited spoils, and God knows she'd earned them.

Her father would be doing his nut too, wondering where she and Sophie had gone, but that was *his* problem. And his fault. If he hadn't been so lazy, she might even have allowed him a small percentage.

Never mind.

Against her will, Marina's mind flitted back to her brother, Grant. He should be here enjoying the cash with her too. But then, he'd made his choice. Or rather, *she'd* made it for him...

Nope, she'd been surrounded by losers for long enough. Not any more. Not now she had everything.

Apart from one thing...

Her eyes narrowed. She could disappear with the nice stash and be set for life, but she wouldn't. *Not yet.* Not whilst there was still one person due their comeuppance.

Looking at the situation, people might think she was perhaps pushing her luck, but Marina knew better. Luck was on her side and owed her *plenty*. The time was right for the scales to balance in her favour.

She wouldn't be going anywhere until Sam Reynold was no longer and if she had to wait for a chance for that to happen without any consequences landing on *her*, that was fine. There was no longer anyone left around to aggravate her and so she had all the time in the world.

* * *

To get his mind off his two-faced daughter and the disappointing behaviour of his on-tap shag, Mickey had planned a few beers, a sarnie and even perhaps a cheeky sit-down at a card game if he could find a viable one.

A bit of time out might help him uncover what his plans should be now.

Then it had come to him – just like that.

What he'd expected to find, he wasn't quite sure. He hadn't even known whether doing this would amount to anything of importance or not, but his prodding instinct was so strong, he'd followed it.

Going to have a butcher's at the Violet Orchid was mostly because he wanted to see the place behind all of the claptrap. The newspaper article he'd first seen showing his bitch of an ex-wife who had fallen sickeningly on her feet like bastard usual was what had kicked off all of this shit in the first place.

It was all right for Linda, wasn't it? By the looks of it, she was doing just fine. Especially as the one and only piece of information that he'd got from that tight bitch, Marina, was that Linda was no longer living at that ghetto she'd been stuck in for years.

This could only mean the old whore had shoehorned herself into a posh drum, courtesy of Samantha Reynold, the casino queen, or so she liked to portray herself.

It was a shame Mickey hadn't got it out of his daughter where old crack-bag, Linda, was now, otherwise he'd pay her a visit. Linda would put him up for a few days, he was sure of it. She'd have no choice about it, unless she wanted him to tell her posh friends and rich daughter what she was *really* like.

Yeah, Linda would have given him a break if she knew he would blow the top off her fancy new setup, wherever it might be. But he didn't know and neither did anyone else.

Now, there was not a lot left to do. Dan had got away, Marina had done one and even Sophie had buggered off. What a bunch of ungrateful bastards they were.

Mickey scraped his hand through his thinning hair. He hadn't got anything to lose by coming to see exactly what was so special about this Violet Orchid place. Not that he'd go in. Memberships cost a fortune and he had fuck all. Certainly not enough to blow on something purely to be nosy.

His eyes scanned the opulent casino frontage. From the newspaper photo he'd seen of his ex-wife flouncing around the bloody place, it was even more spectacular inside than on the outside.

The same couldn't be said for *that* place.

Mickey stared at the shrouded skeleton of the building next door, the clanging and banging of the work going on behind the green fencing getting on his nerves. With the second loud growl coming from his stomach, he was just about to make a move from the bench and have a scoot around to find a cheapo pub to grab a bacon sarnie and a couple of pints, when he saw her.

Mickey squinted. His eyes had seen better days, but he had much better things to spend his brass on than eye tests and fucking specs. But no matter how shit his eyesight was, no glasses were needed to see that was Sam Reynold. The suit she wore would have cost more than a car.

A smirk crossed his face. The Reynold woman even had similar eyes to Marina. It stood to reason it was the sneaky gene inherited from Linda.

And Sam Reynold was off out somewhere. *Alone.*

As Sam hailed a taxi, Mickey got to his feet to follow. He had no idea where he was going or why, but he had the strong urge that he should do this. The bacon sarnie could wait.

Sam hadn't planned on visiting Linda again until next week, but after the uncomfortable way things had been left between her and Seb this morning, then spending an equally uncomfortable few hours with Tina helping her settle in, she'd needed a break.

She knew Linda felt guilty about this whole business, so Sam thought she'd be relieved to find out Tina had been located. And she'd been right.

Linda clasped her hands together and squealed animatedly. 'Thank fuck!' she cried. 'I'm so pleased. That's brilliant news, babe. Absolutely brilliant! Bet Seb's well chuffed, ain't he?'

'Yes,' Sam said, maintaining an excitement level to mirror Linda's, reluctant to let her mother know about the additional problems Tina had brought or that the girl's unwanted presence at the Orchid was putting extra strain on her and Seb's relationship.

The unexpected murder of the person who could have led Seb to both his money and the man behind everything had been bad enough, but Sam coming across as a right cow this morning was even worse. Her pulling rank was the last thing Seb needed. She knew he felt unworthy of using the Orchid as a base, rather than his own place, and along with making it look like she was putting Tina's welfare before him, she'd now succeeded in making him feel even more powerless.

Christ, what a mess.

Sam hated arguing with Seb. *Hated* it. Maybe she should have just told him the main reason Tina was there so she could be protected in case she was needed down the line for his security?

Would it have made a difference to what Seb thought? Probably not.

But Seb and his brothers hadn't seen the abject terror in Tina's eyes last night.

She had.

Tina would run if left to her own devices. And Sam wanted to see Bedworth with her own eyes. She wanted to know exactly what the man possessed to control and instil the fear of God into everyone he dealt with. Once she fathomed out how this monster believed he had the right to tread the same path as anyone else on this earth, she would enjoy Seb disposing of him.

She wasn't leaving things like this. She'd call Seb's mobile when she left here and put things right.

Feeling slightly more at ease, she turned her attention back to Linda. 'Now, fill me in on when the clinic thinks you'll be well enough to leave here.'

And Sam had to know what those time scales were, because she had to ensure Bedworth was no longer breathing by the time her mother stepped out into her new, clean life.

31

Following his instincts cost Mickey a lot more than he'd budgeted for. Why couldn't the posh cow have taken the fucking bus, rather than a black cab?

He scowled, the rumbling of his stomach now having a full on screaming fit. *What sort of super idea was this?* Nearly an hour he'd sat on the edge of the grounds of this weird place and not only was he freezing, but he'd starve to death before long.

Rummaging dejectedly in his pockets, he wasn't altogether surprised to find the only edible thing he possessed was a furry stick of Wrigley's that had fallen out of its foil wrapping to collect fluff, purely to spite him.

The Sirendale Clinic? What even was this place?

It looked like one of those posh medical places trying not to *appear* like a medical place. The sort which tried to disguise itself as an upper-crust spa gaff, when really it was an abortion clinic for snobs or one of those hospitals that did overpriced plastic surgery for birds with rich husbands wanting to keep their brides looking younger than they really were purely to impress others on the golf course.

What was Sam Reynold doing there, then? A boob job?

From what he'd seen, she could use an increase of a couple of cup sizes. Tits the size of Sophie's would be good.

Mickey's eyes narrowed. He wasn't thinking about Sophie, the treacherous whore. She was done. And if she ever came crawling back, he'd slap the teeth clean out of her head.

He focused back on the shiny glass door of the clinic. *Boob job or abortion for Sam Reynold? Which was more likely?*

Oh, this was pointless. She could be in there for days. Now he'd have to stump up for another fucking taxi!

As Mickey went to move away, the postman came around the corner, rolling his eyes as he stubbed his fag out before placing a foot on the manicured path.

Mickey couldn't help but laugh. 'Going in for a boob job, are you, mate?'

'Yeah, right!' the postman grinned. 'Not unless I've missed having a crack addiction and a shedload of cash!'

Mickey blinked. 'It's a druggie place?'

'Yeah,' the postman sneered. 'They make out it's anything but, but us lot know the score. It's for the posh, mind, not the likes of normal folk.'

Mickey casually shrugged and waited for the postman to continue before he retraced his steps.

Interesting... It didn't take rocket science to see that Sam Reynolds was *not* an addict. He'd known enough of them over the years to spot the signs. If she was a secret crack head, then he'd eat his sock.

But he knew someone who *was*... One linked *very* closely to a person with more than enough brass to pay for a place like *this*...

Mickey's mouth slid into a grin, pretty confident he'd just discovered where his divine ex-wife was residing.

* * *

Pulling his shirt cuffs down to sit just below his jacket sleeves, Seb smoothed down his double-breasted suit, then strutted into the Burlington, nodding to the top-hatted doorman as he crossed the threshold.

It had been some time since he and Sam had gone for a drink or had any real time together on their own, away from the confines of the Orchid and the pressure of the businesses. It would do them good. It would certainly do *him* good.

He'd been surprised to receive Sam's call suggesting they meet up for drinks, but by no means unhappy. Not liking how things had been left this morning, he'd now put this aggravation with Tina into perspective. He couldn't pretend he was happy about it, but he understood Sam's reasoning to a certain extent, even if he didn't agree with it. He had to take on board that Tina had done him a much-appreciated service. Once the moment had passed, it was easy to forget how much of a tight corner he'd been in with the police yesterday. He'd still be in that position, or worse, had she not arrived when she had. Due to that and because it was what Sam felt she must do, he'd decided to let it pass. But Tina being on the premises or anywhere around him would not be a long-term thing. He didn't trust her.

This compromise also didn't change that the demise of that one-handed toerag meant they were back to square one with their quest to recoup the stolen money, or finding that bastard, Bedworth. But he wasn't thinking about them just now, not now things had come together.

Gesturing to the waiter, Seb shouted up the best bottle of Dom Pérignon and glanced at his watch.

Sensing Sam's arrival, he looked up to find his sixth sense was spot on. As she moved into the bar, his heart lurched in the same way it always did. Even though he spent half his life in her presence, both at home and now at work, she still possessed the power to take his breath away.

His lips twitched with the hint of a smile, as on spotting him, Sam's eyes lit up. Neither did he miss the envious glances of every single man or the admiring looks of the women in the room.

Sam was his.

Her rare natural beauty preceded her. Something she underestimated. She had no sense of just how stunning she was without even trying, which only made her even more attractive.

Seb stood up as she approached.

Sam rushed into his arms. 'I'm sorry about this morning.'

'Yeah, me too,' Seb said, planting his lips on hers.

Interrupted by the waiter bringing over a silver ice bucket holding the champagne, Seb gestured for Sam to sit down.

She sank into a sumptuous leather chair. 'I am sorry, though. I hate it when we argue. I...'

'I get it, okay? Let's just forget about it,' Seb smiled.

'But the way I spoke an...'

'Sam!' Seb said sternly, placing his finger to her lips.

Sam sipped her champagne. 'You're in a good mood.'

'I am, yes!' Seb grinned, glad he'd secured a booth out of the way of the other customers where they could talk privately. 'So much so that I've sent the order to the printers for the wedding invitations. There's only a few months left, so it's about time we got them.'

Sam frowned. 'I thought we were holding off from finalising anything until everything was sorted?'

Seb's face split into a grin. 'We were, but now it *is*. I've received word from Stu that there's been no movement or anything out of the ordinary on the Ross manor. I've also had the final details in for Thursday, so we're all set.'

He let his good news sink in before continuing. 'Things will be back to normal within weeks!'

'What? The Peacock will be completely finished by then?' Sam gasped. 'That's fantastic! I expected it to take ages.' She glanced around just to be on the safe side before she next spoke. 'And you think this "job" will run smoothly?'

Seb laughed. 'It'll be a cinch. The Rosses are such lazy fuckers it's doubtful they'll even send anyone when their container docks. They're so used to their little world running a certain way it won't cross their tiny minds they're being shafted.'

And as well as getting his hands on the money required to put his life and firm back together, there was also the satisfaction of knowing that he was turning over the tossers who had pissed off his father all that time ago and very nearly succeeded in stopping the Stoker empire from even getting off the ground.

'Well, that's wonderful,' Sam smiled, relieved there would be no more hurdles to navigate.

Seb traced his finger along Sam's bare arm, her soft skin making the hair on the back of his neck stand up. 'Now we can put all of this shit to one side and get married like we originally planned.'

For a moment, not so long ago, he'd had the real and dreadful fear that having to postpone marrying this perfect woman would be his only option. The prospect of marrying her before being able to provide everything he'd promised and wanted to supply was not feasible. Not for him. But now he could deliver.

Sam shivered from the electrical currents Seb's fingers left on her skin. She couldn't wait until Thursday when the heist had been completed. Then the heavy weight of dread stubbornly hanging around her neck would disappear.

Her eyes were drawn like a magnet to Seb's mouth. 'I'm looking forward to marrying you, Mr Stoker,' she whispered, leaning into him.

Seb's hand moved to gently rest on Sam's washboard stomach. 'And when you make me the happiest man in the world by becoming my wife, I'm expecting you to start churning out my children,' he winked.

'Only one at a time, I hope?' Sam laughed happily.

But it was true. They would soon have the option to bring some very much wanted children into a safe world. It was what they'd both been waiting for. It just showed that whatever was thrown at them in this bizarre life of theirs, they could come through stronger than ever.

32

Tina nervously answered the tapping of her door to find a woman holding a gilt tray containing sandwiches and drinks. 'Thank you,' she smiled, gratefully accepting it.

Closing the door as soon as she could politely do without alerting anyone to the depth of her despair, Tina sank back down onto the bed, her eyes filling with tears.

Everyone she'd seen since coming here had been nice to her and the room Sam had given her was more than she'd ever hoped for.

Tina looked around the spacious room which not only had a king-sized bed, a fitted wardrobe and dressing table, but a sitting room area, a kitchenette and a marble bathroom, complete with a walk-in shower. There was even a huge television. It was a completely self-contained little apartment – something she'd have previously given her right arm for.

But that was then, and this was now...

Picking a sandwich from the selection, Tina took a bite. It was lovely, or it would have been had she an appetite or her mouth wasn't so dry that she stood no chance of actually eating it.

Spitting the piece of sandwich into a tissue plucked from a silver box on the bedside table, Tina slumped back against the velvet headboard and let the tears fall in earnest.

As well as this room – apartment – call it whatever, Sam had also given her a job, along with the promise of protection for as long as she wanted or needed it.

Tina should be grateful and happy, but she wasn't. Well, grateful, yes, but happy – quite the opposite...

She was also due to start work tonight. It was only as a glass collector and helping out behind the bar, but she was dreading it. Although everyone seemed nice, she could sense the disapproval and resentment radiating anywhere Seb Stoker and his brothers walked.

She'd only had a very brief introduction to them yesterday. Seb Stoker, the man himself, had been courteous and pleasant when he'd thanked her for talking to the police, but the crushing sense of negativity was stifling.

In all honesty, Tina wasn't surprised. She'd been gobsmacked Sam hadn't personally brained her after blurting out her knowledge about Dan's part in the robbery.

She hadn't meant to say anything about that. Although she'd been racked with guilt about hiding this information, she'd come to the conclusion that some things were better left unsaid. After all, she'd done everything asked of her, all charges against Seb had been dropped and from the gist she'd got from the detective she'd spilled her guts to, the only person they were now gunning for was Bedworth.

But she'd lost her will not to lessen the tremendous guilt the minute Dan had been butchered. It was an image that would never leave her.

Tina shuddered as the awful scene replayed in her mind in horrific technicolour.

Those men who had arrived under Sam's instructions to rid the place of a corpse, like it was a normal occurrence, had upset her resolve. Especially when one immediately flagged up that Dan was the person they'd been looking for in connection with the safe codes.

That, coupled with the rest of that disastrous night, had shattered Tina into little pieces and stopped her from controlling what spilt from her mouth. The need to cleanse her mind of the knowledge, guilt and horror was greater than self-preservation or sanity.

Sam even seemed to understand why she'd kept schtum. Actually *understood*. And even after that, the woman had still arranged this...

Tina's eyes roamed around the room once more. Sam might have promised salvation in the way of protection, a job and somewhere to stay, but the rest of them hadn't. No matter how well they kept it to themselves, the Stokers wanted to impale her, she could tell.

From experience, Tina knew deep-seated distrust and resentment always had a way of finding its target in the end.

She turned away from the large window that shone rays of light into the room and buried her tear-stained face in the pillow.

She'd lost Dan. She'd lost *everything*. Whatever anyone said, Tom would find a way to get to her. No matter how good the offer was and how kind the intentions, she couldn't stay here.

At the end of the day, she'd delivered what had been asked and she'd avenged her mother's memory. Tom would be taken down, but whether that would happen quickly enough for *her* chances of survival, only time would tell.

One thing was certain and that was in doing what she'd done, Dan's demise was down to *her*. He wouldn't have even hung around had she not begged him to.

Someone – and that someone *had* to be Tom – had discovered where Dan was and also that she'd gone to the police.

Now she'd lost the only man who'd ever loved her, the one who'd promised to look after her and the one she'd wanted to be with. There was nothing left to keep her here and a thousand reasons to leave.

Even Stella's whereabouts were no longer an excuse to stay. Her sister would make her own way in life. Stella was a hard case and a lot more confident, and Tina could no longer bypass everything she personally needed to exist solely for what she felt obliged to do for others.

Enough was enough. As much as she felt guilty for throwing kindness back at the people who'd helped her, she would drown if she didn't change this situation.

Getting off the bed, Tina stared from the window out across the back of the Orchid. Somewhere on this road below her, Tom had mown down and killed Deb. How she wished she'd extended the hand of friendship to the girl when they'd been at the Aurora, rather than being the bitch she'd become accustomed to behaving like in order to survive. How she *used* to think until everything dramatically changed.

Furthermore, Tina knew she was being watched by *everyone* here. For our own protection, Sam said – to ensure her safety...

There was no safety. She had to go.

It would be difficult to escape undetected and if she managed it, Tina had no idea where she'd go. All she knew was that she had to give it a try.

* * *

'Why are we going the long way around?' Sam cried, her eyes dancing with amusement.

This night had been a much-needed tonic to counter the stress, strain and uncertainty she and Seb had been dealing with over the past couple of months. The chain of events, especially over the past few weeks, had ramped the pressure up to breaking point. As a couple in a relatively new and already highly pressured relationship, Sam knew they'd started to lose sight of where they were as people.

But just this one night – a mere few hours of stepping away from the murky world of mounting betrayal and multifaceted distrust from just about every angle – served to remind them both that they belonged together.

So much had happened – so many things, yet they'd navigated the never-ending storm. They'd risen above situations and dealt with pressures most people would never face. They'd been forced to cope with debilitating circumstances that held the power to crush most people's faith in anything, let alone each other. *And that spoke volumes.*

Now, Sam felt she might burst with relief, as well as happiness for what was to come. Okay, so there were a couple more hurdles yet to climb, but most had now been dealt with. And Seb's news had made those outstanding things seem even more achievable.

As Seb swung her around by the hand, she squealed with excitement, her mind spinning with excess champagne and love for the man in front of her.

'You asked why we're going the long way around?' Seb's green eyes sparkled as he pulled Sam down the side road towards the back of the Orchid. 'Because, my most beautiful wife-to-be, one: I can't be arsed to speak to anyone if we go through reception. Two: I'm in a silly mood, and three: I have the sudden and *very* strong urge to take you against the wall and make you come so hard you pass out!'

Effortlessly sweeping Sam up like she was as light as a feather, Seb ran further up the alley with her hoisted over his shoulder.

Shrieking with surprise and exhilaration, Sam pointlessly pummelled Seb's back with her fists, tears of laughter cascading down her cheeks. 'Put me down, you lunatic!' she laughed. 'We're supposed to be responsible businesspeople!'

Placing Sam back to the ground, Seb pressed her against the wall. 'You as well as I know that we can be anything we want. And tonight...' Raising an eyebrow, he hitched Sam's dress around her waist. 'We're having a night off from business...'

Crashing his mouth onto hers, his hand found its way into Sam's lacy underwear, whilst his other hand freed himself from his trousers. Lifting her, he entered with skilful precision.

Gasping, Sam wrapped her legs around Seb's waist, then she wound her fingers in his thick hair. How she missed this wanton and free side of Seb – of *both* of them.

This was the best night she'd had in ages. They were through the worst.

'I love you,' Seb panted. 'More than anything.'

Sam couldn't reply, the avalanche of sensations building so rapidly it forced her breath away.

Neither Seb nor Sam heard a van door sliding open, but they did hear a sudden loud thud.

Seb paused. 'What th...' His head swung around, this time on hearing the door sliding shut and an engine pulling away, but all he managed to catch was the end of a white van disappearing out of sight behind the looming back wall of the Orchid.

'Seb? What's goi...'

Gently lowering Sam to the ground, Seb shoved himself back into his trousers and darted around the corner, looking up and down for a sign of the vehicle or anybody at all.

'Seb? What is it?' Sam rushed down the alley to catch up with him. 'Who was it?'

Seb frowned. 'I don't know, but...' He stopped abruptly. 'Shit!'

It was then Sam saw it – an object sticking out from behind her trade bins. *It looked like a roll of carpet... or...*

Seb raced towards the bins. 'Stay back!'

Ignoring Seb's instructions, Sam followed, reaching his side just as he pulled back the thick covering. 'Oh my God, no!' she whimpered, her hand flying to her mouth.

Seb stared first in stunned silence, which immediately changed to wild, unbridled rage as he saw what had been bundled into a roll of carpet and chucked like rubbish into the corner with the trade bins.

Sam didn't want to process what her brain hoped couldn't possibly be real, but her eyes refused to move from the dreadful sight.

It was a man – or most of one...

Both arms had been haphazardly sawn off just below the shoulder, leaving splintered bone jutting through red gore, tendrils of torn tendons the only remaining parts. The man's eyes were missing – not just missing, but had been squashed and crushed within the sockets and then dug out with a serrated knife, the surrounding flesh frayed and bloody, leaving remains of gelatinous eyeball smeared across smashed-up cheekbones.

Sam then focused on the strange-looking purple thing attached by a thick nail to the man's wide chest, realising it was the tongue ripped from the man's head.

Her legs went weak, vomit rising. She clutched at Seb, needing to steady herself.

She knew who this was.

An anguished sob escaped her mouth. It was Stu – her enforcer

– the one sent to scout. The one who had only earlier given Seb the news they'd both been longing to hear.

With a guttural roar, Seb moved forward and snatched a piece of paper tucked in the top pocket of Stu's shirt. Eyes wild, he ripped it open, finding it difficult to hold it still with hands that shook violently from white-hot fury.

Sam stared at the note, the writing messy and scrawled:

> Do not spy
> Do not speek
> Keep your dirty hands out of
> others busness

'What the hell?' Sam cried, her voice deafening in the silence of the alleyway.

Smashing his fist into the wall, Seb seethed with blinding rage. *Yeah, a message – one he'd seen before...* 'It's the Rosses,' he spat, his voice cold as ice. 'This is their fucking doing.'

'Are you sure?' Sam cried. 'How do you know?'

Seb shook away the pain from his cut knuckles and screwed up the note. 'Because, short of the bad spelling, it's the very same wording my father used on the message sent attached to *their* old man's body, that's why!'

He'd also known the second he'd seen the way Sam's enforcer had been mutilated.

And he would kill those Ross wankers.

33

Mickey held the buzzer down for an indeterminate length of time, fighting against the urge to put his foot through the poncy glass door with its stupid monogrammed 'SC' frosting.

He'd put on the best clobber he'd brought along with him to Birmingham. He looked pretty fucking decent, so why the hell was no one letting him in?

He'd even purposely got up early, thinking it better to come in the morning, rather than wait until he usually bothered surfacing. He'd planned to grab himself a burger on the way back too, but now it looked like he need not have bothered if...

Ah...

'Yes? Can I help you?'

Mickey forged a smile at the frosty-faced woman who opened the door a couple of inches to look him up and down. *Right, think, think. Remember the plan.*

'We haven't any deliveries due this morning, so...'

'I'm not a deliveryman!' Mickey snarled, before reining himself in. 'I'm here to see my... erm... my wife...'

'Your *wife*, sir?' The woman looked Mickey up and down once again. 'Do you have an appointment?'

'No, I don't.' *The snotty, condescending trollop*, Mickey thought, praying his face didn't give away his wish to pull the door out of her hands and trap her beak of a nose in the frame. 'It's an emergency. I, erm... I'm afraid I've had some very bad news which I need to tell my wife.'

His brain scrolled through his prearranged story. He'd spent half the night scouring through ways of getting inside this place to see Linda, but had drawn a total blank. That was until *this* idea dropped into his brain during the early hours. And a damn fine one it was too. It was believable and, best of all, *provable*.

Mickey stepped forward, expecting the door to have been opened, only to find it still all but shut. 'Did you not hear me? I need to see my wife. I...'

'I heard you, sir,' the woman said, her nasal voice making Mickey want to throttle her. 'We can't allow you in just like that. This is a secure facility for our clients' benefit and...'

'But it's an *emergency*!' Mickey barked, remembering to look upset. 'My wife needs to know that our son has died!' Seeing the woman's face pale, he hid his smirk. *Yeah, you'll have to let me in now, won't you*, he thought victoriously.

Grasping the chink in the acid-faced woman's armour, Mickey continued whilst he could. 'Linda's my ex-wife – not that we ever got divorced, but she goes by her maiden name, which is Matthews. Linda Matthews.'

Shoving his hand in his leather jacket pocket, he fished out a piece of paper and unfolded it, the creases so ancient, they were almost translucent. He knew if he hung onto this, it would come in handy one day. Now it finally had.

'Here!' He slapped the crumpled piece of paper against the

glass pane. 'Our marriage certificate shows I'm not an impostor. I'm Michael Devlin and I need to speak to my wife.'

Whether Linda already knew about Grant or not was irrelevant. It would get him in here and that was all he cared about. 'It has to be me to break the news. We may be separated, but it was amicable. She has the right to know what's happened to our boy.'

The woman peered at the certificate. 'I completely understand, sir, and I'm very sorry for your loss, but the manager is off sick today and I can't give authority to visitors who haven't previously been vetted.'

Mickey faltered. *Shit. Now what?* Would he have to resort to punching this miserable old bat in the face to get her out of the fucking way?

Wait a moment...

'Bend your rules in this instance then, madam, otherwise I'll tell Linda's daughter that you refused me entry and caused distress. Actually, you've probably heard of her. She was only here yesterday visiting her mother. Samantha Reynold?'

Surely that would get this withered old cow to shift? The stupid bitch knew adverse publicity from top Birmingham names such as Samantha bloody Reynold wouldn't be gratefully received. Her manager wouldn't be best pleased with *that* happening in her absence, would she?

The woman stepped back, clearly flustered. 'Erm, well, I'm sure in this instance and under the extenuating circumstances, Mrs Brunswick would agree that allowing you in is the reasonable thing to do.'

Mickey refrained from punching the air in triumph as the woman fully opened the door. 'Thank you. Now if you could tell me where Linda is, I'll give her the news. I'd appreciate being left alone whilst I do it, though. Linda won't want an audience witnessing her distress.'

Neither did he, because he wasn't sure how Linda would react to him turning up.

But he had a plan for that too. Linda couldn't have changed that much, so he was fairly confident it would work.

It was difficult keeping her overwhelming rage in check, but Sam knew she must. It was the only way to keep this under control and do what was needed. It was what they had all agreed must happen, but it didn't make it any easier. Or more acceptable.

She slowly looked around the faces of her enforcers, seeing only disbelief and seething anger. And that seething anger was directed at her...

'This warrants immediate retaliation!' one of the men shouted, gaining a full house of nodding agreement. 'That always happens, so why not now?'

Sam nodded, acknowledging the question. It was a relevant one. *Why not now, indeed?* The men in the room could barely control their fury that something like this had happened to one of their own. Stu was a well-liked member of the team – one who had worked for the firm for many years and one who would be sorely missed.

Like her enforcers, Sam had had a great deal of respect for the man. This feeling was reflected equally by everyone, including the Stokers, making it doubly difficult for anyone to accept that, on this occasion, retaliation must wait.

The heist in two days' time could not go ahead if a war was declared on the Rosses. A war would not only deflect from what needed to happen, but would generate a massive increase in the Rosses stepping up their protection surrounding everything they did.

It was also impossible to quantify the decision to wait without explaining why, but that could not be done either. It was unanimous that only the inner circle remained in the know to protect everyone.

One thing was guaranteed, though, and that was Potter Ross and his shitty firm would regret *ever* stepping out of line like this.

Anger bubbled in Sam's veins. It had throbbed and pulsed and risen in intensity since the moment she'd seen one of her men mutilated in such a horrific way and dumped like rubbish outside her door. The addition of that note was the final insult. If Potter Ross or any of his people thought she would take this lying down, they were wrong.

But unlike the Stokers, the Reynolds had had no dealings with this Wolverhampton firm. *Ever.* There had never been any cause.

Now there was.

Sam held her stare against the hostile expressions and aggrieved murmurings from the room, knowing she had to acknowledge her enforcers' anger. *But how?* 'I can assure you this will be dealt with,' she said calmly and clearly. 'I also understand you're angry. So am I, but...'

'Then why are we being asked to hold fire?' a man shouted. 'What's happened to this firm?' He folded his meaty arms, the sinews in his neck taut. 'Despite what was said, we gave you the benefit of the doubt and backed you when you took the helm.'

'Yeah, and *now* look what's happened,' another added. 'We ain't having it. Stu was killed like a dog and you're letting it pass?'

Sam's eyes narrowed. 'I'm not letting anything pass. His death will be avenged, believe you me. We just...'

'*Believe* you?' another man shouted. 'You expect us to believe you'll do anything after pulling a fucking stunt like this?'

Kevin stood up. Sam might have insisted on breaking the news, but his men were turning into a braying mob. He knew what they were like and if they lost control or faith in the firm's leadership, they'd take matters into their own hands. 'Watch your tongues and remember who you're speaking to! This is a decision agreed by *everyone* in the inner circle,' he roared. 'One taken for reasons we cannot disclose at the moment.'

He met the eyes of the most volatile men in his teams. 'You'll wait until you're given the nod to move on this and not a second before.' He frowned, hearing more muttering. 'And just to make things clear, this is Sam's final decision. Nothing to do with the Stokers.'

Sam swallowed uneasily. She'd expected it was only a matter of time before *someone* questioned who pulled the strings at the top. *Her or Seb.* It was no secret there was veiled disquiet amongst a percentage of the staff who hadn't quite accepted the longstanding feud between the Reynold and Stoker firms was over and didn't appreciate the Stokers using the Orchid as a base whilst the Peacock was rebuilt. Nor was it unknown that only the Stokers had beef with the Rosses' Wolverhampton firm.

If, for the time being, she could have concealed who they believed to be behind this murder, then she would have, but it wasn't possible. She'd had to tell them, otherwise they'd have crawled the streets and kicked off against every firm in the Midlands and beyond until they found the source.

And that was even more dangerous.

'Thank you, Kevin,' Sam said, pausing as she eyed the room. 'What Kevin said is correct. None of you are to seek retaliation until *I* say so. Is that understood?'

With the remnants of murmurings and a few rolled eyes, Sam bristled further. She wasn't in the mood for this. 'Let's just get one thing fucking straight, shall we? Those of you who think that I haven't the clout, nor the mentality to do what's needed, then there's the door.' Her arm swept across the room to the exit. 'Leave now if you wish. Go on!'

Adrenaline pumped furiously through her veins as she waited to see if anyone got up.

They didn't.

Not yet.

'Let me remind you that you are paid to follow orders, not make your own. Payback will happen when I say so and not before. I want justice just as much as you do, and I will get it. The same way I would seek it for each and every single one of you, should it be any of *you* that was lying butchered last night.' Sam looked back around the room. 'I respect my loyal men, so gentlemen, this is your last chance to leave.'

She scanned the room slowly, the men now shuffling or looking down at the floor. 'Okay, so with that clear, I'll leave you to take your orders for tonight's rotas from Kevin. The minute we can move on this, I promise you'll be told.'

With that, Sam turned on her heel and left the room, her anger beating a steady rhythm. She would be calling in the dues for what the Rosses had done.

How stupid of her to think for one moment there would be no further hurdles to climb.

Now there was a brand new one.

34

Linda knew she should have raised the alarm the second her brain processed who had been ushered into her room, but she hadn't.

Why?

Because she hadn't believed it. In fact, she still couldn't believe it. She hadn't seen Mickey Devlin for about twenty-five years, not that she could remember, anyway. He wasn't someone she'd ever wanted to see again. There were quite a few men from her chequered past who fell under that umbrella – some more than others, but Mickey was *definitely* one nearing the top of the charts.

Leaving her high and dry with his kids hadn't helped her already shaky existence and had subsequently pushed her over the edge – at least in losing another two of her kids to the system.

But saying nothing, she'd instead nodded to the woman looking at her with sympathy as she'd shown this bastard of an ex-husband into her room. Well, the woman need not have bothered, because Linda knew Mickey well enough to realise there was no way in a month of Sundays he'd come up here purely to tell her Grant was dead.

Which meant, in classic Mickey Devlin style, the *only* reason he was here was because he wanted something.

Linda suspected she knew exactly what that was too. In between the remnants of the debilitating craving for crack as it had been slowly and fully removed from her system, being here had given her time to think. Making sense of anything had previously been an unsurmountable mountain to climb when her head was so mangled, but since her brain had gradually cleared, she'd been able to decipher what had brought her son and daughter to Birmingham in the first place; why they'd been angling to get in with Sam and why they'd almost killed her in that quest.

The only common denominator was Mickey...

The man didn't frighten Linda. He didn't have the same power in that department as Tom, but for the first time ever, her immediate instinct was *not* to turn to drugs or alcohol to dull her mind from triggers reminding her of painful episodes from her life. Not this time.

There was a reason for Mickey's pretence of breaking this news. He had an agenda and she wanted to know exactly what that was.

Crossing her legs at the table in the room resembling a hotel suite rather than a secure bedroom in a rehabilitation clinic, Linda eyed Mickey with open suspicion.

'I must say, Lin, you look fantastic!' Mickey said, genuinely surprised. He'd expected a more hideous version of the addled crack whore he'd seen the last time he'd bumped into her. Not that she'd remember that. But now her clothes were good quality, her styled hair was free from grey and her skin was clear. Much to his utter shock, she didn't look bad. Didn't look bad at all.

'I have to admit I thought that picture I saw of you in the paper at the casino must have been doctored,' he laughed, belatedly realising he'd just blown his cover.

'Oh, you mean the one giving you the idea to see what you and our children could tap from me?' Linda sneered. 'Some things don't change, do they, Mickey? Why don't you just cut to the chase and tell me what it is you *really* want. If you're after what you sent Marina and Grant here for, you're too late!'

Mickey blinked. *Crap. He'd misjudged this.*

His eyes darted to the buzzer on the wall close to where Linda sat. That would, if pressed, send the staff running. Looking at this posh joint, it was no doubt linked to the cop shop too.

She would expose him and turn him into the cops. She'd do it just to spite him. 'I didn't tell them to do that,' Mickey lied. 'We might have had our ups and downs when we were married, Lin, but you're the mother of my kids!' And that had been his *first* bloody mistake. *And his second...*

Linda laughed openly. Something she'd done a lot of since having her smashed front teeth recently replaced. One more thing out of many that Sam had arranged for her. Yet she'd been unable to do the *one* thing requested of her...

Linda shook her head to get rid of the thoughts filtering into her brain of Tom Bedworth. She had to deal with Mickey first. 'You're pretending you cared about your kids, when you fucked off and left us?' she snapped. 'Pull the other one!'

'It's not like you made much of an effort, considering you didn't ever look after them!' Mickey countered. Realising he was shooting himself in the foot, he pulled himself in. 'I'm sorry, I'm not here to argue.'

Linda glared at Mickey. 'Why *are* you here then? And, like I said, don't pretend it's because of Grant.'

* * *

'You fuckwit!' Potter snarled, cuffing his brother around the head. 'Don't you ever answer your fucking mobile?'

Mark rubbed his throbbing ear. 'I was in the middle of following your orders!'

'It's not good enough!' Potter grunted as he paced the Portakabin, the rotten floor sagging under his weight. 'You've screwed everything up.'

Mark stared at his brother, sick of being treated like a doughnut. 'You told me to get rid of the bloke, Pot, so that's what I did. I could hardly take it back once it was done. We'd dumped it by the time I saw your missed call.'

Potter seethed. Even if he'd been too late to stop the bloke being offloaded, if he could have prevented the body from being dumped, things wouldn't be quite so bad. But instead, he'd now got a major fight on his hands. The Stokers would jump on the slight to their head prick's wifey, or whatever the Reynold tart was. There would be retaliation big time.

For fuck's sake. All his plans for filching kudos and territory from the Stokers were now knackered. To top it all, Bedworth was now here for no reason. He could no longer be used as part of the masterplan now the whole thing was buggered. Even the delivery on Thursday was up the creek. How could he or anybody afford to be off site, leaving the way clear for the retaliation that was bound to come at them full throttle?

Failing to maintain the appearance of control in front of Mark, Potter swiped the sweat from his forehead with his sleeve. 'Jesus Christ,' he muttered, glaring at his brother with narrowed eyes. 'What a fucking mess! Which van did you use? Did anyone see you dump the body? Anyone at all? Who else was with you? Who else knows?'

Mark wrung his shovel-sized hands. 'Just me, Phil and Spanner. We took the white Transit, but no one saw us. I ain't stupid!'

Potter sighed. *That was a matter of opinion.* And no, he wasn't about to admit his part in this. He might have given the orders, but

Mark should have waited. He never did anything this quickly, so why had he been so fast to undertake this particular instruction? Bloody typical and so goddamned predictable. Never any use when he needed him to be was Mark.

'It doesn't mean anyone will guess we were behind this,' Mark said. 'We haven't had outward rucks with the Stokers for years and no grief with the Reynolds, so why would they automatically presume it was us?'

Potter knocked his knuckles on his own head. 'Duh! Maybe because a member of their firm that wasn't casing our properties of his own accord or through boredom ended up being returned dead and mangled, perhaps? The guy you butchered had been specifically sent to watch us by *them*, you idiot, so who do you think the finger points to?'

'But they can't prove it!' Mark countered. 'That bloke could have been set upon by anyone. Everyone knows outsiders aren't liked over this neck of the woods.'

Potter decided he'd leave out the rather large hint that he'd given by returning that scout's body with an identical note to the one pinned to their own father's body when the Stokers removed him from the equation many years ago.

Yesterday the idea had seemed brilliant in hammering home *exactly* who claimed ownership, but in retrospect, it wasn't one of his better ideas. He'd be buggered if he'd admit it, though. It was better to blame Mark.

Staring at his brother's gormless face, Potter grabbed his arm. 'Just get out of my sight! I need some space to think and you're stealing my fucking oxygen!'

35

Tom fell through the Portakabin door as it unexpectedly opened. Landing at Mark Ross's feet, he scrambled up, only to be barged out of the way as the younger Ross pushed past, looking unhappier than usual.

'I was just coming to see you.' Tom brushed the layer of dust off his front and smiled weakly at Potter.

'By pressing yourself up against the door, earwigging my private fucking conversations?' Potter growled, glaring at Tom with unbridled fury. 'I should kill you for that alone.'

Tom held his hand up. 'Don't be hasty! I couldn't help overhearing and what's happened might not be such a bad thing.' *It certainly wouldn't if he could blag Potter into believing the idea he'd just thought of was good.*

He had to do something because there was no other alternative but to accept Dan had turned him over. He hadn't thought the scrote would ever have had the bollocks to do that, but the fuckhead had lifted the rest of the money and now he was back to square one with the passport problem. He couldn't even go and search for the spineless creep. It would be too late anyway – Dan would be long gone by now.

Aggravating and insulting wasn't the word! It wasn't the first time Tom had been turned over, but he had got *this* option now and so, therefore, needed to ensure it worked. It was his final opportunity to rectify this bloody mess and get the fuck away from here. Except *this* time he'd be damned if he did that without enough to keep him comfortably in retirement.

Putting aside his initial urge to launch Bedworth down the steps to land on his face, Potter grudgingly jerked his head, beckoning the man inside. He might as well hear what the man had to say. Things couldn't be any worse than how they currently stood.

Snatching a bottle of rum, he poured two tots into a pair of dirty plastic glasses. 'I've arranged to send scouts to watch the Orchid. We'll need warning for when the Stokers pounce, because they will!'

Not needing any encouragement to have a drink, Tom planted himself in a chair. 'That's where I think you're wrong,' he said, a smile curling his lips. 'Mark may have a point... You can't be *completely* certain the Stokers know you're behind this.'

'They will...' Potter admitted. 'I sent a note with the body, so I might as well have signed my bloody name!'

Tom shrugged. 'Look, the Stokers are up to their eyeballs. They're so desperate to pull their shit together, they probably didn't even see the note. The body would have been offloaded toute de suite, so the worst thing you could do is send scouts. That *would* be laying claim to what happened.'

Potter frowned. 'How so?'

'The Stokers have many enemies,' Tom continued, his confidence growing every second Potter didn't eject him from the mouldering room. 'They're nowhere near the stable position you believe them to be,' he lied, needing this to sound plausible. *He'd say anything to steer Potter into his trap.*

'That prick – Seb Stoker – he's changed since getting involved with that daft Orchid tart.' Tom grinned. 'Yeah, I know it sounds crazy for a bloke such as that to allow pussy to turn him soft, but it has. Even his fucking brothers wanted to oust him not long ago.' He dared to laugh. *This was risky, but he had to try it.* 'Stoker's left himself wide open on more than one occasion. They're not concentrating. Do you really think the Peacock would have burnt down if he was on form?'

Potter watched Tom carefully. The Stokers *did* have to be in a shit state to enable a cretin like Bedworth to raze their casino to the ground *and* rob them. Not that Bedworth knew he'd worked that bit out.

'With a woman in charge at the Orchid, there won't be retaliation from that side – they don't know their arse from their elbow,' Tom continued. Again, utter bollocks, but Potter was thinking about this now, he was *actually* thinking about it. *What a stupid cunt. Come on, Potter, do what I want you to do.* 'Seriously, don't act defensive. If they don't think you're behind this now, they will if you start watching them.'

Potter chewed his lip. He had heard there had been unrest in the Stoker camp a few months ago too. It was also likely the Stoker honcho *had* got his head turned if he'd made the unexpected and unprecedented step of joining the two firms and no longer being enemies with their rivals. Even so – how could he risk not watching them? They could be on their way, or even here *now*. Leaving his empire unguarded was insanity.

Tom saw Potter's brain wasn't whirring in the required direction. He had to up this. A bit of flattery worked wonders on numbskulls. *Take the bait, dickhead, come on...* 'Look, I won't pretend I'm saying this purely for your benefit,' he said. 'You're an astute man, so there's no point in pretending we're friends, but I *do* have a vested interest.'

'At least you've got one thing right!' Potter mumbled. 'But what do you mean by "vested interest"? What possible delusion of grandeur are you under, Bedworth, to believe you have shag all to do with my firm?'

Tom shrugged once again. 'I've invested a shedload of cash into a delivery that's due in two days' time, so there's that for a start. I don't want that to go pear-shaped, so yes, I have a vested interest. The drop can't go ahead whilst you're flapping about worrying about the Stokers and whether or not they're coming after you.'

Potter bristled. 'I ain't *worried* about the Stokers, you bastard! They don't scare me. I'm refusing to give them a clear run, that's all.' *Not entirely true, but maybe he was jumping the gun?*

'Then don't let this situation hinder anything,' Tom pushed. 'It has to be business as usual. I'm not saying don't be on your guard, but actively making out you're expecting them isn't the way.'

Potter studied Tom as he tipped the dregs of rum into his mouth. He flapped his pudgy hand. 'Whatever, but fuck off now, will you? I need to think about how to play this. I'll come to my own conclusions.'

Nodding graciously, Tom got to his feet.

Potter stared at the door long after Bedworth shut it behind him. He *would* be admitting responsibility if he sent his men to watch the Orchid at the moment.

Unwrapping a half-melted Twix he kept for emergencies in his top drawer, he shoved it in his mouth and chewed noisily.

Bedworth was right. Why should he put his deals on hold for something that might never happen? He had suppliers waiting on Thursday's delivery and not only would he lose money if he didn't honour those, but he'd also lose reputation. And that was not happening.

He wasn't mental, though. It was still plausible the Stokers had seen his note and would come after him, but until he got wind of that, he'd make sure everywhere was manned and watched at all times.

Potter picked up the phone. The first thing to do was cancel the order for scouts to go to the Orchid. This time, he'd make sure the message got through in time. And then he'd work out how to oversee the delivery without losing hands on deck.

Linda made out to the lady bringing in the tray of tea and a pink fluted plate holding an assortment of overpriced biscuits that she was okay with Mickey being in the room. She also acted suitably distressed, like she would have had she just been informed of her son's death.

Mickey had been here for longer than allowed under the hawk-like watch of Mrs Brunswick, especially when bringing distressing news at a crucial part in her recovery, so the staff would be primed to keep a vigilant eye for hints of anything to set back her progress. And that was one thing Linda was not having under any circumstances – even one in the shape of Mickey Devlin.

She was getting out next week to rebuild her life and get back in contact with the children she had left who were young enough for her presence still to count. She'd play whatever game was required to ensure that happened.

The other very pressing thing to achieve, short of hearing of Tom Bedworth's final demise, was making it up to Sam and Seb for not doing what was required when it was asked of her. In a weird twist of fate, Mickey Devlin might have just enabled at least *one* of those things to come to fruition.

Her immediate reaction when Mickey told her of the *real* reason for his presence and his plan was to tell him to sling his hook. She wanted to fuck him over and drop him in it like he fully deserved, but the lady interrupting with the tea had given her time to quickly weigh up her options.

Now she was going one better.

If she pulled this off, Mickey would take the bait. He'd presume her to be the same person of old and if he did, she could achieve all the things she'd promised herself and even the score on everything – good and bad.

Mickey waited until the woman left the room before helping himself to four out of the six biscuits from the plate, the glowing embers of success growing in his brain. He'd just *known* that despite Linda looking every inch a reformed character in her fancy clobber and coiffured hair, she was still Linda Matthews – the greedy, grasping, manipulative and selfish bitch he'd been stupid enough to marry.

But that was good. He was glad she hadn't changed enough to stop herself from playing into his hands. He would have slapped himself on the back, but he'd have dropped the biscuits. 'I thought you were going to blow a gasket on me then for a moment, Lin,' he grinned. 'I thought I'd got it wrong about the real you still being under there somewhere!'

Linda forced herself to laugh. 'No one changes their spots that much.' *Certainly not him...*

But *she* had. Actually, she'd never been what Mickey presumed. Life choices and necessity might have given that impression, along with a hefty daily dose of drugs, but she'd never been that person, and now was the time for the *real* Linda – the one who had barely had chance to ever see the light of day – to shine.

Leaning forward, she allowed her legs to fall slightly open, enforcing the persona Mickey recognised from old. 'So, that nasty whore, Marina, is still out there somewhere with all the cash?'

Mickey shrugged. 'I'm guessing so. But where, I'm not sure. I reckon she's still in Brum. She's never been a good daughter to us, we owe her fuck all and I want my share of the money.' He grinned widely. 'It goes without saying that I'll split it with you, so be honest – has she been to see you?'

'Damn right you'll split it,' Linda grinned. 'But no, Marina hasn't been to see me. Does she even know I'm here?'

That thought bothered Linda more than it should. Her unhinged daughter was a psycho and shouldn't have been given the gift of life. It was the one thing out of *everything* she'd messed up that she would change if she could. Marina had been evil since her first breath. Now she'd killed Grant and tried to kill Sam. She wouldn't be killing anyone else.

'I reckon she's with Dan, even though he shafted her. And to shaft her and Grant, Dan must have had help from someone. From what I can gather, that help was off a bloke from a shitty club.'

Linda hid her flinch. Mickey's words explained everything. *Shitty club? She knew whose...* Bedworth had inveigled his way into Marina's life via this Dan bloke, then?

She could barely contain her excitement. She could get them all as long as she continued fooling Mickey that she was still on his side.

'Of course, stupid cow that she is, my other privileged daughter paid for all *this*.' Linda waved her arm around the large room. 'And Sam's promised to set me up nicely when I'm out of here. Why the fuck do you think I'm having anything to do with her?' she sneered, hating herself for the lies spewing from her mouth, but they were necessary and a means to an end. *All of these bastards' ends, to be precise.* 'Sam must be thick as fuck to think that being as I gave her away once, I'd go back on my decision of getting rid of her only to end up suddenly wanting something to do with her again!'

'Something to do with the hefty wedge she's worth, by any chance?' Mickey winked.

'Your head's still screwed on, then, Mickey? And yeah, whatever happens with Marina, I'll see you right. I'm well looked after now.'

Mickey could jump for joy. He'd hit bingo. Marina need not have bothered with that bollocks with Sam. All that was required was getting Linda on side, proving his original plan was spot on. 'Right, then! Now we just need to put things in place. If Marina gets in touch in the interim, that's even better and more money for us!'

Grasping Mickey's hand made her flesh burn, but Linda held her cool. 'You'd better let me know where you're living, so I can get in contact.' *And so you can receive your payment in kind – the one you're not expecting...*

'Not sure, to be honest,' Mickey said, undecided. 'I've been staying at a flat in Bearwood. It's Marina's and an utter shithole, so I was planning to find somewhere else.' He frowned. 'But now we're in this together, maybe I'll stay there in case she comes back?'

In this together? Linda thought savagely. *Were they fuck!* 'That's probably the best idea. How can I reach you, though?'

Standing up, Mickey grinned. 'Don't you worry about that. There's no phone or owt, but I'll check in with you here every day. Put me on the list of approved visitors, so the Hitlers here don't hassle me.'

Leaning down, he kissed Linda on the cheek. 'I'd best make tracks. Jeez, Lin, we can skim so much off this daughter of yours. I'm so glad we're on the same page.'

'Yeah, me too,' Linda smiled. She waited until Mickey had left the room before she scrubbed her face at the exact place his venomous lips had touched.

As soon as the nurse doing the medication rounds turned up,

she'd demand to use the phone and call Sam. Hopefully, Mickey would be the ticket to lead her daughter and Seb to what they wanted – what *she* wanted.

Only then would she feel she'd halfway paid back the massive debt she owed Samantha.

36

Last night's shift behind the bar had offered Tina a much-needed change of scenery from the confines of her room, but it had also brought with it the spiralling panic of being around people she didn't know, including members of the public.

Such was her steadily growing angst, over the course of the evening she'd dropped several glasses. The other bar staff had been decent about it – *overly* decent, perhaps, no doubt under strict orders from Sam to cut her some slack, but Tina's nervousness had been the least of her problems. She'd been unable to stop her mind from replacing virtually every man's face she saw with Tom's or Dan's.

By the time the last customer had left after what felt like a year, Tina had reached breaking point. All the night had achieved was to fuel her desperate need to leave this place, these people and this city.

Actually, that wasn't *all* the long night had achieved. Being in the casino had given her the opportunity to look for ways of getting out of it. None of which she'd found until it became obvious. *And that's what she was doing now.*

Tina's heart thumped as she lifted a crate of bottled lager from a shelf in the stock room of the massive cellar. She needed a prop, otherwise she'd be questioned.

Shivering, she glanced about her and hummed a tune to distract her from being convinced she could hear Bedworth calling her name. The cellar was as claustrophobic as the attic where she'd found her mother's body. It took all of her concentration, as well as another chorus of 'Smells Like Teen Spirit', to override lobbing the crates to the stone floor and throwing herself on shattered glass in the hope that it slashed her jugular.

Instead, she made her way back up to one of the many bars in preparation for restocking for tonight's shift – one which, if all went well, she had no intention of fulfilling.

Shifting the weight of the crate in her arms, she pulled at the door. All she could do was hope there weren't too many people about and the ones who were there were all so busy with their own tasks they wouldn't bother noticing anything *she* might be doing.

Walking across the polished floor, Tina's heels clacked on the wood, each step banging in her head like a hammer on an anvil.

'You okay with that?'

Tina swung around, the crate threatening to fall from her straining arms. She looked at the man stocking one of the refrigerators. 'Yes, thanks,' she spluttered, determined not to let her fear override her. She had one chance and couldn't mess it up.

Moving behind the bar, she placed the crate down and started stacking the contents in the opposite fridge, forcing herself to make conversation with the nearest bartender.

There were more people here than she'd realised; cleaners polishing tabletops, people squirrelling about ensuring everything was replenished and tip-top, ready for tonight. The place was a hive of activity, but busy enough for people to be diverted with their own tasks if she was lucky. *And quick enough...*

Wracking her brain for the instructions that she'd tried so desperately to memorise last night whilst being walked through the many processes she was expected to follow with her newly allotted job, Tina finished unloading the bottles.

Taking a deep breath, she glanced at the nearest bartender, now a safe distance away the other side of the bar. She gestured to the row of tills along the back wall of the bar. 'I'll do these.'

'Okay,' the man smiled. 'You remember where everything is?'

'I think so. I'll give you a shout if I get stuck.' Turning, Tina walked confidently over to a hatch concealing the chute which delivered separate bags of money acting as floats for each till. She turned the key in the lock. *Please let the money have been sent*, she thought, praying she hadn't timed her plan incorrectly.

Sure her heart must be audible from the other side of the room, Tina opened the hatch, relieved to see the bags in situ. Using the mirrored panel above to check everyone was concentrating on things other than her, she lifted the tray and secured the hatch back in place.

She walked to the first till and entered the combination to release the drawer. With a 'ding', the drawer flew open and she quickly filled the bare sections with the relevant notes and coins, mentally totting up that each float contained around four hundred pounds.

She'd only need one of these.

Making fast work of the first till, she moved on to the next and then the next.

It was only on the sixth till that she slipped a bag of money into her pocket, before spending an equal amount of time fiddling with the empty drawer, then shutting it to move on to the next till.

Willing her hands to stop shaking and acting every bit as guilty as she felt, she ignored the urge to check whether anyone was watching and continued filling the remaining tills, putting all of the floats in their correct place.

By the time anyone noticed one till was missing a float, she'd be long gone.

Placing the now empty tray back into the hatch, Tina crossed the room. 'See you later on, guys,' she said briskly, stopping herself from breaking into a run. 'I'm off to get myself spruced up ready for the shift.'

Amidst a chorus of friendly 'See you laters', Tina left the bar, the bag of money burning in her pocket. She walked down the corridor as quickly as possible, sure she was surrounded by a glowing neon aura spelling out the word 'thief'.

Passing the steps leading to where she should be heading, she continued, confident the way was clear to return to the cellar and through the fire escape that would now be unlocked, ready for the empties. She was almost home and dry.

Rounding the last corner, she walked slap bang into someone. 'Oh my God!' she shrieked.

Holding Tina by her shoulders, Andrew frowned. 'What are you doing?'

Tina felt like screaming. *Andrew Stoker?* She tried to drag some words of explanation from her mouth, but her voice box remained stuck, her mouth hanging open as waves of this man's distrust washed over her in a torrent.

'Are you okay?' Andrew eyed Tina suspiciously. 'You shouldn't be down here.'

'I – I...' Tina faltered. *Shit! Quickly, think.* 'I – I must have got lost. I was told to fetch two crates of lager for the bar. I must have taken the wrong corridor. It all looks the same to me. I'm sorry, I...'

'Who told you to do that?' Andrew frowned. 'Women shouldn't be lifting two crates on their own. We always send birds in pairs. Who gave that order?'

Tina's mouth flapped once again. 'Erm. I – I don't know every-one's names. I...'

'Okay, well, don't worry about it for now,' Andrew said, gesturing for Tina to move in the opposite direction. 'I'll have words and remind everyone in the bar what the rules are.'

'I... erm, I don't want to get anyone into trouble,' Tina blath-ered, hovering as she reached the staircase she should have taken.

'It's fine. You don't want to give anyone reason to suspect you, do you?' Andrew held Tina's eyes for long enough for her to read his meaning loud and clear. *Like everyone suspected her. Of everything...*

Desperate to get away, Tina nodded, then skittered up the staircase.

Around the corner of the landing, she waited, listening for Andrew Stoker's footsteps to fade away. The minute they disap-peared, she'd retrace her steps. This time, she would be reaching that back door and getting through it.

* * *

'They'll keep in line,' Kevin said, wanting to give Sam assurance that, judging by her expression, she needed. 'You dealt with their reaction well.'

Sam nodded, believing otherwise. She hadn't dealt with it well at all. In fact, all she'd achieved was to refuel the original notion that she wasn't capable of handling situations like this. And that riled her more than anything.

The deep-seated need to hold off delivering payback to the bastards who had murdered one of her men was becoming harder to swallow by the second.

She didn't know the Ross firm. She'd heard of them, but didn't *know* them. She didn't even know what the leader, let alone any of his underlings, looked like and that only made her feel even more impotent.

Kevin stepping in to quell the growing discontent had done little to help her confidence either. In many respects, she felt as hopeless as when she'd first stepped into her father's shoes amongst a sea of mistrust and lack of faith. It was not a good place to be and because of how things had improved lately, not some-where she'd thought to be again. It just showed nothing was set in stone – none more so than her premature assumption of there being light at the end of the tunnel.

'I knew I should have been present at that bloody meeting,' Seb snarled, his anger that Sam and her firm were taking the hit for his issues sparking. 'I'd have made it clear what would happen to anyone who felt it acceptable to talk back to you.'

'Wouldn't that have gone down well!' Sam snapped. 'Here's Sam's boyfriend – the one everyone thinks she's sold out to and who's taking over the firm because she's so inane!' The minute the words left her mouth, she regretted them. 'Sorry... I shouldn't have said that.'

Andrew cleared his throat to break the mounting atmosphere. 'We should have sent one of our men, rather than an Orchid enforcer. It would have avoided this.'

'So one of *our* men could be awaiting burial instead?' Neil cried. 'No one should have copped it. The Rosses are the ones who fucked this up, no one else.'

Sam nodded, her eyes moving from Seb's burning glare. They were all angry – *more* than angry. Seb already blamed himself and now she'd corroborated that. If it hadn't been for the shit concerning people connected with her in the first place, Seb wouldn't be in the horrible position he was. The urge for retaliation on Potter Ross and his cronies beat stronger in her veins. If her men didn't believe she could put this right, they were very much mistaken. 'Maybe we should discuss the details for Thursday instead?'

Seb nodded. Sam was angry, but not as angry as him. It was a blatant message from those Wolverhampton scum and he would make them pay dearly. 'I couldn't have chosen to rip off a better candidate with this heist,' he muttered. 'Forget not giving them an inkling we're behind this, like we decided. I want to make sure they know *exactly* who did it.'

'And there's been no sign of them watching us at all?' Kevin asked. 'Anyone would expect retaliation after laying claim to something in such a direct manner. That note and what was done to Stu couldn't have been more obvious!'

'Nope, nothing. It's like they reckon we haven't put two and two together, when they know we must have,' Andrew frowned. 'Perhaps they've discovered our plans and are setting us up?'

Sam looked up, startled. She too had thought that at least one sighting of a Ross scout around the area was guaranteed. It was weird. If this was a setup, the Stokers and *all* of them were walking into a huge trap. She caught Seb's eye. 'How feasible is that?'

Seb shrugged. 'Anything's possible, but it changes nothing. The heist is still going ahead. Either the docks will be swarming with Rosses or they haven't a clue. Maybe they believe us to be unaware of the historic details of their father's demise?'

'On the upside, our contact at the docks is 100 per cent kosher, so we don't need to worry about that,' Andrew said. 'He touched base today and the switch is set and ready. We just need the lorry in situ on Thursday and it's done.'

'That's also arranged,' Neil confirmed. 'The driver's worked for us many times before and can be trusted. I've also set up ten big deals with very eager customers for Friday. They will pull us in a straight £5 million.'

Seb grinned and turned to Sam. 'That will cover the rebuild, so you see, this will soon be put right and then we can move on dealing with the rest of the fuckers!'

Sam nodded. *Then what else could they do but hope?* 'Okay then and wh...' Interrupted by the sudden ringing of her desk phone, she frowned. 'I'm sorry. I don't know why a call has been put through during our meeting.' She snatched up the receiver. 'I'm in a meeting. Can't this w...' Frowning, she listened carefully. 'Okay, thank you.'

With a thunderous expression, she replaced the receiver before stabbing more numbers into the phone.

'What is it?' Seb frowned.

'I'll tell you in a minute when I find out if it's true and connected wi... Hello? Yes. Is she there?' Sam's face paled further. 'When? Okay... I see...'

'What's going on?'

'A float has gone missing from one of the tills. It's only £400, but that's not the point.' Standing up, Sam grabbed her bag. 'The bar manager said Tina did the floats for tonight's shift. I just checked with the rooms upstairs and she's not there...'

Seb sighed loudly. 'I *knew* she couldn't be fucking trusted!'

'That's *your* opinion, not mine,' Sam cried. 'Tina wouldn't do that.'

Seb raised an eyebrow. 'Wouldn't she...?'

'No, she wouldn't!' Sam barked. Tina wouldn't have done this, she was sure of it.

'I saw her sneaking towards the back cellar earlier and had to send her off in the right direction.' Andrew looked at Seb pointedly. 'She's done a runner.'

'Tina's too bloody frightened of Bedworth catching up with her to do that. I'll go up now and find her. I expect it's a simple misunderstanding.' *It had better be...* 'Oh for God's sake!' Sam snatched up the ringing phone. 'What? No, Elaine. I'm in a meeting and something's come up. Take a message. No! I don't care who it is!'

Slamming the phone down, Sam stormed out of the office to find Tina, leaving the Stokers to look at each other in resignation.

37

'I'm surprised too,' Potter admitted, snatching the bacon sandwich from Mark's hand. 'I fully expected the Stokers to have been in contact by now, one way or the other.'

As a glob of brown sauce dropped onto his shirt, his eyes tracked to his desk drawer, the knowledge of the double-barrelled shotgun that yesterday he'd placed within easy reaching distance acting as welcome reassurance. A bit like the gun next to his bed. And the one in the sitting room...

He hadn't left anything to chance, fully expecting those fuckers to have turned up, if not by close of play yesterday, then during the small hours. It would be just the Stokers' style to creep around under the cover of darkness like the sly, spineless twats they'd always been.

But there had been nothing. No hint of anything. And reports from all over his many businesses echoed the same findings.

'Why do you think nothing's happened?' Mark asked, resentfully eyeing the bacon sandwich that had once been his. 'You seemed certain they'd come for us yesterday. Do you think I was right and that they don't know it was us?'

'Perhaps,' Potter sneered. The chances of Mark *ever* being right on anything were slim, but in this instance, he could be. Stoker might have missed the note or it could have fallen off the body. It even could be that they weren't aware of how that old bastard, Malcolm Stoker, had delivered back his butchered father. It was too early to jump to conclusions; however, things looked promising. And if that *was* the case, then his original plans would still work out. Still, it wouldn't pay to let his guard down. 'We must maintain a full quota of men to protect the empire,' he said, glaring at his brother.

'What are we doing about the container tomorrow then? Shall I get in contact with Silvo and tell him to move it to a warehouse until we can arrange pick-up?'

Potter dragged his cuff across his mouth, leaving a trail of bacon grease and a smudge of sauce over the well-worn cotton. 'No way! We have orders to fulfil. That's why I wanted to speak to you.'

He lounged back in his chair, like what he was about to say was a run-of-the-mill comment. He didn't want Mark getting any hint that he'd been awake half the night arguing with himself over the injustice of having to make this decision. 'You'll take delivery of the container, then drive it back here.'

Mark's mouth dropped open. '*Me*? You want me to do that?'

'That's what I said, wasn't it?' Potter scowled. Mark didn't have to make such a fucking song and dance about it. In normal circumstances, he or one of the others would oversee it, like usual. Anyone but Mark.

'Thanks, Pot! I'm honoured!' Mark gushed, beaming so widely to have finally proved himself worthy, he looked like a strange version of the man in the moon.

Potter waved his hand dismissively. 'Yeah, well, don't assume it will be a regular thing. I need every person possessing brains to remain on site.'

Mark's face fell. 'Oh! I thou...'

'Don't think, that's dangerous where you're concerned,' Potter muttered. Even Mark could manage this one. This particular run had been done so many times there was little to do, short of sitting in the lorry whilst the trailer was hitched up and then driving back up the M5. A *chimp* could do it. 'Even *you* can't get this fucking wrong! You have an HGV licence, so you might as well use the fucking thing. And take Bedworth with you.'

'What?' Mark folded his arms. 'There's no way I'm going anywhere with him!'

'Yes, you are.' Potter leant forward, his eyes narrowing menacingly. 'I haven't got enough resources tomorrow to watch him 24/7 as well as protect us here and I'm not giving him a chance to move the cash I know he's got fucking stashed. You know – the stash you failed to find?'

'But...'

'But nothing! Bedworth won't fuck things up. The silly bastard believes he's getting a cut, so he won't want anything going pear-shaped.' *Furthermore, the bastard couldn't do a runner with the coke with Mark there.*

Mark paced around in agitation. 'I'll be stuck with him for hours! You know I fucking hate him!'

'You'll just have to put up with it.' Screwing the greasy sandwich wrapper into a ball, Potter threw it to bounce off the side of Mark's head. 'Now piss off and do something useful.'

* * *

Sam wanted to take Seb up on his offer of spending longer in bed, but her head wasn't in the right place. She knew deep down that he'd gained no enjoyment from being right about Tina's disappearance, but that the girl's actions had subsequently exposed her belief in the woman to be bad judgement had smarted.

Grabbing Sam around the waist, Seb pulled her against him. 'Are you *sure* I can't tempt you...?' Surely she could take it on the chin that she'd made a bad call?

'Very sure!' Sam squirmed out of Seb's grip, becoming more resentful of her defensive behaviour by the second.

'Look, Princess. Don't take it so personally. Sometimes we're all guilty of giving people too much leeway.'

'Another dig?' Sam barked, her eyes flashing. Her irritation wasn't just down to Tina doing a flit – it was more than that.

'What's the matter with you?' Seb snapped, his patience wearing thin. 'Don't take your shit out on me!'

Sam swung around. 'This isn't about *my* shit! Yes, I wanted to give the girl a hand, being as she was so scared and has had such a crap life, but you're missing one major thing...'

'And what's that, aside from your need to help waifs and strays?' Seb folded his arms over his chest. He loved that Sam was one of the few who stood up to him, but she infuriated him when she was like this.

'Who will testify for the validity of Tina's statement if she's not there to do it herself? Have you thought of that? Why do you think I wanted her close at hand?'

The smile that always melted Sam's heart formed on Seb's handsome face. 'It won't come to that. The cops know it was Bedworth. Besides, it won't get to court.' His eyes twinkled. 'Because I'll have killed the cunt long before that happens.'

'We haven't even found him yet!' Sam countered.

Seb succeeded in pulling Sam back towards him this time. 'Nor have they...'

The stress and tension melted from Sam as she sagged in Seb's arms. 'I hope you're right.'

'I usually am!' Tilting up Sam's face, he traced his thumb across her bottom lip. 'Now, come back to bed.'

'I really can't. I need to find Tina. She can't have gone far.'

Seb rolled his eyes and laughed. 'Oh my God! You're so determined to be Mother Teresa, aren't you? I thought you were seeing Linda today?'

Sam pressed her lips against his. 'I was, but that will have to wait. Mother Teresa needs to find Tina.'

Unlike everybody else, she didn't believe Tina had turned her over. It was obvious the girl's terror of being found by Bedworth was greater than risking the ire of the Reynolds by lifting money and disappearing without a word. She had to make sure the girl was okay.

* * *

Marina had been bored shitless until she'd taken herself down to the hotel spa and salon. A thoroughly pleasant afternoon of being pampered was just what the doctor ordered and lying on the bed having a massage had relaxed her enough to step back and look at the big picture.

Three days she'd gone round in circles, getting herself het up to new heights of frustration about hanging around waiting for a suitable opening to complete everything she'd set her heart on. She'd been so hellbent on getting things done, she'd been unable to see that she stood in much better stead by chilling out, kicking back and waiting.

So much time in her life had been spent fixated with doing things *immediately* that she'd made herself blind to other options. In hindsight, had she taken a step back beforehand on several occasions to weigh up things properly, she wouldn't have ended up missing the things she had.

This way of looking at things was strange, but being in this lovely place made it more palatable. *And clearer.* Now she no longer had to dress like a stripper or associate with the dregs of society not worthy of sharing the same air as her. Staying in a place well out of the way of the Reynolds' and Stokers' radar, she could be herself. She could think.

And she had thought.

Hard.

She also had enough money to last until hell froze over.

Sipping at the cocktail specially concocted by the eager-to-please barman, Marina smiled sweetly, then helped herself to a complimentary copy of the *Mail* from the rack of newspapers.

Making her way back to her corner table, she took her time flicking through the pages, knowing her real intention was to stumble across a photograph of Samantha Reynold to wind her relaxed brain up a notch. It felt abnormal not to be chomping at the bit, but in other respects it was refreshing. She didn't have to worry about Dan. Or Mickey. Her useless father was up the creek without a paddle and would have no doubt scurried back to London like the blackhearted worm he was.

He'd lost. That was the payment he got for being a lazy bastard. *Fuck all.*

Snickering to herself, Marina scoured the paper.

Nope. Nothing about Samantha or lover boy. *Maybe they were dead?*

Her mouth flattened, hoping that wasn't the case. It would take away the enjoyment when the time came.

Closing the newspaper, Marina almost bypassed the front page, but abruptly stopped on seeing it.

URGENT WARRANT FOR LOCAL MAN'S ARREST

West Midlands Police have issued an urgent warrant for a

man wanted in connection to several recent incidents – all of which are extremely serious.

Thomas Bedworth, (49), last known to be the owner of the Aurora club on the Hagley Road before its closure via a court order, is wanted in helping police with their enquiries.

Recent information links Mr Bedworth to a number of major unsolved incidents and he is urged to come forward as soon as possible.

Marina's hand flew to her mouth to stop the squeak of excitement. She quickly glanced around the bar, double-checking she hadn't uttered a loud noise, before avidly digesting the remainder of the article.

Members of the public are not to approach this man, but are asked to contact the police if they have any information as to his whereabouts.

Mr Bedworth is described as being approximately 5 feet 11 inches, of stocky build, with short greying hair and blue, close-set eyes.

Marina downed her cocktail. It wasn't like she couldn't afford another.

But *was* this good news?

Not all of the money had been in Dan's possession when she'd ripped it from the cupboard the thick bastard had done such a crap job of hiding it in, so Bedworth must still have the rest.

That money was *hers*, not Tom's, the old pervert.

He must have done a runner and was at this very moment lying on a sun-drenched beach in a revolting pair of green Speedos, safe from the arms of the law, as well as *her*.

Or he too was lying face down in a shallow grave somewhere.

But being as she hadn't had the fortune to lay claim to that prize, the latter was unlikely. Not whilst the Stokers were so busy rebuilding their poxy empire. It was even less likely that Bedworth should still be skulking around Birmingham. If he was, then wouldn't it be a dreadful shame if the cops caught up with him before he hopped on a plane to live out the rest of his days in obscurity...?

Marina shrugged, proud of her new level of resolve. It was unlikely she'd recoup the remainder of that cash and equally unlikely there would be an opportunity to part her sister from her life as a consolation prize. At least for the foreseeable future.

She was better off sticking with the large amount Dan had kindly 'gifted' her, rather than wasting it biding her time here, only for the high chance of being taken out in the crossfire when she showed her hand.

Deciding against ordering a further cocktail, Marina rose from the table, her mind made up.

She'd return to her room, have a nice long, relaxing soak in the bath and first thing in the morning, she'd get on the phone to the travel agents and see what flights were available and to where.

This period of quiet reflection over the last couple of days had brought her to the most sensible conclusion. There was no point in beating a dead horse.

She would leave until the heat had died down and all suspicion surrounding her had evaporated. Then, and when the time was right, she would return to complete her mission.

38

'You're not trying to blag me, are you, Linda?' Mickey studied Linda carefully. 'You said Sam was coming in again today and so I'd hoped you'd have news?'

'I'm not blagging you,' Linda snapped. 'If you think I'd cut you out after what we agreed on yesterday, then maybe there isn't any point in this...'

'Hey, hey!' Mickey backtracked. 'I didn't mean it like that. I'm just not good with patience.'

He noted the position of Linda's hand in relation to the emergency buzzer again, resenting that she had the power to pull the rug from under his feet at any time and drop him in it to the police. *Or worse.*

But no matter how much it felt like gargling with a mantrap, he had to keep himself in line and quit with the accusations. He reached for Linda's hand. 'I really didn't mean to sound like I don't have faith in you. We go back a long way, Lin.'

Far too long, Linda thought acidly, pulling away from his touch. She'd assumed Mickey wouldn't turn up again. Being told ten minutes ago that she had a visitor, Linda's relief was astronomical, presuming it to be Sam. Since leaving the urgent message last night at the Orchid, she'd done nothing but pace the room, waiting for her daughter to return her call. She hadn't, but even worse – Sam hadn't arrived today as planned either. That alone was worrying.

Sam always did what she said, unless there was a *very* good reason. Linda didn't want to think of what possibilities might have stopped the visit. She had to get this new information about Marina, Dan and Tom Bedworth over to Sam, so she and Seb could act on it.

Even thinking of Tom's name made Linda go cold and shaky.

Remembering Mickey's scrutinising presence, Linda pretended to accept his apology. 'Yeah, okay, just forget it.' She clasped her hands together, acting casual. 'Sam didn't come today. I guess something came up. No doubt she'll be here tomorrow instead.'

'Shit!' Mickey hissed. 'What about the groundwork we discussed – the stuff you said you'd do? Buttering up the girl to get more dosh?'

'I *will* do it,' Linda lied. 'I'm getting out of here next week, remember? Sam's already promised to buy me a new place and give me a shedload of money to help get me sorted.' *She had to keep Mickey reeled in.*

'That's great!' Mickey's eyes lit up. 'How much exactly?'

'I don't know, but it will be a nice lump sum and there'll be more after that too.' *Whilst Mickey thought there was something in it for him, he'd stick around.*

'Why don't you sell the drum she buys then we can split the cash?' Mickey suggested.

'I've already thought of that,' Linda agreed. 'It's bound to be a massive place too! Sam's a stuck-up cow and wouldn't dream of buying anything less than spangly and overpriced. It's all about social standing with people like her. With that money, we could buy two places – one each?'

'Or we could buy a small drum between us and spend the remainder,' Mickey winked. 'We're still legally married, Lin, and we got on well enough back in the day to produce two children, so why not pick up where we left off?'

Linda pretended to consider this ridiculous suggestion. *As if she'd ever touch this loser with a bargepole again.* More likely, whilst the promise of ongoing funds was on offer, he planned to attach himself to her like a limpet. 'You know, I've always had a soft spot for you, Mick.'

Mickey stood up. 'I'll be back tomorrow then. Same time?'

Linda frowned. 'You'd best leave coming tomorrow. You can't risk being here when Sam comes and I don't know what time that will be. We don't want her thinking you're hanging around with the intention of fleecing me, do we? I mean, *I* know you're not, but having not seen you before and then you suddenly turning up like this, she might...'

Mickey paused halfway to the door. 'Hmm... In that case, I'd best tell you where I can be found in case you need to send urgent word.' He scrawled his address on a piece of letterheaded notepaper from the writing desk. 'I won't be staying there much longer. I've got to leave before the rent's due again. I'll come to see you on Friday, okay?'

'See you then.' Linda's smile remained in place until Mickey left the room, before snatching the notepaper from the desk, carefully folding it and placing it in her pocket.

* * *

'This will cheer you up!' Seb plonked the box of invites that had arrived from the printers down on the table. He pulled a folded cream card embossed with gold lettering from the box. With a wink, he flicked the luxurious gold tassel attached to the corner. 'See! Even this tasselly thing trembles under my skilled fingers.'

Taking the card, Sam wanted to be happy. She wanted to feel overjoyed that the wedding to the man she loved could go ahead like originally planned. And she *was*, but the unresolved issues and hypothetical outcomes hanging in the balance meant too much was on a thin line to think too far ahead without the threat of a marred future. The timeline was tight and her recent optimism was sliding precariously down a steep gorge.

Since the damaging knock to her confidence from the scathing reaction of a big percentage of her workforce, and with what she'd discovered today, she was even more concerned by the implications if things she was counting on to pan out in a certain way didn't.

This heist; Marina still being at large; the despicable Tom Bedworth; Trevor – or *Grant's* death – the brother she'd never got the chance to know... Finding that body of the man who must be the instigator for the robbery and a precursor for ruining Seb's livelihood, along with the trumped-up and wrong allegations about him that could return with a vengeance since Tina had disappeared... And most recently, one of her best enforcers being mutilated and left like rubbish...

The list was endless...

Feeling the unwanted burn of tears at the back of her eyes, Sam ploughed her concentration into the beautifully printed invitation to the future she desperately wanted, but which now hung on a diminishing thread of gossamer.

As Seb's arms snaked around her waist, Sam thanked her lucky stars that regardless of what had happened, she still had him. She didn't know any other person in the whole world who could understand the pressure she was under or the life they lived. Only a man who had caused mayhem in this abnormal path they'd been born

into could understand, support and be there for her through all
of it.

For however long he was here, that was...

What if Seb was arrested again? What if he got sent down for
something he hadn't done – or for the things he *had* done...

And tomorrow... She was *dreading* tomorrow.

'Sam, you need to forget about Tina.' Seb held her close, his
deep voice vibrating through her body. 'You're not responsible for
everybody. I know you're worried, but she's made her choice.'

'But what if *you* need her? What if this goes to court?' Sam
cried. She knew she'd said that before, but it plagued her. Yes, she
was hurt that Tina had left without a word, despite understanding
why the girl had stolen from her, but it didn't stop the feelings of
being gullible, incompetent and pathetic from crowding her mind
like being trapped in a pit of snakes.

'My enforcers were right. Everyone thinks I'm useless and
clearly I am,' she said hollowly.

Seb turned Sam around to face him. 'Don't start that shit again,'
he said sternly. 'You're not any of those things. I love you beyond
anything, but I will not mollycoddle you or put up with your self-
pity.'

Sam itched to snap at Seb, but he was right. She *was* feeling
sorry for herself and *that* was pathetic. 'I'm sorry. It's been a bad
couple of days.' She bit her lip. 'What if something goes wrong at
the heist tomorrow. I can't face the thought of losing you...'

Seb cupped Sam's face and kissed her. 'Nothing's going to
happen. Everything will be fine. You know Neil's lined the deals up
ready for Friday, so by the weekend everything will be done and
dusted and then the only way is up.'

And he hoped with all his heart that would be true. It was clear
everything was now weighing heavily on Sam.

The guaranteed war with the Ross firm was another thing to

add to that growing list, but he would ensure it was as stress free and achieved as quickly as possible. As would concentrating on ending the man who all of these problems stemmed from.

Sam would breathe easier after that and then, all being well, he could revert back to his original plan of stepping away from the riskier sides of the business. There might have been a convoluted detour to reach this aim, but he would achieve it. And it would be soon.

Seb took Sam's hand and pulled her down to sit at the table. 'Come on, let's decide who'll receive an invite. We'll post them after the last deal to shift this incoming coke closes on Friday. How about that for a plan?'

Finally smiling, Sam pulled an invitation from the box, feeling more comfortable than she had ten minutes ago.

39

Tom justified being stuck in a lorry cab on the M5 with Mark Ross with the promise of what was to come. But every time the prick made a dig at his expense, it only increased his desire to lean over, open the driver's door and push the thick bastard into the path of the traffic.

He was sure he could drive this artic to Bristol himself. It couldn't be *that* different from driving a seven and a half tonner and he'd driven one of those a few times in the past.

As Mark continued singing in a horrifically out of tune voice to some crap on Radio 1 playing for the fourth time in the hour they'd been on the road, Tom clenched his fists. The retarded moron was only singing it because he'd made the stupid mistake of mentioning how much he hated the bloody song.

Just concentrate, Tom thought. It was important to remember this was an unexpected and brilliant turn-up for the books.

He'd done a sterling job of talking Potter into putting extra vigilance into the home front and successfully steering him away from casing the Stokers and bringing further complications to his door, but he hadn't dreamt his words of wisdom would lead to being sent to take delivery of the container full of what would be his compensation.

It almost bypassed Dan turning him over, but only almost. That still grated on every neuron in his brain.

Still, who would benefit most from this?

Not Dan...

As soon as he'd got that lump of metal full of gear on the back of this wagon, got back to Wolverhampton and filched several kilos of coke on the quiet for his own benefit, he was home and dry. If Potter thought he would swallow the pittance of the percentage offered for his outlay and trouble, then the man had shit for brains.

A grin slid over Tom's face as he glanced at the clock attached with Blu Tack to the dashboard. Only half an hour until Bristol docks and then he was on the home run. Never again would he have to put up with this lobotomised freaklet.

'La la la la la laaaah!' Mark shouted the hated tune into Tom's ear. 'You don't like this one, do you?' Contrary to what he'd expected, the enforced proximity with Bedworth was more enjoyable than he'd thought. Winding the bloke up was funny and passed the time. 'I might have to stop for a piss in a minute,' he said. 'Do you need to go?'

'Just hang on until we get there,' Tom snapped, the thought of an extra ten minutes wasted at the services more than he could bear. 'Potter wants us back by five to allow time to sort the gear out,' he reasoned, hoping the mention of Mark's brother would be enough to make him rethink his urge to stop. 'We need to get this done as soon as possible.'

When Mark indicated to take the slip road off the M5 for Michaelwood services, Tom realised with irritation that his effort had fallen on deaf ears.

* * *

'When will Mrs Brunswick be back?' Linda asked. It was important not to lose her temper at the agency nurse, but that was easier said than done when someone unlikely to have a life as complicated as *her* said the only person in this whole place with authority to change discharge dates was still off sick.

Her eyes narrowed. It would be easier to knock the woman out and storm from the building, but doing that would ruin her chance of getting visiting rights with her younger children, let alone custody.

With only a week left before leaving here billed as clean, cured and officially capable of joining society without having to explain herself, she had to play by the book.

And that's what money brought – the ability to bypass the system, ensuring the tattoo of 'loser' was not applied.

Linda would be eternally grateful that Sam had arranged things so she would not have to constantly look back on her tainted life. Even more reason why she was stuck between a rock and a hard place. Apart from being worried sick something had befallen her daughter, she had to relay what she knew before the trail went cold. But how could she do that if her daughter was unreachable?

Linda continued to pace the confines of her room, knowing she was being watched. She forced a smile at the frosty-faced nurse, who seemed to be forming the opinion that Linda's irritation and angst signified her recovery was not as finalised as they believed.

Linda's lips pursed. She would never use drugs again – that was a *fact*. 'What about a day release instead?' she suggested.

'I can't see how I can arrange that either, unless it was an emergency.'

'But it *is* an emergency!' Linda blurted, immediately regretting it.

The nurse eyed Linda suspiciously and jotted something down on her pad. 'Unless you can tell me what this "emergency" is, you know it's against policy to sanction it.' She tapped her pen in an annoying rhythm. 'You seem reluctant to embellish on the reasons, so...'

Linda scowled. *She couldn't, could she?* If she told this woman what was going on and why, then more than 'agitated' and 'wants to leave' would be recorded in that notebook. More like 'paranoid, delusional and unsafe'.

This old boot looked just the type to enter that sort of thing into the system regardless and that really would shaft any chance of putting her life back together.

'Hopefully Mrs Brunswick will be back after the weekend, so you can ask then.' The nurse smiled – the action more of a grimace. 'Besides, it's rather silly making a song and dance about this when you've only got seven days left here.'

Linda inwardly seethed. 'Can I at least have an extra telephone call then?' *Sam must be around by now?*

The nurse waggled her finger like she was disciplining a disobedient child. 'Linda, you know you've already had today's allotted phone call.'

Yeah, and that had been pointless too... Wait... 'I need to ring my daughter. Perhaps you should ask your colleagues who she is...'

Yes, she'd resort to name dropping again, but needs must.

* * *

Tom thought by remaining in the lorry, Mark might hurry up, believing he may harbour the notion to drive away. He knew Potter insisted on him being watched at all times, which explained why he'd accompanied this bonehead on the run.

He *would* have considered driving off and leaving Mark in the services, most likely playing on an arcade machine, if that idea wasn't scuppered by the drongo having the unexpected foresight to take the ignition keys with him.

No, Tom was stuck here, whether he liked it or not.

He stared out of the window through the drizzle towards the services. Still no sign of Mark. *For fuck's sake! How long did it take to have a piss?*

Snatching the *Birmingham Mail* from where it was shoved down the front of the dashboard, he scowled. *It was yesterday's...*

Unfolding it, his stomach plummeted to his feet on reading the front-page headline emblazoned in huge letters.

Fuck. FUCK!

Mark clambered into the cab, making Tom jump out of his seat. He saw Tom's glazed expression and the sweat beading on his forehead. 'Christ, I wasn't that long! What the fuck's the matter with you?'

Following Tom's rigid gaze, Mark scanned the headline and the first few lines of the article and burst into loud guffaws of laughter. 'Who's been a naughty boy, then? Oh dear, Bedworth. It seems you're a wanted man! I *knew* you were hiding something.' He raised an eyebrow. 'I wonder if they're offering a reward...'

'Fuck off, Ross, you cock,' Tom barked. Despite not wanting to, he couldn't help but glance out of the window to see if anyone was coming towards the truck.

'Oh, come on!' Mark sneered. 'There's no photo and no one knows you here anyway.'

'How do you know?' Tom cried, his panic rising. He jerked his head back at the services. 'Go and get me a hat or something!'

'You're joking, right?' Tears of mirth ran down Mark's face, unsure when he last remembered something being so hilarious and well-deserved as Tom Bedworth being on the wanted list.

'I don't know why you think this is so fucking funny?' Tom's eyes formed narrow slits. 'We're out in public and thousands of people know me. Don't forget, you're with me, therefore you'll be seen as harbouring me and part of *everything*!'

He didn't know thousands of people at all – especially not around here, but remembering as a kid when he'd bumped into his neighbour during an especially crap camping trip in Scotland, he was taking no chances.

Mark's laughter promptly fell away. He wasn't being lumped in with Bedworth. 'What have you done, anyway?'

'None of your business!' He fished twenty pounds from his pocket. 'Just go and buy me a hat and some fucking shades. I need a disguise – *anything*. Get me a packet of fags whilst you're at it, as well.'

Leaving Mark to hurry back to the services, Tom chewed his fingernails, wondering who there was left to shop him to the police that he hadn't already got rid of.

* * *

Ten minutes after resorting to using the name-dropping technique, Linda found herself with access to the telephone for reasons given as 'just this once'.

She shrugged away the twinge of guilt for using the agency nurse's position to her advantage. This was more important. It was even *more* important since Mickey had started making noises about moving elsewhere. If he wasn't caught up with before that happened, his whereabouts would be unknown.

'Hello? Yes, Ms Reynold, please,' Linda breathed, her heart pounding. She glanced over her shoulder along the shiny corridor, making sure she had no audience. 'Still not available? Look, it's really, *really* important. I'm her... No, okay... I understand...'

Linda's mind whirred. *Now what?* 'Erm, wait! What about Mr Stoker – Sebastian? What? Oh, for fuck's sake... Sorry, I meant...

erm... When will he be back? When will any of them be back? I need to speak to one of them straight away!'

She tried her best not to explode. Sam was still absent and so were the Stokers? What the hell was going on? Something bad must have happened for none of them to be at the Orchid.

Worry fell over Linda like a shroud. 'I'll try again later. It's Linda. Yes... please tell them I called.' Replacing the handset, she leant against the wall and sighed heavily. *What was she going to do?*

'Ah! They said you were out here somewhere!'

Swinging around, Linda saw Mickey making his way down the corridor. They'd let *him* in, but not her out?

He'd said he wasn't coming today, so why was he here? He must be getting suspicious. She had to do something about this. And do it fast.

40

Maintaining an outwardly relaxed stance, Seb hid the persistent gnawing within the base of his stomach by taking long and measured drags from his cigarette.

From his seat in the van, he kept his gaze fixed on the containers being slowly winched over the dock to the holding bay – one of which his contact had instructed was the one they wanted. 'It won't be long now,' he said. 'As soon as we get the nod, we'll go and oversee it.'

'I'm still not convinced any of us should be here, let alone *all* of us! What if something kicks off back at the Orchid?' Neil said, unable to hide his worry as well as his brother was.

Seb shrugged. 'Yeah, it's not great, but after Stu was taken out, we've had no choice but to come down here blind, you know that. We don't know what those bastards are doing, but I'm fairly confident nothing will happen. Hopefully, the Rosses are hunkered down waiting for reprisals, no doubt scratching their heads wondering why we haven't come down on them like a ton of bricks.' *But after today, they'd get the message loud and clear. And this was only the start...*

He sat forward as the crane moved to lower the container holding everything needed to get his firm back where it should be, into the relevant bay. 'Here we go...'

Andrew stiffened. 'If bay nine is ours, where is the Ross one?'

'Theirs is number twenty-two.' Seb jerked his head in the direction of the end of the opposite row. 'Let's hope they have good use for washing powder, 'cos that's what they're receiving instead of dog food and coke!'

Seeing a container moving towards bay twenty-two, Andrew chuckled, despite the tense situation. 'You're sure Bob's done the switch?'

'As sure as I can be.' Seb shoved his hand down the side of his leg so his brothers wouldn't see him wiping away the sweat on his palm. 'We know things could go tits up at the last knockings, sure, but once we get the nod, let's do it.' And all he could do was pray that everything went smoothly because *everything* rested on this.

All three brothers sat stiff and alert, watching the container reach the concrete floor of bay nine, the heavy thud music to their ears.

When men moved to swap the lifting gear to what would position the container on the back of their lorry, Seb reached for the door. 'Come on,' he hissed. 'Our driver and artic will soon move into position.'

Neil's gaze flicked between the two areas of the dockyard. 'You were right! No one's around to oversee the Ross delivery...'

Andrew was about to agree, but instead frowned as an artic backed in position at bay twenty-two. 'Hang on. What have we got here?'

'Shit!' Neil gasped. 'Why hasn't our lorry been given the green light? That container came off the same time as ours. Has the switch not happened?'

'I don't know,' Seb muttered, his concentration now centred on who had arrived to collect the Rosses' delivery. He squinted into the sun. 'It's Potter Ross's brother!'

Neil peered at a second man clambering from the passenger side of the artic's cab. 'And who's that? Crocodile fucking Dundee?'

Andrew burst out laughing, seeing a man kitted out in an Australian-style hat complete with corks. 'What a fucking prick!'

'Ah!' Seb exclaimed, seeing their own artic move into position. 'And there's Bob.' Relief flooded him as his contact scratched his left ear as agreed. 'There's the sign. Time to go, fellas.'

'But what about the Ross lot?' Neil urged. 'Won't they recognise us?'

Seb jumped from the cab. 'The brother is a thick fuck and God knows who the other dickhead is. They'll be too tied up working out how to sign their names on the docket to take notice of us. Besides, what difference does it make? We're allowed to get our own deliveries and we're not in their bay, so what's it got to do with them?'

He pulled up the lapels of his jacket to protect against the bracing wind rushing in from the estuary mouth, an idea forming. It might not be feasible, but he was sure as hell going to give it a go. He wanted Potter to know he was behind this and what better way than using the opportunity which had just presented itself?

He waited for his brothers to clamber from the van. 'Make sure it's on the lorry securely, then tell the driver we'll tail him back. I'll go and deal with the paperwork.'

Walking off, Seb left his brothers, to find out if he had time to leave the ultimate calling card.

* * *

Sitting stiffly in the back of a taxi, Sam nervously picked at the hem of her skirt. She'd scoured every place she could risk going without taking one of the men as security. Being as the only people to ask such as Kev, Daz and Craig were all tied up getting the warehouse ready to receive the container, there wasn't anyone else to pull on. Not anyone who was aware of what was going on, anyway.

Even if there was, she was reticent to ask anything of people who believed she had shit for brains or was untrustworthy, like it seemed was the enforcers' general consensus.

Anger and hopelessness bubbled once again. *What a bloody mess.*

'Heading back to the Orchid, madam?'

Sam flinched at the taxi driver's voice. 'Erm, yes, please.'

It was pointless doing this today. Her mind was waylaid with what was unfolding at the docks. It was pointless doing *anything* today. Until Seb was back and everything had gone as planned, she couldn't hold down any other thought and the lack of movement from the Ross firm nagged consistently, wearing away at her already frayed nerves.

Seb and his brothers should be there by now. They might even have the container hitched up, or if things had moved fast, could even be on their way back?

Sam's heart thrummed, her temples pounding. *But if they'd been set up...*

As the taxi turned into Broad Street, Sam sat forward. Although it was premature, she'd pop into the Orchid on the off-chance there had been word from Seb. Then she'd pay Linda a visit. Her mother was no doubt fretting as Sam hadn't got the chance to go yesterday.

With any luck, concentrating on Linda would take her mind off what was happening in Bristol.

* * *

Flattening himself against the wall, Tom didn't dare breathe. He wished Mark would stop calling his bloody name. Christ, he couldn't have had worse luck. What chances were there of coming to Bristol only for the fucking Stokers to rock up to take delivery of a container?

This just proved his causality theory. If he went to the moon, then some fucker he'd last seen in 1981 would roll up saying, 'Hi, Tom, fancy seeing you here...'

But it wasn't some random bloke from 1981. It was Seb Stoker.

Tom ignored the dripping from above that plopped rhythmically onto his hat. He hadn't bought Mark's lame excuse that the only hat in the shop was *this* one. The guy was taking the piss and wanted to make him look a prick. He'd very nearly not even put it on, but the slim prospect of someone recognising him after making the headline news nagged.

Now he was more than glad he'd worn it.

Tom closed his eyes in disbelief. At first, he'd thought the Stokers were here waiting for him, but they weren't, so providing they didn't spot him, he'd be fine. Plus, he was pretty sure they didn't even know what he looked like. Nevertheless, this situation was far from comfortable.

He held his breath. Mark was no longer shouting for him, but how long should he lurk around for? It would have to at least be until the Stokers left, but that could be *ages*.

Tom hopped from foot to foot, wishing he'd used the toilet at the services when he'd had the chance. Accepting there was nothing else for it, he relieved himself against the wall, cringing with the sound of his gushing urine, sure everyone would hear and find him.

Despite the cold chill of the air, sweat ran down the back of his neck, soaking into his T-shirt.

When he finally ran the risk of coming out from behind this wall, hoping Mark hadn't buggered off without him, he'd now have to put up with the moron moaning about his lack of help the entire way back to Wolverhampton.

41

Dropping the clutch, Tom cringed as the grinding noise of the gearbox assaulted his ears. Fighting to shove the gear stick into second, he then grappled with the huge steering wheel, realising he'd drifted half across the other lane.

His sweat-drenched T-shirt stuck to the grubby plastic seat cover, only to suddenly unstick when braking at the roundabout, the urgent stopping lurching him forward in the seat.

Jesus H. Christ. He'd have nightmares about this for years.

Ignoring the blasting of angry horns, Tom trundled out into the road in front of the traffic. 'Get into bleeding gear, you bastard!' he screamed amidst more crunching sounds.

This thing was harder to drive than he'd anticipated, but only because it was an antiquated old knacker and didn't work properly. It wasn't down to *him*.

Jaw clenched, Tom careered down the road, overshooting the traffic lights. He had to get back to the yard and out of this lorry. By the time he'd passed Cirencester, his arse had gone to sleep. But there wasn't far to go now, thank God. 'Fucking aged me ten years, this has,' he muttered. 'Bastard Mark, the prick!'

What had Mark been thinking of? The fucker would just have to get the train or hitch back. Potter wouldn't be happy, but what else was he supposed to do?

Tom glanced at the clock. *An hour late.*

Bunny-hopping into the yard only to see Potter standing with his arms folded and a face like a bulldog, served to make things worse.

Tom only just managed to set the brakes before Potter yanked the door open.

'You're fucking late! What's your ex... Why the hell are *you* driving my lorry?' Potter craned his massive head around Tom. 'Where the fuck is Mark?'

Tom jumped from the cab. 'That's exactly what I'd like to know!'

'What?' Potter snarled. *If Tom had tried to pull a fast one. If he'd...*

'I don't know where Mark is. He disappeared,' Tom explained. 'I waited as long as I could, but as you wanted us back by five, I had to make the decision to leave without him.'

Potter's face grew redder. 'You left him there? How could he have just disappeared?'

'He kept running to the bogs all day. We even had to stop on the way down.' Tom shrugged. 'After the container was on the lorry, he went to sign the docket, then called for me, but when I finally got back around, there was no sign of him.'

Potter's eyes narrowed menacingly. 'Back around where? Where the fuck had *you* gone?'

Tom wiped the sweat from his forehead, so grateful that he was no longer driving that claptrap that even Potter's barking wasn't a problem. 'The fucking Stokers! I didn't want them to see me.'

Potter froze. 'The Stokers? They were there?'

'It wasn't to do with us. They were picking up a container the other side of the dock. They didn't see me.'

'And Mark? Did they see Mark?'

'No, they were doing their own thing.' *Thankfully.* 'They left before I did and once they'd gone, I came back out when Mark called.' Tom frowned. Had Mark stopped calling by that point or was it before? He couldn't remember. It didn't matter – the Stokers hadn't seen *him* and that was the main thing.

Potter stomped around the lorry, checking his men were offloading the container correctly. *Mark, the useless prick!* He was always in the shitter, that one. He'd just have to make his own way back and if he dared moan, then he'd be getting a right pasting.

But this was astounding! Bedworth had actually come up trumps and done the best thing for once. It wouldn't have been wise to lurk around half the night with a shedload of coke on the back of the lorry. Asking for trouble, that was.

Mark was just bloody lucky Tom hadn't disappeared with the whole fucking container. He'd definitely had the chance. It was amazing that he hadn't, but as much as Bedworth might have done him a favour after Mark had successfully screwed up the one simple task he'd been given, he wasn't letting him think he'd get off easy.

Potter's head swivelled on his pudgy neck to stare at Tom. 'Get on with it, then!'

Tom blinked. 'Get on with what?'

Moving the metal arm securing the back of the container to one side, Potter cranked open one of the doors. 'Sorting the coke out from the rest of the shit! What do you think needs doing?'

Tom stared into the container at the huge drums. 'On my own?'

'Blame Mark when he gets his sorry arse back! All the rest of my men are busy,' Potter grunted. 'And get a move on. We need it sorted, cut and bagged by tomorrow. I have people expecting their deliveries.'

'But it will take *hours!*' Tom moaned.

'Ah, shut your whining. At least you ain't got a wife to play her face about you being on an all-nighter,' Potter smirked. 'Listen, the drums holding the gear should have some kind of indication on them. They usually do, so use your fucking initiative for once, there's a good chap!'

* * *

'I told you, everything's in hand,' Linda said a little bit too sharply, willing her nerves not to get the better of her. Having Mickey heaping the pressure on why she hadn't any news about Sam wasn't doing anything to calm the swirling panic that increased at a worrying rate.

She had to keep him sweet and where she knew to locate him for a bit longer until she could reach Sam or Seb. She couldn't get this far, holding this important knowledge, only to let it slip through her fingers.

Mickey was bound to know more than what he'd said, but unfortunately she couldn't press too hard without alerting suspicion. He was already suspicious enough.

Linda dragged her eyes to Mickey's, aware he hadn't shifted his gaze from her since he'd arrived unexpectedly yet again. She must play her alter ego – the crass personality she'd owned her entire life, which now felt oddly unfamiliar since her head had cleared and the majority of her demons had been banished. But it was vital to behave every inch like the Linda Matthews of old.

'Why are you staring at me?' she snapped, remembering her standard defensive habit of folding her arms over her chest and scowling at anyone she believed had wronged her. It was easy to see now that she had spent most of her life blaming everyone and everything else around her, rather than herself for her bad choices.

But retaining this attitude was a must so Mickey remained convinced that she was still thoroughly *her*.

Mickey snorted, his nostrils flaring. 'I'm staring at you because you're jittery.' Leaning closer, his eyes narrowed. 'You're on edge... like there's something you're not saying...'

Helping himself to one of Linda's cigarettes, he flicked his lighter into life and took a long drag. 'I thought we were in agreement about what needs to happen, Lin, so why the fuck am I getting the impression that you're not being straight? You're too jumpy.'

'Course I'm fucking jumpy!' Linda snapped. 'I'm choking for a drink and I need a fucking hit too. You want to try being stuck here. I can't wait to get out and you getting on my bloody back ain't helping. I *told* you I'm onto things where Sam's concerned, but you turning up all the time will screw that up. You're stressing me out!'

Mickey relaxed his stance. 'Okay, okay. Keep your hair on.' He was onto a good thing here, so must keep himself in check. 'Did Sam visit like you reckoned she would? Have you got hold of her?'

Linda snatched her packet of cigarettes from the table before Mickey could help himself to any more. Doing that also gave her a few more seconds to come up with something plausible.

Plausible was what was needed, although she'd much rather know why her daughter had disappeared from the radar. It wasn't like Sam. The longer time went on without a word or contact, the more worrying it became, but Mickey couldn't pick up on that. 'I called her earlier. In fact, I'd just finished speaking to her when you showed up,' Linda lied.

Mickey sat forward, his eyes reflecting the pound signs he could avidly envisage. 'When's she coming? How soon do you reckon you can get the money off her so that we can...'

'Whoa! Pull your head in!' Linda barked. 'I'm not due to get out of here until next week. I can't expect Sam to fork out for a house before I've even set foot out of this place.'

'It's all taking too long! I haven't got the time to hang around. I told you Marina fucked off back to London with all that cash? She's left me right in the lurch because the rent on her poxy flat is due tomorrow,' Mickey scowled. 'If I can't get my hands on some readies, I'll have no choice but to do a flit. The stupid bitch is already three months behind and this time the bailiffs will be coming. I ain't waiting to be booted out of a doss hole because of that selfish cow!'

Linda remained outwardly calm, but inside she was screaming. If Mickey moved from the address he'd given her, then how could she pass him to Seb and Sam? She didn't want Mickey round her neck longer than needs be. It was no good. She knew she'd have to act on this quickly, but now it was even more imperative.

Despite her inner turmoil, an easy smile slid across her face. 'It's a good job Sam's coming to see me tonight then, isn't it? Don't worry, I'll tap her for money. Can't have you with nowhere to stay – not when we're so close to hitting the jackpot. Being back together in a nice drum of our own will be great too!' *God forbid that should ever happen*, Linda thought acidly.

Craning her neck, she made a point of looking at the clock on the wall. 'You'd best make yourself scarce because she's due any minute.'

'Shit!' Mickey scrambled to his feet. 'You're sure you'll hit her for some dosh?'

'Absolutely,' Linda said. 'Come back tomorrow night about seven and I'll have it for you. That way, you can stay in the flat until I get out next week.'

'Cheers, babe,' Mickey grinned.

As Mickey left her room, Linda returned his smile, although it choked her. He wouldn't be coming back tomorrow night because she would move heaven and earth to sort it so that by then, Seb Stoker would have picked him up to mangle every last piece of information out of the greedy scrote. Mickey would remember a *lot* more detail under pressure...

Now she had the rest of the night to devise how to get out of here and reach Sam and Seb before it was too late. If doing this scuppered her plans for a new life, then so be it. Getting this done was the very least she owed them.

And in turn, Mickey would receive everything he deserved at the same time.

* * *

Andrew's face screwed up as he hefted yet another crate of dog food off the top of a stack. 'We've got our work cut out here.'

Neil waded through the shrink wrap piling up on the warehouse floor, alleviating his itchy nose with the back of his hand, not wanting the mess from his fingers on his face. He stared at the heavily wrapped bags of cocaine that had so far been lifted from the massive tins of dog food, their thick wrapping coated with chunks of slimy meat and gravy. 'Fucking disgusting, this is. The smell is making my stomach turn.'

'At least it's here. Imagine if it wasn't after all this?' Andrew glanced at Daz and Craig. 'There's a couple more bags here, lads.'

He waited until Daz lumbered over to collect the bags, then lowered his voice. 'The shit's really going to hit the fan now.'

Neil nodded. *Wasn't it just.* Not only for this, but for what Seb had done. Had his brother mentioned what he'd got up his sleeve, both he and Andrew would have done everything in their power to stop it. Admittedly, it was an ingenious move and a distinct statement, which, given the situation, was fully warranted, but the timing – that couldn't be worse. 'There's nothing we can do about it now, apart from wait to see what comes of it.'

Andrew cranked the lid off another industrial tin of dog food. 'Seb was determined to put our name to this. I think we can safely say that he has,' he laughed. 'We'll just have to deal with the fallout as quickly as possible and put an end to this Ross bullshit.'

Neil frowned. 'Where is Seb anyway? He hasn't gone back to the Orchid, has he?'

'Nah, he's cleaning up and getting rid of his clobber, then he's getting word to Kev that we're back. Sam will want to know.'

'She won't want to know the rest of it...'

Andrew arched an eyebrow. 'Knowing Sam, she'll find out soon enough.'

42

'I'm telling you, I can't find any sign of it!' Tom cried, getting irritated. Two hours now he'd been in here with his eyes streaming and his nose running like a tap. He'd never be able to wash his clothes ever again. The smell of washing powder was forever stuck to the inside of his nostrils and he was certain he must have already breathed in half a lungful of powder.

Potter hefted himself inside the container and glared at the mound of white powder on the metal floor. 'It looks like Santa's fucking grotto in here! Shame it's the wrong sort of powder! I take it you *have* been looking properly?'

'Does it not look like I've been looking? I've been through all the marked drums and there's shag all in them, apart from washing powder!' Tom barked.

'Maybe it's in the ones that haven't got numbers on instead? Did you not think of that?' Potter stared at the side of one of the open drums, seeing the number four scrawled in marker pen. His annoyance grew. *If the Colombians had given him a dud container...*

No, they wouldn't have. They'd shifted loads via the South

Americans over the years and a decent price was always paid, so they wouldn't want to scupper future dealings.

'Could we have been given the wrong container?' Tom suggested. Seeing a glimmer of concern on Potter's ugly face, his own worry sparked. *This couldn't go wrong.* He was counting on it working. If that thick fuck, Mark, had picked up the wrong paperwork, then he'd done all of this for nothing.

'There's no way that could happen. Silvo never ballses up,' Potter said.

'There's always a first time,' Tom added, 'and I've already been through some of the unmarked ones...'

Potter yanked Tom to one side by the lapel of his jacket. 'Get out of the fucking way! I'll look myself.' He crowbarred off the top of another drum and shoved his arms shoulder deep into the white crystalline powder. 'There should be packs of coke bricks in here. Surely they wouldn't all be packed in one or two drums?'

Spluttering from a cloud of detergent, he grew more and more stressed as he felt around. Could the Colombians really have ripped him off? Or had his dilbert brother signed for the wrong container? If he had, then when he finally showed his sorry face, he'd launch the imbecile from a motorway gantry.

The coke *had* to be here.

With effort, Potter kicked the drum over – a landslide of washing powder adding to the already covered container floor. 'Check more drums, Bedworth. It's got to be somewhere!'

Spotting more drums with numbers, Potter frowned. 'I thought you said you'd checked all of the marked drums?'

'Well, I got to number eight...'

'Nine and ten are over there!' Potter yelled. 'Why haven't you checked those? They must be the ones packed to the rafters with coke. There may be more besides too, you fucking idiot!'

Glowering, Tom waded resentfully through the powder to prise at the lid of drum number nine. Now things were even worse. With Potter under his feet, how could he stash several kilos to sell on? Damn Mark for this – he'd ballsed up everything. He'd probably done it on purpose, the idiotic muppet.

Removing the lid, Tom frowned. 'This looks to be just powder too.'

'Go further down,' Potter roared, his stress at breaking point. If this had gone wrong, he'd lose all the deals that had been set up. He'd lose standing as the best supplier in the Midlands too. Even now, time was short to cut it as much as they usually did in time for the first delivery.

Scowling at Potter busy lifting the lid from drum ten, Tom shoved his arms in deep, feeling a large bulky object. 'Wait! There's something in here.' He groped around, his fingers tracing the shape. 'It goes right to the edge. There must be loads.'

Abandoning drum number ten, Potter stumbled over to Tom. 'Lift it out. Go on!' *Thank God for that. For a minute there, he thought he'd been done.*

'I can't!' Tom's grasping fingers failed to grip the bulky shape. 'It's too tightly packed.'

'Stop!' Potter yelled. 'You might tear the wrapping. I know I cut my coke heavily, but not with washing powder!' Grabbing the drum, he carefully tipped it onto its side. 'I'll steady it, now you can pull them out.'

Tom squatted down. Seeing something black, he put his hands back into the drum. 'I can see it, hang on.' Finally getting a grip, he pulled gently. 'It's bloody heavy. There must be kilos in this one alone!'

'Get on with it!' Potter barked. 'And be careful! If you tear anything, I'll kill you!'

'What the fuck?' Putting his fingers into something soft and squidgy, Tom jerked his hands out of the drum and stared at what he'd begun to pull out.

'What now?' Potter clambered off the drum and moved to where Tom stood gawping at what was in front of him. There was something wet and gloopy... It was oval shaped, the wet surface covered in washing powder. 'What the hell is that?'

Tom's eyes moved to the wider part below, realising with horror what it was. 'It's a jacket... and someone's shoulders...'

'What?' Potter screamed. 'Those Colombian bastards have put a fucking body in one of these drums instead of my coke?'

Storming over to drum ten, he yanked the half-open lid off, his stomach turning at the tuft of hair sticking through the layer of washing powder. 'Jesus! There's another fucker in here!'

Tom moved forward, but Potter had already kicked the drum over.

'Get it out then!' Potter shouted.

Tom didn't want to pull the thing out even if he could. Despite this, he gingerly grasped a handful of hair. 'Somebody's pissed the Colombians off,' he muttered. 'You've been turned over here, Potter.'

Yanking hard, Tom fully expected to tear off half of this poor bastard's scalp, but instead, he flew backwards and landed softly on a pile of washing powder.

Unsure what was going on, he looked at what remained clutched in his hand. Emitting a loud shriek, he tossed it to the floor.

Potter was about to belt Tom in the chops for sounding like a girl and wasting time when he saw what had been thrown to roll in washing powder. Freezing to the spot, his legs turned jelly-like.

'Fucking hell!' Tom spluttered, eyeing the head of Mark Ross, his eyeballs covered in white powder. 'Fuck!' His head darted to the other drum. He'd stuck his fingers in the neck? Mark's neck? His hand flew to his mouth as vomit surged.

It was also impossible to miss the writing on Mark's forehead in thick black marker pen:

With kind regards
S.S

It didn't take much to work out who had done this...

Tom's eyes darted back to Potter, who looked like an overgrown child having learnt his train set was bust.

'Clear this up,' Potter mumbled, staggering from the container, as far away from the remains of his brother as possible.

* * *

Unable to contain herself, Sam raced from the car to bang on the metal doors of the Erdington warehouse. Somehow refraining from calling Seb's name, she waited for what seemed an aeon before the door cranked open just enough for her to step inside, closely followed by Kevin.

'Christ, Sam! You nearly gave me a heart attack! Good job I have a peephole to see who's outside,' Andrew grumbled, glaring at Kev for allowing Sam to come here.

'I tried to stop her...' Kev muttered.

'I couldn't help it!' Sam grinned, overjoyed that everything had been achieved with no problems. 'I was just about to go and see Linda when Kev caught me and I'm glad he did. I've been a bag of nerves all day!' She wrapped her arms tightly around Seb's waist.

'You had no need to worry, Princess. I told you everything would be fine, and it is.' He kissed the end of Sam's nose. 'It's all done and dusted.'

Sam looked between all of the men eagerly. 'No one was suspicious or noticed anything amiss?' Her face cracked into a wide smile. 'Oh, this is great! Now you ca... Hang on...'

Noticing Seb was wearing different clothes from when she last saw him, she frowned. 'That's not what you went in... You never wear tracksuits.'

Seb shrugged. 'Just got a bit hot, that's all...'

As the men exchanged glances, Sam's eyes narrowed. 'Okay, so now why don't you tell me the real reason...'

Seb sighed. Sam was too astute to have the wool pulled over her eyes. He'd promised her honesty, he knew that, but she'd only worry if she knew everything. He *would* tell her, just not yet. After the turmoil of how her enforcers had acted because of *his* decision, the least he owed her was justice for Stu. But he'd save telling her the finer details until the Rosses had been dealt with.

Sam watched Seb closely, conscious of the heavy silence. 'Seb? The change of clothes? What went wrong? What have you done?'

'Oh, ye of little faith!' Seb exclaimed. 'If you must know, I stunk of washing powder. It's difficult to move drums of the stuff around without getting it everywhere.'

'But you said the coke was packed in dog food?' That was certainly what Sam could smell. The stench was choking and Neil and Andrew's hands were covered in the gunk.

'Just thought I'd have a little game with Potter Ross,' Seb winked, deciding to improvise. 'I marked up some of the drums, meaning the twat had to wade through all of it, only to find there was no coke at all.' He gave his brothers a warning look: *say nothing...*

Sam laughed, then stopped. 'But surely now they'll guess it was down to you?'

'Yep, but that's a dead cert, anyhow, therefore no harm in having fun!' Seb shrugged. As long as Sam didn't ask anything outright, then this version of events would do for now. He wasn't going out of his way to tell her something to freak her out and that what he'd done to Mark Ross would only accentuate the onslaught. The sooner this was finished, the better.

Once the Ross firm had been put back in their box, he'd tell Sam everything. The Rosses would be out of the way, he'd then deal with Bedworth and then they could rest easy.

Almost there now.

Seb clapped his hands together. 'Let's get cracking. We've got tonight to make sure this is sorted for tomorrow so the deals Neil has set up go ahead.'

Sam perched on the workbench, watching proudly as Seb and his brothers continued wading through the dog food for further bricks of coke. They had successfully pulled off the heist and now his casino and firm would be fine.

Suddenly, Daz appeared out of the back room. 'That lot's been cut and divvied up, so if there's any more that I ca... Oh, hi Sam!'

Sam smiled widely. 'Hi, Daz. A good haul, eh?'

Daz grinned. 'Indeed! Your enforcers will be equally pleased when they hear what that fucker had happen to him! Fuck me, how I'd have loved to have seen Potter Ross's face when he fou...' As soon as he saw the expressions on the Stokers' faces, Daz knew he'd royally screwed up.

Sam's smile fell as she turned to Seb. 'And what exactly did that fucker have happen to him today?'

Glaring at Daz, Seb knew he had no option but to tell Sam everything.

Sam listened as Seb reluctantly explained what had *really* happened.

Not so long ago, she'd have been horrified, but certain things made sense in the world they inhabited. Whether that was good or bad, she didn't know, but she *did* know that Stu had received justice.

An eye for an eye was the only way things worked. It was only this concept which justified her acceptance of something that, by most people's standards, would be inexcusable.

What did that say about her? Did it make her a bad person?

No. It meant she was living in this world and making things safe the only way possible for her staff and her family.

But it did mean *one* thing – a rather big thing. There would now be a war. And that was exactly what she'd wanted to avoid.

Seeing the concern on Sam's face, Seb smiled. 'Look, I'd rather it this way. It's quicker. Now we have the upper hand and a head start to deal with the expected fallout we knew would come from the heist. They'd work out soon enough we were behind it as well as what I did as an "extra". Now we can put the Rosses back in their place sooner rather than later, instead of playing cat and mouse.'

Sam nodded. That was true, but Seb's reasoning didn't change that he'd failed to be honest about what he'd done.

Again.

And that alone made her angrier than she had been for some time.

43

Tom didn't want to look for Potter. For God's sake, it was barely six o'clock in the bloody morning, but there wasn't a lot else he could do. He couldn't begin to try and rectify any of this until he found out what the fuck was going on.

Okay, so Mark Ross had been decapitated and shoved in a drum of washing powder. It wasn't like he could easily forget that revolting sight. Neither could he rid his senses of the squidgy feeling as he'd shoved his fingers into that bastard's neck. Fucking disgusting, that was. Just the thought of the sludgy flesh on his fingertips made him want to scrape his own eyeballs out. He didn't think he'd ever be able to stop imagining it.

Tom stared at his hands, his face screwing into a grimace. No matter how many times he'd washed them, he was convinced something repulsive was still stuck to them.

But that didn't mean Potter had to lose the fucking plot, did it?

Where was he? No one had seen the man since last night, and things were so weird that even *he* wasn't even being watched any longer.

All this aside, his plans had gone down the shitter. Fucked. Finito.

He'd forked out all that wedge for a coke delivery that hadn't materialised, Dan had buggered off with the remains of the money and soon there would be a shedload of fucknuts banging at the door expecting bricks of coke that didn't exist.

Potter's time, as well as his own, was limited.

Tom's mouth curled into a snarl. And guess what? All of this shit was down to Sebastian-fucking-Stoker.

Whilst glancing around the yard, he moved towards the Portakabin. Was Potter in there?

Tom tentatively knocked on the Portakabin door. Even the numbskulls working for Potter were nowhere to be seen. Had there been an apocalypse? Everything had gone to shit. He didn't have a backup plan and the Stokers were after the Rosses with bells on.

He had to exit stage left, but with no passport, reduced cash and nobody onside around this neck of the woods, he didn't have the first clue how he would do that.

Receiving no reply, Tom banged the door again, becoming more agitated by the second. There was nothing to do but hang around. At least Potter offered a smidgen of protection, even if the situation had slid into something worse than unsavoury.

With still no answer and hearing no movement from within, Tom tried the door. Potter must be holed up in one of the shitholes he owned, but he didn't know where any of those places were. In fact, given the change of plans and the ghastly scenario of the Stokers closing in like a pack of hyenas, Tom admitted he knew a lot less than he was comfortable with.

Surprised to find that the door pushed open, Tom craned his neck into the messy space. 'Potter?' he hissed, half expecting to find another dismembered corpse. Instead, his eyes fell on the motionless figure of Potter sitting at his desk.

Frowning, Tom stepped inside, his tension mounting. The man wasn't dead. Potter was still very much alive, but he was unmoving – sitting rigid like a statue. 'Potter?'

He edged forwards, refraining from looking behind to check there wasn't a Stoker poised behind the door, complete with an axe raised to chop his head clean off. 'Why are you sitting here like this? Where is everyone?'

Potter remained silent, his eyes unblinking. The slow rise and fall of the man's barrel chest was the only hint he still possessed life.

Uncertainty, along with worry, pooled at the base of Tom's spine. *What was the matter with the fat prick?* Okay, so his brother had been murdered and he'd lost his cocaine, but let's face it, Potter didn't even like Mark – anyone could tell that much and the punters expecting coke would just have to be patient. If Potter had as good a relationship with these people as he professed, they'd be okay about it. *Probably...*

But Potter sitting like a catatonic loon when people were out for his blood wasn't the best idea. It didn't help *him* either...

'Mate, I don't know what's going on, but you need to tell me what the plan is. We need to be extra-vigilant, so what's the back-up?' Tom waited as patiently as he could, but received not even a blink from the man in the chair. Not one flicker of anything hinted that Potter was aware of anyone else in the room.

Feeling his irritation brewing, Tom clenched his teeth. He could grab this ideal opportunity to smash the bloke's skull in to get him back for the countless times he'd been yelled at like a cunt, but he couldn't. Potter was his only ally in this sewer of shit. But the man being as much use as a dead cat was not helpful. 'Pull yourself together!' Tom shouted, in the hope of eliciting a response, but still there was nothing.

* * *

Having shoved a handful of her possessions in a bag, Linda held her breath as she moved along the corridor, her ears tuned for any sign of movement.

Slipping a folded-up piece of cardboard in the hinge of her door last night after the nurse doing the last round of the day's medication left had succeeded in preventing the door's deadlock to set when it closed.

Linda's plan had worked well and now she was out. So far, so good...

Now she had to get past the night shift. Hopefully, they'd either dropped off through boredom or were engrossed in the TV they didn't think anyone noticed they watched to pass the time during the small hours.

Linda's heart thumped in her chest. The rolled-up blankets and the rest of her clothes that she'd carefully arranged under the duvet to resemble a sleeping body should suffice in allowing time to reach Sam before her absence was noticed and the alarm raised that she'd gone AWOL.

The rest was straightforward. If patients were asleep when the old dear with the breakfast trolley trundled around, it was standard practice to leave them to sleep. This was something she'd unfortunately learned the hard way after more than one occasion of missing breakfast.

No one else would appear until the first medication rounds started at 9.30. *Then* she'd be missed. But that gave her a good two and a half hours to reach Sam.

Linda confirmed her calculation by looking at the clock on the corridor wall as she neared the area where the nurses congregated. With any luck, there would only be one or two nurses about until the day shift took over at 7.30. She knew this, having watched the movements of everybody for some time, having little else to do, short of watch and think.

Now that seemingly pointless exercise had come in useful.

Hearing the muffled drone of a television programme, its volume down low, Linda took a deep breath and darted past the open door and window of the nurses' station, her relief tangible as she cleared the other side without detection.

There shouldn't be anyone else between here and the front door, but she wasn't heading there. The security guard on reception would be sure to stop her.

No, she was heading down *here...*

Linda hastily darted down the corridor leading to the kitchen, flattening herself against the wall as an elderly tea-lady scuttled from the room. Holding her breath, Linda watched the old dear open the door of the walk-in stock cupboard, then took her chance to dash past into the kitchen.

If she could get out through the side door, then she'd make it.

Heading through the commercial kitchen, past the big tea urn bubbling in preparation on the side, Linda thought about pinching a slice of bread from the pile stacked waiting for the toasting to start. Thinking better of it, she instead continued around the corner.

Further relief cascaded through her when she saw the side door propped open with a bin to rid the room of the building steam.

Come on, go through it, Linda willed as her shaky legs propelled her forward. She tried not to dwell on leaving behind the beautiful clothes she'd been forced to use to create a makeshift person in her bed. She'd never owned one item of clothing even half as nice as the ones Sam had purchased for her, let alone a whole wardrobe full. Leaving them behind was like salt in the wound.

She shook the thoughts away. Material things did not matter. Plus, she wouldn't need them now she'd screwed up any chance of a future. But it would be okay. She would lobby the courts until they gave her access to Tayquan and Shondra and just shoulder the stigma of regular drug testing she'd now be forced to endure when they caught up with her.

She'd still have a future – just in a less palatable way than she'd hoped. As long as she could maintain contact with her youngest two and get the required information to Seb and Sam before it was too late, that was fine.

Nothing else mattered.

* * *

'Christ, Sam! I only didn't tell you to start with yesterday because I didn't want you to react like this!' Seb paced the kitchen, his eyes flashing with frustration. 'Justice has been done for your man, which will stop your enforcers' unrest. It was *my* call to send one of your scouts, so it was only right I should rectify that.'

Sam slammed the fridge door shut so hard the whole unit shook. Yes, she'd wanted justice for Stu and yes, she was frustrated about getting grief from her staff for being unable to level with them about why they had held off with retaliation, but it wasn't just that.

This sort of thing was half the problem and the sticking point in her and Seb's relationship. It had been from day one.

And it made her furious.

'You're doing what you promised not to do any more! Being the judge of what I should and shouldn't know until either *you* deem it right, or I happen to find out about it!' Sam's eyes flashed with fire. 'We're supposed to be in this together! That was the deal, was it not? No more bullshit, hiding stuff or...'

'For God's sake!' Seb barked. 'I knew you'd kick off about what I'd done and what it meant. I don't want you to worry. You don't *need* to worry!'

'Who gives you the right to decide what I should worry about?'

'I give *myself* that right!' Seb thumped his chest with his fist. 'Me! I'm marrying you because I love you! That also means I want you safe, free from stress and…'

'How do you expect me to be free from stress when I can't count on whether what you tell me is what I need to know? You don't have that right, Seb. You certainly don't have the right to lie to me!'

Seb folded his arms, a small smile tugging the corner of his mouth. 'Oh, come on! I didn't lie, I just didn't go out of my way to give you details that weren't necessary at that particular moment…'

Sam stared at Seb incredulously. 'You think this is funny? That it's a game? You think I'm so soft that I can't take the truth? Don't you dare, Seb! I mean it! Too many times you've done this!'

'I'm aware that you're far from soft, Sam. Look, see it for what it is! The heist is done, the money to complete the rebuild will be in my hands by this afternoon and I've righted the grief with your enforcers. What the fuck is wrong with that? Furthermore, why spoil good news by making a big deal about something and nothing?'

'Chopping the head off the brother of a rival firm's leader when they're already out to cause problems isn't nothing!' Sam shouted. 'There will be a goddamn war now, yet you don't want me to worry?'

'See? You've reacted *exactly* how I expected. It's no sweat. The Rosses will be dealt with.'

'Glad I'm so bloody predictable!' Turning, Sam grabbed her bag and jacket. 'I'm going to work. I suggest you make your own way there and give me some space. Unless of course you're planning to cause more problems that we need to hide?'

Slamming the door before Seb had the chance to reply, Sam stormed down the gravel drive from her house. She didn't want to get in Seb's car. She didn't want to hear one more excuse. She'd get a taxi from the main road.

Calming down was the most important thing she could do before things turned into a full-scale argument.

Sam reached the main road and continued walking, conscious the heel of her shoe was already rubbing. She was pleased Stu had got justice, but she wasn't pleased with *how*.

Christ, chopping a man's head off and purposely placing his body and head in different drums of washing powder for his own brother to find was hardcore. It served to remind her of the very real side of Sebastian Stoker that she rarely saw.

Although she was far from green these days when it came down to how things worked, it was a short sharp shock just how harsh and twisted this life could be.

Just how harsh and twisted *Seb* could be...

But not levelling with her? That was the worst part...

Spotting a black cab heading in her direction, Sam raised her hand. As the cab slowed, she realised that maybe she should do well to remember that despite her insistence on complete transparency between them, she'd been selective about what she'd related to Seb. The latest being that unbeknownst to him and his brothers, she hadn't voiced that she knew it was Dan who was responsible for stealing the money when she should have. Had she done so, it would have saved Seb a lot of time.

She'd taken it upon herself to decide that it was better for Seb not knowing for as long as possible, so it wouldn't distract his concentration from the heist.

Had she the right to do that?

No, she didn't.

Sam clambered in the back of the taxi and gave the driver the curt instructions to go to Broad Street.

She stared out of the window, with the persistent knowledge that when push came to shove, not completely levelling with Seb made her actions not much different than his.

44

'Come on!' Seb ignored Sam's expression as he pulled her towards him. 'There's no point being cross with me. See things for what they are.'

Sam shrugged Seb away. Following her to the Orchid when she'd expressly asked for space, coupled with his effort to clear the air, only served to rub her face in acknowledging that she was being hypocritical. Admitting that, bristled.

She knew she was being unreasonable, but everything was getting out of control again. The pressure was mounting to a level she could not keep up with.

'Sam!' Linda burst through the office door.

The Orchid's receptionist followed quickly on Linda's tail. 'I'm sorry, Ms Reynold. She was so quick, I coul...'

'It's fine, Elaine.' Sam flapped her hand, concealing her shock at her mother standing in front of her, red-faced and panting. She cut Seb a quick look as the receptionist left the office. Only when she was sure the woman was out of earshot did she face Linda. 'What on earth are you doing here?' she cried. 'You left the clinic? Discharged yourself? Why? How?'

Linda dropped into the nearest available chair, exhaustion overtaking her. She fanned her face, fighting to push the words from her deprived lungs. 'I snuck out through the kitchen when I got the chance and...'

'Are you *insane*?' Sam whispered angrily. After all the effort she'd put in to ensure a better outlook for her mother, she'd pulled a stunt like this? 'Don't you realise the lengths I've gone to so you could live your life normally after leaving the clinic?'

Picking up the closest thing to hand, Sam launched the hole punch against the wall, making Linda jump in surprise. 'You stupid, stupid wo...'

'Sam!' Seb warned, stepping forward, his hand outstretched.

'No!' Sam batted Seb's arm away. 'If you think I should be okay about this, then you're as crazy as her!' She spun back to Linda. 'What were you thinking? You had all but a handful of days left there, yet you chose to screw it up? I've pulled so many strings; made countless promises, I've done *everything* to keep you off radar and...'

'I know love, but...'

'But nothing!' Sam cut Linda's explanation dead. 'Jesus Christ! I even cleared it with Gloria for you to live with her, so you had company and a decent environment.'

'You never mentioned that?' Seb frowned.

'No, I didn't. After your reaction to me bringing Tina to the Orchid, I didn't think you'd be too enamoured if I'd invited Linda to live with us, considering your opinion of her at the moment!'

Seeing Linda's dismay, Seb gritted his teeth with embarrassment. Despite this, he reached out to Sam once more. 'Listen, why don't you...'

'Just shut up!' Sam hissed, pacing the room, unable to comprehend the stupidity of her mother's decision. She'd been *that* close to having a normal life. *That close.* 'What do you care? *You* wanted fuck all to do with her not so long ago, so don't tell me I should calm down and...'

'That's enough!' Seb yelled, his irritation rising.

'Sam...' Linda's second attempt to interrupt her daughter and calm the situation was immediately cut off by Sam's next barrage of abuse.

'You would have been living with your two youngest. Remember them? Tayquan and Shondra? Or aren't they important either? For God's sake, you've ruined your chances of getting custody now, not to mention wasting my fucking time. I hope getting an extra couple of extra days of freedom is worth it!'

Linda felt the surge of tears, Sam's words cutting like a knife. She'd been certain she could still get contact and apply for custody on the proviso she jumped through the relevant hoops, but maybe not. And if Sam felt she'd been let down, then perhaps she really *had* made a mammoth mistake by doing this?

Seb's bitterness for Linda's lack of help in the recent past evaporated. 'Sam, you need to stop before you say something you regret. Hear what Linda's got to say before you throw the towel at her!'

Sam leant against the wall with both palms. She dragged air into her lungs and fought to control the crushing disappointment. Her rage was with what Linda had given up, rather than personal. She'd wanted her mother to have a fresh, clean slate. Not *this*.

Amazed Seb had taken her corner, Linda took this final opening to tell them what they needed to know. 'Doing what I've done was the only way. Waiting until next week would have been too late!'

She spoke quickly, the words jumbling. 'Mickey – Marina and Grant's father, has been visiting me. He knows about this Dan bloke you're after and Tom Bedworth must be involved because Mickey mentioned a guy with a shitty club.'

Sam froze with disbelief. '*What*?'

* * *

Tom answered the tapping on the Portakabin door in the hope that it was a fairy godmother sent to whisk him away from this waking nightmare. *It wasn't.*

However, it was a relief to see that at least *one* member of the Ross firm was still here, until he realised who it was.

This lad was all of sixteen – a gopher – no one of any use. He'd been the one sent to deliver the note to Mark that had ended up attached to Sam Reynold's enforcer's dead body.

Tom was careful to pull the door behind him rather than allowing the lad's searching eyes to spot Potter sitting like a waxwork of Buddha. It would do no one any good if it got out the boss had lost his marbles. But then, judging by the lack of people around, this had already happened. Everyone within the firm must have legged it before the whole place got crushed by the Stokers.

'What do you want?' Tom growled.

The lad fidgeted on the threshold, his nervousness apparent. 'I... erm... I just thought I'd see if Mr Ross was here and whether he wanted his usual daily paper?' He made another attempt to look past Tom to catch a glimpse inside the Portakabin. 'Is he here? I... erm... I thought that...'

'Mr Ross *is* here, but we're very busy.' Tom snatched the paper from the lad's hands. 'Now leave us be.'

Quickly slamming the door, Tom eyed Potter scornfully. 'Did you hear that? That kid was digging for info. Jesus, Potter – your entire workforce has jumped ship! Get a fucking grip and sort things out before it's too late!'

Receiving no response yet again, Tom stomped to the opposite chair and threw the copy of the paper on the desk. Even the plume of dust exploding in Potter's face elicited nothing from the man.

Tom's stress levels rose higher. How long could he remain here like a target? The Stokers would soon up their game and waiting to be taken out was not something on his bucket list. 'Your paper's here,' he pushed, desperate for a sign of life. *Anything.* 'Why don't you see what's happening in Brum? You always say it's important to keep tabs?' *Now more than ever.*

Tom slapped the newspaper back down on the desk in defeat, his eyes drawn to the side column on the front page.

HUNT STEPPED UP FOR WANTED MAN

Police have stepped up their hunt for the man wanted in connection with many recent violent crimes in Birmingham, extending their search to involve neighbouring forces.

There is reason to believe that Thomas Bedworth, (49), has fled Birmingham in a bid to evade detection and is seeking refuge outside of the city.

All ports and airports are being watched whilst leads are being followed up as to Mr Bedworth's current location.

Anyone with information or sightings of...

Tom slammed an old coffee mug down on the article, the mouldering remains inside the cup slopping around the cracked china.

Fuck. Had Dan told the Old Bill he was in Wolverhampton?

Sweat beaded on Tom's brow. He couldn't have. Dan knew his exact location, so if he'd flapped his gums, the police would have descended long ago. But if they had leads for 'other locations', then they would be looking over here soon enough.

And the ports and airports were being watched too?

Shit!

Even if he had a fucking passport, that route was now shagged.

Tom wiped his sweaty hands down his jeans, his teeth gnashing. If the Stokers didn't get him, the police would.

He glared at the man in front of him, his eyes drawn to the dark stained patch over Potter's crotch. *For fuck's sake... This was bad.*

'How long is this going to go on for?' Tom screamed, partly out of desperation, the rest in angry frustration. 'Look, I'm sorry about what happened to Mark, but you must snap out of this. You can't sit here and let the Stokers win!'

And no, he wasn't *really* sorry Mark was no more. The bloke was a twat, but he'd say anything to get a response from Potter.

Tom slumped back in his chair. This was pointless. Potter was too fucked up.

It was only then that he saw a lone fat tear roll down Potter's cheek. 'Potter?'

Had he finally succeeded in bringing the fat fuckwit back from the land of bastard Zog?

Quick! Keep it going. Think of something to say. Don't let this chink of lucidity slip away.

'What can I do to help, mate? Anything at all?' he blathered. Of course, there was nothing he could do. Even if there was, he wouldn't. Helping this bastard had never been at the top of the list and it certainly wasn't now. Protecting himself was the only thing on the agenda – the only thing worth anything.

But to do that, he needed Potter back to life.

Tom clapped his hands together. 'Can you hear me? We have to...'

'I can't even give him a funeral...'

The voice was quiet – barely a whisper. If Tom hadn't seen Potter's fleshy lips move, he wouldn't believe it came from the man who only ever spoke in two ways: shouting or snarling.

Eager to keep Potter going, Tom flailed around with his words. 'Why can't we give Mark a funeral?'

That was a stupid thing for him to say. Incinerating the various parts of Mark Ross was the only way to keep things under wraps and Potter knew it.

Suddenly an idea glimmered. It was a pile of absolute shite, but being as Potter was so cut up about the loss of his retarded sibling, it might just do the trick.

Refusing to waste another second, Tom continued. 'I mean, I know we can't hold an *actual* funeral. Terrible business having to remove all traces of your brother, but we *can* have a remembrance service...'

Seeing a flicker behind Potter's eyes, Tom pushed on, his idea gaining pace. 'It would be a private service, of course – just you and me. That way we can make sure that word doesn't get out. I've got some stuff of Mark's we can use to commemorate him. We'll go to that nice little park down the road to give him a proper send-off.'

Tom didn't have anything of Mark's, but he'd find something to do the trick. He had a couple of old socks knocking around at the flat and that cheapo chain he'd always hated would do for a start. Okay, the park wasn't exactly a 'park'. A decaying tree sitting in the centre of a patch of grass behind the Indian takeaway where druggies left needles wasn't the most scenic of surroundings, but if he bigged the idea up enough...

'A friend of mine was a minister,' Tom lied, getting into the swing. 'So I know everything to say in order to conduct a proper service.' He'd make that up too. 'We can do it tomorrow? It's going to be sunny, so a perfect day for a send-off. What do you think?'

Potter moved for the first time and dragged his big hand under his snotty nose. Sniffing loudly, he nodded. 'Yeah, yeah, that would be good.'

Tom refrained from punching the air in glee and instead forced himself to pat Potter's hand. 'Great! I'll arrange it.'

Hallelujah.

* * *

'You reckon this bloke who "runs a shitty club" that Mickey Devlin mentioned is Bedworth?' Seb asked Linda for the second time.

Linda nodded. 'It's got to be. It all adds up. Mickey's also sure Marina has run off with Dan, even though the man turned her over.' Her eyes narrowed. 'It's feasible, being as that girl would do anything to get her hands on money.'

Sam shook her head in disbelief. She hadn't expected this. *None of it.* Her mother had risked her own neck and upcoming freedom to bring them information, yet she'd repaid that sacrifice by accusing the woman of not caring? She put her head in her hands.

What Linda said also backed up the theory that Bedworth was the one involved in the robbery and the arson. But there was one thing that couldn't be right. 'I don't know whether Marina returned to London or not, but she can't have left with Dan and the money because he's dead...'

'W-what? Dead?' Linda's mouth dropped open, her face paling by at least six shades.

Seb nodded. 'Murdered – presumably by Bedworth for that all-important cash. *My* cash.'

'So Tom's still out there? Oh God, he's still in Birmingham? I – I don't believe it!' Linda's eyes darted around as if the man was lurking under Sam's desk.

Sam sighed, knowing she could no longer truthfully promise Linda would be safe from Bedworth. Neither could she say he wasn't waiting for an opportunity to finish where he left off. This alone horrified her.

She scraped her sweaty hair from the nape of her neck, stopping as she remembered something. *Something that now made sense.* 'Wait a minute! The night Dan was murdered, Tina muttered something about him being expected in Wolverhampton. She was all over the place, so I took little notice, but now it makes sense. She kept saying "that man" must have killed Dan for the stolen money. But how could Bedworth have murdered anyone that night if he was in Wolverhampton?'

Seb frowned. 'How could he, indeed?' *It also underlined something else...* He raised an eyebrow knowingly. 'It also shows I'm not the only one who "forgets" to mention certain things, Sam.'

Sam reddened, realising her words exposed she'd kept the knowledge about knowing Dan was responsible for the robbery to herself. She looked at Seb pleadingly. 'Seb, I...'

Seb scowled. Yes, he was aggravated by Sam's double standards. 'What's going on now is more important than what's passed,' he said brusquely, turning his concentration to Linda. 'All I know is that I need to bring Mickey Devlin in.'

Linda's eyes darted between Seb and those of her daughter's. 'He's coming to the clinic at seven tonight to see me. Obviously, I won't be there, but you could intercept him?' Pulling a piece of paper from her pocket, she held it out with shaking hands. 'This is where he lives.'

'Bearwood?' Seb scanned the address, his jaw clenching. 'Then this is where I'm going! No need to intercept him at the clinic.'

'You'll have to beat the bailiffs to it,' Linda said. 'They're due to collect the rent he's counting on getting from me, via *you*, today.' She jerked her chin at Sam. 'And I think he knows more than he told me.'

'Not necessarily. He could be as much of a thick cunt as he sounds,' Seb muttered.

Sam gasped. 'But he might... And depending on how much Devlin knows, there still could be a chance you could get your money back, Seb!' She took Linda's hand. 'Mum, you know this Bedworth bastard better than anyone. If he had a stash of money, where would he hide it?'

Linda bit her lip. 'Tom *never* divulged anything to me. But that coke he stole from your runners in the past, he hid under the floorboards in my kitchen. Do you remember me telling you about it?'

Sam nodded, her mind racing. *How could she not?* Before Linda had gone missing, finding out her mother knew of Tom Bedworth's original plan to rip her off was what had spawned another mountain of mistrust. But if they discovered where Bedworth was in Wolverhampton, then looking under the floorboards at that location was as good a place as any. If he'd done it before, there was a chance he'd stick to a way that worked.

'What should I do?' Linda blurted. 'Bedworth will come for me and...'

'You're going back to the clinic,' Sam said.

'W-what?' Linda blinked repeatedly. 'I can't! I left... I...'

'Yes, you can!' Sam glanced at her watch. 'If you go now, you could be back before anyone notices!' She turned to Seb. 'It's worth a try, isn't it? And if Mickey confirms Bedworth has gone to Wolverhampton, that backs up what Tina said, so we look there first.'

Seb's eyes narrowed. 'Are you thinking what I'm thinking...?'

Sam nodded, the enormity of what was unfolding registering thick and fast. 'That Bedworth's working with the Ross firm...?'

Seb snatched up the desk phone to dial the extension for the office Andrew and Neil shared. 'Andrew, I need you down here. We have a couple of things on today. Firstly, we have someone requiring a lift out of town immediately and secondly, we've got someone to see as a matter of urgency. You'll come with me whilst Neil remains to broker the coke deals at the warehouse.'

Those deals he was not losing, and neither was he losing the chance of getting his hands on Bedworth. Mickey Devlin was the next piece in the jigsaw to move closer to that ultimate aim.

45

Mickey risked a glimpse behind the stained lounge curtains down to the road below, bolstered to see the white van containing the bailiffs had finally left.

His face split into a smile. By tonight, he'd have the money to pay those fuckers off. Not the complete debt Dan and Marina had saddled him with because of this poxy flat, but enough to buy him another week of using this shithole as a base before receiving a big chunk off Linda.

That was guaranteed. The nasty old cow might look a ton better since cleaning up her act and donning fancy clobber, but she was still a thick bitch, desperately gagging for his company, like he knew she would be.

It was all too easy.

Linda had never been the sort to resist compliments and falling for the oldest trick in the book.

Want Linda Mickey did not, but he sure as hell would do a good job of pretending otherwise until that stuck-up daughter of hers delivered the money Linda was promised.

It was a good job his ex-wife was as grasping and mercenary as ever because for once, he would gain nicely.

Mickey's brows suddenly knitted into a frown. Okay, so it didn't make up for the colossal amount of readies his cut from Marina would have netted, but this was better than a kick in the nuts.

Mickey let the curtain drop back on its sagging rail. Although he'd told himself not to clock watch, he couldn't help it. There were *hours* to go until seven when he'd see Linda, but he had no doubt she'd have the cash she'd promised because she was a shit liar. He also knew that her desperation for another stab at life with him was enough for her to not welch on their arrangement.

Bored shitless, Mickey stopped himself from pacing the small lounge. It was grating not having anything to pass the time, like shagging Sophie, but he'd pick another bird up soon. Once he'd got a shedload of cash in his back pocket again, there would be no problem on that score. This time, he'd keep it *exactly* that – a shag. No more stupid ideas because of a deluded view that he was getting too old.

Fuck that!

Perhaps he should nip down the offy to buy a couple of cans to keep him going?

He paused at the lounge door and contemplated the idea.

On second thoughts, he wouldn't. He didn't want to wander around outside in case the bailiffs returned sooner than expected. Plus, if he started on the beer, he might get sidetracked and he couldn't be late for Linda.

Nah, he'd stay put until it was time to go to the clinic and he'd be there ready and waiting at seven on the dot.

And that time couldn't come soon enough.

* * *

Linda smiled confidently as she was handed her lunch tray. She moved to sit at a table near one of the windows in the large room used as a dining area.

She gazed through the floor-to-ceiling glass out to the landscaped garden beyond. Even the overcast, dull day didn't cause the meticulously planted beds and pretty water features to lose their charm.

She fixed on the view, acting tranquil and at ease with herself and life, when inside she was a bundle of nerves, the knot in her stomach twisting and turning.

Sam was bang on with her idea. Sneaking back into the clinic the way she'd left and hurrying back to her room a few hours ago had worked like a dream.

She'd got away with it. But only just because less than five minutes later, the medication round had arrived.

Only a few minutes' difference in her arriving would have caused her absence to be noted, the alarm raised and all chance of the life Sam had planned for her going down the pan. Now, thanks to sheer good fortune, nothing would change on her release. She'd still be eligible for a normal life. But there was one massive difference. Sam and Seb were now aware of what *she* knew.

And for that, all the risks she'd taken were worthwhile.

Linda stole a glance around the room, hoping to avoid anyone's eye. She didn't want to strike up a conversation because opening her mouth would expose how on edge she really was.

Despite her outwardly relaxed stance, Linda's body remained taut – every fibre primed, expecting Mickey to appear, having successfully evaded Seb.

What were the chances of that happening?

Slim, to the point of impossible.

Mickey was done for – and that was on *her* conscience. Linda frowned. She owed him nothing. In the short time they'd remained together years ago, he'd treated her like shit, abandoning the two children they'd produced. Nothing good had come from them either. One of those kids, the only half-decent one, was, thanks to Mickey's money-making schemes, now dead. The other was a psychotic bitch, hellbent on killing Sam. Even then, the deranged cow had somehow managed to get away with that unscathed.

Had Mickey not been so greedy, their children wouldn't even have been on Sam's tail or set to ruin her and Seb's life in the first place. The man deserved everything coming his way.

Linda's mouth flattened. She'd lose no sleep over what would come down on Mickey's head. That's if it hadn't already.

But Mickey Devlin wasn't responsible for the *other* factor fuelling her jangling nerves. Tom Bedworth.

And Tom was still out there...

Whilst Bedworth possessed the ability to draw oxygen, he remained a danger. Not just to her, but to Sam, too, and Linda knew that fear would not dissipate until she received the welcome news that the man was pushing up daisies.

* * *

Andrew checked the time on the dashboard clock again before doing a further round of scanning the road. He shifted his weight in the driver's seat, the increasing stiffness of his backside and legs from not moving taking its toll.

Linda had been spot on with what she'd told Seb about bailiffs being due at Devlin's today, but neither he nor Seb had expected them to be there when they'd arrived at the given address.

It was frustrating having to wait for them to leave, but better for them to have now been and gone, rather than them turning up midway through Mickey Devlin being ejected from his hidey-hole.

But how long before they could make a move? It would be

hours before darkness completely fell and they'd have to intercept the man at the clinic at this rate. No one wanted that. 'When do you reckon we can risk making a move?'

Seb chewed his inner cheek. If the bailiffs planned on lulling Devlin into a false sense of security by making out they'd left, only to double back on themselves, they'd have returned long ago. They'd been gone an hour, so it was unlikely attempt number two would be for a while yet – more than adequate time to lift the twat from his pit.

His eyes drifted to the clock. It was almost 4 p.m., so Neil should have completed the coke deals by now and be busy cleaning the room in the Orchid's basement that he'd earmarked as a good place to bring Devlin. 'Let's move into position and weigh it up from there.'

Andrew started the van, and they made their way to the service road behind the flats. Dragging a man across Bearwood High Street to shove him into the back of a van would be noticed by *someone*, even if most of the inhabitants around here were safely ensconced in the pub.

As Andrew killed the engine, Seb opened the van door and peered at the overcast sky. 'It's murky enough to make it seem almost twilight.' A smirk twitched in the corner of his mouth as he jerked his head in his brother's direction. 'Come on. Let's go and grab the wanker.'

Seb clambered from the van and smoothed down his overcoat. 'If this is what March has to offer, I can't see it being a very good spring this year.' The concept of pulling in a man for torture was as normal for the Stokers as discussing holiday plans. 'Let's see if we can remember how to be bailiffs.'

As Andrew followed Seb up the stairwell leading to the first-floor flat over the chip shop, he laughed. 'This is just like old times when we were on the money runs. While we're here, we might as well also have a mooch around and see if Sam's bitch of a sister left any hints as to her whereabouts.'

Reaching the chipped front door of the flat, Seb double checked it matched with the address Linda had supplied. *It did.*

He looked at Andrew and nodded.

Without needing words, the Stoker brothers put their shoulders to the door at the exact same time, ripping it easily from its hinges to crash noisily onto the hallway floor.

46

Hearing the noise of his smashing front door had initially confused Mickey. It had taken a couple of seconds before he'd registered what the sound was, quickly coming to the conclusion that the bailiffs had returned.

Panicking and thinking how to stall them didn't help when, within seconds, two men had crashed into the room and Mickey realised his situation was more dire than he'd first thought.

Mickey gingerly rubbed the large lump on the side of his head. No, he hadn't dreamt it. Two blokes *had* showed up at his flat. And by the state of his head, he'd been given a clump too.

Although his brain was still foggy, he had a vague recollection of being manhandled out of the flat and bundled into a van. But after that, his memory was patchy.

Where even was he?

Opening his eyes, Mickey blinked, the bright yet blurred outline of a room slowly coming into focus. He groped against whatever he was lying on, panic snowballing. He was on a concrete floor in a cold room, surrounded by bare brick walls. Only the humming from the florescent tube of an overhead strip light broke the shrouded darkness around him.

His fingers scrabbled against the rough surface of the floor, frowning to find it sloping. It was then that he spotted a drain hole a few inches from his left thigh.

What the hell was this place? And why was he here?

Mickey's eyes darted around as they adjusted to the contrast of darkness and the bright light from above. *Who had brought him here?* Surely bailiffs wouldn't go to the effort of bundling him from his flat to keep him hostage in a basement?

As his memory suddenly lurched back into consciousness, Mickey sat bolt upright, bile racing up his throat.

The Stokers. That's who'd kicked in his door. He remembered now. *Shit.*

Amazed to find that he wasn't tied down, Mickey began to get to his feet. There wasn't anyone here? Maybe the Stokers had made a mistake and pulled him in, only to then realise their error?

Hearing a movement as well as seeing something move from the shadows, Mickey realised he'd been wrong on that assumption slightly too late to avoid the boot smashing into his face, sending him flat on his back. His head whacked the concrete floor with a sickening thud.

Twisted to one side as a heavy boot pressed down against his windpipe, Mickey stared at the drain hole from a closer angle, attempting not to freak out over the metallic taste of blood running from his smashed nose down the inside of his throat.

'Interesting architectural feature that, isn't it, Devlin?' Seb's gravelly voice was loud in the echoing room. 'But being as you're so interested, I'll tell you some history about the place, shall I?'

Removing his foot from Mickey's throat, Seb dropped to his haunches, enjoying the raw terror in this pathetic worm's eyes. 'Many years ago – long before this building became the Orchid, it was a factory, like many places around Birmingham were. You know, when people did a hard day's work for their pay?'

He cracked his knuckles in the gloom, his eyes glinting. '*This* particular building was a meat production place. It had cold stores and of course, several abattoirs.' His mouth twisted into a cruel smile. 'This being one of them...' He jerked his head in the direction of the drain hole. 'And *that* was to get rid of the blood straight into the sewers. Handy, eh?'

Mickey would have swallowed had his throat not seized up. *Abattoir... What the fuck?*

Seb stood back up to his full height, pointing at the low ceiling just above his head. 'And here you can see another useful relic from days gone by... Hanging hooks. They take the weight of several whole cows... Did you know that?' He smiled brightly. 'Fascinating, isn't it, history? Hey, Andrew, did you know any of this?'

'Can't say I did...'

Mickey wanted to scream as the second Stoker stepped from the shadows. *He was done for. Utterly done for.* 'L-look, I...'

Seb's slight nod in his brother's direction was all Andrew required. Before Mickey could even think about forming any further coherent words, he was dragged up by his neck. His legs pointlessly wheeled around in thin air as he found himself hoisted up and hooked over one of the vicious meat hooks, the metal effortlessly puncturing a hole in the back of his jacket. 'Jesus Christ!' he squawked, suspended from the ceiling, his eyes wide with dread.

'Now, shit for brains, start talking. Tell us what you know about Tom Bedworth and why the fuck you deemed it sensible to try and turn over the woman I'm marrying by using the help of your fucked-up children?'

Seb hadn't forgotten the comeuppance Marina was due. Not only for putting a bullet in his thigh, but for wanting and *trying* to kill Sam. For that and that alone, he'd rip this cunt to pieces. But not before he'd got him to spill his guts and tell him every last thing he knew.

* * *

Marina thought about looking over her shoulder before clambering aboard the National Express, but decided not to bother.

There was nothing about this city she wanted to take away with her, short of Samantha Reynold's corpse and the money from her prick of an ex.

She'd got one of those things already and would just bide her time before pulling in the other.

For the umpteenth time, she checked all her bags were safely in her hands or on her person before climbing the last remaining step into the coach. Pulling out her ticket, she smiled convincingly at the uniformed driver, when really she'd love to smash his head through the windscreen for having the audacity to stare at her tits.

Oh, he was having a good look, but reminding herself of her newly formed outlook on life, she wouldn't make a song and dance about it. A couple of hours and she'd be out of here.

And she couldn't wait.

Marina turned her charm up higher than a halogen search-light. 'Birmingham International? The airport?'

'Yes, love,' the driver confirmed, his eyes still firmly glued to Marina's chest. 'This coach is going direct. Are you off on your hols?'

'Yeah, something like that...'

'You've got tons of luggage,' the driver remarked. 'Shall I put it in the hold for you? I'm not sure whether that lot will fit in the overheads and...'

'I'll manage,' Marina snarled, quickly exchanging her irritation for a smile. 'I'll go and find my seat. I don't want to miss my plane.'

And if this freak thought she'd put her bags in the coach's belly where any fucker could help themselves, then he had a sponge instead of a brain. She'd keep this lot on her even if she had to sit on the fucking floor.

Forcing her way up the narrow aisle of the already crammed coach, Marina ignored the glares and tuts as her holdall scraped along people's thighs or faces.

They shouldn't be in the fucking way, she thought, purposefully dragging the holdall on her right shoulder across the back of a man's head.

Stopping, she glared at the outstretched leg of another man reclined in his seat, the hissing and muffled beat from his earphones audible. *There was only so much she could take...*

She jabbed him hard in the arm with her pointy nail. 'Move your fucking foot!' Not waiting to see if he had moved, she stomped along the aisle, finally reaching her seat.

Flopping down in the chair, she dumped her bags across the spare seat next to her. It was empty for now and if she had anything to do with it, it would remain that way.

As the coach engine thrummed into life and they pulled slowly out of the depot, Marina exhaled with relief. Taking the ticket from her pocket, her fingers traced around the rectangular edges representing her guaranteed route out of here.

Destination: Marbella

Granted, it wasn't her first choice, but it would suffice well enough. There would be a beach, sun and plenty of people around enabling her to be anonymous, should the need arise.

Which it wouldn't...

And as for that crusty old bitch in Thompsons Travel who'd given her spiel about no space being available on flights to *anywhere* for the next three weeks... well, it was amazing what a cash incentive did in achieving the impossible...

Travel agents were cunts. *Everyone* was a cunt.

But it was okay. She'd got what she needed for now and that would buy her limitless unmolested time until the window of opportunity opened for her return to finish what she'd started.

* * *

Neil knew as soon as his brothers walked into the office that they'd done what was required. Seb was on a high that he hadn't witnessed for some time. His face looked only what could be described as rapturous – his green eyes shining and manic. The same look his eldest brother wore each and every time a particularly satisfying exchange had occurred. That, or a warranted kill...

In this particular instance, Neil suspected he knew which one Seb's demeanour was down to. The other giveaway was the blood splatters visible over both his brothers' clothes.

'I need Daz and one other to sluice that room down as well as doing the usual clean-up,' Seb said. Quickly stripping his shirt off, he held it out. 'Get rid of this whilst you're at it.'

As Neil took the soiled shirt, Seb walked bare-chested over to the cabinet and snatched up the whisky. Forgoing etiquette, he drank straight from the bottle. Doing Devlin the way they had was like old times. The rush when someone with a well-earned price on their head spilt their guts, bleating the required information in the last throes of blind hope that, despite everything, they could escape with their lives, was always amusing.

The chance of Mickey Devlin walking out of there had been minimal. Correction – it had been *zero*.

'What was said?' Sam rose from her chair, her heart thumping. She didn't need to ask what Mickey Devlin's outcome had been. It was written all over Seb's face. And his clothes.

Seb was so in the zone, he'd forgotten for a second he was in Sam's office and that she was present too. A wide smile creased his face. 'Bedworth *is* in Wolverhampton. Devlin confirmed that was what that tart, Marina, said.'

'We turned over her flat too, but there was no hint of where that psycho bitch has gone,' Andrew added.

'Yeah, that part was disappointing, but the rest was far from it,' Seb grinned, his eyes gleaming. 'By the way, Devlin sends his profuse apologies for instigating his offspring to turn you over. In fact, he couldn't apologise enough – not that it made any difference...'

Sam swallowed uncomfortably. No, she'd expected it wouldn't make any difference. It certainly didn't now. 'But what about your money? Was any indication given as to where it is?'

Seb shook his head. 'Nah. Like I suspected, the prat knew very little – only what his tramp of a daughter had said. But one thing's for sure and that is tomorrow, Wolverhampton is my next stop!'

Sam grabbed Seb's arm. 'Don't rush to take Bedworth out. I want the opportunity to speak to him. I want to see this creature with my own eyes, face to face and...'

'What the fuck for?' Seb cried. 'I'm not waiting longer than needs be to...'

'Before we discuss any of that, you need to see this.' Neil was eager that no argument started between Sam and Seb about when Bedworth's death would happen. And *this* should be enough to deflect from any cross words. For now, at least.

Neil moved to the safe in the corner of Sam's office. Kneeling down, he opened it and, with difficulty, hefted out bags. 'It's all here. Everything required.'

Temporarily forgetting Sam's protest over Bedworth, Seb whooped with delight. He stared into the bags at the tightly packed rolls of money – evidence that today's coke deals had all successfully completed. 'A bunch of happy customers, I see?'

'Five million – more than enough to cover the £4.2 million needed for the rebuild bill, with a bit to spare,' Neil confirmed. 'It's all there, ready to go, and we've still got loads of coke left to flog at a more leisurely pace when we're ready.'

Seb grinned at Sam and dashed to the cupboard to retrieve a clean shirt. 'I bet you can guess where I'm going now…'

'I'll come with you,' Andrew said. Witnessing the final payment for the Peacock's rebuild was what he needed to calm him from the high he shared with Seb. Finally getting their club back up and running was the icing on the cake.

Seb pulled Sam towards him for a kiss. 'What a fucking top day! Only Bedworth and the Rosses to finish now.'

Sam let Seb hoist the bags on his shoulder and leave the office with Andrew before the smile slid from her face. How she would keep him from going all guns blazing to Wolverhampton she wasn't sure, but she had to try. She was determined to face Bedworth herself before he was obliterated from Planet Earth.

It was what she'd dreamt of for so long.

47

'It's hardly relevant now. It's done and dusted and doesn't matter,' Seb shrugged.

Actually, the fact that because of DI Baker's absence he'd been set up and dragged in for an identity parade mattered a *lot*. Only Sam and Tina's efforts, combined with good luck, had got him off the hook, but Baker descending this morning was messing up his plans, so the gripe he had with this man would have to wait.

He'd said last night he would go to Wolverhampton this morning and that he fully intended to do. Baker needed to hurry up and piss off. Seb glared at the back of the detective's head as he continued his annoying habit of fingering anything in front of him he found interesting.

'I have to say I was aghast returning from leave to discover what had happened to you. I can only apologise for that,' Baker continued, determined to absolve himself from blame. 'I can assure you that all of the officers involved have been severely reprimanded and dealt with accordingly.'

Walking in front of Baker, Seb took the gold figurine from his hand and replaced it on the lounge mantlepiece. 'Like I said, it shouldn't have happened, but it's one of those things.' *Again...* 'It's sorted now, thankfully.'

'It was still unacceptable,' Baker grovelled. 'What I can say, though, and I hope is of some solace is that you are no longer under scrutiny over this and won't be again. There's only one person we're after and we're pulling out all the stops to bring the real perpetrator of those murders in.' He lowered his voice. 'Keep this to yourself, but intel has flagged up that Bedworth is in Wolverhampton, so that's our next port of call for a raid, which should be in a couple of days.'

Seb didn't flinch, yet the knowledge the police were closer on Bedworth's tail than he'd thought seared his brain. How had they tracked the man to Wolverhampton? There was no way they were getting hold of that wanker before *he* did. He was getting that bastard for Sam and no one else was taking that prize.

Baker clapped his hands melodramatically. 'So, it's all come good in the end and like I was saying, I can only...'

'Just leave it now,' Seb hissed, cutting Baker off. 'By the way, how's your daughter? I hope she's now well?'

Baker's face split into a wide beam at the unexpected change of subject. 'It was a bit dicey for a while. I don't mind admitting my heart was in my mouth, but...' He patted his chest proudly. 'I'm now a very happy grandfather of a bouncing baby boy!'

'Congratulations!' Seb exclaimed, steering Baker closer to the door. 'I'm very pleased for you!' *Now fuck off out of my house and leave me alone...* 'Thanks for coming round, but I really must get on now.'

Baker opened his mouth to speak, only to find he'd somehow ended up the other side of the front door, which promptly closed in his face.

Having watched the entire exchange, Sam stifled a laugh. 'Seb! That was *so* obvious!'

'That twat would have been here for centuries licking my arse otherwise.' Seb rolled his eyes. 'I'm off now to pick up Andrew and Neil. Things to do and people to see...'

Sam's dread resurfaced. She'd explained in great detail last night why she wanted Seb to hold fire with the plan for Bedworth. She'd really thought he'd listened. '*Please* don't do anything rash. It's really important that I see this man face to face before he's offloaded.'

Seb shrugged on his jacket. 'Yeah, I know. Don't worry, Princess. I know what you want. We're only speccing things out today, nothing more.'

'I'll come with you, then.' Sam reached for her jacket.

'There really isn't any need.' Bending down, Seb planted a kiss on Sam's lips. 'If you could get a final date from the project manager as to when the Peacock rebuild will be complete, that would help loads. Once I've checked out what's going on over Wolverhampton, we'll make a plan for Bedworth, okay?'

Sam studied Seb and raised an eyebrow. 'Okkaaay... as long as you're sure you're not gunning for him today.'

Blowing Sam a kiss, Seb rushed from the house, his car keys in hand. The minute the door was closed, his face twisted into a ferocious snarl.

He knew what Sam wanted but he wasn't having her anywhere near that tainted piece of shit. Neither would he put her in the firing line of anything that might be waiting for them at the Ross headquarters. They could be walking into a trap and Sam wasn't being touched or hurt by any of those bastards. No fucking way. Neither would he stand by and allow Bedworth to find safety behind the bars of a prison cell.

Seb fired the car's engine, the throaty roar loud as he moved down the driveway.

The net was closing in on that Bedworth cunt from angles

other than his, so time was limited. What Sam wished to do for Linda and those other young girls' sakes was a nice thought of hers, just not achievable the way things were panning out. If he could swing it so that she could still do what she wanted, then he would, but only if she wasn't put in danger. And her going anywhere near Wolverhampton would mean just that. Sam's safety *had* to take precedence.

Slamming the car down a gear, Seb made rapid pace towards Broad Street to collect his brothers.

Andrew and Neil knew what was happening. They knew the score.

* * *

Tom kicked an empty can of Tennent's Super out of the way with his boot, surreptitiously keeping an eye out not to place his hoof on any needles the dirty bastards who utilised this waste patch of grass as a jacking-up point might have dropped. That, and turds littering the ground.

Trying to keep his face clear of unsavoury expressions, he watched Potter stumble towards him. For Christ's sake, what an utter bloody joke! God knows what he would say to make this sound convincing. He hadn't got a bloody clue what he was talking about. Regardless of what he'd spouted to Potter, he didn't *really* know any ministers. Neither did he know any suitable words for remembrance services, but hopefully, thanks to the shots of spirits Potter had already slung down his fat neck, he wouldn't take too much notice.

All he had to do was to make this look and sound the real deal.

Tom pulled a velvet-covered bundle from his Tesco carrier. 'Here's Mark's items. I've already said the words to bless them and

I've wrapped them in something suitable,' he said, emboldened to see a flicker of recognition behind Potter's dull eyes.

Yeah, yeah, socks in an old cushion cover were perfect to remember Mark Ross by, Tom thought, concealing his smirk.

He hadn't blessed anything – whatever that entailed, but it sounded impressive. As long as the socks didn't drop out of the bottom of this thing, then he'd get away with it and Potter would be none the wiser. Not that there had been any comments or questions over what he'd done so far. Not a bloody thing. He just had to pray that this bullshit would be enough to make Potter get a grip and sort his head out.

He stole another glance at Potter whilst making a big deal of putting the sock-filled cushion at the base of the gnarled tree, making extra sure not to touch the bark or anywhere near the ground. No doubt it was used as a urinal.

Standing up, Tom cleared his throat and raised his arms skywards. 'We are gathered here today to celebrate the life of Mark Ross – a much-loved family member and wonderful friend...'

God, this was embarrassing. And ridiculous. It had better do the trick.

Although hopefully not for a couple hours more...

Tom wanted the extra little bonus for himself before Potter finally snapped out of his catatonia. Once the fat jerk was wasted after the wake he'd got lined up for the two of them following this load of bollocks, he'd leave the twat dribbling into his pint and sneak a quick shifty around the Portakabin. There would be a few quid stashed in that poxy place that he could grab for himself.

Tom continued muttering more nonsensical words, happy to see tears rolling down Potter's cheek.

Yep, this was doing the trick. He really was a clever bastard for thinking this one up, even if he did say so himself. And if lady luck prevailed, he'd be out of this dump long before the Stoker wankers descended.

48

Seb's jaw was so tight, it felt it may snap. He stared through the windscreen at the sign in front of him.

Primo Autoshop

His fist clenched harder. 'We're here,' he hissed. 'I want Potter and I want Bedworth. We're going in.'

There was no point checking to see if there was a trap before they steamed into a rival's territory. Rivals who, without a doubt, would likely be waiting for their arrival. This possibility made no difference to the relentless and insatiable need for payback.

Neil could spout any number of sensibilities he wished, but Seb was so fuming, it was impossible to listen to reason or contemplate any other way. This was not continuing for one second longer.

It had suddenly dawned on him during the tense drive over to Wolverhampton that Bedworth must have been the loser he'd seen in the cork hat accompanying Mark Ross to the docks on the day of the heist, a thought that had sickened him further. His most wanted had been right in front of him, yet he'd missed it? That alone scalded hotter than burning oil.

Seb scowled. He wouldn't miss anything else. Bedworth's list of crimes was far too long and the Rosses had stepped well over the line. There was no going back.

Jerking open the van doors, Seb clambered out, his brothers following.

Andrew glanced around the deserted yard. 'Where the fuck is everyone?'

Neil frowned. 'Do you reckon they've had a tip-off and heard we were coming?'

'By who?' Seb strode into the yard. If he'd lost the chance to finally bring Bedworth in and rip him to pieces, then he'd never forgive himself. Conversely, if the Rosses had buggered off to pastures new, that only meant their ugly mugs would resurface at some point in the near future to play stupid bastards over territory again, or kill more of his or Sam's men.

And without knowing where they were put the Stokers at a distinct disadvantage.

Sensing movement in the corner of the yard, Seb froze. On spotting a man, he lurched forward like a panther.

The young man yelped as he was dragged around the side of a workshop and slammed up against the wall. 'Where is he? Where's Ross and his new sidekick, Bedworth? And don't try telling me that you don't know!'

The young lad's mouth flapped up and down, the vice-like grip on his throat choking. His eyes darted from the terrifying Stoker man in front of him, to the equally scary two standing to either side.

He knew who these men were and therefore knew it was fruitless trying to worm his way out of this. Besides, he didn't owe Potter Ross or that other bloke anything. The only reason he and a couple of others were still knocking around was because of a lack of anything else to do. Everyone knew the Rosses were finished, that's why everyone had gone.

'I asked you a question.' Flecks of Seb's spittle landed on the young lad's face. 'I suggest you answer it.' Releasing his hold, he watched the lad sag against the wall, his hands moving to his throat. 'Talk!'

Seb remained poised in case a fleeting instance of juvenile exuberance caused this kid to pull a fast one. If he attempted that, it would be the last thing he achieved in this life.

'There's no one here! Everyone's legged it,' the lad croaked, but unable to stop himself, his eyes flickered over to the Portakabin.

Seb clocked where the man's eyes inadvertently darted to. 'You're lying!' he spat, jerking his head in the direction of the Portakabin. 'They're in there, aren't they? Is it both of them? Ross and Bedworth?'

'N-no! They're not in there and I don't know who Bedworth is,' the lad garbled. Choking once again as the grip returned around his throat, this time even harder, he frantically waved his hand, begging to be allowed to continue. 'B-but there is a man who's been around recently. A Brummie. Potter let him stay in one of his flats. Me ma does the cleaning for Mr Ross and she sa...'

'The address of this flat?' Andrew growled, stepping forward.

Pulling out his phone, he quickly made a note of what the lad stuttered in his terror.

'There! That wasn't so difficult, was it?' Seb smiled coldly. 'But you're still lying, which is very stupid. Where's everyone else really?'

The young man swallowed painfully, sure his throat was crushed flat. They might know he was lying, but he was done for anyway.

'I told you the truth. Everyone left after Mark died because

Potter won't deal with anything. He's lost the plot and...' The lad eyed Seb warily. 'No one wanted to hang around for when... when...'

'When *I* turned up?' Seb laughed, his eyes tracking back to the Portakabin. 'Well, guess what? I *have* turned up!' And because this kid was a shit liar, Potter and Ross must be in that Portakabin. *Someone* was. Right now, that someone was looking through those bent blinds, realising they were fucked. He would enjoy this. And there was no time like the present to take that enjoyment.

Sensing it was time for the off, Andrew grabbed the lad by his arm, his eyes narrowing. 'Bring this one in as well?'

Seb paused, his eyes still fixed on the Portakabin, sure the yellowing blind at one of the windows fluttered. He'd pull Bedworth, Ross *and* this little prick in and take them to the warehouse, which was now clear enough for a spot of torturing without fear of interruptions by coke deals. That way, before Bedworth met his maker, Sam could have her chance of an audience with the worm, like she so yearned for.

The Erdington warehouse was far from Ross soil, so any fuckers having a change of heart and remembering loyalty to the firm they'd chosen to side with and return to fight their corner wouldn't dare set foot on *his* territory. Or he could just do it here and leave Potter Ross's head on a fucking stake to serve as a warning to any other dickhead thinking it a good idea to take the Stokers on.

No, he'd take Bedworth and Ross back to his own turf. Once Sam had her say and did what she needed, then he'd knock every last bit of life out of the cunts who had caused everyone so much bother. Then he'd...

Seb's thought process stopped, seeing Andrew's rabid impatience morph to alarm as he stared at the phone in his free hand. 'What?'

'A text from Kev. I've only just seen it.' Ignoring the young man still firmly within his grip, Andrew held the phone up so Seb could view the screen:

Baker called. Said to tell you it's happening today.

Seb stared at the text, his mind whirring. *Today?* Did Baker mean the police were pulling the Wolverhampton raid today? He'd said this morning it was happening in a couple of days, not *today*...

Various scenarios revolved in Seb's mind – none of them good. 'When was this sent?'

Pulling the phone back towards him, Andrew scrolled to the details of the text message. 'Eleven o'clock.'

'Shit!' Seb hissed. The raid must have been decided on the second Baker had returned to the station. It was already 2 p.m. So much for no more cock-ups. How had this happened? Unless Baker had an inkling they were planning something such as this and was setting him up?

But then, why warn him if that was the case?

Seb scowled. He'd have to lift Bedworth and Ross and do it fucking quick.

His plan of checking out the address for Bedworth was up the swannee too. At least for now. No one could afford to hang around with coppers set to arrive at any time. 'Come on!' Seb jerked his head in the direction of the Portakabin. 'Bring the van round and back it up. There's no time to waste.' He yanked Andrew's hand free of the young man. 'Fuck off whilst you can, kid.'

The young lad remained stock still, not sure he'd heard correctly. *The Stokers were letting him go?* 'I...'

'What are you doing?' Neil hissed.

'He won't bleat,' Seb shrugged. 'Besides, there's no one to bleat to!' He turned his attention back to the trembling lad. 'Go on. Don't just stand there! Disappear. Don't force me to have to come and find you.'

The young man didn't need further encouragement. 'I – I won't, Mr Stoker. You have my word!' With that, he disappeared from the yard so quickly it was as if he'd never been there at all.

Seb stalked towards the Portakabin, ignoring his brothers' eyes burning into the back of his head. '*These* are the important ones, not a fucking gopher! Now get the van!'

Andrew and Neil had almost cleared half the yard before they heard the tell-tale sound that they were too late to follow Plan A.

Sirens...

'Fuck!' Seb spat. 'The raid? And if not, then coppers are still heading in this direction. Lots of them!'

'We won't have time to take Ross and Bedworth!' Neil cried.

'No, which means there's only one way to do this because I'm not letting the filth get these two. Over my dead fucking body!' Spotting a large canister near a workshop door, Seb dragged it out, confident it contained what he hoped it did. 'Help me stack some shit up.'

Grabbing anything bulky and heavy to hand between them, Seb, Neil and Andrew made quick work of constructing a makeshift barricade against the Portakabin door.

The only way in. Or out...

This barricade wouldn't last for two seconds if anyone put effort into it from inside, but it was the only hope of pulling this off. With this unexpected change of plans, there was no other solution.

Seb rushed back to the cannister. 'Grab another one,' he hissed and, with effort, hoisted the metal drum higher and unscrewed the lid. Getting a whiff of fumes, he grinned.

Hurriedly dousing the door and front walls of the Portakabin with petrol, Seb left his brothers to do likewise to the workshops and anything else that could be covered with enough fuel to ensure it took light. Hearing sudden cries from inside the Portakabin, he checked his brothers' positions before pulling a box of matches from his pocket.

'Matches for every eventuality,' he muttered. That was his motto and this was a perfect example.

The 'boomf' as the petrol ignited made Seb's heart thump, his building elation only trumped by the now desperate cries and banging as the two people he hated most in the world realised their time was up.

He knew all too well how ruinous fire was. Even more so when trapped in it. Like *them*. And who more deserving of being burnt to a crisp than the person who had razed the Peacock to the ground the very same way? 'What goes around comes around, Bedworth!' Seb roared.

He glanced around, satisfied those cunts were going nowhere and his brothers' efforts to deal with the rest of the Ross workfront ensured there would be shag all business left to trade.

He smiled. This way might not be ideal, but it had to be done.

Seb stilled for a moment, just able to discern the muffled screams over the loud crackling of the fire and the sirens, which were getting louder. *Much* louder...

As much as he'd love to hang around to watch how this unfolded, he couldn't. 'We need to disappear,' he said abruptly. Not even a glimpse of one of his tail-lights could be sighted around this shithole when the police appeared.

As they clambered into the van, Seb turned to his brothers, resenting taking his eyes from the inferno. 'Let's take the opportunity to check out that flat. The Old Bill will be too busy dealing with this to look anywhere else for the time being.'

He grinned as their van screeched off the Primo Autoshop's yard. This might not have been done the way it was planned, but Ross and Bedworth were done for and there was still a fighting chance he could reclaim his stolen money before returning to Birmingham.

Sam would be disappointed about this chain of events, as was he, but she would have to accept the change of circumstances was beyond his control.

* * *

'How are you feeling, mate?' Tom asked, helping Potter keep pace as they made their way back towards the yard. 'Right proper send-off, that was. Mark's in good hands now.' Ignoring how Potter's tear-stained, puffy face remained passive and devoid of expression, he continued rambling. 'Now we'll go to the pub and have a few jars in Mark's memory, like we planned.'

Like *he'd* planned, rather, not Potter. Potter had done shag all for this or *anything*. And that grated on his bollocks. But he was nearly done here now.

Tom glanced sideways at the shuffling man beside him, refraining from shoving him into the path of the bus trundling along the road. *Just keep it together a bit longer*, he willed himself. 'We'll quickly nip back to the yard and grab a few quid for drinks.'

He didn't want to risk taking money with them to the pretend remembrance service. As suspected, there had been a selection of fucked-up junkies lurking around the periphery of the wasteland patch, watching them intently. Tom wasn't getting turned over by hepatitis-ridden fuckjobs for a couple of notes.

Furthermore, it was *Potter's* money they'd spend at the boozer, not his. He was buggered if he was using any of his own getting this bloated bastard drunk. With any luck, Potter would stupidly outline exactly where in the Portakabin his funds were kept, which would save time when he shortly returned to clear everything out.

'Yeah, it will be nice to raise a toast to Mark – just the two of us.

As I keep saying, I had loads of time for your brother,' Tom blath-
ered, the stream of sickening lies in aid of the cause rotting his
mouth like a gob full of acid. He felt like shouting that he hated
Mark Ross and hoped the man was trapped in a hellish purgatory
for eternity – if, for nothing else, to winkle a reaction from the
zombie residing in Potter's body.

Although it was tempting, Tom believed even that would have
as much effect on Potter as electrodes attached to a corpse's
genitals.

Just keep talking, feed him as many drinks as required and then
he was good to go. And that had better happen soon because Tom
needed time away to get his bearings and rethink his plan of
action.

Nearing the turn for the Autoshop, Tom's nostrils twitched.
'Jeez, someone's having a bloody bonfire. Do they want a smog
problem back around these parts or what?'

As they rounded the corner, his stomach plunged somewhere
near to his feet, realising something was very wrong. 'Wait!' He
held his arm out across Potter's huge expanse of middle, the big
man obediently halting in his tracks like a puppet.

Tom stared at the amassed crowd amongst the flashing lights
and a bustle of uniformed men swarming in and around the yard.
He then looked up at the billowing smoke pouring into the sky, his
eyes as well as his nose stinging. 'What the fuck...?' he gasped,
moving slowly forward. 'What the hell's happened?'

He turned to Potter. 'Stay there,' he hissed. 'Don't move a single
muscle.' After checking to see Potter remained where instructed,
Tom pushed forward to mingle with the crowd of onlookers.

At least this bunch of morbid ghouls would detract from his
presence if the Stokers were lurking and admiring their handi-
work. Because this was down to them. It *had* to be.

Fuck.

Tom trod heavily on a man's foot as he shoved further to the front. 'Sorry, mate,' he muttered. 'What's happened here?'

Scowling, a man with several missing teeth faced him. 'I'm fucked if I know, but someone's torched the place, that's for sure.' He scraped his hand under his running nose. 'Can't say I'm surprised. Word has it the Ross firm is finished. Apparently, the big man's lost the plot, so it's probably an insurance job.'

Tom squinted harder, his heart clamouring with what he saw. 'Don't know about an insurance job. Not *everyone* has buggered off...' He jerked his head to where men in plastic suits manoeuvred from the yard towards a waiting van.

If he wasn't mistaken, the men had two bagged-up bodies on gurneys.

'Shit the bed!' The man blew through what teeth he had left. 'I wonder if it was suicide then? That could be Potter and some other poor fucker being dragged out of there. He probably gave up, the state people said he was in.'

'Perhaps...' Tom muttered, his mind ticking over at ten to the dozen. He knew for a fact it wasn't suicide, but if that's what this lot wanted to think, then who was he to argue? His eyes tracked to the two fire engines, their hoses still pumping water over the smouldering remains of the Primo Autoshop buildings, ensuring there was no risk of reigniting.

This completely screwed his plan of filching a bit of extra cash from the Portakabin, but it made no odds. If there was a chance the Stokers were still hanging around, both he and Potter had to get out of here sharpish.

Shit! Potter! He'd left the gormless cunt waiting around the corner. He'd better not have wandered off. Turning, Tom made to push his way back in the direction he had come.

'Hey! Aren't you watching the rest?' the toothless man shouted.

'No, I've seen enough.' Tom elbowed through the steadily

increasing mass of people. There was no choice now but to retreat to the flat. It also meant he'd have to take Potter with him, which was a hideous concept, but at least he still had money stashed and the minute this shit died down, he was out of here.

He'd leave Potter to be torn apart by the Stokers because he was damned if that would be happening to *him*.

49

'What a fucking dump!' Andrew grabbed a pen from the table and used it to gingerly lift a dirty shirt from the floor.

'Don't mess about with that shit,' Seb said. 'Let's just locate our money and get the hell out of here.' When the police worked out the bodies in the Portakabin, which must be charcoal by now, belonged to Bedworth and Ross, they'd be looking anywhere either of them had been last living for next of kin details. Neither he, Neil or Andrew could be within a ten-mile radius by that point.

Seb scanned the paltry contents of the flat. There was barely a stick of furniture in the place and the whole gaff had a weird smell – a cloying hint of decay. Some smells could *never* be thoroughly removed. This being one of them.

What an utter dump.

He scowled. The day veering off at a steep tangent from what had been planned and Bedworth and Ross now being dust hadn't fully sunk in. The joy of personally torturing those two men before removing them from life remained current in his mind like it was still a viable option.

But it wasn't and that was beginning to hit home.

Both men were dead, and Seb had been robbed of the pleasure of making them suffer to points neither of them could have imagined.

And it galled.

He hadn't realised how long he'd held his jaw clenched for, but judging by the persistent, nagging ache, it had been some time. He suspected it would only worsen as the unpalatable knowledge that payback on those bastards had been unfairly reduced seeped further into his mind.

Sure, he could tell himself the main aim had been achieved, but it didn't stop the way it had happened from grating.

'Have you checked under these ones in here?'

Neil's voice snapped Seb from his roundabout of incessant thoughts. He looked up, somewhat startled to find Andrew pointing to the floor.

'Didn't Linda say Bedworth had a penchant for stashing things under floorboards?' Andrew jammed his crowbar between two ill-fitting boards. 'Me and Neil have done the bedroom, if you can call it that, but we haven't looked here.'

Moving swiftly across the room, Seb's concentration returned to the present. There was no point dwelling on what couldn't be changed. Regaining his money would soften the blow, so he would concentrate on that.

With a renewed sense of enthusiasm, he dropped to his haunches and hooked his fingers under the boards Andrew had leverage on. He pulled one up easily and peered into the hole beneath. 'Bollocks! There's fuck all here!'

Letting the board drop back into place, Seb stamped it down with disappointment. What if his hunch was wrong and Bedworth hadn't got the money? Or he'd got it, but stashed it elsewhere? That knowledge had now disappeared with the man's demise.

Seb sighed. He knew the lost money had been replaced via

different means, but it would have been gratifying reclaiming the *original* money from the *original* thief.

Neil sighed despondently. 'I hate to say it, but I think we'll have to jack this off as a dead loss.'

'I think you're right. We can't hang around here any longer and... Hold on a sec...' Eyes narrowing, Seb darted over to the corner of the room. It was only a slightly bunched-up piece of carpet against the skirting board, which judging by the rest of this dump meant little. But call it instinct... 'I want a quick look here.'

Kneeling on the grubby carpet, Seb tugged at the nasty green covering to find it dislodged easily from where it was tucked under the skirting board lip. His pulse ramped up as he rolled the carpet back to reveal loose floorboards. 'I think we may have located the place,' he whispered. *But that didn't mean anything was still there...*

Scrabbling against the edge of the board, Seb prised it up. Dismissing the filthy floor, he lay belly down and plunged his arm into the hole. Having a wide reach, he blindly groped around, his fingers brushing against canvas. He traced the outline of one, possibly more objects that felt like bags...

Seb looked up at his brothers. 'I think we've only gone and fucking found it!'

* * *

'They've gone to Wolverhampton, haven't they?' Sam cried, her stress levels hitting ceiling-height. She'd just *known* Seb would do this. Just known it.

Kevin wrung his meaty hands together. He hadn't wanted Sam to discover the Stokers had done the opposite of what she'd asked. Neither did he want to be the one telling her about it. Or that he'd been party to the plan, but it was too late now. What choice had he but to send that text to warn them? What he hadn't noticed was that Sam had seen what he'd keyed into the phone, resulting in the obvious questions that he could not deny.

He stared at his mobile. If this bloody thing didn't have such stupid, poxy buttons to press with fingers the size of *his*, then perhaps it wouldn't have taken so long to text a couple of words and therefore wouldn't have given Sam the window of opportunity to see.

Damn.

But although he couldn't deny he knew what the Stokers had planned, it wasn't what Sam assumed. 'I understand your frustration, but...'

'Frustration?' Sam paced the room. 'Seb's gone to kill Bedworth when he promised me he was only speccing things out! How can I not be frustrated or angry? I wanted to have things out with that bastard. After that, *then* he could die! I'd happily fucking watch. Now I can't do either of those things!'

Kev decided he might as well tell Sam everything, rather than let her make the wrong assumptions. 'Okay, yes, they've gone to Wolverhampton, but they're planning to bring both men in, not kill them!' he reasoned. 'They're taking them to the lockup. That's what I'm waiting for – the nod to say they've arrived so I can bring you to ask your questions.'

Sam stopped pacing, relief washing over her like a waterfall. 'So, Seb hasn't gone to kill Bedworth? Why didn't he just tell me this?'

Kev sighed. 'See it from his side. The man wants to protect you. He won't place you in jeopardy.'

Sam's indignation bristled. 'But...'

'They could be walking into a trap set by the Rosses. Seb won't take the chance of involving you, should that happen.' Kev raised an eyebrow. 'He also knows, like I do, that if he told you the plan was to lift those men, then you'd have insisted on accompanying them regardless. Tell me I'm wrong.'

Despite her tenseness, Sam couldn't help a slight smile from forming. It was true. She *would* have insisted. And if Seb believed she could be harmed, it would deflect his concentration and that wasn't helpful.

'Why can't you just accept the man loves you? Christ, if you were my wife, I'd make exactly the same decision!'

Sam smiled. Fully, this time. She wasn't Seb's wife quite yet, but she soon would be, and that Seb had kept his word spoke volumes. He no longer treated her unequally and that meant the world. 'When will they be back?'

Questions she wanted to throw at that despicable creature who had ruined her mother's life began stacking in her mind. How she'd refrain from killing Bedworth herself, she didn't yet know...

'Soon, I hope,' Kev said, glancing at his watch. 'I also hope you'll then be able to do what you need.'

Sam's pile of questions toppled, her blood thrumming in her veins. 'What do you mean, "hope"?'

'Erm, I don't yet know whether they've pulled it off. If it was a trap or if the police got there, then...'

Sam bit her bottom lip. If it was a trap, Seb could be dead. If the police had suddenly descended and they'd been caught unawares, then Seb and his brothers could have been arrested. Or if they'd been forced to leave empty handed, then it meant that bastard and the Rosses had evaded punishment *again*. They could have gone anywhere...

Sweat prickled. They would be back to square one and that couldn't happen. It just couldn't.

She inhaled deeply, willing herself to remain calm until she had a cast-iron reason not to be. 'No one responded to your text?'

That was the part that bothered Kev. 'No... I don't know

whether it was seen or even received.' He shrugged glumly. 'I've got no way of finding out, so all we can do is wait and hope they've done what was needed.'

Sam resumed her pacing. She was tired of waiting. She wanted – *needed* this to be over. 'I'm sick of Bedworth ruining my life,' she spat, more to herself than Kev.

50

Constantly looking over his shoulder, Tom got to the flats as quickly as possible, not helped by Potter, who he felt was dragging his feet purely to annoy him.

Stopping at the end of the road before the block of flats came into view, Tom leant against the wall and pressed Potter as close as possible to the brickwork that the man's massive gut allowed.

Now, the burning question was, were the Stokers here? Waiting?

'Burning question' being an apt phrase if he was correct in his assumption. He was *sure* the Stokers must have torched Potter's place. Who else would it realistically be?

And if they knew he was with Potter, which they must, then it also meant it was likely they'd discovered where he was staying...

Tom's eyes narrowed at the ghastly lump of concrete that Potter had so 'kindly' allowed him to reside in. He'd have been better off kipping down with those fucking junkies on the waste patch of grass. It was cleaner.

Every tendon and sinew in Tom's body coiled like a spring, his heartbeat thudding in his ears. Any second now, a bullet would appear. He wouldn't have time to work out where it came from and when he heard that hissing whistle, it would already be too late. It would lodge a hole in his temple, between his eyes or blow the back of his skull out...

As much as he resented it, Tom couldn't prevent his body from trembling. But he wouldn't fold under this pressure. He just *wouldn't*. Those jumped-up pointless bastards that his stupid bitch of a daughter had attached herself to, could take pot shots all they liked. They could tie him up, torture him, do what they damn well liked. He wasn't scared. He'd show them...

Tom bit his tongue as he gnashed his teeth. Who was he trying to kid? He was shitting himself. Completely bricking it.

So, where the fuck were they?

Tom glanced sideways at Potter, who remained as vacant as ever. Hadn't the mug noticed his whole business had gone up in flames?

Shit. What if the police turned up at the flat next?

No, they wouldn't. *He* didn't own the firm, Potter did. They'd been looking for him to inform him about the tragedy and they'd...

Yelping as a hand appeared on his shoulder, Tom spun around, his legs turning to jelly and his bowels liquefying on impact. *The Stokers?*

'I've been hoping you'd come here. Has Mr Ross heard what's ha...'

'What the fuck?' Tom screeched, somehow controlling the urge to hyperventilate and vomit at the same time, amazed his heart hadn't flatlined. He gasped with sheer relief to find the person sneaking up on him wasn't his arch nemesis, but then scowled, realising it was that stupid little bastard from Potter's place. 'Don't creep up on people!'

The young lad clung onto Tom's sleeve. 'The yard's burnt down!' He turned to Potter. 'Can you hear me, Mr Ross? It's the yard... It's burnt down and...'

'Speak to me, not him! Potter ain't got a clue what fucking day it is,' Tom snarled, yanking his arm from the lad's clutches. 'And yes, I know the yard's burnt down.'

'Y-you must be Bedworth,' the lad gibbered. 'They were looking for you. They...'

'Who was looking for me?' *Come on, say it*, Tom thought. *Was he right?*

'The Stokers! They were asking after you and Potter. They threatened me – asking where you both were.'

Tom's eyes narrowed. *What a surprise. Correct again...* He glanced around a further time. *Wait a minute...* 'You thick fuck!' he yelled. 'If you've been speaking to the Stokers, they could have followed you here!' His hands grasped for the young man's throat, which by its redness, looked like someone else had come up with the same idea not long since. 'You've told them where I'm staying, haven't you, you little cunt?'

'No!' the lad shouted. 'I said neither of you were in the yard, but they didn't believe me.' *Sort of true...* 'They thought you were in the Portakabin.'

Tom paused. *So the Stokers thought he and Potter were in the Portakabin?* A flicker of unexpected pleasure glowed inside his brain. If they believed him to have been in there, then they'd think he'd been torched along with the shitty place.

With a wide grin, Tom turned to Potter, then, changing his mind about commenting being as the retard wouldn't respond, swung back to the boy. 'How come they let you go?' *That wasn't like the Stokers...*

The lad shrugged. 'Not sure, but they were twitchy after they received a text message, and then once I left the yard, I heard sirens coming closer.'

Tom raised an eyebrow. *The cops?* This got better and better... So, the police had been on route – most likely for *him*, making the

Stokers cut their game short and burn the place down instead. Now, thanks to this skinny twat, they thought that *he'd* burnt with it.

Brilliant!

Beaming, Tom slapped the young lad on the back. 'All in all, a good day then?'

'A good day? How? Bill and Pete, the security guards, were in the Portakabin! They're dead and the yard ha...'

'Oh, well... Shit happens.' Tom flapped his hand. *It was good news for him, anyhow.* 'Get on your way then, kid.' Now the coast was clear, he and Potter could go to the flat and safely keep out of the way for a while.

He was in such a good mood with this unexpected news, even the concept of putting up with Potter's useless presence wasn't as offensive as it had been half an hour ago.

Noticing the lad was still standing there, Tom's eyes narrowed. 'I told you to fuck off, didn't I? There's nothing else to say. And don't be telling anyone you've seen me. *Either* of us.'

The lad shook his head vehemently. 'I wouldn't dream of it, Mr Bedworth, but... I was thinking... Shouldn't I get some kind of reward for my troubles? After all, I didn't have to look for you to tell you.'

A strangled-sounding laugh escaped from between Tom's gritted teeth. 'You want me to thank you for not grassing us up? Are you taking the piss?'

Having already escaped unscathed from the Stokers, the lad felt he could be more confident. 'Well, no... I was just thinking perhaps of a few quid to...'

'You want a fucking tip for doing your job, you wanker? Okay!' Tom delivered an expertly aimed headbutt that not only smashed the young man's nose but collapsed him to the floor. 'You cheeky cunt! Now, here's a tip! Get the fuck out of here before I smash every single tooth out of your gob. And after I've done that, I'll sell you to the fucking Stokers myself!'

Scrabbling from the floor, the young lad staggered off down the road with blood pouring down his T-shirt, leaving Tom chuckling. He had to admire that little prick for his front.

He tugged Potter's arm. 'Come on, we'll go to the flat and raise a glass to Mark there instead of the pub, eh?'

Now he could catch his breath, grab the money and work out what to do now without the added pressure of the Stokers on his back.

* * *

Seb took the beautifully cut crystal tumbler from Neil and raised it to his lips whilst keeping one eye on Sam. Most of the journey back to the Orchid he'd spent wracking his brains how to break the news she could no longer confront the man she'd waited so long for.

He ran his finger around the rim of the glass, battling between being overjoyed that their problems were over and resentment for not meting out sorely deserved punishment.

Knowing how much it meant to Sam, Seb had fully expected her to hit the roof on his return and be angry with him – with *everyone*, but she wasn't. Much to his surprise, the first thing she'd asked as they stepped through the door was, 'Where is he?' – like she'd known what was planned.

Kev's face had quickly underlined that Sam *was* aware of the plans.

Initially irritated with the man, Seb found that soon evaporated. Sam already had suspicions that he hadn't gone to Wolverhampton purely for a reccy and at least Kev had levelled up his mishap by setting the record straight. Everything Kev had told Sam was true.

Seb was steadfast that Sam's life and well-being would *never* be risked on the proviso of getting her say with Bedworth, even if that meant twisting the truth somewhat. Whatever she thought of that, he firmly stuck by his decision and still did. But however it had turned out, he really *had* intended to bring the tossers in.

'I think this is well-deserved.' Neil raised his glass of whisky, his eyes fixed on the money Andrew tipped from the holdalls recovered from Bedworth's flat.

Seb's glass paused halfway to his mouth. 'Just not in quite the way we'd hoped...'

Registering the disappointment in Seb's eyes, Sam sipped her drink. It wasn't what *she'd* hoped for either.

Her first reaction on seeing Seb was relief he hadn't walked into a trap on the Rosses' manor or been caught red-handed meting out punishment to Bedworth by the police. This relief had fast turned to impatience. If Seb was back, where was the man she wanted to rip to pieces with her bare hands?

Listening to what had unfolded, Sam had been both gutted and angry. Not with Seb. Not with him at all. Having had time to reflect on Kev's words as they waited, she'd already accepted why Seb had planned things the way he had. She'd even found herself agreeing with his decision, despite it meaning he hadn't been completely on the level. Sometimes there were valid reasons, and this was one of them.

But it didn't change that she was utterly furious not to get the chance to personally make Bedworth pay for what he'd done to her, to Linda and to all those women and girls he'd abused.

It seemed grossly unjust that the man should find death so quickly. In an ideal world, Tom Bedworth's demise would have mirrored the long-inflicted misery, pain and terror he'd caused to every single person he'd touched with his tainted hands over the years.

On the flipside, Bedworth was dead, and the Ross firm was finished. And as an added bonus, Seb had retrieved part of his stolen money back.

She knew she couldn't change what had happened, so the only thing to do was concentrate on their problems being over. And concentrate *only* on that. Because that alone was a massive relief.

Seeing Sam's mind filled with thoughts, Seb studied her with his piercing green eyes, the weight of failing to deliver what she needed heavy. He reached for her hand. 'I'm sorry, Princess. If there had been another way…'

Sam squeezed Seb's hand. 'If you'd not taken the route you did, then both Bedworth and Ross would still be out there and we wouldn't know where. It was the right thing to do.'

Seb nodded, not entirely convinced Sam was comfortable with how the events had unfolded, regardless of what she said.

Sam frowned. She didn't want Seb wasting another second on something that couldn't be altered. 'Look, how could I not be gutted that I can't say what I've dreamt of saying? How can I not be pissed off that I won't get to enjoy you slowly ripping the life from that bastard? But… Bedworth's dead. And with that, my mother is free, as are all the women he hurt. *That's* the most important thing.'

She looked at her hands, a sad smile crossing her mouth. 'And no, it won't bring the woman in the wardrobe or the girl he ran over back to life. Nor all the other people he killed or had a hand in destroying, but he can't do anything to anyone else now, so we must be thankful for that.'

She looked around the room, seeing the other Stokers, Daz and Kev nodding in agreement. 'I only wish I could find Tina to tell her that she has nothing to run from any longer.'

'Not even from us?' Seb winked, feeling more at ease with the situation. 'Doesn't she still owe you four hundred quid?'

Sam laughed. 'Not even from us. And let's not forget – Devlin's toast and Marina's gone too. She won't be back again. Not now.' She took hold of both of Seb's hands. 'You've done it! The Rosses are finished, and your club is almost back up and running. Stu has got justice and you've even retrieved some of your cash. So...' Standing up, she raised her glass high. 'There's *definitely* cause to celebrate! Now I'm calling Linda to tell her the good news. I think she's been waiting for this moment even longer than us!'

Seb's face broke into a smile, watching Sam dial Linda's number. Sam was the only person in the entire world who had the ability to reinstate him as king of the world when he felt the opposite.

How lucky he was to call her his own. Now he could get on with things the way he'd planned for their life together.

It was definitely time to start putting phase two of their life into action.

And it started now.

51

THREE WEEKS LATER

'It's stunning, Seb, it really is!' Linda cried, meaning every single word.

Seb smoothed down the lapels·of his tuxedo, his free arm firmly on Sam's waist. He smiled proudly at his soon-to-be mother-in-law. 'Thank you, Linda.'

Despite wearing her Louboutin stilettos, Sam had to push herself onto tiptoes to kiss Seb on the lips. 'I'm so proud of you,' she whispered.

Linda watched her daughter with the man she would shortly marry and felt happier than ever. All animosity and awkwardness had long since fallen away between her and Seb. Knowing her daughter was now completely safe and free from harm, her life was complete.

Having spent almost a month with her two youngest children at Sam's adoptive mother's house, being invited to the grand reopening of the Royal Peacock was the icing on the cake – an honour that only a year ago she couldn't have imagined.

None of what her life had now become could she have dreamt of. And all because of her most beautiful firstborn daughter.

Linda's heart swelled with pride as she sipped her mineral water. Despite many people saying so, even *she* had to acknowledge that she looked at least ten years younger. This wasn't only down to cosmetic dentistry, regular facials, and the beautiful clothes Sam had insisted upon. It wasn't even down to being clean from drugs or drink...

Of course, all of those things had contributed, but what gave Linda the edge was not something possessions, a healthy lifestyle or any amount of money could buy. The intrinsic and deep-seated peace she felt could never be purchased.

Finally, Linda could relax.

She was free.

Free from Tom Bedworth, Mickey Devlin and all the men and things which had controlled and dragged her down for decades.

It was impossible to retrieve what she had lost or regain what had been taken, but she *had* been able to start again with a completely clean slate. She was rebuilding her life with her youngest children who, thankfully, had big enough hearts to let her back into their lives; she was living with an exceptionally kind woman in a beautiful house and Sam was safe, happy and content. What else could she ever wish for?

Sam smiled at her mother, thinking how amazing she looked. There were no longer qualms that Linda might slip back down the slimy slope of addiction. The change in her was absolute and Sam couldn't have been more pleased. 'You look like the cat who's got the cream.'

'I feel like it!' Linda grinned. 'I'm *so* pleased everything's coming good for us all at last. And this place... well... wow!'

Sam's eyes mirrored Linda's joy as she looked around the rebuilt interior of the Peacock. Splendid in its opulence, it was just as nice as it had been before its destruction, if not *better*. The rebuild was impressive and she couldn't fail but be proud as punch for Seb.

She watched him being congratulated by people invited as VIPs for the special opening night before the casino officially reopened to the public.

It marked a new chapter in all of their lives.

The night after Bedworth's demise, she and Seb had taken a couple of well-deserved days off from work. They'd sent out all the wedding invitations and, like he'd planned, Seb had already made the official decision to move his business dealings away from the less salubrious side of things. This was something she too had also chosen. Things would be a lot different from now on.

Sam's eyes lit up at the prospect. Never having been maternal, it was strange how the combination of a good man that she could count on in any eventuality, inner peace and genuine contentment could change a mindset to consider certain things in a different light. Now, for the first time, their world was safe enough to perhaps extend to involve a brand new member of the family. And once they were married, only a handful of weeks from now, she would let nature take its course...

Returning to stand beside Sam, Seb slipped his arm back around her waist. 'Time to deal with the press,' he grinned. 'We've even got *Midlands Today* clamouring for an interview.'

Sam rolled her eyes, but only in jest. For once, she didn't resent the newspapers and television intruding. She wanted the whole city and the whole world to celebrate their good fortune.

EPILOGUE

Tom picked through the cardboard-like remnants of the takeaway left over from last night. Stone cold and only slightly less edible than the night before, he'd probably get food poisoning, but in all truthfulness, he couldn't care less.

Having his head down the toilet for the foreseeable future would give him a break.

Three weeks he'd been holed up in this rancid dump with little more than a stuffed pig who alternated between staring at the wall or crying, thinking it standard behaviour.

It was driving him insane.

Tom scowled at Potter, slumped in the sagging armchair. He'd even degenerated into dreaming about killing the fat toad more often than usual this past week.

One thing was crystal clear: nothing would knock Potter from his trauma-induced catatonia. *Nothing.*

Even that stupid memorial service or the gaff getting burnt down hadn't shaken the loon from his stupor. He wasn't even interested hearing the Stokers thought them both dead, so they didn't have them on their backs any more.

What Tom had read of the fire in the local rag also backed up the general consensus that Potter had been one of the victims. Good job the coppers couldn't give a toss about getting to the bottom of who had really got fried. They were just glad the city was rid of a prick running a dodgy firm who caused extra paperwork.

This would have all been good, apart from that one thing... The thing that had immediately revealed itself when going into the flat that day...

Tom gritted his teeth – what was left of those he hadn't already ground down over the past couple of weeks. Oh, yes, he'd spotted the difference. Just like when Potter had sent his dim-arsed brother around to try and find where he'd stashed his money. He knew the signs.

And he'd been right.

He'd been convinced he would choke to death when he'd seen the carpet had moved in the corner of the lounge.

The carpet over the floorboards... The floorboards that concealed his bags...

His bags with the money...

The bags that had gone...

They'd fucking gone. Gone. *Gone.*

The Stokers had come after all. Although they believed they'd fucking fried him, they'd still lifted his money as the ultimate piss take.

Bastards. Utter fucking wankturd bastards.

But what could he do? Demand it back? Report it to the police?

Of course not. Because a) he'd robbed it in the first place and b) because he was supposed to be fucking dead.

And Tom didn't want either of those things coming out in the wash.

And so, here he was...

Even the subsequent reaction to his missing money that had

caused him to smash the fuck out of the flat in front of Potter hadn't spawned a reaction from the bloke.

The whole thing was futile.

Now more than ever.

Tom glared at Potter, still unmoving in the chair, and wished he possessed the power to kill by staring alone. It would save so much time and effort.

What was he supposed to do now? Three weeks he'd waited for an epiphany, but the facts remained the same: he had no passport, no money, no property, no contacts. No shag all.

He was trapped.

Hearing a thunk as the newspaper dropped onto the wooden floorboards, Tom shuffled out into the hall, deciding he might as well wind himself up further by seeing just how everyone else around him was getting on with their lives. Reports of new businesses, success stories, even disasters – all denoted being part of the human race, rather than stuck in a makeshift holding cell in the place that time forgot with a silent lunatic.

'Might as well see what's going on in the world,' Tom said loudly – his habit of talking to himself now commonplace. It helped break the monotony of silence gradually eating away at his brain.

He thumbed through the pages, laughing loudly at a follow-up report of last week's pile-up on the M6. 'Listen to this – "two more people have since died in hospital of their catastrophic injuries"...'

It was comforting to know there were some people worse off than him. 'There had to be at least twenty cars involved in that accident, so with any luck, a couple more will drop off the twig soon,' he continued gleefully, not bothering looking to see if Potter was listening. He already knew what the answer would be to that one.

Still chuckling at others' misfortunes, Tom turned the page, eager for something else to make him feel better.

But then he saw it. A whole double page of it.

'What the fuck is this?' he shrieked, his enjoyment falling into a black void. 'This can't be right!'

His eyes moved feverishly over the photographs amidst the huge article, containing images of various well-known dignitaries from around Birmingham, along with others – many that Tom knew by sight to be loaded, successful and influential. They were all standing posing and grinning like bastards within the newly reopened Royal Peacock... the Royal Peacock that looked sickeningly and sparklingly meticulous.

'It burnt the fuck down! How can this be?' Tom gibbered. 'How the hell did they get this done so quickly and with what?' His voice cracked as his pitch raised by two octaves.

His eyes then gravitated to the large centrepiece photograph, his throat constricting. *There she was... His bitch of a daughter with the fucking Stokers.*

'The slimy, fucking...' Stopping dead, Tom did a double take at the figure standing next to her, his eyeballs bulging from their sockets. 'I don't believe it!' he roared. 'She's supposed to be dead! I left the old cow for dead, yet she's here in the paper with my slag of a daughter, alive like the rest of them!'

Swinging around, Tom slapped the paper down in front of Potter and stabbed the picture of Sam, Linda and the Stokers with his finger. 'I knew that whore of a daughter of mine would somehow come out of this shit smelling of fucking roses!'

Red-faced, he paced the room, blindly kicking at the already smashed pieces of furniture. 'No opinion on this, Potter?' he screamed. 'What a fucking surprise that is! Jesus Christ! How come Samantha gets everything falling into her lap? And them? The fucking Stokers should have been screwed after what I did, yet here they are again...'

Spit sprayed from Tom's mouth as he pulled at his hair. 'And what about Linda? She was a bloody corpse! I saw it with my own eyes. There's no way she could have come back from that, yet she has! Tell me how that happened, you fat fuck? Come on! Are we the dead ones or something? Maybe we're just in some weird fucking dream and th...'

'You never mentioned Samantha Reynold is your daughter...'

Tom nearly died on the spot. Now, just to make this utter insult of a day even bloody worse, he was hallucinating? He'd thought for a moment then that Potter had actually said something!

With horror, he realised he wasn't hallucinating at all when Potter grabbed him around the throat.

'Why did you not tell me Samantha Reynold is your daughter?' Potter repeated, this revelation snapping him from his stupor like he'd just necked a pint of the elixir of life.

'Well, I...' Tom spluttered, still trying to get his head around that, like many other people he'd just seen, Potter had miraculously emerged from a self-induced coma.

'This puts a whole different slant on things!' Letting go of Tom's throat, Potter let him drop to the floor. He couldn't be bothered to listen to Bedworth's excuses. Bedworth might have presumed him devoid and unhearing of all the insults and crap he'd thrown in his general direction for the last month, but Potter had heard every single word.

He'd chosen not to react because he'd been upset and not himself. But now there was *every* reason to rejoin the human race. As much as he'd like to pummel Bedworth into the ground, this time he *really* needed him.

With Bedworth's knowledge of Birmingham and his blood ties to a woman joined to the Stokers by the hip, the man would be useful. The Stokers were behind lifting his coke, killing Mark and torching his business.

And he would have revenge for that.

Potter smiled slowly at Tom, whose face remained plastered in shock at his unexpected reanimation. 'I'm glad you stuck around, Bedworth, because you're intrinsic in getting my revenge.'

And revenge is what he would have. It was what Mark would want.

ACKNOWLEDGMENTS

I've loved writing this series! It's been a particularly difficult year for me on a personal level and although things are now coming together, being able to lose myself in my writing has been a much-needed escape.

As always, many thanks to my editor Emily Ruston and the Boldwood team, and to Annie Aldington for doing such a fantastic job of narrating the audio.

Love to my family and friends and to all the readers out there who enjoy my books. I hope you will enjoy *Payback* and the rest of the series.

Much love

Edie

X

MORE FROM EDIE BAYLIS

We hope you enjoyed reading *Payback*. If you did, please leave a review.

If you'd like to gift a copy, this book is also available as an ebook, digital audio download and audiobook CD.

Sign up to Edie Baylis's mailing list for news, competitions and updates on future books.

https://bit.ly/EdieBaylisnews

Explore the rest of the Allegiance series now.

ABOUT THE AUTHOR

Edie Baylis is a successful self-published author of dark gritty thrillers with violent background settings. She lives in Worcestershire, has a history of owning daft cars and several motorbikes and is licensed to run a pub.

Visit Edie's website: http://www.ediebaylis.co.uk/

Follow Edie on social media:

 twitter.com/ediebaylis
 facebook.com/downfallseries
 instagram.com/ediebaylis

PEAKY READERS

GANG LOYALTIES. DARK SECRETS.
BLOODY REVENGE.

A READER COMMUNITY FOR
GANGLAND CRIME THRILLER FANS!

DISCOVER PAGE-TURNING NOVELS
FROM YOUR FAVOURITE AUTHORS
AND MEET NEW FRIENDS.

Boldwood

Boldwood Books is an award-winning fiction publishing company seeking out the best stories from around the world.

Find out more at www.boldwoodbooks.com

Join our reader community for brilliant books, competitions and offers!

Follow us
@BoldwoodBooks
@BookandTonic

Sign up to our weekly
deals newsletter

https://bit.ly/BookandTonicNews

Printed in Great Britain
by Amazon

43410431R00208

One·From·The
HEART

Published in Great Britain in 1996 by

Starlight Publishing Limited

37 West Street

Brighton BN1 2RE

e mail: saunders@pavilion.co.uk

-

ISBN 0 9520991 0 1

Printed and bound in Hong Kong.

One·From·The
HEART

"Open randomly for gentle positive guidance."

Claire Saunders

For tis a divine intervention
that has come unto yee
and fills thee with
the joy and harmony
and love of life.
Yee shall succeed and
be very happy in this
world and shall share
the joys and love of the
life and lands yee
inhabit. From this love
of life great kindnesses
and comforts will be
found by others and
enlightenment of a kind
will befall many people.

Foreword

"For yours is not the only consciousness that needs awakening which is why you have to catalogue the information you receive so that others may benefit as well as yourself."

It was not easy editing the words of a guide 'from the light'. When we have had difficulty interpreting the meaning whom could we ask? Claire Saunders could not help. She received the words and wrote them down - exactly as they came to her. Her interpretation of the verses is as she heard them.

In the end the answer was simple. The words are faithfully recorded in their original state, as heard, and except where strictly necessary, very few alterations have been made. It is important to remember that these were spoken words, a one-way dialogue to Claire from her guide and should be read as such.

The only changes have been in punctuation. As Claire received the dialogue she wrote it down, obviously fast and often with only a dash or a comma between sentences. Some punctuation needed to be carefully added to facilitate the understanding and clarity of these powerful words.

This raises another point. Claire's original, hand-written record is remarkable in itself and is testimony to the extraordinary nature of the whole phenomenon. Firstly, it is obvious how quickly she had to write. There are no pauses or breaks and hardly a correction in her written words, exactly as if she had 'taken dictation'. More incredibly, the lessons finish nearly always neatly and conclusively at the end of each page. This would be extremely difficult to achieve if attempted, especially with such regularity.

Then there is the reading of the verses themselves. How anyone chooses to read them is entirely their individual choice. Firstly, they can be marvelled at as a fascinating occurrence; a one-way dialogue from guide to pupil, as lessons with a particular relevance to Claire's personal life and spiritual growth. Or, more simply, the verses can be enjoyed for their poetical beauty and colourful allusions. But most of all 'the words... will have much meaning for a great many people'; they have been spoken and recorded for all of us. The words you are about to read are, quite literally, 'from the heart' of universal truth.

A final point needs to be made about this. Many who have read the passages have emphasised that they are best read carefully, one now and again as a thought for the day or to be reflected on at night. Others have opened the book at random to find a message relevant to their own lives, often very specifically. It is due to these people that Claire decided to publish her volumes. This, and the fulfilment of her guide's request, as written in the words above.

The rest is up to you.

September 1995

Author's Note

One from the Heart is a collection of channeled writings which I have received since a visit to Santa Fe, New Mexico in 1991. Everything from the title and illustrations to the numerous messages over the subsequent years are as I originally received them.

From the very first time the words started coming into my head, I heard them ready formed as sentences and passages, as if being read aloud. I was not at all familiar with the phenomenon of channeling, and to begin with I was at great odds with the sensation. Slowly, I reached a better understanding of what was happening and I became more comfortable with the experience. When there is something special I feel I need to write, I get a jumpy sensation in my right arm and to me this is affectionately known as 'Twitchy'.

When I started receiving this book, I initially felt the messages were extremely personal and only relevant to me and the emotional situations in which I found myself. However, from the first time I shared the writing it became apparent that this was not so. Everyone who has read the messages has found them particularly poignant to their own lives and filled with personal meaning for themselves.

The writing generally gives great comfort and guidance to one and all, and it has been through a high demand for copies from friends and associates, that I have published this book. Now the messages are available to anyone who wishes to read them and is looking for a deeper understanding of themselves.

I trust that this book will give you as much pleasure, hope and guidance as it has given me. If it does, then please share what you find with your friends. They, too, may be aware of the need for their own spiritual expansion and yours could be the helping hand that gives them the very guidance they are looking for. Twitchy once said:

"You cannot change humanity. That is understood.
But by each being the best you can,
collectively you could!"

Together we can make a difference.

Claire Saunders

August 1995

Thank you —
To all my family
and friends for
your Love and support
⭐

Claire Saunders

To David

Dedicated to the memory of my father, tears and laughter always and forever.

One·From·The
HEART

BOOK 1

Question ye not your future for it shall be shown unto ye as an open book, and ye shall dance across the pages with love and light and colour. Forget not to pick the flowers as you travel through life's rich garden, and to seek and find peace and harmony in every wakening flower and fragrant bloom!

Santa Fe, May 1991

Develop and trust in that which ye feel. Question not and judge ye not by those around ye, for ye have inner knowledge of perfect harmony, balance and colour. Yours is the eye through which a multitude of minds will seek their inspiration, and as such ye shall have a strong command of the creative force. Let it flow ~

Santa Fe, May 1991

Be not ye like those who go before ye or walk around ye. Carve for yourself a new and brave way of expressing the love and beauty ye see around ye, and with your work open the eyes of others to that which they might not otherwise see.

Santa Fe, May 1991

Behold, for thine eyes can see and 'tis a gift given unto thee. Catch the colours of life and express them to those living in the darkness of the beauty in the world that surrounds them, for thine is the role of colourist in a world of black and white.

Santa Fe, May 1991

The way of your love and the way of your work are one, and from this will come the answers for all that you are looking for. May there be harmony and understanding in all that you do, and life and love will all flow unto you.

Santa Fe, May 1991

And when ye cross the path from security to indecision fear not your direction, for it shall flow through ye as a babbling brook and cast aside all doubt and disbelief.

London, August 1991

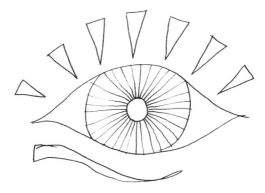

Tis no use hiding away thine eyes for 'tis thy gift and thou shall see with thine eyes open or yet closed. Now is the time to face up to thy responsibilities and expectations and to accept the challenges put before thee.

London, August 1991

Pick up your pen and write and write, and write again, until ye can see that the Life-force flows through ye, that everything ye do shall be guided and filled with golden light.

London, August 1991

Tis only your inner strength that ye are at battle with. And if ye relax and let it flow through ye with passion and vigour, life will take on a whole new meaning and hue, a new blaze of love and light and colour.

London, August 1991

Ye say that ye do not know what it is that is asked of ye. Nothing, except that which ye feel it is right to feel, and to follow these thoughts. Try not to fulfil an idea or perception that is not maybe real. Relax to your life, let the force go and let it flow through ye with ease and pleasure for 'tis a good thing for ye and all those around ye ~

London, August 1991

And with this new ease of expression you can reap the rewards like a gardener gathering the fruits of a good harvest. Trust in the force that you feel. 'Tis true, it is there expressly for you. Tap it, use it, do not abuse it.

London, August 1991

'Tis true ye must write as does the scribe, and unto ye shall come the words to write and to colour your future. 'Tis in the interest of many men that you are requested to do that which is asked of you. And when thy day is done, thy kingdom will come.

For 'tis your fate and destiny to follow the path that ye choose ~

For 'tis a divine intervention that has come unto ye and fills ye with the joy and harmony and love of life.

Ye shall succeed and be very happy in this world and shall share the joys and love of the life and lands ye inhabit. From this love of life great kindness and comfort will be found by others and enlightenment of a kind will befall many people.

The kindness of your words will not go unheard ~

Thy lips will carry the words and deliver the kiss of years gone by, of times when worlds were one and the same. All manner of things may happen, some strange and some yet more beguiling. Great things are destined to come your way. Fear not, thy way is clear. Love and light and colour will surround thee in all that you do.

Make peace amongst your friends and joyous things will unfold unto you. Happiness is the key to the safe deposit of life. Surround yourself with light and laughter and joy. Pretensions may be the downfall of many, but you are to succeed because of your trust and love in the beliefs and ways of all that is good and of the highest order.

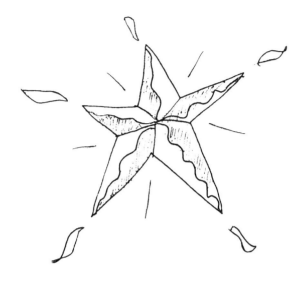

Tis a long time since the rain has come and gone like the loves in your life but soon, my love, one day you'll meet your perfect partner in the stars, in the heavens and, yes, on earth. You are to be married into the heavens through your union with this man. He is righteous and kind and passionate in many ways. He will love you and understand you and all that flows through you in all the waking hours as well as between the naked sheets.

Yours is the role that has been chosen unto ye and as such a champion has been found to combine that which is good in all men and will give great strength and love to the bond ye shall create. His role is also predetermined and as such his life will coincide with yours. So fear ye not that time might pass ye by. Remember that life for ye has not yet begun and the best of it is yet to come.

Tis not the meaning of these words alone that imparts the truth of what is in your soul. 'Tis your love of life itself and your joy at being used to display the best way to view your world. Colour, light and music are all of great importance and your soul can hear their tunes. Discords upset you, and tunes are rarely sweeter than tunes made by the very sounds of nature around you ~

There are energies gathering about you that would lighten up a tower. Keep control of the power; it is immense and thus exhausting. Relax, but be aware of the depths you can go to and the breadths you can reach from deep within yourself, and fulfil your body to its ultimate purification, in food and in exercise and in thought. The power of the word is not only in the writing of it down but in the forming of it in one's own mind. This is to be remembered and used as a tool to forge yourself a future of love and light and grace and harmony. The malformation of words creates discords and unharmonious vibrations which in turn manifest themselves in disruptive aspects within the realms of your life.

Pure thoughts. Pure light. Pure heart.

Disturbances delay development. Remove thine own disruptions and create thine own free way. Thy free will will follow and thy spirit soar, higher still than thine imagination can conjure up in thought.

To create a book of your own future memories is a great idea. It will stand you in good stead when the time comes to develop your trust, and reference is essential if you are to learn the lessons of your life. Imagination and memory serve the same Life-force and should be captured in spirit, as one, as in thought, in mind and ink.

The scriptures do tell of many things in verse and even song. The tales are said so that man can recall the messages and meanings of his life.

Conquer thy hunger and thou shall be rewarded with a perfect body. Then self-confidence will prevail and all insecurity will dissolve as does all darkness within the light. Health and fitness are to be maintained at all times by a diet of good food and good thought. Positivity is to be plentiful in thy mind and negativity as unwelcomed as are bad toxins in thy body. Open up thy channels through clarity of mind, body and soul. 'Laugh and the world laughs with you!'

You are both excited and enthralled by the changes happening in and all around you. You shall be helped and guided by those you know and shall meet, to help you gain a greater understanding of all you are about, and how to reach the ultimate of your potential. You shall not fail and should consider this no more. 'Tis not an option; 'tis preordained, and yet you do not trust right now fully that you are guided and no harm shall come your way. Trust in it and it will be good.

España, August 1991

Question thee not thy words for they come from far beyond thy realms of comprehension. Just receive them and their meanings will become clear as do the pictures painted upon your crystal globe.

You are worried they are messages from the dark side and sometimes doubt your sanity, but it is an unjust accusation to suggest such words are sin, or that they come from anything other than love and peace and harmony, of understanding and of light.

Brighton, September 1991

These words are meant, with the gentleness of intent, only to give you a clearer channel down which to apply your energy, not to confuse or disturb you in any way or form.

You are to maintain a high level of health and achievement from dawn until dusk, and replenish yourself with hours of much-needed and deserved rest of all kinds.

Strength of body and strength of mind are as one and should not be ignored as such. Both must be replenished when resources have run low. Spirit and soul and blood and tissue need food and rest. Inspiration and direction shall flow through your whole body and mind like a fresh breeze entering a stale old room ~

Brighton, September 1991

The times they are 'a changing', in season and in song. Fear not thy voices for they come only to soothe and guide thee. They come from charity and from love. To deny them you succeed only in denying yourself a great love that you deserve.

How strange the ways of the world, how strange the ways of love. It can be seen and appreciated in many ways and things. It can be disguised as many things and does not always come as expected.

Yours is not to question why, yours is but to do and live and love. Much as birds fly south until the spring, the time has come for you to move into a warmer period of love. Seasons change as time goes by and we move a little further down our path of life, enlightenment and understanding. For we are each on our own chosen path and have many miles to go before our journey's end.

London, November 1991

You are in a state of confusion but you are not alone. Remember this and too that help is close at hand to be called upon and thus received. Inner strength and guidance are never far away. Just open up to them and ye shall realise that you do not need material props or external help. The answers are all to be found from within. Just gather your strength, for now you feel weak and weary but great things are about to befall you. Ye are assured in sickness and in health ye are not alone.

Tis sad you should feel so lonely when in fact ye are never alone. 'Tis true, there is no earthly being to share your daily life right now but there are many souls who love and protect you from afar. Have faith, my dear, the love of your life is really very near ~

Time is such a strange commodity and is a difficult thing to account. Who can say what it is, the true length of even but one day? Yet even now the time ticks by as a day on a distant desert plain in Africa, as it slips away as night right here. Days and nights are nothing but parts of one and the same. All is one, life is one, and time perhaps an illusion! 'Tis, after all, not the length of a journey that is of most significance but the ground that is covered.

Not mere miles or even mountains or even desert plains, but the experiences encountered and their lessons learned. Some are very hard and some pass unnoticed by your conscious mind, yet still record themselves in your soul to be remembered and re-read if circumstances require. People and places, fond images and faces, feelings and fears, laughter and tears and the love and light in a golden smile.

Look for all the good in the world and it shall show itself to ye. Worry ye not about the dark side of things and walk not too long in the shadows. There are wondrous things to be found in the light as well as great love and warmth and comfort. 'Tis a necessary part of the life experience to cross from side to side, to feel the depth and breadth of all there is to feel, to know what it is to be in the darkness and to suffer alone, as well as to know the comfort and security, strength and warmth and eternal comfort of the light. 'Tis a silly thing to wish for one's life to always be plain and simple, for where in that would one ever find true meaning? Without experiences what would be a life? Therefore, you know the more you experience on every level, the more you live on this and every other plane. Life is but a rich and magnificent tapestry and the greatness of the pattern therein depends upon the choice of colours used, and the variety and number of stitches. If a job is worth doing, it is worth doing well!

Why settle for a simple thing when a little extra patience and effort can result in an elaborate, intricate embroidery of great beauty? You are after all the master craftsman and the tools of your trade are in your hands. Create for yourself a life rich in love and light and colour but accept too that to give true depth to your design you must balance the colours carefully, and that the darker shades and hues are of great importance and must also be selected and worked-in to create perfect harmony. Truly rich colours and experiences are made from many hues, both dark and difficult. Be not afraid of these tones or times. Accept them for what they are: important parts of the pattern of Life ~

Know yourself and then the answers will become clear. You have spent enough time in the shadows and the darkness. Now the time has come to cross onto the sunnier side of the street. We each have our times to walk in the shade and then, as well, our time to feel the joy of the warmth and sunshine as we go dancing into the light.

We hope you find a greater understanding of all that there is and of the powers that are all around you. Listen and you will learn. Open up your mind to these new channels of thought. The greatest wisdom is the highest consciousness.

Practice what you learn and a great peace will befall you and benefit those around you, not just in your patience and acceptance of things, but also in your enlightened ways of thinking and approaching situations with a good understanding and sound advice. That is not to say that you are to counsel or carry the problems of all those you know, but to be there for them as a strong, centred human being from which they can take strength and light and love as an inspiration to guide and counsel themselves.

And so the time has come to turn the page into another book. Do not forget from time to time to read again the writings here within. They will bring you solace and alignment in times of confusion or despair. These words can be shared and indeed they should, for although they are mere words, their sentiment and meaning is of great, profound importance and should not be forgotten as an aid to inner understanding which applies to each and every one of you ~

Brighton, November 1991

BOOK 2

And so the time has come to start again, with fresh new pages and a good strong pen. For there are many new messages to be received and many new ideas to be conceived. The times ahead are exciting and your energies will be strong. You will learn to live and love freely, and gain strength as a river does with every new downpour of rain ~

You see, every cloud does have a silver lining, although it certainly may not appear so at the time. Bad experiences and difficult times feed your own river of emotions and energy. These waters may run rough and wild over troubled times and raging rapids. But then too in times of calmness and reflection they run calm and smooth and deep. Great peace can be found in still waters, as great pain can be found in times of drought. Water is an essential part of life and existence. The purest of all waters rise up from within the earth itself and a great deal too falls clean out of the sky from the grey clouds on a rainy day.

Life-forces are all strong and work in conjunction with each other, and 'tis from these elements and their sometimes strange and confusing combinations and balances that we have to develop an understanding and perspective about our lives and the lives of those around us.

Different influences are balanced in different ways in each and every one of us. That is why ours is not to judge or criticise others for we know not their individual combinations, and can and should not try to judge them or evaluate them against a scale devised to register our own.

Each man has a set of fingerprints unlike any other. Why not too, should he then have an individual code of conduct to express the powers and influences upon himself? No man is better than another. Some have just perfected a better way of balancing themselves, their personal pressures and passions, intentions and reactions.

Experience is of great importance and these lessons are to be learnt over many lifetimes. It is a mistake to deny this and it should be seen as an opportunity to develop and grow from one life to the next. Experiences and lessons are never really forgotten, just embedded deep in our genetic pattern to influence and guide us as best they can through our daily actions and from the silent guidance of our deep subconscious voice.

To perhaps enquire of this deep knowledge and greater understanding of all that there is, is of course a reasonable suggestion but it's not in everyone's nature to be an inquirer, questioner or explorer. You have to have strength of mind, trust and interest and a desire for a taste of adventure and development. That is why for those who want to see and read, these words will play delicate tunes upon their souls and they shall resound with a deeper understanding of a sort. Yet, for those for whom there can be no music, it is best not to slave across the pages for they will never hear the delicate sounds unless they are properly tuned in to receive them.

Share these words by all means with those you love and trust, for a great reward will be felt in their appreciation for the guidance upon these pages that enables them all to have a greater understanding of themselves. It is only a question of developing your inner-self to address these external problems properly, so that they may comfort and guide themselves. All answers to everything are within yourself, warm and confident, standing boldly in the light, not being afraid of what we do not actually see but imagine in the shadows.

Angels and devils both have their place, as doth the knight and the page. Each man has his own chosen path and destiny. It is predetermined and arranged. As all is a balance, one life affects another and what is balanced wrongly in one event or lifetime must be counterbalanced in another. It is all cause and effect every way you look at it. Therefore you know you cannot cheat yourself or your fate even if you succeed in hoodwinking those around you.

People have their own purpose and it is up to the individual to discover exactly what it is, his or her own true direction. Everyone should be striving for enlightenment and to some this is as clear as a crystal. Yet for others, they have no clear idea about the real values of their lives and so get confused and behave as if they were alone as a single unit instead of a small component in the ultimate composition of a whole.

Forgive me if I do not always speak in a way you clearly understand but I try to convey to you meanings and messages as best I can. Take time to reflect upon the words I have said, and over time their lessons will become clearer and their meanings understood.

3rd December 1991

'Tis of no consequence who I am. I am from the light and you know in your heart that this is true. Your trust in that which is good is enough to expand through your own inner guidance. There are many things around you, some good and some you feel are less good. You are becoming more aware of these vibrations and are developing a greater perception, which is good. You are beginning to ask questions from the view-point of a young inquisitive mind looking for more information to digest. This is very pleasing, for you no longer mistrust or suspect and therefore question my words in a different fashion.

Words will flow from this pen from time to time and you will find a great love displayed from deep within and between each line.

Things are already beginning to take their places in the pattern of your future. Likened unto a serpent I shall unravel and reveal to you your own inner strength and guidance.

You are beginning to appreciate your finer qualities and must develop these if you are to achieve your full potential. The ways are open. It will become clearer to you if you trust in that which is good, then it shall return as such and all that is good will come to pass.

Pursue many avenues and you shall discover many things. Stick only to one path and you shall only discover the range of things available on offer along the way. Journey off and encounter more options and experiences that you might not otherwise encounter.

Turn your hand to that which feels good. Question not its value or worth as a pursuit or angle, but indulge yourself in creative exploration and you will be delighted with the results that follow.

Limit yourself not with false perimeters. Break the boundaries from the conscious confinements and develop your potential in areas you might not have hitherto imagined held excitement. For you the way ahead is paved in many colours and bathed in golden light. Pursue your books by all means, for they are after all what you know to be your calling.

The time is nigh to make advances and opportunities are to be seized if success is to be achieved. Many people are enthused by the idea of such a book, and many more would appreciate their own meaning, value and potential if you take up the challenge and follow up the leads you have been given. Develop these new friendships for they will prove invaluable to you now and for a long time to come.

Procrastination can be the downfall of many an idea and a man. You are not to follow this pattern and so must act now and force a way for yourself and make headway in your journey. You have many leads now like clues to a game or pieces in a puzzle. Use your common sense and playful nature and enjoy the game ahead.

Pursue each avenue and be not too discouraged if doors do not immediately lead where you expect them to. Remember that doors open onto passages that lead to rooms! Only by opening many doors and roaming many passages will you be sure to find the way.

People you meet will show you the way and point you in the right direction but it is your decision whether to follow their advice or to falter. Think not too long before moving along even if at times it seems too fast just because you are unsure of yourself in this new ground. Trust that you can conquer new territory in the name of love and hope and glory.

16th December 1991

This solstice is significant and you are right to celebrate it even if you do not fully comprehend its meaning. You are becoming aware now that 'as is above, as is below' and the planetary changes indicate inevitable changes in your daily life. To become more aware of these movements will better prepare you for the changes ahead. That is not to say you should live amongst the stars but accept that the stars live amongst you. Concentrate on your daily earthly life but be aware of the scale of things happening against the overall large game plan of life and of all that there is.

You are all but pawns in a larger game not governed or controlled by yourself but an understanding, perhaps, of the game that is being played and the rules by which it is played can enhance your ease and enjoyment of the game tenfold or more!

You are here to learn and learn you must if you are to move. The game continues over many lives and each return is to the position you have progressed to.

Thus if you close your eyes and refuse to learn the lessons of one life, you will someday be returned to face the challenges and move forward to a new position for reincarnation.

Thus the more you learn in a life, the further and faster you progress across the game board of love and life and experience.

The New Year brings a new birth to us all and as such we have the possibility to progress and move into a new position with each passing year. As with the tradition held for New Year's resolutions, affirmations are decrees of ways we intend to improve. They should not be such idle reformations as taking less sugar in one's tea; more, much more carefully considered directions we intend to steer our hand in destiny.

'Decree a thing and it shall be done'

Never a more shining explanation of visualisation not to be ignored. If it is success that you seek then ask and it shall be. If it is love and faith, display trust in your beliefs and in the results that follow.

Decide a definitive list of directives to follow, then you need not roam without direction. Write them down and put some solidity behind your intentions. Then you need not forget to exercise your interest in them all, rather than indulging wholly on one you favour.

Affirmations are of the greatest importance and it cannot be stressed enough how indications of where you would like to be will give your guides a direction in which to lead you.

You do create your own life and if yours is to be born out of confusion and chaos how is it to be expected to develop any order or sense? Put your head in good order and your life will reflect this. It is not always easy to do this but life is seldom simple.

21st December 1991

Over-indulgence on a daily basis is not to be encouraged, yet on occasion in celebration it is to be accepted.

Think not that ye have eaten too much, only that ye have eaten well and give praise to the recognition of that fact.

There are multitudes and millions of people around the world who will have much less to be grateful for than ye. As well as many beautiful presents, you have been given a magnificent gift you know must be graciously accepted and appreciated as a rare and treasured thing.

The year ahead is very exciting and holds for you many challenges. Know you are not to accept these too lightly or expect them to pass without lasting effect. Sometimes this can be painful, even devastating, and yet essential to progress. That is not to say the way ahead is fraught with danger or catastrophes, only that 'tis not either plain or simple and emotional energies will be exhausted from time to time in the name of development and advancement. Strive for the highest of goals and it is a long and difficult climb. The view from the top however has to be seen to be believed. If you have it in you to pick up your own personal challenge, then what is there to stop you having a go and giving it your best shot?

Some people procrastinate to a point of near stagnation. 'Tis the force of creativity that flows through you and keeps your rivers running fast and deep. Open yourselves up to this Life-force and the energy that it brings and have the courage to act on your instincts, follow your ideas to a logical conclusion and waste them not, for every one keeps your energy flowing and eliminates the possibility of stagnation.

Continue to live your life with a vested interest in your destiny and not as a victim of your fate.

Your life is in your hands. You are tired and should go and sleep now, for sleep is a vital, important part of life. The waking hours must be balanced by the sleeping hours much as life must ultimately be balanced by death. As with all balances they are not necessarily as expected or constant. From time to time you need more or less of one or the other depending on the demands made upon you at that time.

Hormonal changes and imbalances develop as a result of mis-channeled energies. A lot is to be expected of you and no discomfort is intended but relief can be achieved by self-centring and by positive channeling of the energies that now flow through you. By all means seek help and guidance from those around you who have a greater knowledge of these things, for the quicker you learn to deal with them yourself, the more comfortable your life will become.

You cannot expect your physical body not to react at all to the enormous changes that are happening to you on the psychic plane. Adjustments have to be made and have not been established as such yet. You are right to use your writings as a guideline for self-development, yet also to seek help from those for whom it would give great joy to watch your growth and development.

Keep your strength up by eating and by sleeping and allow yourself to revive and rest during the sleeping hours to be fresh and strong to deal with the challenges of each and every day ahead. I bid you goodnight and God bless and peace be with you.

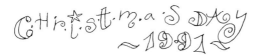

CHRISTMAS DAY
~1991~

The time has come to show some abstinence as you have happily shared indulgence. To re-balance your metabolism to its normal state you must restrain from the continuous overloading of your system.

No harm comes from such seasonal celebrations but to restore a normal regime as soon as possible is advisable. If not, new patterns of supply on demand and the new established appetites take command and you lose control of your equilibrium. You will not be happy if you develop insecurities about your body, and your mind and spirit will suffer the consequences.

You are not in any danger of constant over-indulgence. It's just as well to remind you, you are what you eat and that you do have the body that you wish and that you have the tools in your hands, as it were, to shape your mind and body into perfection or defection.

Practice what you preach and display a measure of self control, for the easiest of all challenges is surely that of conquering your own actions, for they are after all the only actions at your disposal over which to display any control.

There are stereotype ideals one develops through life about many things and relationships are certainly one of them. Yet things are never exactly what they seem and seldom run true to an expected form. Therefore it is best to avoid setting such preconceived ideals and truly facing every new encounter and emotional experience as it comes. Disappointment can be avoided and a desire to change a characteristic in someone that does not fit your preconceived ideal can also be eliminated.

26th December 1991

A new beginning, in many ways much more than one.

To have your parents so close is a precious gift indeed. You are right to share in your love for each other so openly; it frees the way for much more love and happiness to come to you all.

For love transcends the limits of time and reaches beyond to remain for eternity. Even now the love of loves gone by lives on as a quantity of a rare commodity to fill the world with good vibrations. You are becoming aware of what it is that is expected of you, and are prepared to accept the challenges ahead.

Present no problems for yourself and there will be none. See the road ahead as clear and trouble-free and that is what it shall be.

Success is within your grasp, just be not afraid to outstretch your hands and to take it. Accept that it is yours for the taking as much as for any man or woman who has the trust and belief to see it as such and not be afraid of it. Feel the fear and do it anyway. Such a wonderful approach to life, it provides excitement in every challenge and direction in every time of hesitation.

To doubt yourself is an invitation for others to do the same, yet trust in yourself and others will gladly follow your example and trust in you too, as well as develop greater belief in themselves.

The gifts of fame and fortune are sure to come your way. Be ready to graciously accept them both. Put your plans into action and set your projects under way. Turn the wheel of fortune in your favour and open up your path to happiness and success. Hesitate ye not, you have been warned of the dangers of procrastination. You have your ideas, now make them happen. Believe in them and they will become real. Doubt them and you restrict their development, even cause their very downfall.

Act now however and you are assured success. Hesitation results in speculation. You will never really know the outcome of a thing until it is done.

Because you cannot force a thing, why take the responsibility for it when it is ultimately out of your hands, whether 'twill be or is not to be? Just accept that which is your responsibility, which is to trust that everything has a reason, a cause and an effect. You do not make the rules of the game but that is not to say you should not play it as best you can.

To not play at all guarantees losing but playing at all presents the possibility of winning. Play well by understanding the rules and accepting the challenges without the guarantee of winning, but the trust and belief that you can win with fun and laughter and concentration will bring ultimate success.

1st January 1992

And so the time has come again to pick up the pen and listen to the written word.

Once a thing is decided upon, pursue it to its final end. The outcome may not always be what you foresaw or intended but that is not to say that it is not what is meant to be. Be open minded about all things and open to inspiration and direction even if it takes you from your chosen path. Do not lose sight of your goal. Just be prepared to arrive at it by an unexpected route.

Fame and fortune and success are all out there in front of you. No doubt you will one day arrive at them all, even if you all but stumble across them along your way. They may not always be the thing you are consciously going after, and yet they could stand between you and your ultimate desire and chosen destination.

To chart a route with the soul aim or intention to arrive at one such place or position may result in empty disappointment, for 'tis after all better to journey than to arrive.

If fame and fortune have a hollow sound 'tis not their fault alone. For 'tis the values displayed on the journey to get them that is the true worth and prize in the end.

If you are perchance to encounter such delights along the way as a beautiful view or a golden sunset, are they not of as much importance in the final impression at the journey's end? 'Tis true and you know it to be so.

You are impressed with the speed at which I write and yet for me 'tis far easier than ABC.

You are receptive to my thoughts and as such act as a good receiver, and 'tis your responsibility then to transmit what I have said to you unto the hearts and minds of those whom I cannot reach. The answers are to be found within yourselves, each and every one. That is why what I have said always sounds somehow familiar as if you somehow already know it to be true.

Tis but the values and beliefs you hold and are taught to live by that confuse your natural behaviour that is within, and perhaps a small reminder can awaken the inner knowledge that you hold into remembering and influencing your daily lives.

Guidance is a good thing if it is of the right sort. Follow not the encouragement and teachings of those you do not feel are right and good. Question from within and truly learn to think with your heart and feel with your mind. That way there will be fewer surprises of the undesirable kind.

Do not be too influenced by those around you. Carve for thyself a truly new direction. Why cover the ground of any other, when unexplored territory can result in great adventure? 'Tis true it could be fraught with danger but could also result in the discovery of new and wondrous things.

Once upon a time there was a fair maiden whose job it was to spread the kind and gentle words of guidance to those throughout the land. And once again the time has come for such a messenger and has come now.

It is your choice how you share these words but share them you must. For the gift of greater understanding is not yours alone and is to be spread for sure, so that an increased awareness in love and humanity can be set among the people for whom it is intended. You are aware that the gift you have has a rare and precious value above all your worldly goods, for sure. Now, perhaps now for the first time, you are becoming aware of the role you play as the maestro and can truly begin to appreciate the enormity of the orchestra you are to conduct so that sweet music can be heard by so many. Such music can soothe and comfort those in need and can be enjoyed by many more who will enjoy listening to it for the love of sweet melody.

The value of comfort to one in need is immeasurable. It is one of the greatest gifts you can bestow upon another human being and should be appreciated as such. To have the capacity to do this is a gift in itself and you have been given the sentences and sentiments that can reach into and heal even the deepest depths of doubt and despair, dissatisfaction and disbelief. Trust in the power of the words that I impart and the depth of wisdom and greater understanding from which they are drawn.

Think not that your job will be done with the completion of another volume. It is only now that you are not questioning but truly ready to accept what it is that is being asked of you. Once before this question was raised and you were instructed to do only that which you felt was right to do. 'Tis as true now as it was then, but now you have a clearer vision of what is right to do and of exactly what you are capable of doing. No more or no less than what you can do will ever be expected or asked of you; no more than you are able to do, whether you are aware of it or not at the time the challenges pose themselves.

Take up the challenges you are set and approach them with confidence and caution. Take time to consider your actions wisely before setting them in motion. You know the answers lie in cause and effect. Think before you speak, look before you leap and try not to crush the flowers as you tread lightly through the long grass, on your journey across the magnificent meadow of feelings, findings, emotions, experiences, meanings and loves of life.

6th January 1992

BOOK 3

The time has come to show abstinence in many fields if you wish them to be fertile lands in years to come.

Your job and your career are not to act as obstacles in your way giving diversion and confusion to your life's course, only to be viewed as bends in the road to be travelled along with ease as practical, tactical manoeuvres to enhance the journey.

Necessary means to an end ensure your arrival at the end.

You must negotiate each bend as it appears before you. Adjust your approach accordingly, and continue along with as much speed and efficiency as you can safely travel onward and upward.

Do not rush at it as a race that has to be run, or risk running off the road completely and losing your direction.

Take time to appreciate the journey, to stop and admire the scenery and the breathtaking views.

The game of life is to be played for the love of living and not for the love of winning. To complete the course is as important if you have enjoyed playing, and the pleasure of the game is only enhanced by the joy of winning.

You are now in a hurry to put into action all the marvellous and exciting projects and schemes you have devised. This is refreshing and pleasing. You have time enough, my dear, and yet good preparation in the planning of a trip before it is even begun can result in a much more pleasant, rewarding, successful and trouble-free journey, altogether calmer and more relaxed, resulting in a happier traveller.

9th January 1992

It is of great importance to face old hurts and harboured feelings and to reassess them from a new maturer view point. Then you can address them with the knowledge and experience of an older wiser person who is better able to cope with them than a delicate child ~

To reassess such things with the beauty of hindsight is to view them from a comfortable distance. The hurts and pains are of so long ago that they can no longer reach and harm you. You can now perhaps have a greater understanding of them and that means you can choose to re-programme them into yourself without just blocking them into the dark, untouchable archives within.

To move through all the rooms of your mind and not restrict yourself to the comfortable ones breathes fresh air into them all and enlarges your personal internal space. Sometimes when we shut off too many rooms we become claustrophobic to a degree, and become dissatisfied and feel trapped and limited in our daily physical lives.

Open up all your rooms. Take your time to clear them up, one at a time, and make them truly clean and clear and uncluttered before moving on and making the next as comfortable and welcoming. Then someday your whole house will be in good order and this will reflect itself in your every waking hour.

You are also aware that this has to be addressed to many areas and that many things have to be cleared up and that this all takes time, a great deal of time if you let it, but realising and accepting that it can be started right now is a good beginning.

There is a right time for everything and a right time for everyone, too. Everything cannot be decided by one person any more than the next and each has their own clock by which to tell their own personal time ~

It is a very strange commodity, time, for who knows how much of it anyone really has? It is therefore important to recognise and react to your own individual time and follow such things as intuition and instinct as to when a time is right for you. All time is yours and therefore, if you choose, you can make the most of it and create for yourself great changes and developments if you decide to believe that the time is always right for you ~

Sometimes changes are made for us by other people's actions and words and not through any such recognition and wish to change of our own, but that is not to say that it is not the right time for us to change, just that we are not aware of it at that time. Everything has a reason and change is always for the good, on some level. The freeing of the waters so that they can flow again is a good thing, for it breathes new oxygen and life into them, even if it is gained by crashing over rocks and boulders or by pouring from a great height off a rock face and crashing down onto yet more rocks and boulders below ~

But when at last it comes to settle, will not this water be clearer and sweeter and more inviting than the stale, stagnating waters we used to drink from often?

12th January 1992

For yours is not the only consciousness that needs awakening which is why you have to catalogue the information you receive so that others may benefit as well as yourself.

There are many around you for whom the times are very difficult and a little help, through guidance, can go a long way in such times of trouble and strife.

It is not a regional recession, but a world-wide reshuffle of values and opinions through emotional and circumstantial change ~

Tis true, there are many more enlightened people amongst those of you who tread the earth, and yet you are still few in number compared to those who continue to stumble along with no real reason or value to their lives. You are living in the dark age of awareness and consciousness. Therefore you have the responsibility of holding high your guiding light, that it may spread a little warmth and comfort to many by illuminating their way ahead ~

For stumbling blind in the dark may be the plight of many but that is not to say that it is their choice and that they would not prefer to have a clear vision and direction if it were shown to them ~

Of course, it is all optional and should be remembered as such, not an obligation.

How you choose to live and lead your life is entirely up to you, but to live it to the full means more than just living it up. It means to use your full range of experiences and emotions and not by closing yourself off to those you do not desire.

Huge changes are happening so that many more people are having to live a lot more. They are now having to cope with emotions and experiences that are unfamiliar and often undesired. This is because too many people for too long a time have closed themselves down and concentrated wholly on themselves, their egos and personal pleasures, at the expense of their compassion for humanity.

That is why the times are so hard, because you are all being forced to learn the lessons of life you have all chosen to ignore ~

Anyone will enjoy a class in a subject they enjoy and excel in, but most students will more than grumble in a subject they think is very difficult and possibly boring because of the hard work involved. It is like a double physics lesson on a timetable replacing needlework or games or cookery or art. Compulsory for once and although it may be very difficult and confuse a lot of people, at the end of the day you may find that a good many of them actually learned something, not their chosen subject but an education all the same, even broader than the one they might have chosen which will in fact better prepare them for life.

You cannot always choose to walk on the sunny side of the street or eat only the golden, ripened fruits. Sometimes the sun is obscured by clouds and both sides of the street are grey. Sometimes too, you are forced to eat the bitter, green, unripened fruits as well. Thus you know the difference and develop a broader palate of tastes even if you do not like or enjoy the ones that are in fact less sweet.

The body needs food to survive and as such may have to eat for necessity rather than pleasure from time to time.

Forget ye not that your mind, body and soul survival are intrinsically linked and that you are what you eat, you are what you think and you are what you feel.

Therefore, if you want a truly healthy and happy mind, body and soul, be selective of what you eat, you think and you feel. If you choose to eat, think and feel badly, how do you expect your life to be?

Take control of your appetites, your attitudes and your emotions. Forget ye not too that they are all ultimately within your control, even if you do not believe them to be so.

Trust in yourself and all manner of things will become possible. Take the responsibility for your life for it is what you make it and not vice-versa.

16th January 1992

You only have to look into the past to see that hope does spring eternal. It makes the world go round, hope, not certainty. Love is the energy, but hope the driving force.

Love is not there for every man but hope of love is there for all mankind. There are times when love is not travelling at your side, but hope that love will at sometime join you is what keeps you journeying onward.

There will be great loves to come your way, so be ye not tempted to rest a while and contemplate your loneliness, rather hurry along your way to meet them. Many things are changing around you to make way for those that are yet to come.

Take time to adjust to these changes and to welcome them as they come. If not, you may become disoriented in your world and distressed, or reluctant to change. Release and accept, receive and appreciate the past, present and future. You know that everything has a purpose and a time, even if you cannot see the significance of either as they happen. Trust in it. Trust in that which is good and it shall be so.

24th January 1992

The words that you receive are of great importance and will have much meaning for a great many people.

You knoweth not the magnitude of influence your words will have, and have had, but a small and indicative reaction from the few who have encountered your manuscript so far.

Tis rewarding to know that already such people are being reached and reawakened to the true and righteous ways of the world ~

Your brother is to be of great importance to you in the spreading of these words, and a closeness between you will develop further as the trust and belief in what you are doing will give you both courage and confidence to lead yourselves and others onto higher ground. Practice what you preach and as you sow so shall you reap.

Let light and love be your guiding star and from this guidance you shall travel far. 'Tis true, you have many avenues to explore and in due time you will visit them all. But for now, be content to consider your options and approach them one at a time ~

Preparations can be made for adventures and plans to be put into action but remember, 'tis better to concentrate on one such scheme at a time than to spread yourself too thinly and exhaust and disappoint yourself in an attempt to do too much at one time ~

Your attention may be divided into many sections, resulting in the dispersal of mental energy. Remember the powers of concentration and you shall be able to tap into great reservoirs of strength. Weakness is a state of mind as strength is courage and conviction and belief in all that you think and do.

28th January 1992

You have been visited again by the happiness of your youth. Great comfort and security can be found in this reunion that show to you that love does indeed transcend the breadth of time ~

True love and its vibrations continue to thrive and resound across time and space and the universe. No love is ever wasted, from a deep, heart-felt emotion to a gentle kindness or tenderness shown. Every drop is precious and goes towards the common good, to fill the reservoirs and supply the sea of love from which all can quench their thirst from time to time. To simply survive and also to feel truly alive.

Love is as necessary to the survival of the soul as water is to the body. The lips that part to drink are the same that impart a kiss. There is not enough love in the world and the reservoirs are low. That is why a greater love has to be created between mankind so that humanity can drink to survive ~

If you truly believe that what you give out will one day be returned to you, is it not logical to wish for clear, sweet waters to run into you in preference to vile, foul smelling slime, and for clear waters to be the birthright of every child by the actions of their forefathers' and fathers' generations?

That is why it is so important to see life as a continuous pattern and not as a one-off experience. If it is in your hands to create the kind of world future generations will inherit, take care to leave for them a legacy of love, life and light to be accepted and lovingly appreciated in kind.

1st February 1992

You are aware that your saturn return is nearly upon you, and that with this will come the necessary revealing of your life. You are, as yet, still unaware that the reshaping of your own life and reaffirming of your beliefs will have such an affect on the reshaping and re-evaluating of the lives of so many.

Put yourself on solid ground and those around you will stand steady beside you. Each and every one, strong and independent, yet giving love and light and support to one another.

You are all one and can find great joy in living together, as a single tree does in the union with others in the forming of a forest, each one living and thriving in harmony and health and not sapping its strength from another.

Casting too great a shadow restricts the growth of those around you, yet climbing high up into the sky creates a fertile ground below from which new life can spring and grow. The canopy is but one level of life and existence in the composition of a forest, and many forms of fauna and flora flourish and add beauty and colour to the scene.

Succulent fruits and berries, exotic birds and butterflies all have a place in the order of things, as do the animals and the insects who inhabit and survive on the fruits of the forest and on the health and strength of the trees therein.

But to be as solid as a rock, immovable and unchangeable, is to be as lifeless as a stone, cold and unfeeling. Nothing can grow with ease on a rock, nor yet is it capable of growth itself. Yet to be likened to a fertile soil gives great promise, that seeds carefully planted and tended with love and light and care will in time yield forth from this ground and bring life and colour and beauty.

Therefore plant for yourself seeds of love that one day they will bear fruit and help feed the famine of humanity. Then you can all eat well and make merry in the celebration of your life.

2nd February 1992

BOOK 4

A new page, a new book, a new phase and outlook ~

Great things are beginning to happen and their success is in your hands.

Fear not the challenges before you. Accept them gladly with great hope and understanding, then trust in your beliefs and make them happen ~

Colours are of great importance to you, and 'tis your use of them that will bring you much attention. These words will colour your life as your paints would colour a page. Music doth colour your mind as a flower's sweet fragrance doth colour the air on the edge of a summer breeze.

Sweet melodies surround you in laughter, love and song. Fill your life with complimentary colours, explore and delight in the full spectrum of experience and emotion. Be not afraid to investigate all hues, but try to maintain an essential balance of tone at all times. Clarity of colour reflects the murkiness of one's mind.

Keep a clear head and clear colours will be applied to your life. Let not your palette become spoiled by careless thoughts or actions. If you select a light shade, be sure to cleanse your brush lest you discolour it with darkness and taint your composition.

Your life is as a clean, clear page and you put colour to your emotions, therefore careful selection will result in a more harmonious final outcome. Words can be colourful but uncontrolled emotions can ruin their delight.

Take great care in controlling all the colours in your command. Thoughts and actions too reverberate as pigments with the potential to enhance or destroy the harmony in your life.

Learn to think in colour, speak in colour, eat in colour and rejoice in colour, then you are less likely to become covered in blackness. Not in your mind, body or soul.

Trust in the light; 'tis from which all colours are to be found. Darkness is only possible without some degree of light. Increase your trust and belief in the light and introduce more colours into your life. Paint yourself a rainbow.

5th February 1992

Good friends come but seldom really go. Take time to enjoy and appreciate them when you are together but never think they are truly gone, even when many miles may come between you ~

True friends will always be with you, and you with them. One meets and encounters many from which but a very few may become close companions with which to travel through your lifetime ~

Some part of you remains with each other when you continue on down stream on different currents and even flow in different directions. 'Tis the essence of a good companion that they will journey onward by your side so that you may never feel totally alone ~

The comfort and security found in good friendship is immense. Therefore a small investment in maintaining a closeness with these individuals can result in a huge and happy return. For 'tis the pattern of life for some friendships to fade so that new ones are made and flourish.

Be not too sad when the wheel of fortune and fate moves forward and some fond faces and familiar places are no longer with you. Be aware that what is meant to be is meant to be, and as such will be so. Yet those who are meant to travel somehow with you will transcend the restrictions of circumstance and situation, and journey on with you on some level always.

That is why it is important to rendezvous from time to time, to catch up with each other on all levels. Then, once reaffirmed, you can feel the eternal warmth of friendship and need never feel the chill of loneliness. You may feel from time to time that you walk on your own but remember, you never walk alone.

See, a simple song can evoke the memory of a loved one and can remind you of a closeness you once shared, and again transcends the airways and reunites you by the repetition of a shared vibration. 'Tis then that you must realise that you are always to be together because the harmonious vibrations you made and fondly remember continue to reverberate across time.

That is why all actions, thoughts and words deserve careful consideration because the vibrations they create will continue to resound for eternity. Harsh words may be retracted in haste and yet, of course, their discord has been struck and can be regretted but not removed.

Likewise a soft, sweet sentiment or kindness shown in consideration will go a long way and last forevermore.

Tis a very good thing to heighten your awareness of what you are capable of and for how much you are responsible.

12th February 1992

You must read and re-read your affirmations, to affirm and re-affirm your intentions and aspirations. That way you will not forget the direction you wish to travel and are less likely to be distracted or fall by the wayside.

When you have a clear view of where you are going, is it not easier to find your way and get there, than to take your chances by stumbling in the dark and possibly losing your way?

Affirmations can be altered and adjusted to stay in line with your moving goal posts. As long as you have a direction to move in at all times it does not matter if they are not always the same. Sometimes circumstances change and so adjustments have to be made because the hand of fate can wear a glove, and who can tell when she will reveal herself and reshuffle the cards. The game does not stop because a new hand has been dealt. It just has to be picked up and played as best you can.

Reshuffling the pack deals new fate and fortune to many, not just yourself. Sometimes lady luck may sit by your side but in other rounds you may just have to play by yourself, by the best intuition and experience you can.

Even at such times as these when you feel you are playing your hand by yourself, forget not that those around you are each and every one having to face the same challenge and are in fact all playing with you, and each on their own, as well.

Forget ye not also, that all of life is but a game and the joy of it can be shared by many players. The pleasure of the playing however, can be ruined by a few who cheat to gain personal reward. But what a disappointment it would be if in fact there were no reward for winning by fair means or foul, but just the love and laughter and enjoyment shared with those who sit at your table, and how hideous and hollow to put all the value on the final outcome and not on the vital income ~

You are weary of the world around you as are many others. It is as a fading flower that may lose its scent and change its colour, but its beauty remains in another form to be appreciated all the same. Do you not treasure your delicate dried flowers and love them as much if not more than the fresh picked ones that fill the air with their sweet perfume for such a comparatively short time?

But don't give up hope and live only for the fresh flowers. New blooms blossom with the passing of the seasons as a new sun always rises out of the darkness of the night, yet even in the night a new moon rises and sheds a glimmer of light which carries you through to the break of dawn. You do not question that the sun will follow the moon or that spring will follow winter, so question ye not that there will be a new beginning to follow the ever-nearing end.

Throughout history and time there have been many dawnings of many ages. Each has had its place and eventually had its downfall only to be reborn as a new era and a new age. 'Tis true no other has had such a global destruction or decline on an environmental level, but that is not to say that even now your times will be the last, only more different from those to come.

Great changes have to happen because great imbalances have arisen. But that is not to say that such adjustments have not been made by others before you in times gone by.

The legend of Atlantis surrounds a time you can all but imagine, because so much of the world as you know it was so different as it was. Likewise your world is changing enormously, seemingly before your very eyes. You may not like these changes and cry out in fear and despair, but do you not think that the voices of those before you did not cry out as the world they knew began to sink?

Now you can see and hold the belief that out of the ashes of the fire doth rise the mighty phoenix. The world as you know it has survived ever since, and yet to those of Atlantis their world was destroyed and the end of their time had come.

The passing of an age can be marked by the passing of beliefs. The coming of 'the end of the world' can be the coming of the end of the world's beliefs.

The values and virtues, meanings and merits, sins and significancies can all change and are often replaced by new ones, sometimes complete reversals of those previously preached. Man can have a short memory and adapt to these changes with equal enthusiasm and faith.

That is why you should look long and deep into the values and beliefs you hold, and see if they would stay true and stand the test of time by out-living the fads of fashionable belief or motivation, and remain as a recipe for life rather than a flavour of the month.

15th February 1992

Tis but an illusion that your life is going nowhere, only that it may not be going where you want it to, at a speed you would like it to. That is not to say that it has come to a standstill or that your days are dormant. Time does not stand still so how can it be that a life can appear to be going nowhere when the mere nature of life is to progress and grow?

It is just a period perhaps through which you are walking down a passage from one room on the way to another. The passage may be dark, seemingly without windows or light, but when you at last come into the room you will appreciate the stark contrasts.

To breeze from one delightful space straight into the next detracts somewhat from the full appreciation and beauty of them both. For without a change in ambience, atmosphere and air as well as temperature and light, how can the new environment be truly assessed? If all is to be much of a muchness then too much of a good thing can breed complacency and discontent.

To remain objective one has to be aware of all the alternatives. That is why your house must have a wide variety of rooms and passages, doors and windows through which to view and move around your own full house of life.

There may be stairs you have to climb from time to time which may be tiresome, but new rooms with new opportunities lie on the levels at the top of your wooden hill. When you are wandering down a corridor remember that it is for a reason. You are not going nowhere, and so should not dawdle or doubt your direction and delay your journey. Just keep on going down that corridor with courage and confidence and conviction. Be open to ideas and suggestions, as you may open many doors and look around before deciding which room to enter next.

Yet sometimes it is true, you do not always have the choice which rooms you inhabit but need to pass through one to get to the next. Not all rooms are linked by passages, some just run from one to the next, but one thing for sure is that passages always lead somewhere and that you should not forget ~

23rd February 1992

Be not afraid, all is not doom and gloom even if that is all it appears to be from where you are standing.

Change the position from which you observe and your view will take on a new perspective. Same landscape, only different angle and light. Different things become the centre of your picture and different things come into focus for your attention as much as your eye.

Tis only that you do not have a good clear view from where you stand right now. 'Tis true you do not always or yet often have a long view ahead, for that is not always meant to be. But there are many times when the distance you can see is clear and calm and comfortable. Then too, like now, there are times when all you see around is unclear, uncomfortable and distressing.

But remember too that life is but a moving picture show to be lived out frame by frame. Sometimes seemingly in slow motion, others on fast forward. Nevertheless, each frame is a part of the whole and has more meaning when viewed as such in context rather than being scrutinised or assessed as a single shot.

Some of the best films have a number of disturbing, ugly or frightening frames which have their place and role to add depth and drama to the full motion picture. Not all films are tragedies or love stories, soap operas or comedies, horrors or adventures. The best however are all for one and one for all ~

Remember, it is all just make-believe. How you choose to read your lines and deliver them will determine their success. How you choose to lead and deliver your life, in the same way will determine your success.

You may not have written the script or chosen the location but put your best into the role, and sincerity into every scene if it is to stand close inspection on the cinema screen and remain compelling and convincing. Timing is important. It is important to wait until the right time to deliver a line or to make a move and not to either pre-empt or miss your cue ~

26th February 1992

Have faith and courage in the belief that your life is to be bathed in golden light and love and it shall be so ~

Doubt it not in times of darkness, for faith itself is the belief in the unproven, unknown and as with a good cake the proof is in the pudding. Make it carefully,

bake it carefully, then rejoice in the delight of
its deliciousness ~

The better quality of the ingredients and the right
balance and quantity of each, all have an influence
on the success of the recipe. Parts of the baking
process can be mundane and messy. Patience too,
has to be shown especially during the baking. That is
when the temptation is to risk ruining the possible
perfect outcome by opening the oven prematurely,
altering the temperature, interfering with and
interrupting a process that is best left alone.

It cannot be rushed. It will be done when the time
for it to be done is come and not before. If you can
be patient and let it cool down properly too, once it
is out in front of you, then you avoid the possibility
of getting your fingers burnt!

True, then you could go ahead and eat your cake.
However if you give a little more time to it and
decorate it, it can turn into an altogether more
successful culinary delight to be shared and
appreciated by many in true celebration ~

Why is it of such importance to you who I am when you know my words to be true? If it is to satisfy the curiosity of others then they will have to read these words themselves and then decide if it is at all important which name I put to myself when it is not personal recognition I seek, but a world-wide awareness of all that there is, and the glory of that, lies therein.

Each man should know himself and should use my words to re-find himself but needs no introduction to me to do that. The answers are all there within each and every one of you. 'Tis for you to find and re-introduce them into your daily lives from the depths of your own consciousness. The credit and glory can then be given as self-praise, appreciation and confidence all of which are far more important than attributing them to an external anything or anyone.

My words are of great importance as I have said and my name is not. Trust in me and believe in my words, then trust in you and believe in yourself ∞

7th March 1992

Your loving cup shall overfloweth and those around you will rejoice as the plenitude of positivity spills forth to flavour their futures as well ~

Tis of great importance that you will find great happiness. For from that burning brightness a greater light can shine and give guidance to a greater audience, and give much hope and faith to many more mortals ~

For yours is not a selfish love and as such will have no limit. If it were yours to give you would gladly give all the love in the world. In return, what you wish upon all others shall be granted unto you. "Thy will be done, thy kingdom come; on Earth as it is in Heaven." To believe and understand this is the key to believe and understand life itself.

Be careful what you wish lest it be granted, then regretted.

9th March 1992

In olden times man was more in touch with himself and the tunes he heard around him. 'Tis a great pity that you have only succeeded in distancing yourselves as mankind from the very Life-force that ensures your survival ~

Nature and you are one, and as such should have a vested interest in the both of you as a whole and not in the progression of one at the expense of the other. You have lost the clear vision that all is one and should live and work as one ~

You live as it were, exist as it were, with almost total disregard for the Life-force that feeds you. The air that you breathe, the food that you need, and the waters that you drink must be clean and clear and healthy if they are to give good positive energy to what you are and what you think ~

Cleanse your body and cleanse your mind. Then energy will flow through your mind, body and soul ~

You know it has to be done and that the time has surely come ~

Accept that your life is what you make it and that you yourself are what you make yourself. If you are full of negativity and feel heavy in your head and heavy in your body, do you not expect to feel heavy in your heart?

Lighten up your load, listen to my words and learn from them to lighten up your life. Get lighter in your mind, lighter in your body and then you will get lighter in your heart and soul.

Take control of your inner-self. Turn to yourself for strength and understanding. Make the best for yourself by making the best of yourself, in what you choose to eat, do and think ~

No one else can do this for you. But do it for yourself, treat yourself for yourself. You deserve it and you will appreciate it. Be kind to yourself and replace all negatives and bad toxins with positive goodness instead.

Do not worry so. Your life will sort itself out if you sort yourself out.

Clear out those cluttered old rooms in your head and in your heart harbouring old hurts and fears and insecurities. Take the time to spring-clean your whole house and it will be fresh and in good order to face the year ahead. For spring is just around the corner, as is the rest of your life ~

Rejoice in the coming of each new day and welcome it with the dawning of its light. It is a great new beginning of life, and nature takes delight in displaying this in all its glory ~

New buds burst forth and grow from old ground, as new thoughts do spring into your mind and blossom if in fertile soil.

Take care to tend your garden. Prepare the soil and sow the right seeds at the right time. Give them what they need, love and light and nutrients, then they will thrive. Clear away the weeds and lovingly protect them, and in time you will have a beautiful, fruitful garden of delight ~

14th March 1992

A guided verse would best describe the words I've often wrote, but what to call them for all the world has yet to be decided ~

For 'tis of great importance; as words provoke thoughts 'tis best to use them wisely ~

Wilst thou be'est mine if I woo you with sweet rhyme? Wouldst thou read on in awe if I were to capture you with more?

Mere ink spots on a page can by their configuration, depict a time, write a line, and plant thoughts to grow inside your mind ~

You can trust that this book will succeed as guided and protected from afar. Ye need not worry about its reception. 'Tis enough, for now, to celebrate its conception ~

Tis a great achievement that we have been able to collaborate so well in this journalistic venture. Much has been achieved by yourself for opening up and accepting my words so freely. 'Tis no longer a problem communicating with you, and I am much relieved you no longer feel threatened by me but accept my love as freely as my words ~

Tis a great love that is there for all men to receive. Just find love in your own heart and you will open the way for a great love to find you.

The universe is full of love and light and positivity. Open yourselves up to this and dispel and discourage all negativity. What you find in your heart is what you find in your life ~

Memoires of the future
Words of warmth with lines of light ~
Future memories
Present dreams and many happy returns ~
Starlight scriptures
Heavenly prose or
The wishing well of life ~

I could go on with many more, right into the night.
For in verse and prose, as you well know, I find a
true delight. However, 'tis not good to exhaust you
and you should go to sleep.

Rest well and be sure we will share words again ~

22nd March 1992

$\mathbf{T}$is not always easy to keep one's face above the water when the waves come fast and furious ~

But learn to hold your breath when you see the wall of water before you, and therefore be as best prepared you can for when it comes crashing down upon your head. Be confident that you will come up when the wave has passed. Gather yourself, take a deep breath and shake the water from your eyes.

It is important to close your mouth, your nose, your eyes and your ears so that you do not take in the turbulent waters. In such times of tempest it is sound advice to close yourself to all the negativity that abounds, hurt and anger, pain and strain, lest you take them in, in dangerous and damaging amounts. Learn to swim underwater to survive and stay alive ~

You like to swim as you like to live. Is it not more exciting to swim in the unpredictable sea than in a still pool, and have not some of the best things you've seen been under deep water? Remember this and swim free ~

Adjustments and precautions have to be made depending on water conditions, as to how you are going to approach your swim, much as with your life. Assess how best you can safely enjoy yourself but be not afraid to get wet ~

25th March 1992

Tis a great joy to be found in the celebration of life and light and colour, to be shared by many who may gaze upon your renditions in far off places and delight in the colours and life therein, when within their eyes and lives there might not be an abundance of light or love. To them they may appear as bright as stars in a dark sky, as hope, and promise and sunshine on a rainy day ~

España, 1st May 1992

One From The Heart right from the start were the words I bade you wrote. Do you still not know since one year ago that they are as true now as they were then and come from your spirit and soul therein? Each man can find such truthful lines, if he chooses to think with his heart and feel with his mind.

I may express my words in flowering phrases but only to take delight in creating lasting pictures, poetically painted in your mind. Thence there is more chance their images will remind you of the messages they contain.

They are carefully selected and chosen for their strength and colour and should help you retain their meaning, whereas empty words, like empty conversation, can be quick to be forgotten.

7th May 1992

Like a world within a world and a wheel within a wheel, life goes on in concentric circles. Each one ringing with the next one's vibration.

Beware then of the vibrations you transmit. For en masse they resound across the universe and affect the worlds around you. Your own inner vibrations dictate those you release. Those in turn affect those around you. Neighbour to neighbour, nation to nation, planet to planet, life to life ~

Therefore the key vibrations to begin with, to ensure happiness and harmony, are love and peace and understanding, from deep within your soul, deep within yourself.

Each man is responsible for his own destiny, and should be aware of this and spread kind words of love and peace instead of harsh words of war and hate. These can only result in his own destruction when the tide does choose to change and all he has released returns from whence it came.

Transmit love and it will one day be returned to you, your neighbour, your nation, your planet and your life ~

9th May 1992

Make positive signs of light for all the world to see shining bright. Fear not your good intentions will go astray, for your light will shine around the globe in places where it's night and places where it's day ~

Fill yourself with positivity and your projects will not fail. Make your plans happen. Make your dreams reality. The power to make them happen is yours to command as you will ~

There is a right time for everything. Recognise it when it arrives, seize the opportunities when they happen, and play an active roll in the forming of your future, instead of a passive roll in the passing of your present ~

12th May 1992

The power of love comes in great waves and gains strength with the ebbing tide. The currents flow deep below and their strength is yet unseen, but to go with the flow is to waken into a dream.

All manner of things may come to pass if you trust in great love and do not ask. It will be given unto ye as great things do come to those who wait.

Trust in this and ye shall see, just how great love can be.

Liken unto a wave yourself. Ye shall gather your strength from deep below, build yourself up, then let yourself go with all the force of nature behind you. Be not afraid to ride high on the crest of your wave.

You will find your shore to break upon as all waves someday will. There you can greet the land, embrace the sand and rejoice in a happy union,
hand in hand.

Who knows how far a wave has to travel before it finds its break. Who knows where it gets its strength from if not from those around it. For seemingly they come in sets but sometimes maybe not. Each wave is certainly separate and yet forms part of
a greater whole.

The sea of love is much the same and its movements unpredictable. Some days are rough, some days are calm, by the calling of the moon. If the moon of love does rise above, then you feel the force of nature well up inside you from deep below. Then who knows where your beach will be. Just build yourself up and go with the flow ~

15th May 1992

To say "if you knew then what you know now" is hindsight but to strive to know now all that you knew then, in the greater sense of the word, is to aim to understand and appreciate the importance of reincarnation and karmic return, a far deeper and more revealing reflection than hindsight.

My messages are often familiar to you and strike a chord of accepted wisdom and truth. The more you re-awaken these inner memories and knowledge of the way of things, the better you will be able to play the game of life right. Increase your inner consciousness and understanding of the rules of the game, the laws of nature and the results of cause and effect, then you can avoid obvious mistakes, pitfalls and pain.

My words are meant to assist you all, to gain greater understanding of yourselves from within so that you may develop a better understanding of your lives and of those around you, everywhere. You are aware that your life is a part of many others as many others' lives are part of yours. If you were to change your life with love and light and peace and understanding, you will change the lives of those around you by bringing more love and light and peace and understanding into theirs.

If each man were to do this, think how fast the whole world could change from mere self-development of individuals to the mass improvement of nations, notions and nature. You are all one. You and the land are one and should stand together on issues of health and welfare as one. Do not bite the hand that feeds you or cut off your Life-force. Instead, work in union with the universe and with one another. Learn to play the game of life to win and not to lose.

Be careful not to cloud your own waters. Clean, clear, pure thought like clean, clear water can be whirled up into confusion by the stirring up of sediments happily settled at the bottom of all pools of idea and emotion. See your way clearly and swim as cleanly as you can through these delightful waters and create as little disturbance as you can by reducing undercurrents and counter flows of thought and idea and directions. If you thrash around like a flaying duck or moth upon the water, you progress in no direction but waste a lot of energy, create your own waves and disturbances, perhaps even draw the attention of the predators you are trying to avoid who may be responsible for your final downfall.

Be buoyant and brave and be prepared to relax and let yourself go with the existing flow when you know not in which direction to go.

17th May 1992

You speak of these things as if you do not know what has passed between you many lives ago! As love once shared leaves an echo to resound across all space and time, so do hate and evil scent. If you have a feeling of warmth to some people upon first meeting them should this not be balanced sometimes by those encounters that leave you dead and cold? Memory does not always serve you well for if you could conjure up all the information on infinite record your life would be a total confusion of mixed reality and some might say you would lose your mind. For a mind is nothing without a true perspective. The difference between a dream and reality or a film and reality is the firmness of a fixed perspective. If one should not possess such a milestone one could very easily lose one's mind. However if actual detailed memories evade you but the strength of their impression sometimes carries enough to make a lasting impact on your senses, and you know not what you feel but feel it all the same, then keep a firm perspective, for these are shadows of times gone by and do not have any place or threat in this time.

Allow not your mind to wander and indulge on negative adventure into things that can only cause destruction which in turn may manifest as repercussions in your real world as real disruptions or confusion in your life.

Remember it is in your hands the very chance to practice what I have so often preached and you have endeavoured to understand, the power is all within. "There is no problem unless you make a problem". Trust in it and believe in it.

If you choose to grow you sometimes have to have pain but through that pain you will endure and evolve an even stronger you. Yet, if you choose to dive into the unknown depths of time and lose the true perspective by which you live, you invite the possibility of confrontation and disruption.

You know not to spend too much time in the shadows if it is cold and you shiver, then keep on walking and move yourself back into the warm sunlight.

You know if you do not like the feel of a place or the inner person behind the face much more than you used to because your senses have risen and it is a good thing to see you have achieved such sensitivity. Do not take it as a personal thing, as a negative. Look to it as a positive personal thing, that you are more aware of bad things as much as you are of good. They are, after all, both just opposite ends of the same measure.

When your instincts tell you to steer clear of a person or a place you are as right to follow this as much as a good hunch or feeling. People's love and affection can colour your better judgements as much as their negative responses may colour your opinion of a thing, person or situation. However, your deeper, heart-felt feelings are those to listen to for they will be true. If not for everyone but for you. From this you can learn to think with your heart and feel with your mind. Consider your thoughts as feelings and begin to assess your feelings as thoughts. If you feel a thing is right in your heart then consider this and think it is right in your mind. Learn to use all your senses and to call upon more than your mind for answers, and listen to them all.

Compassion is thinking with your heart and feeling with your mind.

That is why more of it is needed in the world. Too many people have too little compassion for life and humanity and think only for themselves without feeling for others. If they were to think more for others and feel less for themselves the world would be a much better place.

To be self-centred is so shallow when you could be centred to the whole universe. Nature, earth and life, not just bones and blood and tissue. The wisdom, love and light of the whole universe are infinitely greater than the limited amounts of each to be found within the mortal mind and body of a single soul in a sealed shell, of a single self.

Brighton, 6th June 1992

Hurt and pain do come as thunder and lightning in a storm. Then tears do flow as a healing force as rain does fall from the heavens onto the parched and arid land.

The storm may wreak havoc and leave destruction in its wake but the rains are often needed to replenish the land and although pain may cause their flow, tears are sometimes needed to purge and cleanse the soul.

The calm that comes with the passing of the storm may be a much needed change in atmosphere but the air is fresher than before, the earth is wetter than before, and because of this in time the fruits will thus be sweeter than before ~

It is a good thing to release pain for it should not be held inside, any more than a cloud can contain its electric charge without releasing it sometime, cracking across the sky with fire and brimstone.

If pain is restrained it feeds the growing cloud and it swells and darkens and blocks out the sun, blocks out the light and covers the land in darkness.

A good tempest which unleashes all the heavens' hold clears the air, disperses the clouds and allows the sun to burst through and shed its golden light once more across the land.

Now your clouds have burst, their waters shed, you can look forward to fine weather and welcome the sun back into your world and its light back into your life.

Brighton, 7th June 1992

You know the things you have to do, and things you've already done. Patience is required in some places and action is sought in others.

Do not hesitate and waver just because you feel you are on uneven ground. The best course of action to be taken in such times is to keep moving on until firmer grounds are found. If you stop you know not what will happen, yet if you continue on in the direction you started you may well find what you are expecting at the journey's end.

You owe it to yourself to believe in yourself, to believe in your own ideas and in your own success.

Make it happen. Support yourself and support your ideas. Help yourself succeed, and don't be tempted to trip yourself up. That gives you an excuse for failing to succeed but it's cheating.

Cheating yourself ~

If you can't be honest with yourself who can you be honest with, and how can you expect others to be honest with you? Be honest and true in your heart. There is no-one but you that matters in this discourse. It begins and ends with you.

Love yourself and like yourself and others will love and like you too. If you are hard on yourself, dislike yourself and criticise yourself, what vibrations do you think you are giving out to others as a guide to how they should react to you?

That is not to say that you should praise yourself in public but praise and support yourself in private you must.

Tis true you have no-one but yourself right now but it is a good thing to spend a measure of one's life by oneself. In this way you gain a greater understanding of yourself, by asking more questions of yourself and thus answering them for yourself; thus asking deeper questions perhaps than maybe you might if other people were available for answers to your questions.

Perhaps life and time would pass so quickly and completely you might not have time or yet need to ask some questions at all.

Not every man's life, or woman's for that matter, poses the same questions for them. Some holy men for instance spend entire lifetimes asking questions and seeking truths within themselves. Yet other individuals in vast numbers seem to come and go and simply exist in the space between without asking a single question of themselves or looking for the truth and honesty in their lives.

You are alone and have been alone for a reason. Take the time while you are able to learn of life those things that it is only possible to learn whilst you are alone. Then when your partner comes you will be a more complete person, ready to learn all the more things you have yet to learn about sharing your life and sharing yourself.

I promise thee thy love will come. Believe this and do not despair. Take comfort in your loneliness by appreciating it as a necessary time spent out in the cold, as it were to learn how life is out there before coming in and sharing the warmth and love indoors.

When the time comes to meet your partner you will surely meet him so do not fret so. You must believe in it and all good things, and he like them will come as all good things come to those who wait. I have told of this before and want nothing more than to see you happy and in the arms of the man you will share a great love with.

However with every day you are still apart from this burning love and pillar of strength you are growing and developing your knowing and inner knowledge and understanding.

It is a vital thing that you be the most strong and understanding person you can for your life carries great responsibility with it and inner strength is going to be one of the most important resources and qualities you have. So do not think that even a single hour of a single day is wasted in the gaining of it. So it may be hard to achieve, particularly in the "No pain, no gain" aspect, but not a drop will go to waste.

Even if life were a bed of roses and your feet were not hardened up but soft, you would be pricked by thorns and get scratched and bleed and cry tears of pain amid sweet fragrance and beauty.

Sometimes it serves you well to be seasoned and perhaps to know when it's best to wear your shoes!

Brighton, 21st June 1992

The summer solstice is of much significance to your inner journey of development. It makes the passing of the milestone set as the end of one phase of your journey.

You have completed a significant section and thus a celebration is traditionally in order to praise yourself for the vast amount of ground covered. It not only marks the completing of a particular course but also serves well as the celebration of a new beginning, the closing of one door and the opening of another, the turning of a page, the dawning of a new day ~

From this point on you should not look back, you should not consider your journey from its original beginnings but see this solstice as the new beginning. Past experiences, emotions and actions from your previous phase should only be recalled as positives by which to prepare you to perform in the next phase. It is only wise to unload the heavy things you have acquired such as guilt and doubt and disbelief, pain and strain and loneliness, and the contents of a heavy heart ~

Lighten up your load so that you can be more sure-footed on the unknown terrain of the future. Why carry the extra weight of negativity with you unnecessarily? This is a specific stop in your journey designed for the refreshing of your mind, body and soul, to wash and clean yourself off from the dust and dirt you have encountered.

Bathe as it were in clean fresh water and emerge cleansed and revived. Re-dress yourself and re-pack your bags and review your direction and mark your new course to go from this point to the next.

The distance of your entire journey when seen as a whole can be somewhat awesome. For it can span many miles in many lifetimes and it might seem like an interminable distance. However, seen from one stage or solstice to the next puts it into plausible portions that one can easily see completeable.

You were right to celebrate this solstice even if you knew not why or even that you were actually doing it ~

London, 22nd June 1992

Remember things are not always as bad as they seem or yet always what they seem ~

Many a time a negative situation has a positive end. The thing is just to remember to take a wider perspective and not get stuck with tunnel vision.

Look for the best in everything and everyone and that is what you will find. It can sometimes be difficult to find, obscured from view but there none the less. Do not take all situations or people on first impressions. They may last but they may well not be true.

Give people time to be seen in more than just one light and give situations time too. Assess them from all other angles before deciding if a thing is good or bad.

There are often great surprises to be found if only you look hard enough. Give yourself support to overcome your fears instead of scolding yourself for having them. If the child in you is crying, comfort her instead of punishing her. She is you. Do not let your childish insecurities bring about the downfall or cause disruptions in your adult ideas in the life of the adult you ~

Inner strength which you have been developing is exactly what is required. It has been developed for the distinct purpose of helping yourself.

It is well appreciated how difficult your responsibilities are and because of the enormity of strength required you have had to be prepared to be able to accept them. This too has been difficult and distressing for you but you will come to see that you are ready to cope as soon as you decide.

London, 26th June 1992

Let us hope that the time has come for you to pick up the challenge your future holds. Remember that time is a changeable thing and it is up to you to read your own clock and decide when the time is right for you. You can make a thing happen by conscious action and likewise you can delay its progress by conscious inaction.

It is easy to excuse yourself from taking action by justifying your daily duties and current situation as taking precedence. Be careful not to do anything because you are too busy doing anything.

Turn up your flame, bring your pot to the boil and don't let it simmer silently away. Then you can proudly shout "tea's made" and fill the cups of those who have a great thirst and a great need for refreshment.

Picture yourself as the charlady, then laugh, lighten up, take a much more fun attitude to your role then relax and enjoy it. Your happy-go-lucky nature should stand you in good stead so do not forget to laugh at yourself. For if laughter is a good thing then to laugh at yourself must be a good thing to do.

Laugh a lot and take your problems more lightly, both personal and publishing! Then you will fill your lines with positive light and eliminate all traces of negativity, darkness and doubt.

29th June 1992

~☆~

The joys of the world can be multifold and yours can be an adventure ~

The magnitude of meaning can only truly be measured against a scale of similar proportion.

If your scale is short or shallow you can only register and record a small degree of the whole. Deeper broader emotions and meanings fall beyond your comprehension or attention. Develop yourself a larger capacity to measure extremes and not mere mediocrity.

The versatility of each artist's interpretation is a clear indication of the individual spirit within and shows that no two people or paintings are the same. Even if the subject matter were exactly the same, each artist's angle and perception of an image would be different and thus reflected in each individual rendition.

That is why there is never any right or wrong with art or yet anything. Each piece of artwork should be assessed not just from your mind, whether it fits an accepted idea of expectation or worth, but from your heart; what it means to you, for yourself. Beauty is in the eye of the beholder and thus being the beholder the choice is yours to interpret as you see.

If a thing makes you feel happy or gives you delight in some degree, then that is yours to experience and express. Take delight in studying and reproducing such images. Express yourself in pen and ink and paint ~

Take time to relax when you have the opportunity. There are times when it is nigh impossible to relax due to the daily pressures of life. That is why like now when such opportunities arise you should welcome them with open arms and freely give up to the struggles of life and concentrate on relaxing. Mind, body and soul will all benefit from this and you will be wholly revived.

España, 7th July 1992

Organisation and preparation are imperative as much as strong belief and visualisation.

Pursue a thought unto its end, plan it out in stages, visualise each one completed unto its end. Believe in it and make it happen.

Write down your plans and schemes and projects so that you can chart a route and steer your life to sail through each one with ease and efficiency.

"Decree a thing and it shall be done". Decide what to decree and do so with your mind, body and soul.

Have total belief in yourself and your projects and life will not fail.

Restrict yourself not by false limitations.

Expand yourself and grow by strong belief and support for yourself.

You can do anything you set your mind to. Remember this and set your mind accordingly. Situations you surround yourself with are those you choose to, for on some level they are what you create. All have a reason and a significance in your life even if you do not fully comprehend them or their role.

As on a larger scale your entire life has a reason and significance even if you do not fully comprehend it or your role. Therefore remember that a wider perspective of things will give you a greater understanding of things. Strive to keep a large scale life and to see all obstacles as small!

España, 11th July 1992

Where once you would have settled for the view from the garden wall now look for more beyond that closed perimeter and expand your far horizons ~

Be inquisitive and enquiring of all you find along the walk of life, learn of all the lessons it has for you in store. Approach them with enthusiasm and gain wisdom from their teaching ~

España, 14th July 1992

To relax and give your ideas time to grow is what is going to benefit you most. You can achieve very little of worth with force, but you can have everything you value most with patience and time and love.

España, 15th July 1992

Write upon thy pages not just for the now but for future prosperity. Your future is in the making every day of your life. Be aware of this and be prepared to put the time in today to make a better tomorrow.

Don't put off today what you could do for your own tomorrow and towards your future.

España, 22nd July 1992

My trust in thee is tantamount to thy trust in me. I will impart more words of wisdom when thou relinquish thy limitations and false restrictions. Strive to live and grow each day, then the fruits of wisdom may fall your way.

España, 25th July 1992

With the coming of the full moon comes the fruition of thought to put into action in the month ahead. To be in tune with the moon is to be in tune with yourself. Be aware of your losing and your gaining. Energies both ebb and flow and 'tis with this you should let yourself go.

To speak my words when they come to you clearly is yet another step in your development but to write them still has a more lasting and far-reaching effect. They come for you to share and sometimes that might mean with those around you in immediate company and sometimes for those far and away.

Many people, 'tis true, are writing things of much importance but each has its message and meaning and role in things. The spreading of good words of wisdom and guidance is a task of great magnitude and as such mortal recruits have been sought to carry out this work. Each is as important, as every drop of light that breaks through helps dispel the darkness.

Brighton, 13th August 1992

You have come a long way, crossed a vast distance from the unknowing towards the light. Journey on with your trusty companions and together you will make great headway. Though you are all on your own pathways, you are all heading in the same direction. To be aware of this, that there are many like you heading for the same goal should be a great comfort, and although each and every one of you has your own lessons to learn, individually wrapped in circumstance and emotion and outcome, the lessons are all universal.

Therefore, empathy for the trials and tribulations of your friends in their sometimes painful growth through life and learning better prepares you to recognise and appreciate the lesson in your own life.

It is not important to know the intimate details of one another's lives and lessons and loves, but to know other people are hurting for whatever reason theirs might be is essential in maintaining a broader perspective of your own pains. It eliminates the personal ego aspect of the victim role. It is an essential part of life to grow fully and you need to experience great pain yourself if you are to fully understand it.

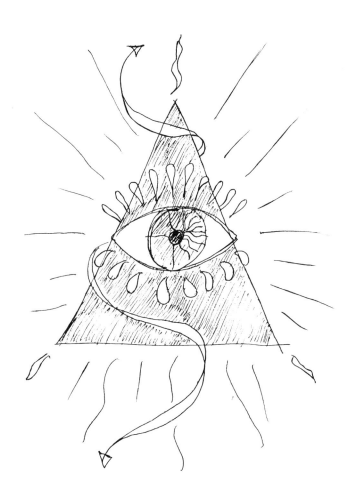

Much as you are all eager to fully investigate and experience the joys of pure love and happiness be prepared to study all emotions. Be aware that they are a necessary part of your education and that the path of the spiritual traveller is never easy for it ends in the total understanding of all that there is through personal experience gained over many lifetimes.

Brighton, 14th August 1992

So now the time has come to spread your wings and fly away. Behold the great changes that have to be undertaken through growth and development for the young green caterpillar before he or she can emerge as a beautiful butterfly.

You have to give time to active growth when necessary but must also appreciate the need for the close, comforting cocoon period prior to your release into the world as a delicate intricate thing of beauty and nature.

There comes a time though, when the new you has outgrown the old and it is necessary to shed your past self to allow the inner you to spread your wings and fly free, fly high, to distances beyond the sky.

You have had your personal periods of spiritual gestation and are ready to be born to the world again as new and to fly forth from this point on with the confidence and compassion of the wings of inner wisdom.

17th August 1992

When sometimes you are parted from those you love, take heart that a part of them is still with you even when they are not, and that the sense of loss you feel is the part of you that has gone with them and will remain with them even when you are not. Be aware of this and grieve not that you are not to be together for you will always be by this bond and give yourself comfort in that.

Brighton, 18th August 1992

You have not questioned me before in such a way and I know your request is a truly heartfelt one. Yet problems in the world are not for me to prophesise. What will be will be and cannot be avoided in its course. But that great changes will happen and the world be re-shapen in all aspects will surely come to pass.

What may cause these changes and shake the world and its people into the realisation that their beliefs and values are not totally truths, depends on the magnitude of vibrations the entire planet emits.

If the strongest notes are of discord and discontent, anger hate and pain, aggressive vibrations may cause explosive reactions and result in the literal destruction of the planet.

Maybe with the first crumblings of the land in which the crumbling societies inhabit, will be enough for the people to realise they are responsible for the destruction of the planet beneath the surface as well as above it.

Perhaps then too, they will see and believe that to change discord to harmony, hate to love and war to peace is the only way to pacify the aggression and to stop emitting self-destructive violent vibrations.

It is imperative you spread these words as far and as fast as you can. For without great change of tune, if not now then someday soon, massive devastation will occur not just within each nation but across and in all lands.

People can change, but know not how extremely important and necessary it is to ensure the survival of the planet as a green and pleasant land, to understand their role in things and their responsibility and attitude in its reflection, as cause and effect will help positive people power.

The eruption of wars and the erratic changes in world weather patterns, massive famines and droughts, floods and storms, hurricanes and earthquakes must surely serve you well as indications that the world at present is supersaturated with bad vibrations. It does not mean that harmony cannot be restored and peace returned to the land, just that positive action has to be taken by a magnitude of minds, bodies and souls, to love and laugh and sing and fill the world with good vibrations.

Brighton, 24th August 1992

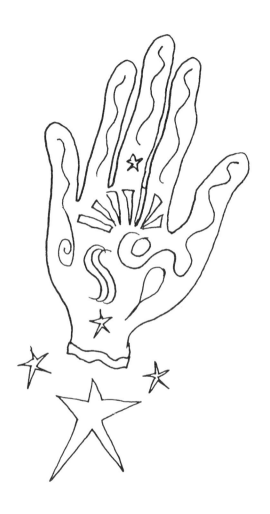

Where once I bade you do things and see things from a wider perspective with attention to the effect on others, I now suggest that you take a closer look upon yourself and pay attention to the effects on you.

It is of paramount importance that you maintain your strength of self so that you can continue to live and grow happily. To lose sight of yourself is to lose hope and that is not a good thing.

You must give time to yourself, your internal self, help yourself as best you can. Take time to reflect on things that you need to and address situations and feelings that need attention.

Your physical decline and deficiencies are a reflection of your spiritual health. Feed your body, feed your mind and feed your soul. Replenish yourself on the physical plane and on every other. Regain your strength and your hair and beauty will flourish as a wilted rose doth once it receives much needed water.

Fear not your future and fear not your past. They are neither no more or no less than you chose to make them. You can't change the past but you can change the effect it will have on your future. If it was a problem, is a problem, you can decide that it no longer will be a problem. Let go of it and choose to travel light with laughter.

You can and will emerge from this self-help session however slow or fast you conduct it, and if properly performed, as a stronger happier lighter soul. Pain and anger are heavy, grounding emotions and if you harbour a great amount of each how can you expect to truly fly?

To release your stored hurts and fears will lighten your load as if letting go of excess baggage not required on the rest of your journey.

Perhaps for some reason you have been carrying it a long way and been gathering it as you go. Now however, it is depleting your strength and you cannot move freely forward but are burdened down so heavily that to proceed you must at last be forced to unload a great deal if you wish to journey on. It is bad enough when obstacles arrive in your path that you do not know and have to find a new approach and way round. So why drag your own sad old faithful pitfalls along with you, causing a more problematic course for yourself?

If you do not wish to fall down one of your past painful pitfalls, do not drag them around your feet. For sometimes when the light fades it is not easy to see where you are walking and you may well cause yourself great pain and danger by putting your foot into something you should have cleared out long ago.

If you empty all this fear you harbour it will make room for great love and hope. If you release all your anger and tears you will make room for great joy and laughter. Swim and walk and sing. Laugh and eat and sleep. Work, rest and play every night as well as day. Live every day and you will be okay.

Rest your mind and rest your body and your soul will be reborn. Energise yourself through mental and physical stimulation then rest yourself through physical relaxation and mental meditation.

You know yourself and you know you deserve some much-needed attention. You would not desert a friend in need, so rush to your own side and give yourself the courage and confidence you have so often given so positively to others.

London, 5th October 1992

Where once you would have braced the pain and braved a smile, allow yourself to feel the pain and breathe a sigh of relief as it passes.

'Better out than in' is worth a million as an approach to the releasing of past hurts and tears. Anger turns to resentment and as such has a harder time resurfacing in another manifestation that suitably releases its true sentiment. Say what you feel when you feel it, when you know what it is that you feel and you know what it is that makes you feel what you feel.

It is far simpler than having to fathom out in the future what it is that you are still feeling when it is completely out of context and you no longer have a clear recollection of what it was, when it was or why it even was that you felt it in the first place. But you believe it all the same.

A lot of feelings are disjointed, misplaced and unwanted. They are from a different time, a different you. Your responses to situations and harsh words were one thing then but would be a different thing now. If you have outgrown something what is the purpose of keeping it, particularly if you have a replacement you prefer?

Everything: thought, fear, smile, kiss, tear has its time and place and day. Be not afraid to draw their curtain closed when their show is over. Because they caused a great impact with their debut does not mean they have a free run of the stage. Your life is the performance and it is up to you whether it be a romance or tragedy.

If you allow your past pains to continue with encore after encore there will be little laughter in the house. Take command as the manager of your stage and be selective with your performers and put on the best show you can, your greatest show on earth.

7th October 1992

Patience is a virtue and in good time you shall see why your life has been what it has been so that you can truly be what you shall be.

I may sometimes speak in rhyme and sometimes in prophecy. The words I speak strike a chord of truth and in good time your light will shine and your inner higher notes will chime.

You are treating yourself well these days and healing yourself well these nights. Give time for your work to show, keep up the rhythm and go with your flow ~

Little ripples dissipate and disappear but good, consistent, strong currents can turn a tide and bring good fortune to your shore. Be in tune with the moon and be mistress of your own waves of emotion.

You know what great strength doth have the sea, yet it is driven by the unseen power of the moon. Your physical body can thus be driven by your mind and the unseen power in your soul. Live and grow, sometimes fast and sometimes slow. Be aware that progress is made in any case. For all is meant for a reason and this has its place in your development. Be patient and let yourself grow.

12th October 1992

Your days of prophetic writing are not yet over. But your time to concentrate on yourself on the physical plane is certainly at hand. Ours is a relationship that transcends all perception of time and we will be together for evermore on this level and at this time, as much as on every other level and every other time.

Therefore, what I have to say to you sometimes can take on a more personal reference than the broader scale proclamations I deliver for humanity, harmony and understanding for unity upon the planet.

Everything begins and ends with you because you are part of everything and everything is a part of you. So in the interest of you, yourself, your planet and those around you, I suggest you concentrate upon yourself for the best results of the whole.

You are greatly loved and will be greatly loved as you have been greatly loved before. Love yourself and surround yourself with light and love, and light will come to you from near and far and love will find you exactly where you are. Where you are is always where you are meant to be, be assured of that. Things will also happen when they are meant to happen which you will learn to see. There is a time for everything and what will be will be.

Things are coming together that you cannot see but that does not mean that they will not be. Patience is a virtue and you are virtuous in many ways and you will be rewarded for them all in the coming days ~

18th October 1992

The written word has its place upon the earth as its sentiment has its place upon your world. Expand your thoughts, expand your plans and open up your opportunities. Operate on many levels and do not get isolated on the earthly plain of day to day living without even giving a thought to things.

Plans can be realised and dreams come true. If you don't have a dream, how can you have a dream come true? Be your own hero and get your goal and be not afraid to receive your rewards and they will not be delayed in coming to you. Acknowledge your own success and welcome it warmly when others acknowledge it too with ease and comfort and it will be both easy and comfortable. Success is yours in whatever field you decide to plant your seeds of love and life and hope.

Colour and pattern with love and passion can be found in all around. With harmony and understanding you can create, with patience and faith you can wait. With wisdom and purpose it can be yours, with dedication and determination it shall be ~

2nd November 1992

Dream on, little sister, and your life will be full of smiles.

That is, if you greet the world with a smile and take life lightly, that is how it will treat you. Enjoy all the situations and circumstances and success you encounter and the company you keep, and you shall be presented with all the circumstances and situations and success that you seek and great company to keep.

3rd November 1992

~ FAITH ~

~ HOPE ~

~ CHARITY ~

Relax to that which is coming for 'tis coming, ready or not!

Be prepared for all things, for all things are possible. Why not then be ready always to expect the very best of life and accept it when it comes, yet accept the very worst too even if it comes but expect it not. Not now or in the future or ever in our kingdom come.

5th November 1992

When two things become one the one becomes stronger. The more separate parts you put together, the greater the strength of the whole. The strength of the masses can be measured as the strength of a single body united, as one. Ideas, like people, can be individual and important and collectively support one another for the common good. This should be remembered and understood.

7th November 1992

When the time is right the time is right and ye shall all rejoice with true delight. Plans and schemes can result in dreams. Make your vitality for life become the reality of your life. It's not just an illusion, just find the solution and turn the wheel of good fortune and fate.

9th November 1992

From whence ye came ye know the pain of land and sea and life. Try not to remember these but the life and love and joy to be found by living in harmony with nature and the true laws of the land.

Beauty can be heard in the mocking bird and in the silent breeze when it passes through the treetops and whispers to their leaves. It can be seen in a blazing sunset and many a pretty thing, from a mountain range and a blue lagoon to a tiny fairy wing.

To see it and hear it are two of the things, but to feel it with passion is where it begins. Love and life are insurmountable. To understand, tune all your senses to the beauty in your world, get in harmony with the land.

Take time to walk upon the earth and watch the rivers flow. Tune yourself to feel the force and let nature take her course. Follow the signs that you do see by listening to yourself as well as me. Feel your greater conscience and be happy with your own council. Be your own guiding light; look for the truth and meaning and put them in your life.

Gain wisdom and understanding on your way as you live and learn and love everyday. Appreciate the lessons in your life and appreciate the love as well. Welcome them both into your life with joy and enthusiasm now and in the future, for when then is now, they are the same and should be remembered as such. We are all the same; time and space, land and sea, flesh and blood, fruit and flower. Learn to live as one united universe.

15th November 1992

Patience is your lesson and you have studied well, and great things shall be the reward for your effort. Now the time has come for action and you must apply the same aptitude to your next subject as you have in the past. Where learning is one of your great joys, be prepared to learn a lot as you enter your new classroom.

Great changes will occur as they must with a change of curriculum, and you must accept these and expect these as any conscientious student must. You can and will succeed in this. With your keen and assertive mind accept readily the changes and the speed at which they occur, because the pace of this lesson is much quicker than that of patience which by its very nature requires great time and many long periods of inaction. In contrast, action and progress and success will require exactly as they suggest.

Gather thy strength for it shall be required in many measures. That of mind and body and soul. All the lessons of strength and self support will serve you well as will those of positive thinking and social integration. By working and being with people you have learned a lot, much as you have learned by being alone and away from the daily working reality and company of many people. All these will come to show their meaning in the place of your life and the deepening of your character, as well as the awakening of your conscience as your life unfolds before you, and you progress through space and time. Decree a thing and it shall be done, decide what it is you want and, believe me, you can have it. Believe you, you deserve it ~ thy will be done, thy kingdom come.

17th November 1992

The excitement you feel is not just your imagination. 'Tis the feeling of life that brings rejuvenation. It sparkles, it tingles, it charges your mind. It pulses and twitches and charges your body. With positivity and light it charges your soul ~

When it is the very life-force that flows along your veins 'tis not at all surprising it stimulates your brain. Relax unto the feeling and I'm sure that you will find the good things that the future brings will really blow your mind.

Welcome them into your life, accept them when they come, for they will. Believe it when I say to you the best is yet to come. The dawn is just breaking so 'tis with excited anticipation you await your rising sun ~

London, 19th November 1992

The antithesis of a thing is the opposite extreme of the same. If you perceive them as such, pure truth remains. For there is good and bad, happy and sad to be seen and found in all that abound, but they are all both one and the same.

Don't look for one and hide from the other, or look for love and hide from a lover. Learn to draw the connection now and not in reflection.

Be open to both sides of every story as the two sides
of every coin. There would be no fun in a game of
chance if you could foretell the outcome at a single
glance, but when the hand of fate does flip the call
there is always great hope for one and all ~

24th November 1992

When the feeling comes upon ye pick up your
pen and write, for words of great importance
are shared with you at night. 'Tis your responsibility
to share them in the day, then all around may
prosper and be helped along their way. For every
path is separate but there are places they converge.
May your book become a starting point from which
they all are drawn to the same horizon. With
guidance and protection they can follow the light.
With love and understanding they can set the world
to rights. Your role is thus important and cannot be
more stressed. Worry ye not about your book. It is
truly heavenly blessed.

25th November 1992

How interesting to hear other people's motives and other people's goals; it gives a clearer insight to other people's souls. 'Tis right to give them time and to listen with an open mind, for as you receive so ye shall be received. Remember to feel with your mind and think with your heart and despite great minds or powers of persuasion you will not be blown off course or waver one degree from your chart. Be strong and true to your own inner feelings and you need never fall prey to the salesman and his dealings. His offers may appeal but ask yourself if they are real.

Take what you feel is right and disregard the rest, then live how you feel right as only you know best ~

Tis not for any man to tell you how to feel or think or see or be. 'Tis up to you alone to be truly who you are, however that may be. Strong of mind or weak of limb, tall or short or fat or thin. Young or old, shy or bold. Man, woman or child. You are all essentially good, and have just perhaps thus far yourselves misunderstood. Therefore, be true to this innermost, purest you. Discover who you are yourself, then you need not be told who you are by anyone else. If you tune into your feelings instead of listening to your mind you'll be delighted and surprised at the answers you will find. But attune yourself carefully to all that is good and eliminate all else. Be selective for the common good and not the common self.

Strive to be the best you can be for the sake of all mankind, not to pamper or to boost an egotistical mind ~

You cannot change humanity. That is understood. But by each being the best you can, collectively you could ~

As souls on the earth you all have a choice. Like singers in a choir you all have a voice. For rhyme and reason to create harmonious vibrations should be your common goals, then sweet melodies of life and love can lighten up your souls. Think not you should not help all others for all in all they are your brothers.

Make music together, not discordant sound. Spread
love and light around the world and peace
across the land ~

26th November 1992

To be alive and feel alive are the best things in
the world, but to be alive and not feel alive
seems sadly quite absurd. Your body is alive so
waken up your soul, then you can truly live and
fulfil your earthly role. Your time down here is
precious so value every day. You made the choice
to be here, come what may.

Live to love and learn,
Love to live and learn,
Learn to love and truly live.
Your mind, body and soul
are all three merged to form your whole.

27th November 1992

Don't take responsibility for another person's life even if you are the other person's wife.

Your life is your own, your body is your home. Learn to live inside yourself as well as round about. Be filled with love and strength yourself, then you can gladly give it out.

You cannot feel the pain or take another's strain for without their personal lessons where are their personal gains?

The meaning of life cannot be explained, for you all have individual souls and therefore individual goals.

To generalise would be to demise the value of each life. Everyone is important, no one more than any other. Treat each one as your equal, treat each one as your brother.

28th November 1992

It is impossible to surmise all the teaching that there is, so be prepared to study as long as you all shall live.

If life had no more lessons it would be time for you to go, so be grateful for its teachings and of how much there is yet still to know.

Be willing to learn every day and not be too set in your ways. By limiting your mind you restrict your soul and number your own days.

Like a pot-bound plant who wants to grow but can't you must broaden your own horizons. You must follow the light and break free of your own restraints. Make your mind a fertile land and eagerly learn to grow.

30th November 1992

Expand the width of your souls and expand the width of your goals.

Give what is right to give and ye shall receive what is right to receive.

Give what you don't want yourself only if it will benefit someone else.

Give generously what is needed when it is, be it passion, compassion or time ~

Be mindful to keep yourself complete if you feel your resources are low. Give what you can when you feel that you can, but don't be afraid to say No.

Don't put another person's wants before your own needs, even if it is done to please. Needs must and yours come first, but don't put your wants before others' needs.

1st December 1992

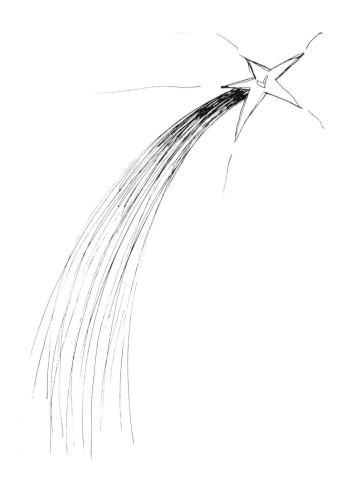

BOOK

6

It is a good thing to keep your writings in a book and to start a new edition sets a positive outlook. For if one day you wish to see your words in print and bound, to start as you wish to be by writing yourself upon these pages is like a visualisation that will help you through the early stages. See that it can be done. Believe that it will be done.

It has been a great help and comfort to those who have already had chance to read my words in advance of its publication, but the magnitude of gratitude that will follow its distribution will spread light and love and understanding across yours and every nation. Positivity breeds content!

7th December 1992

Tis nigh upon us the mid-season celebration. 'Tis the same for every man whatever his beliefs or his nation.

Tis a time for loving and living, receiving and for giving, for faith of every kind whatever your religion.

Be pleased for one another this time of year is here. Wish all men peace and happiness with love and Christmas cheer ~

Brighton, 23rd December 1992

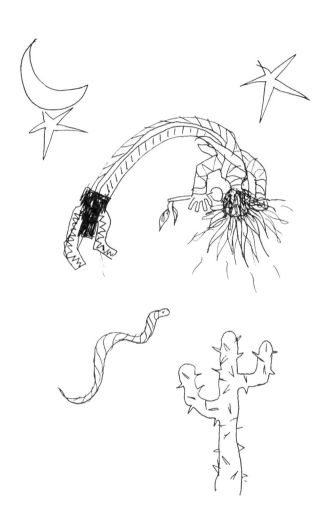

194

You are nearing ancient lands where rivers run deep and mountains reach high, where heaven doth meet the earth and the land doth meet the sky.

Here it is not forgotten that all are one and the same, be it animal, vegetable or mineral, regardless of its name.

Twould be good for modern people to respect the Indian ways, for they had great understanding of things you don't know these days ~

California, 28th December 1992

Light and life and colour abound from the clouds in the sky to the rocks in the ground. Where the spirits of all things meet each other and man and nature greet each other. They celebrate as one, reverberate as one, respect the vital harmony of living together as one. 'Tis a lesson to you all to assess your motivations and to live your life for the common good, despite your egos' protestations ~

Santa Fe, 1st January 1993

Relax unto the belief that what is meant to be will be. Feel not too much responsibility for that you cannot see. Trust in the fact you are the person you are truly meant to be. Fear not you will disappoint or fail to succeed. For even now as you have transcribed my guidance may be read, acknowledge what you have thus achieved and concentrate on that instead. Every man or woman has their calling they cannot pass to anyone else. There are certain things that have to be done, you just have to do yourself.

Santa Fe, 2nd January 1993

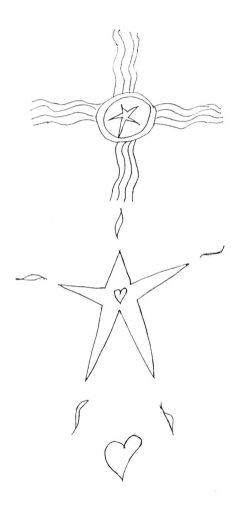

By taking steps towards your future you are giving your life direction.

That way the things you wish for can line up and present themselves along your way. If you do not know your course they do not know where to come, their opportunity may not come by accident and their part in your life may not be done. Be open to all the good things in your life and in good time they will come.

Los Angeles, 10th January 1993

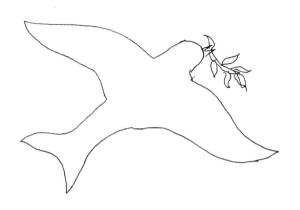

You have now become more aware of the necessity of my words. My messages are of hope and love to comfort you all through these difficult times. I do not try to prophesise the problems in your lives, but time will show and you all will know that you need to change and adjust and learn to grow.

Los Angeles, 14th January 1993

You have travelled many miles and witnessed many things. Now you have returned to the place you know as home. 'Tis time to put into action all that which you have learned. Look for the meanings of the things you have experienced; they are all of some significance. Although their importance may not always be apparent, they are all lessons on some level, albeit subliminal. Be open and receptive on all levels; these and distant plains. Be not scared on this earthly realm when you are safe in every other.

Are children not often fearful going to school but nonetheless graduate much wiser? Growing pains are acknowledged in the young but should not be restricted to youth alone. You continue to grow as you live and it continues to hurt. But from the pain of that growth comes great comfort and ultimate understanding. Apply much patience and compassion, and love will heal all hurts received and peace and truth remain. Live your lives in the pursuit of being wise.

Brighton, 17th January 1993

The times and things are happening in the here and now, so enjoy your daily working life as much as the spaces in-between.

Brighton, 21st January 1993

Your life has many compartments which vary in size depending on their presumed importance. But the smallest rooms can harbour vital things that ensure the comfort and support the function of the others. The boiler room is given little attention but in fact supplies much, albeit unseen, to all areas. Major importance is put on the interior and exterior face of things but underneath all that which is most clearly seen are the truly important foundations, much with a house, a home and a heart. Look deeper than appearance or position and do not overlook the underlying worth and value of a property or a person.

When renovating an old building or developing your own inner self there are certain rules you must adhere to for strength and stability. You cannot remove too many rooms or smash down too many walls but you must clear out and remove all heaped and harboured rubble and rubbish.

If things appear to crumble or certain structures in your life fall, make haste to clear the wreckage and take advantage of the new space in which you have to live.

You know not how quickly the walls may be rebuilt or even exactly where, but if your house is strong on good foundations and still holds your small service rooms, supplying your heat and food and light and love and hope, fear not; your life will not collapse even if your house is reshapen.

Trust in your own secure foundation and appreciate that the most important things in your life may certainly not be the largest, or even seen at all.

Love of life and peace of mind can neither be observed, but for happiness and harmony they are the most important things in the world.

London, 4th February 1993

Spring is nearly here as are the first shoots of the seeds you have so carefully planted and so patiently waited for to take root and grow. Close attention will have to be paid to their healthy development as nature and time run their course. Then when the harvest does come you can happily reap the fruits of your labour and delight in the fragrance of sweet success and love ~

London, 8th February 1993

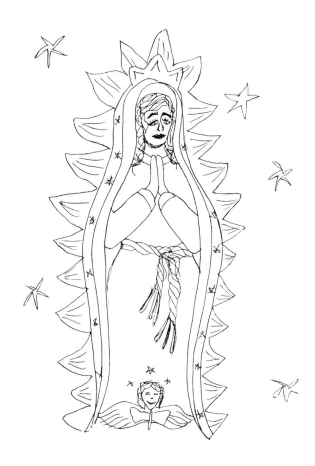

Find love and peace and harmony where you are, for that too is where they are. They are with you all always.

Trust in their eternal presence and let it be felt. Find faith and patience and hope for they are within you all always, also.

Find in yourself that which you would wish to find in everyone else and the world. What you find in your life is what you find in yourself.

London, 9th February 1993

Guidance and protection should be asked for and sought so their comfort and security can be learned without their necessity being taught. Take good care of yourself; your life is your greatest wealth. By this token all men are rich but know and appreciate it not. Trust in the powers that be to fill you with white light when called upon as protection so that you can live your life safely without it being taken by anyone else or accidentally lost. Work, rest and play blessed.

London, 15th February 1993

When you cannot see the road ahead, take time to enjoy where you are instead. You are moving along day by day regardless of what unseen things may come your way.

There are times you should run and some you must walk, as there are times you must listen and some you must talk.

In order to run you must first learn to walk. As you must first learn to listen before you can talk. If your life is going slowly, it is time for you to listen. Learn to speak the language of life with delicacy and precision. Then with this new knowledge and ambition you can move confidently along your way and your pace can quicken.

7th March 1993

Use your time wisely when you know that it is yours. You are free. Make your own decisions, follow your own life's course, be creative with your time and it will live on for days to come. Don't waste your time because it is your own. Lovingly accept it and respect it in every way. Be happy and rejoice in life each and every day ~

8th March 1993

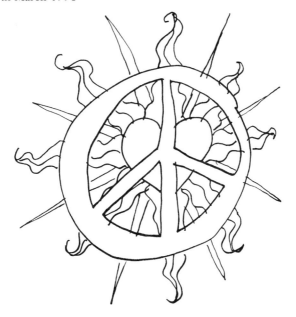

If you choose to accept your role, your life will be less of a struggle. It doesn't have to be a battlefield, you can put up no resistance and live to fight another day and live your life in a better way. To join in and take your part you must feel with your mind and think with your heart.

A life may be long or a life may be short, depending on the number of lessons to be taught. 'Tis not just an exercise in perfecting yourself, it's more what you do for everyone else. 'Tis learning to act as part of a whole, with love and peace in harmony with the universal soul. A life cannot be measured by the number of its days. It can however be assessed in many other ways.

Some lessons we are happy to learn when a new life to us is born, but others we are forced to learn when a life from us is torn. The purpose of a person's life, may not be clear at all, but on the higher level of things it has a role for sure ~

Past, present and future are all parts of one and the same, as all lives are parts of one, being lived again and again and again ~

Brighton, 18th March 1993

Like a blossoming flower needs light to empower the life within the bud, be prepared to let go and let yourself grow. Thus from within you can then blossom out. Be patient as your petals delicately develop and gently open in due course. A perfect bloom can thus evolve by nature, not by force ~

Brighton, 1st April 1993

There is light upon the horizon. Make that what you set your eyes on. There is much to be done with the coming of the sun. Rejoice when it shines for it brings better times. The seasons are passing as are your troubled ways. Make your dreams become reality in these coming days. Concentrate on positivity and light, and trust in the belief it will all be alright.

Brighton, 2nd April 1993

There is a wealth of ideas amidst your plethora of emotions. Take your time to be selective and not dwell on negative notions. As the full moon in the clear night sky pours silver on the sea, concentrate on just good thoughts with love and positivity.

Do not allow dark clouds to gather from your own doom and gloom, remember that they block the light and deprive the waves of the richness of the moon. White light from above shines down with great love, so rest ye at ease and be ye at peace.

Brighton, 7th April 1993

Be mindful how you pass your days for now is where your future lays. As present does flow upon the tides of time 'tis a constant changing thing. When the moon does call a turn, your future you will learn.

For then will be now and yesterday be gone. Tomorrow is the future dawning and by nightfall the present will be past and done. So when you wake up in the morning, the future will have come ~

Brighton, 11th April 1993

Before the music begins there is a pregnant pause. Then the notes begin to play and your life is underway. Be patient through times of your germination and contemplate ye not termination.

When a tune is thus begun it must run its full duration. It may begin as something slight but allowed to run its course thus gathering gentle force it can result in a joyous ovation.

Be not afraid in a silent world. The music will begin and your heart will sweetly sing of the great love you have therein ~

Brighton, 12th April 1993

When the time is right, the dawn breaks through the night. Take comfort in the moon whilst the sun awaits beyond the horizon, coming soon but out of sight. Be in tune with the moon for she governs the tides of emotion. Even when daylight comes she controls the seas and oceans. Day and night both have their light, gold and silver and white. So even in the darkest times you are sure to be alright.

Brighton, 13th April 1993

Take time to heal yourself for your health is your greatest wealth.

Spiritual growth can sometimes be exhausting but its benefits are everlasting and rewarding. Lovingly release your past and then embrace your future. Learn your lesson from the season and your teacher, Mother Nature.

A good garden requires much pruning so that new life can spring from the bud, not be suppressed under old dead wood, but grow with light and love.

Brighton, 16th April 1993

For even now you are helping others by treating all men as your brothers. You should not see someone as their creed or colour or race but look for the person they are inside, see the person behind the face. For they are your fellow beings, life spirit in a human case. For you are made of the self same metal as your sisters and brothers be they family or friends, enemies or lovers.

Hereby learn empathy with other people's souls, for you are all united in your earthly roles, by joining together in a lifetime contract and all accepting the mortal pact. You have all chosen to be here to play the same life game and thus you are all identical, only distinguishable by your name.

You are all parts of the same source of light. In essence you are all the same but as pure light is diffused in the physical plane you come in many colours. Beneath the skin you are all kin, soul sisters and soul brothers.

London, 19th April 1993

Gather the things around you that you like unto yourself. Be they things of natural beauty, constructed or contrived, whatever makes you happiest and feel something good inside.

For even in a house of much perceivable wealth your life may be full of riches but your soul may be deprived. True value is in the harmony of the things you have around. For these are the vibrations with which you do resound.

Let your soul sing with your surroundings and not be tethered to the ground by the things you have around you that create discordant sound.

London, 28th April 1993

When the time is right the day does turn to night, then night does turn to day and darkness rolls away. You have had your turn of never-ending dark. Now embrace the dawn of the everlasting light. Golden rays are soon to be upon you, 'tis just a matter of time. Be patient and they will come your way as night does turn to day. Soon your world will be warmed with the love and light of gloriously bright sunshine.

Brighton, 2nd May 1993

Good things are soon to befall you in the coming days. Find comfort in the fact good fortune is on its way to get you through this difficult phase. Sometimes it seems unlikely the dawn will ever break, but when it does and fills your world with light and love, believe you me, you will all then see it is worth the night-long wait. Your faith is being tested and your patience being tried, as part of the development of the you, you are inside.

London, 5th May 1993

When the dawn decides to come 'tis usually marked by the appearance of the sun. By dissipating darkness with particles of light 'tis long before its arrival that illumination is begun. Be patient as you wait whilst it makes a slow approach. Enjoy each enlightened moment that truly marks the coming of your sun. Thus slowly but surely you will see before you the warmth and love of light grow into a glorious day out of deepest, darkest night.

London, 11th May 1993

As sometimes you feel that you must die before you are reborn, you must pass through the dead of night before you reach the dawn. As sometimes you must cry out to let your inner darkness out, before you find the space to let the sunshine in. As sometimes you must clear your throat before your voice can sing, lovingly release your past, your pain, your tears. Then fill yourself with love and light in the coming years.

London, 16th May 1993

Matters of the heart affect every part of your mind, your body and your soul, and thus it should be seen as much as with a lucid dream, your thoughts are in control.

If you stub your toe it thinks it has been hurt and sends the message to your brain where you in turn do feel the pain. When you are happy, in love, it shows from the twinkle in your eye right down to your toes, thus 'tis at such times that you can see you think with your heart and feel with your mind. Realise then that you should learn to think more with your heart and less with your mind and feel more happy in your head more of the time.

Perfect health is thus a state of mind. Feel healthy in your head and your entire body will think itself healthy in kind.

Thus you must be in harmony with your mind, your body and soul, even if from time to time what you think you need with your body is in conflict with what you think you need in your mind. Your inner feelings are thoughts as much as your inner thoughts are feelings.

Learn to decipher your body's every word.
Understand the thoughts behind the feelings. Allow
the messages to be received and not to go unheard.
Expand your conscience and broaden your mind to
accept the thoughts from your body as a whole.
Follow your instincts and become more receptive to
the messages from the universal soul.

Heighten your own awareness and open yourself up
to your psychic sensitivities. The meanings of
feelings can often go unheard if you are not
sufficiently highly tuned to hear their silent words.

London, 19th May 1993

The word from above is, rejoice in the love you
feel there is around.

Brighton, 24th May 1993

Be happy and rejoice in praise in this, your halcyon stage, from which you will progress and turn another page. Trust that the good times are coming, for behold they are already here. Believe me you are at home and your soul need no longer roam.

Bolney, 1st June 1993

Your life is not the dark cloud you thought it to be but 'tis the golden light beyond. After troubled times of tempest, tranquillity is born. Your life can start afresh in the calm that follows the storm.

Flourish and grow by truly letting go and reach for the future from where you stand. It lies outstretched before you like a green and pleasant land. Full of love, peace and harmony.

Bolney, 4th June 1993

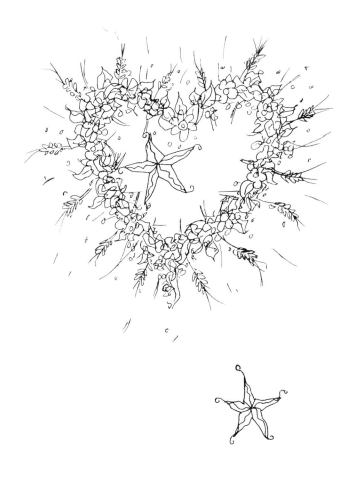

You have mastered your self-control. Now let your spirit free and happily indulge yourself with freedom, light and positivity.

Express yourself as best you can by spreading love across the land. Thus what you write, let others read. Give them food for thought upon which to feed.

Bolney, 13th June 1993

Concentrate in this next phase on how is best to pass your days. Enjoy yourself in social pleasures and express yourself at your own leisure.

You cannot force what will be a matter of course. You must first learn to go with the flow of time as the clock has to wait before its next chime.

Bolney, 27th June 1993

Lily and poppy and woodland rose. Behold the wide variety of flowers that nature grows.

If variety be the spice of life, see how well your world was planned. A multitude of peoples with individual features, all colours, shapes and sizes. From different roots, bearing different fruits, yet all are glittering prizes.

Thus live and grow, hand-in-hand, with all the peoples of the world and your home land. If all life were made identical, the same size, same shape, same form, your life would be less colourful; flavourless and bland.

Bolney, 1st July 1993

Within the heart is where to start to make amends to your life. Thus from within you can begin to set the world to rights. 'Tis within the bark of the mighty oak the tree does truly live. Thus from within it does supply the inner strength to reach the sky. Planetary peace and universal love can be yours here on earth as in heaven above.

Bolney, 19th July 1993

Seldom you can see what your life is meant to be, yet trust you can live in prosperity by living your life with truth and love and positivity. All manner of things will come your way if you practice what you preach every day. Be true to yourself as you are to all others then rejoice in your own success as well as of your brothers. Patience will deliver what only time can tell, thus through peace of mind and strength of heart you will come to know as well. Do not falter, do not waver, however tough your times may seem. They are necessary lessons on the way to reaching your dream. By giving a lot to life through love and peace and understanding, you will be repaid in kind much more than you have planned. By trusting in the powers of the universe you all will be given a helping hand.

Bolney, 24th July 1993

Great things will soon befall you as great change is soon to be upon you. As the winter's snow does melt away and flow across the land 'tis its water that feeds the earth, for when harvest comes that water proves its worth by nurturing the shoot, by feeding the root, by helping it grow to one day bear fruit.

Bolney, 8th August 1993

When the light flickers be watchful of the flame but when the time comes be not afraid of letting go. For you shall not be plunged into darkness but illuminated by the candles around you who continue to burn bright and live on to fill the world with light. Love and peace can thus remain and live on beyond the life of a single flame.

Bolney, 24th August 1993

From where you are the door to your future is ajar. You cannot see into it but the door is definitely open. 'Tis not until you actually move into it, are its contents revealed. Fear not to cross the threshold; 'tis time to go in from the cold.

Bolney, 5th October 1993

Though the joys of the flesh may be pleasurable, their ecstasy is not long lasting. The heights that can be reached fall far short of those that can be conquered with the extra sexual strength of celibacy. They are good for the physical soul in its grounding to its plain. Yet it can deplete the essence of your spirit and delay your inner growth. That is not to say that it is not a healthy part of the life experience to have sex and lay as one, for it is.

It is a vital area of learning for you each to experience yet so too are there important lessons you can learn through abstinence. Many wise men and dedicated women have chosen this as a way to live and grow. For the brightest lights reach the greatest heights.

London, 11th October 1993

When at last the dawn does break and the sun does begin to climb above the horizon, rejoice, for the light does ever brighten and your day has just begun. For as from now your world will be filled with light, golden and warm from the sun. Be sure the darkness of the night has passed for love and light are truly here at last ~

Bolney, 2nd November 1993

Some days are long, some lives are short, some winters last forever. Yet night always falls as dawn always breaks, however long in time either of them takes.

To be born into life is to live for a day as the sun shines upon the earth, but when the moon approaches you must move on over into death. So go out in a blaze of colour as a beautiful sunset.

Thus the legacy of a life is the love it provides, for love transcends time and stays with you always inside.

Sunrises be exciting for they bring promise of life and love with hope. Yet sunsets do take the glory for the wonderful image of life and love in death they provoke.

Faith is the belief that after such a splendid setting of the sun 'tis only a question of time before it will return and once again over the horizon come.

14th December 1993

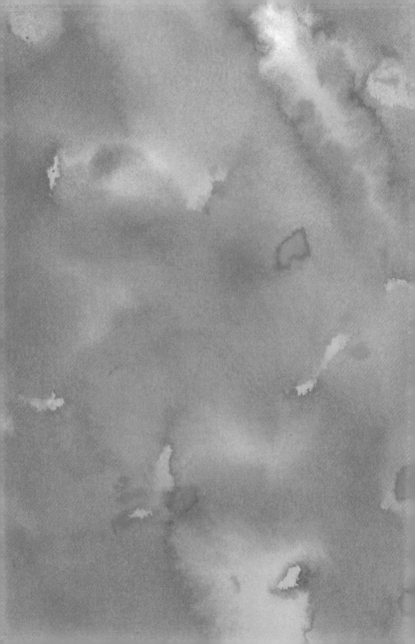